Lost Legends of Nothing

Katherine Tegen Books is an imprint of HarperCollins Publishers.
HarperAlley is an imprint of HarperCollins Publishers.

Lost Legends of Nothing

For information address HarperCollins Children's Books, a division of HarperCollins Publishers, 195 Broadway, New York, NY 10007.
www.harpercollinschildrens.com

ISBN 978-0-06-283950-3 — ISBN 978-0-06-283951-0 (hardcover)

The artists used Adobe Photoshop to create the digital illustrations for this book.
Typography by Fanny Rodriguez
22 23 24 25 26 GPS 10 9 8 7 6 5 4 3 2 1
First Edition

For the one soul I'm lucky enough to share
my life with nothing but love, laughter, and
adventure. For everything and always.
Thank you.

—Ale

For my dearest, the one who always keeps
me from getting lost through sidequests.
Thank you for making nothing so
wonderful.

—Fanny

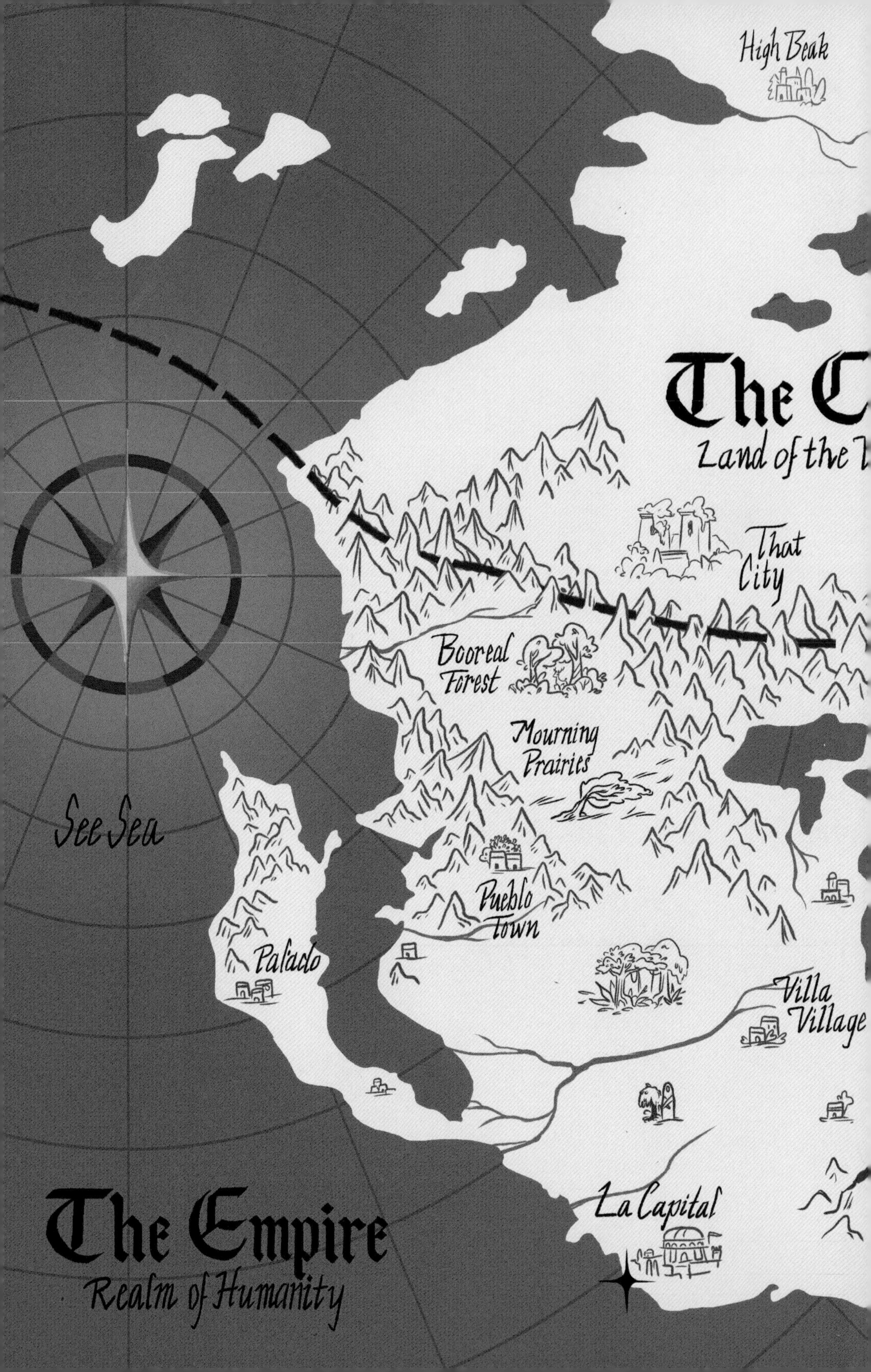
High Beak
The C
Land of the
That City
Booreal Forest
Mourning Prairies
See Sea
Pueblo Town
Palado
Villa Village
La Capital
The Empire
Realm of Humanity

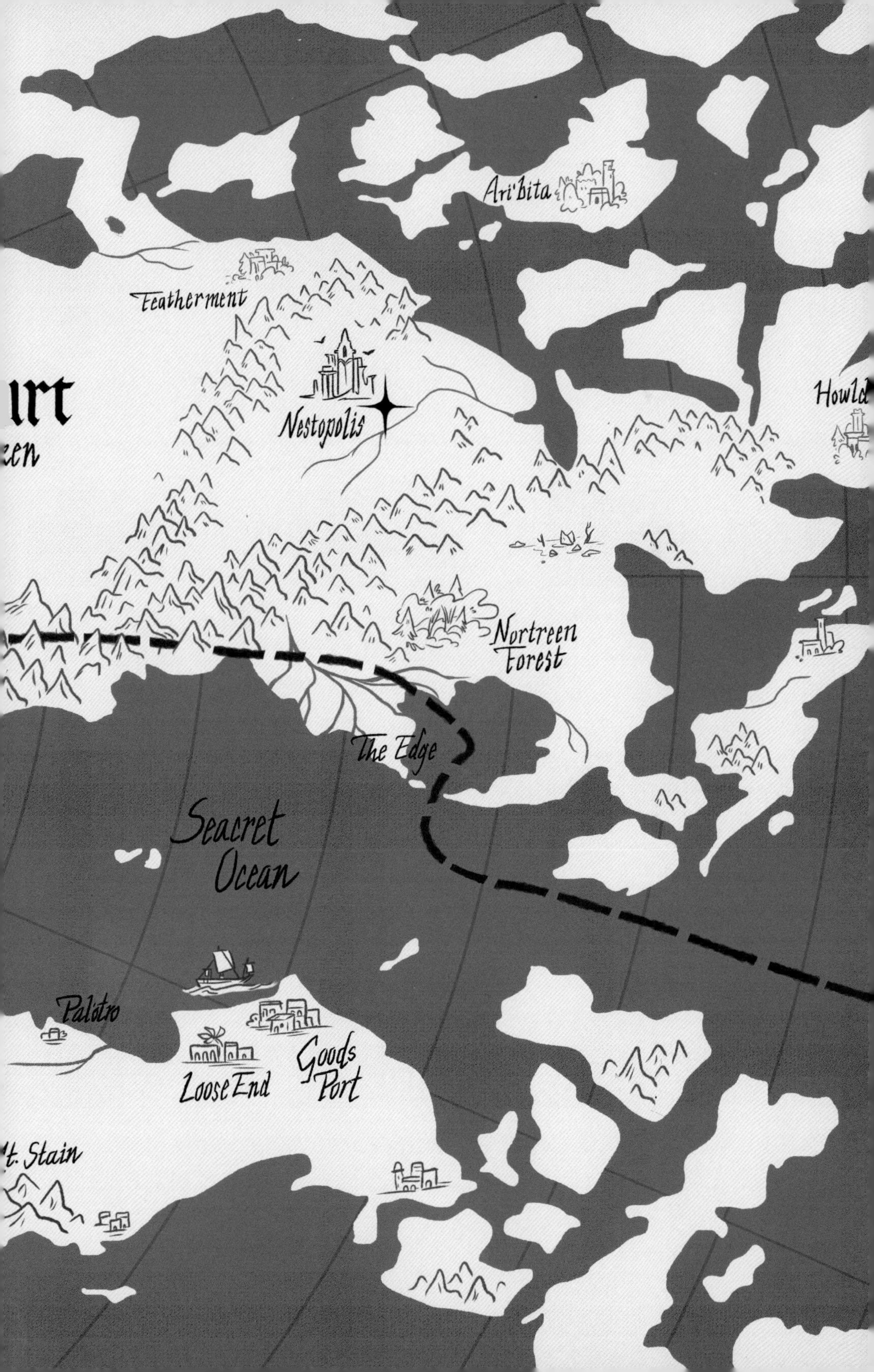
Ari'bita
Feathermen
...urt
...reen
Nestopolis
Howld
Nortreen Forest
The Edge
Seacret Ocean
Palotro
Loose End
Goods Port
...t. Stain

Alejandra Green & Fanny Rodriguez

Lost Legends of Nothing

KATHERINE TEGEN BOOKS
An Imprint of HarperCollins Publishers

HARPER
alley

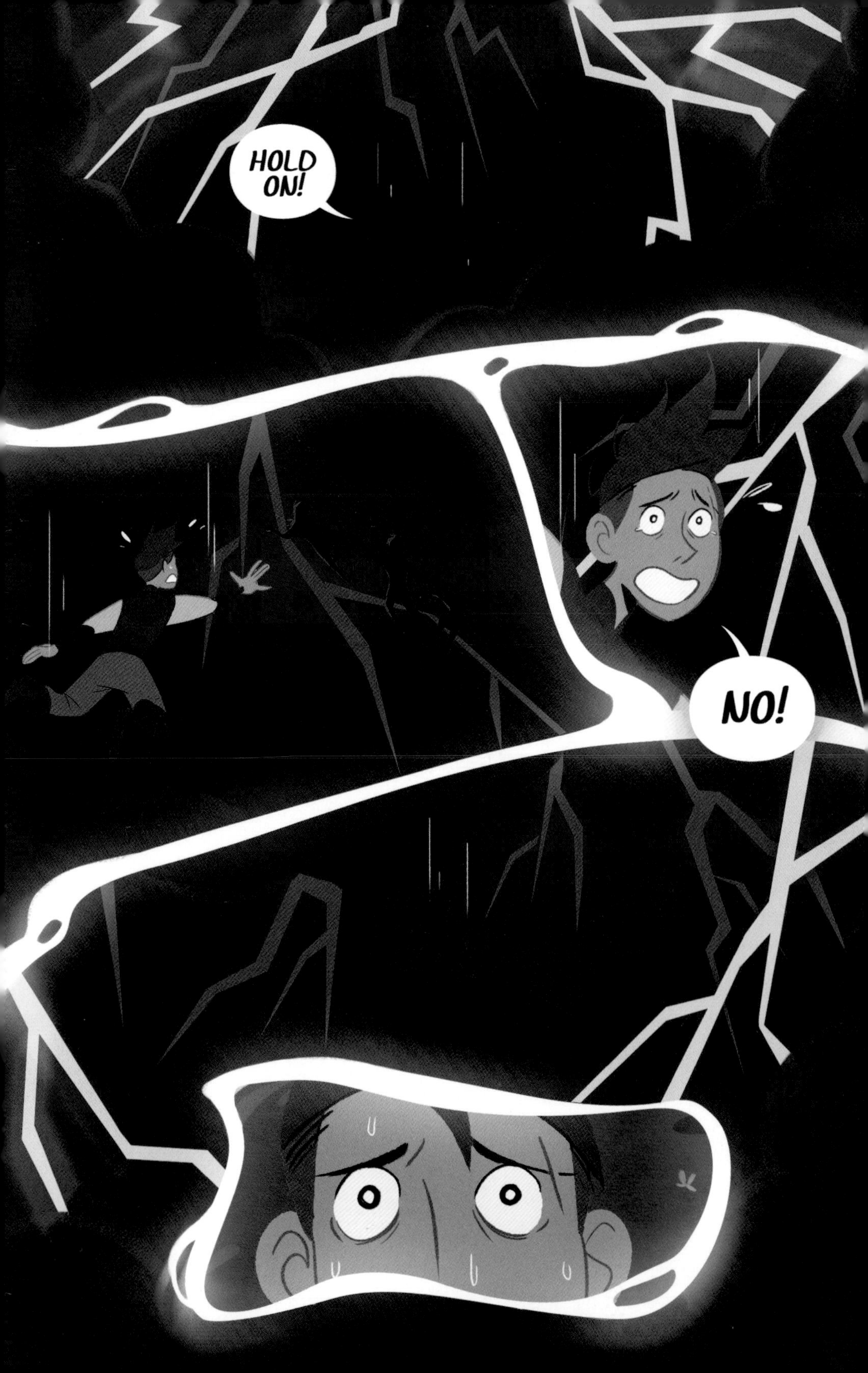
HOLD ON!
NO!

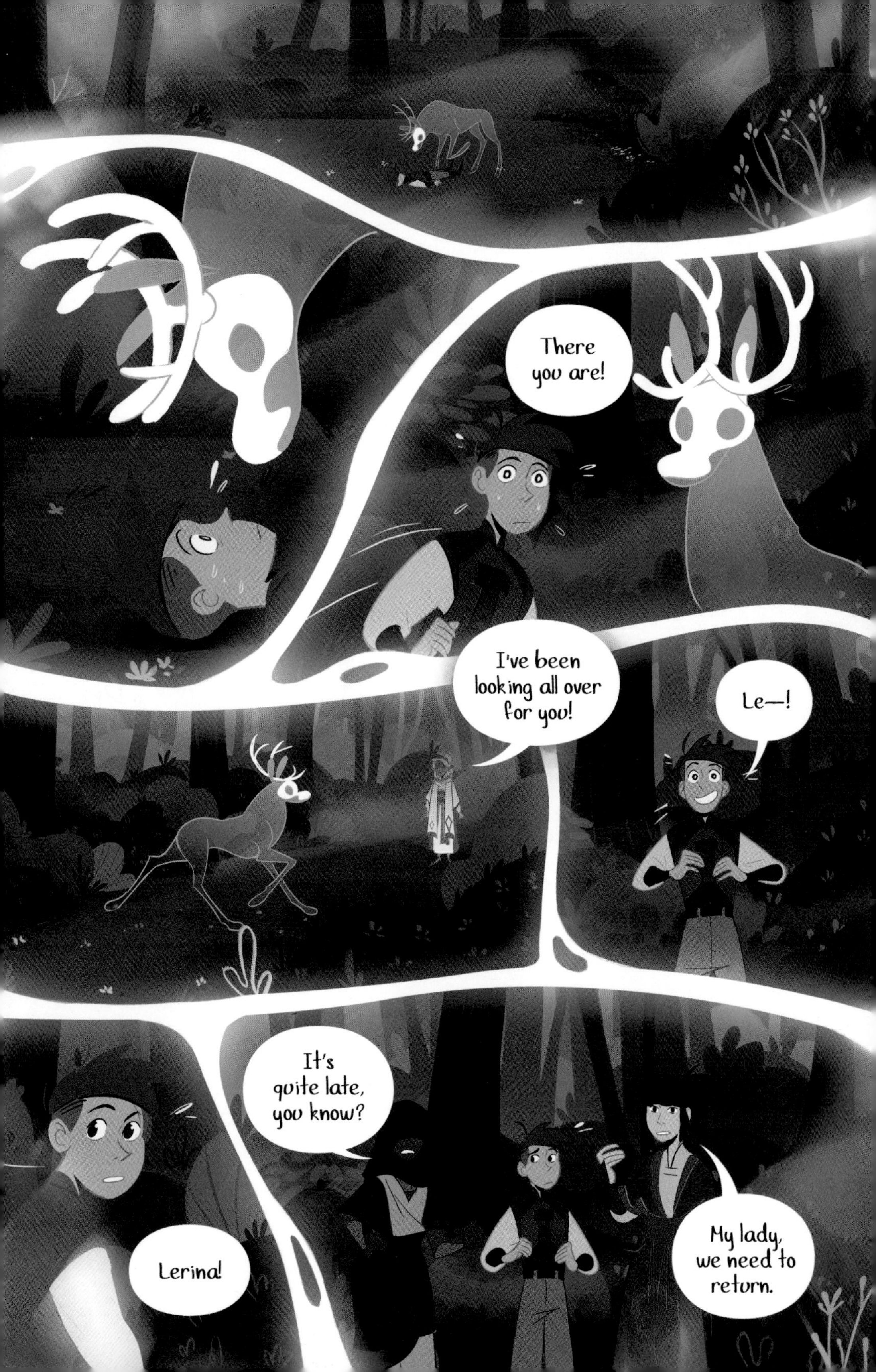
There you are!
I've been looking all over for you!
Le—!
It's quite late, you know?
Lerina!
My lady, we need to return.

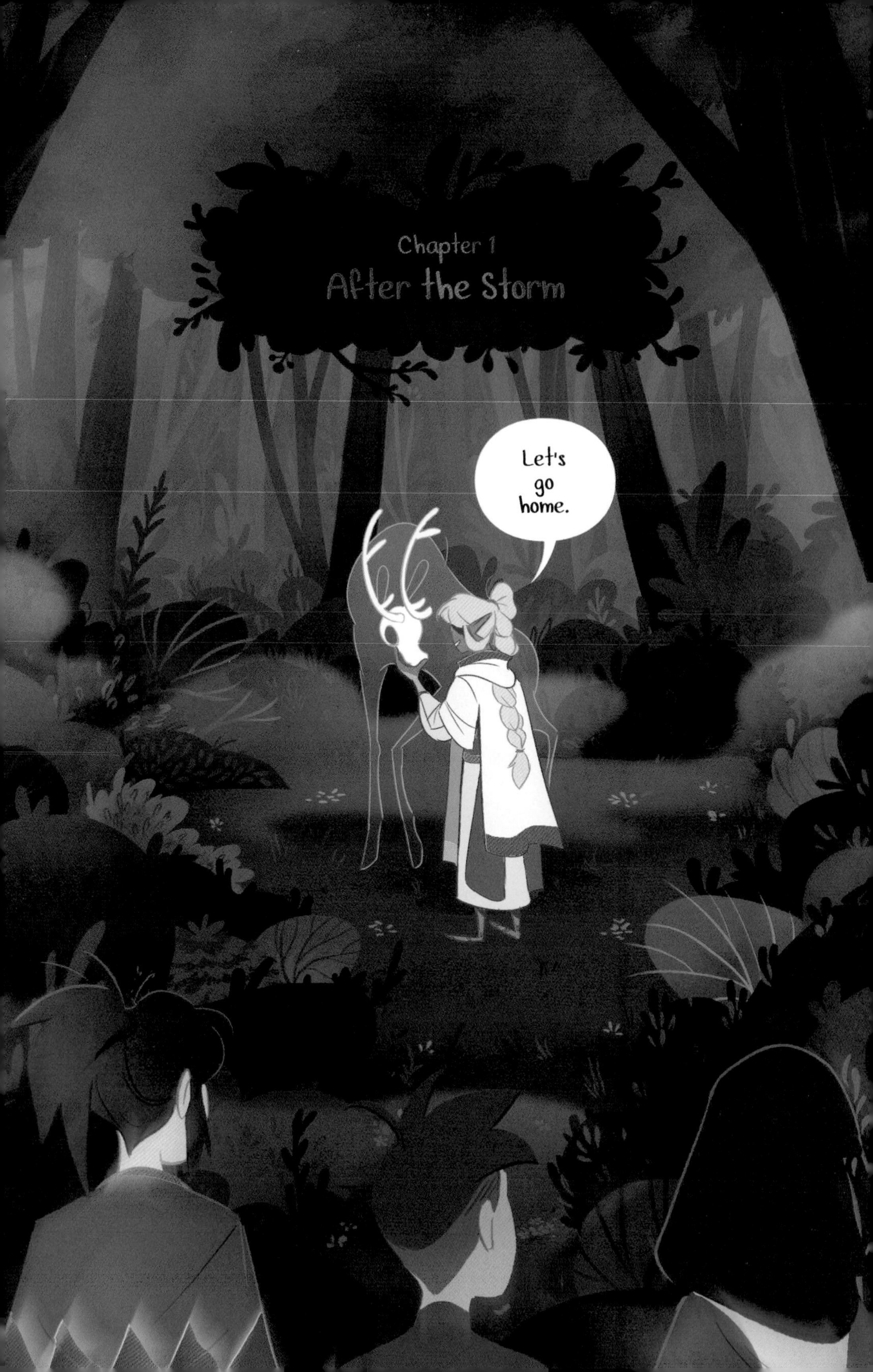
Chapter 1
After the Storm
Let's go home.

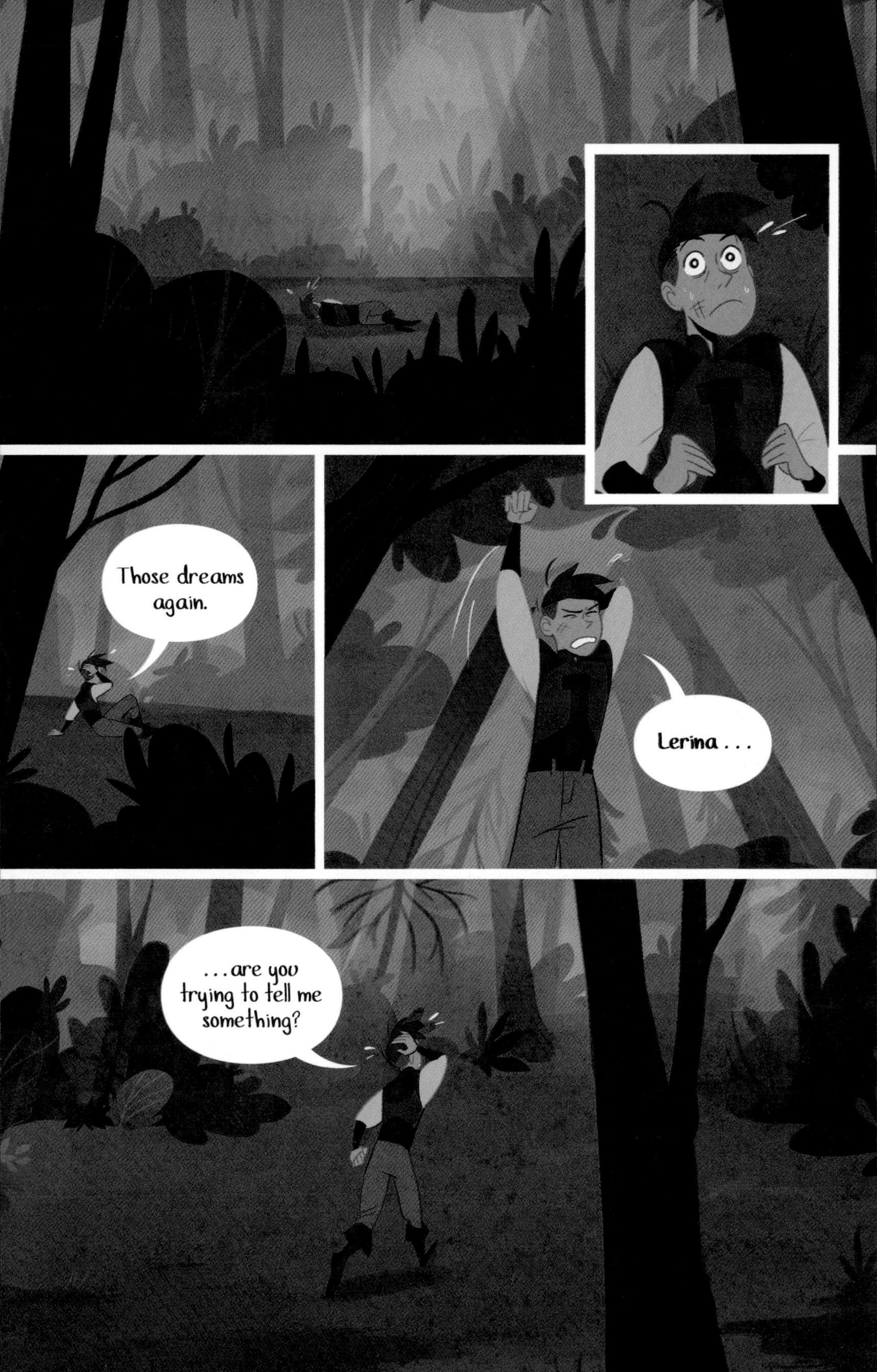
Those dreams again.
Lerina . . .
. . . are you trying to tell me something?

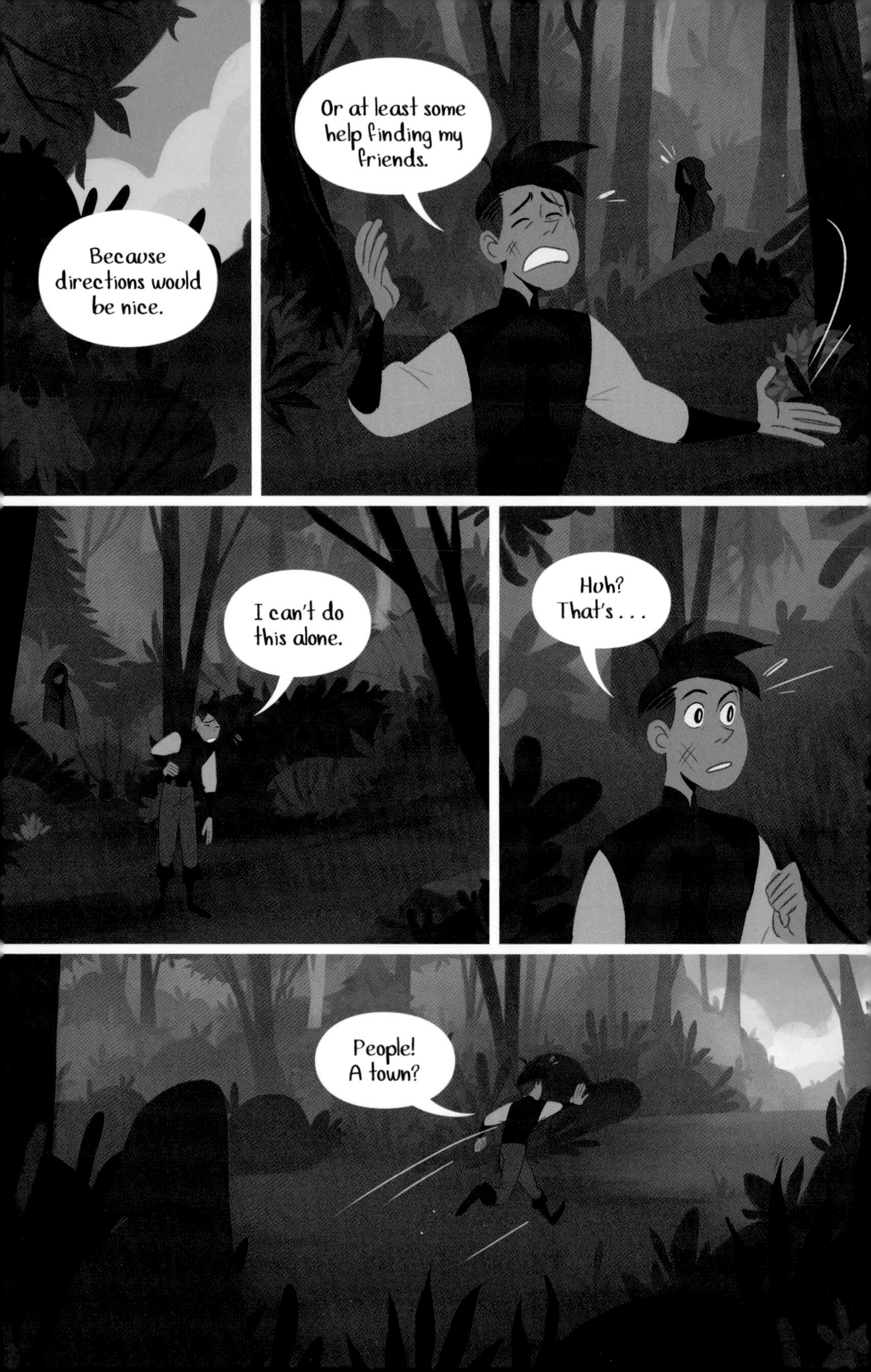
Because directions would be nice.
Or at least some help finding my friends.
I can't do this alone.
Huh? That's . . .
People! A town?

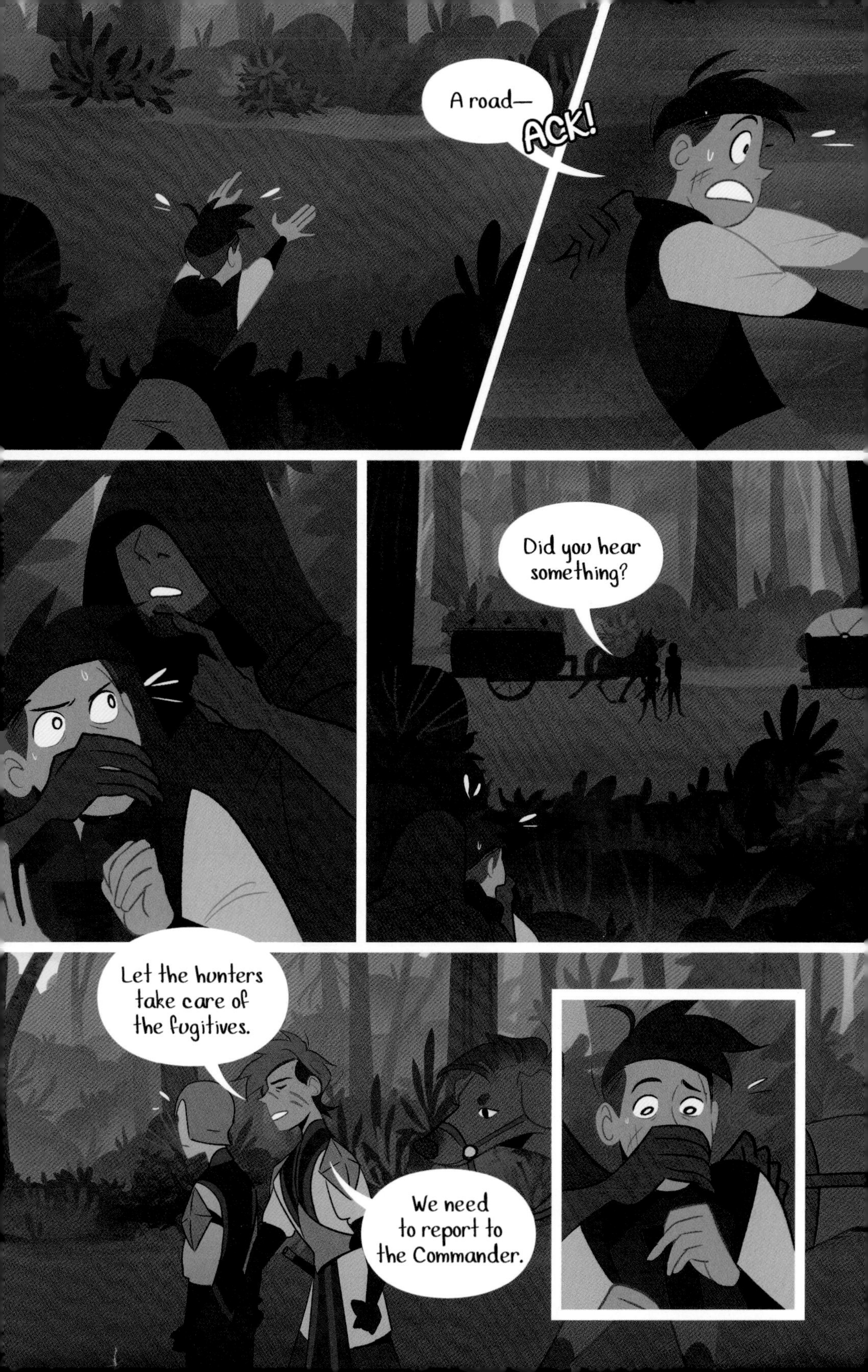
A road—
ACK!
Did you hear something?
Let the hunters take care of the fugitives.
We need to report to the Commander.

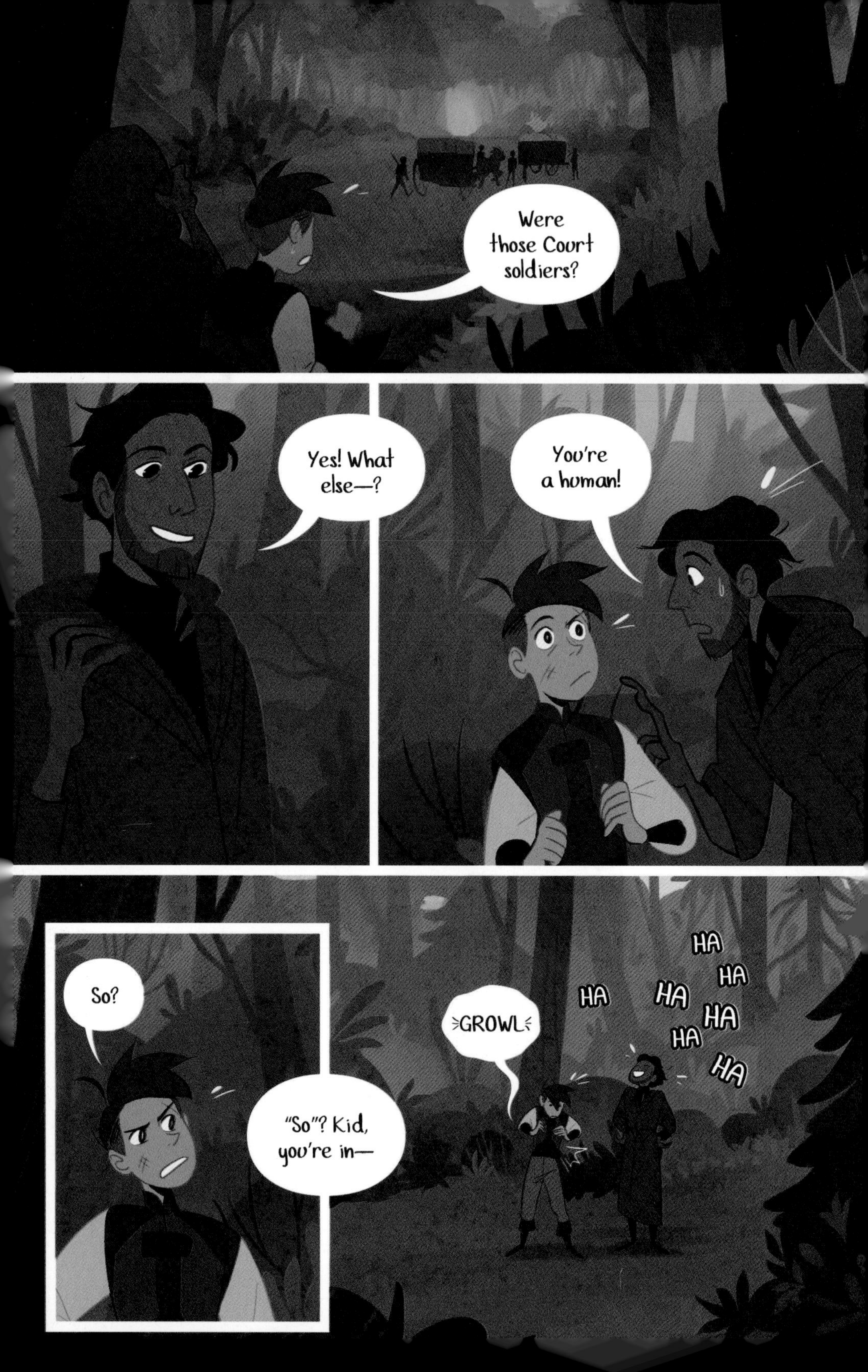
Were those Court soldiers?
Yes! What else—?
You're a human!
So?
"So"? Kid, you're in—
GROWL
HA HA HA HA HA HA HA

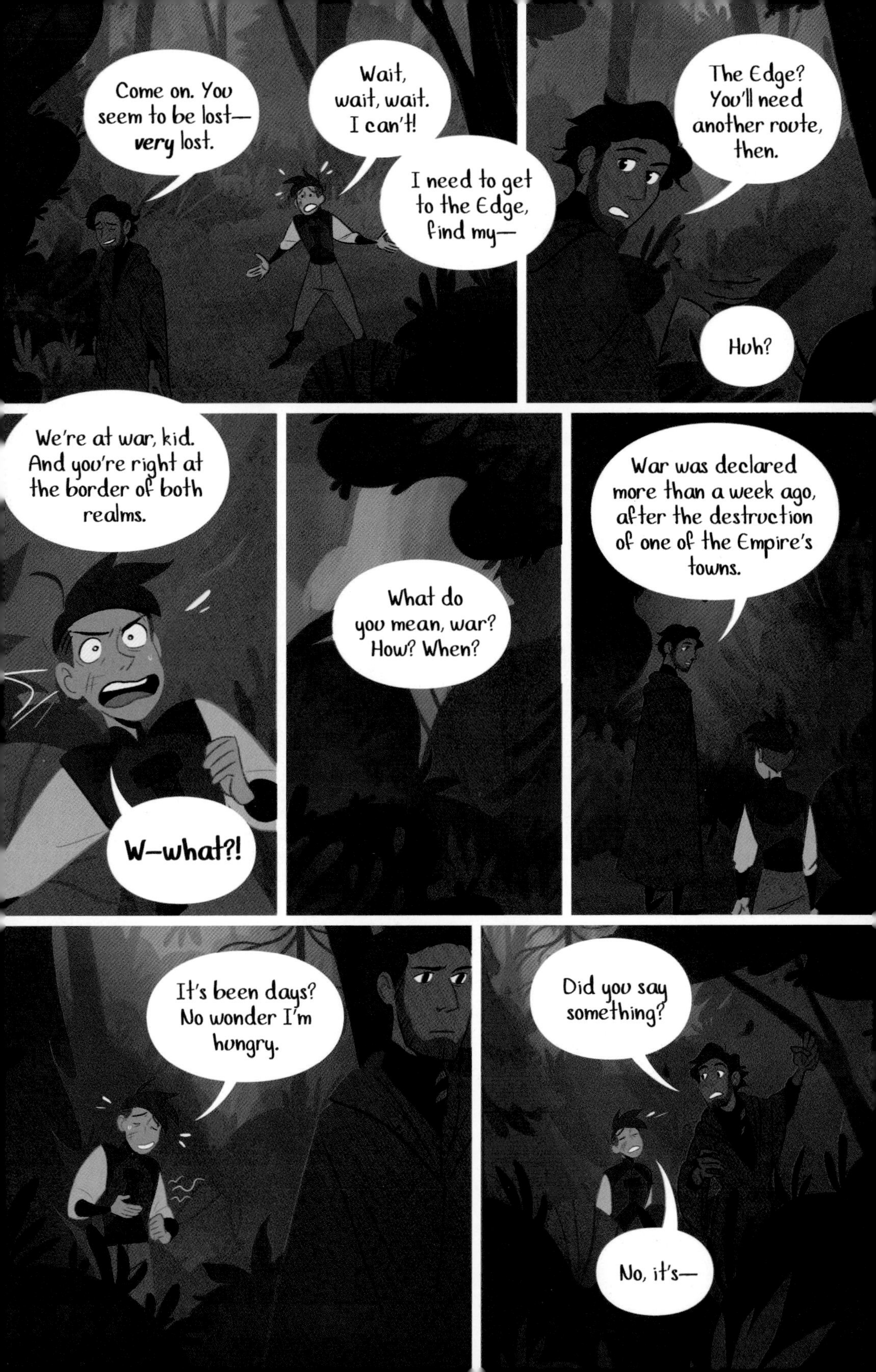
Come on. You seem to be lost— *very* lost.
Wait, wait, wait. I can't!
I need to get to the Edge, find my—
The Edge? You'll need another route, then.
Huh?
We're at war, kid. And you're right at the border of both realms.
W-what?!
What do you mean, war? How? When?
War was declared more than a week ago, after the destruction of one of the Empire's towns.
It's been days? No wonder I'm hungry.
Did you say something?
No, it's—

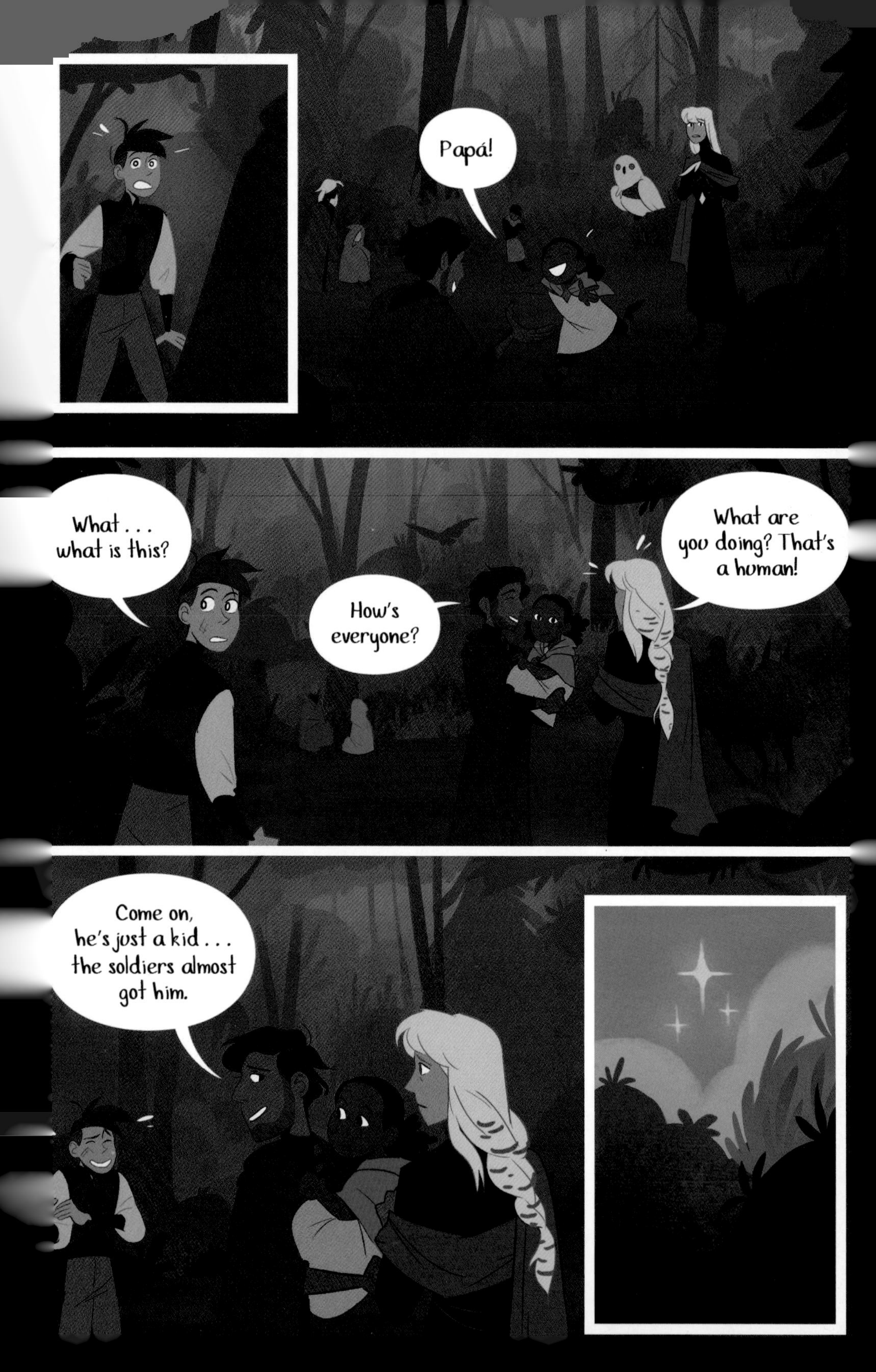
Papá!
What . . . what is this?
How's everyone?
What are you doing? That's a human!
Come on, he's just a kid . . . the soldiers almost got him.

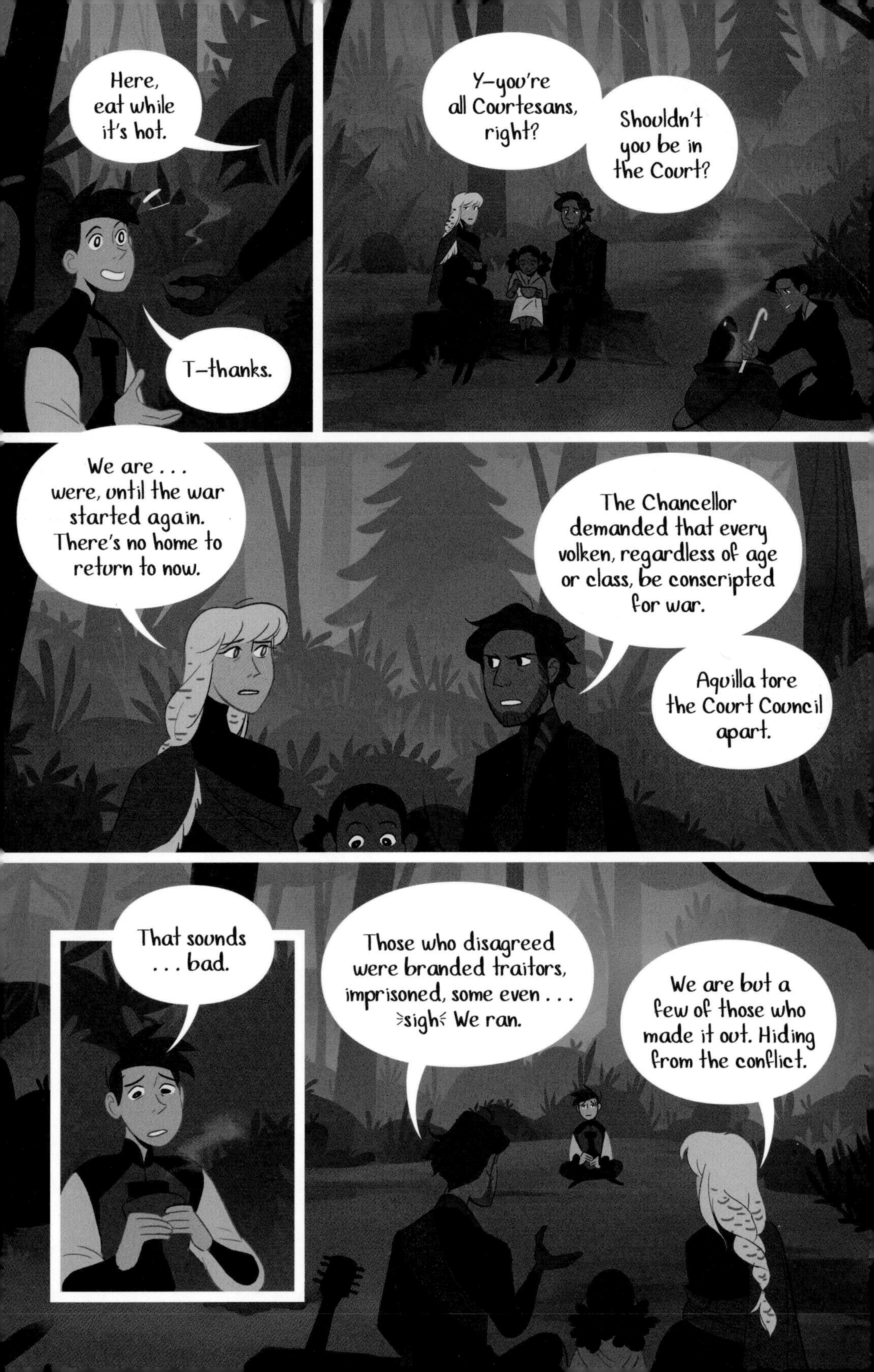
Here, eat while it's hot.
T–thanks.
Y–you're all Courtesans, right?
Shouldn't you be in the Court?
We are . . . were, until the war started again. There's no home to return to now.
The Chancellor demanded that every volken, regardless of age or class, be conscripted for war.
Aquilla tore the Court Council apart.
That sounds . . . bad.
Those who disagreed were branded traitors, imprisoned, some even . . . ≽sigh≼ We ran.
We are but a few of those who made it out. Hiding from the conflict.

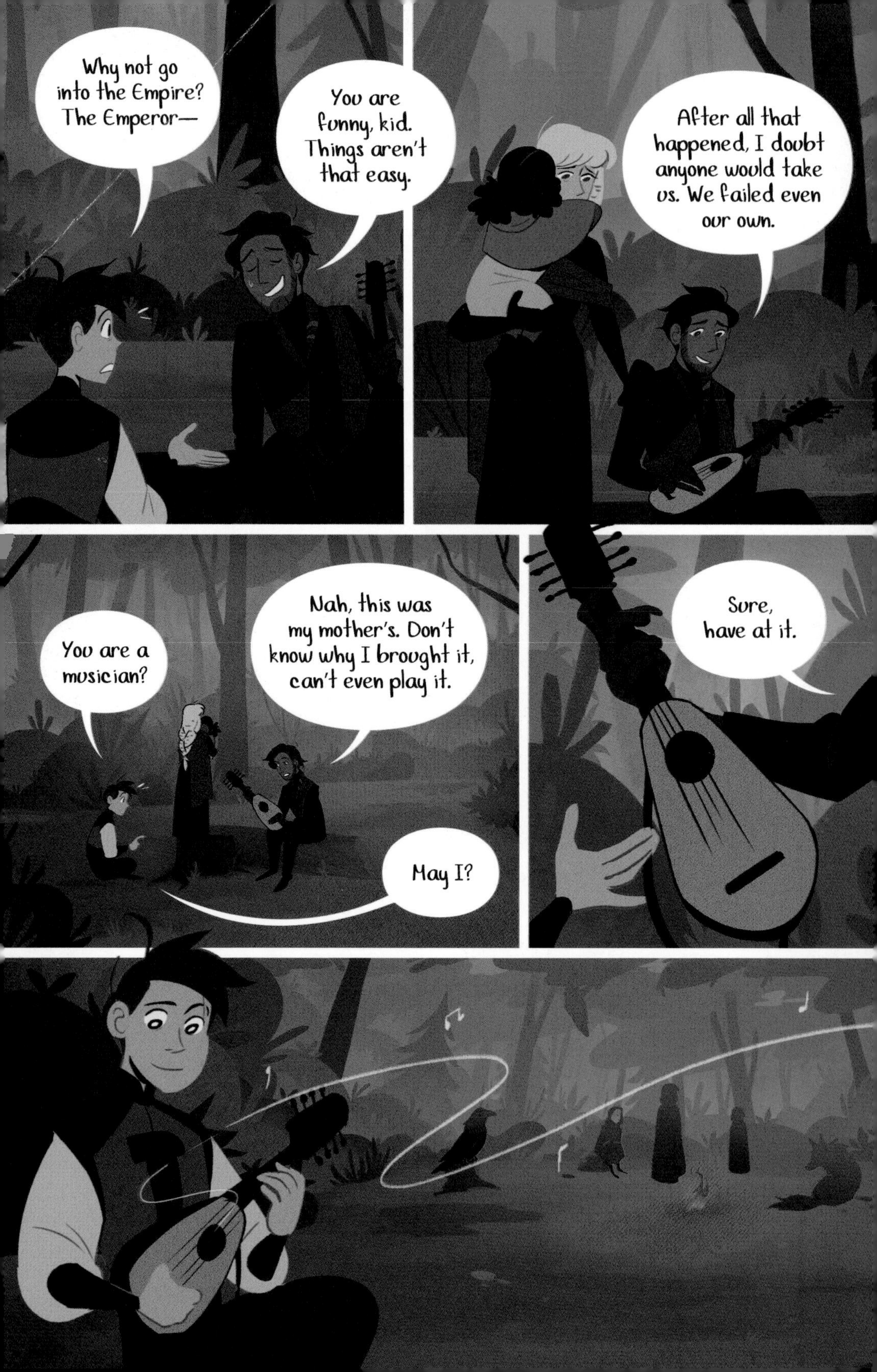
Why not go into the Empire? The Emperor—
You are funny, kid. Things aren't that easy.
After all that happened, I doubt anyone would take us. We failed even our own.
You are a musician?
Nah, this was my mother's. Don't know why I brought it, can't even play it.
May I?
Sure, have at it.

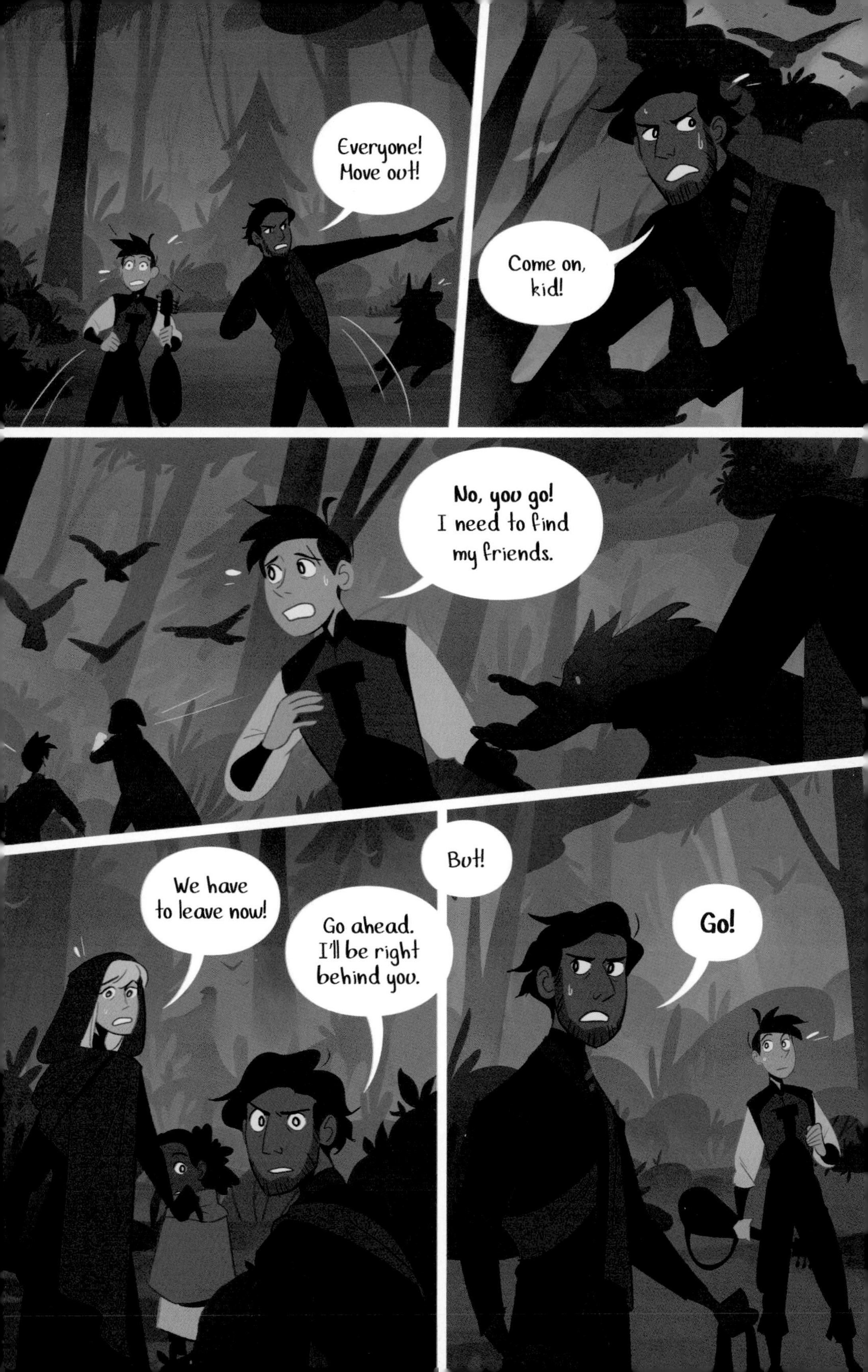
Everyone! Move out!
Come on, kid!
No, you go! I need to find my friends.
We have to leave now!
Go ahead. I'll be right behind you.
But!
Go!

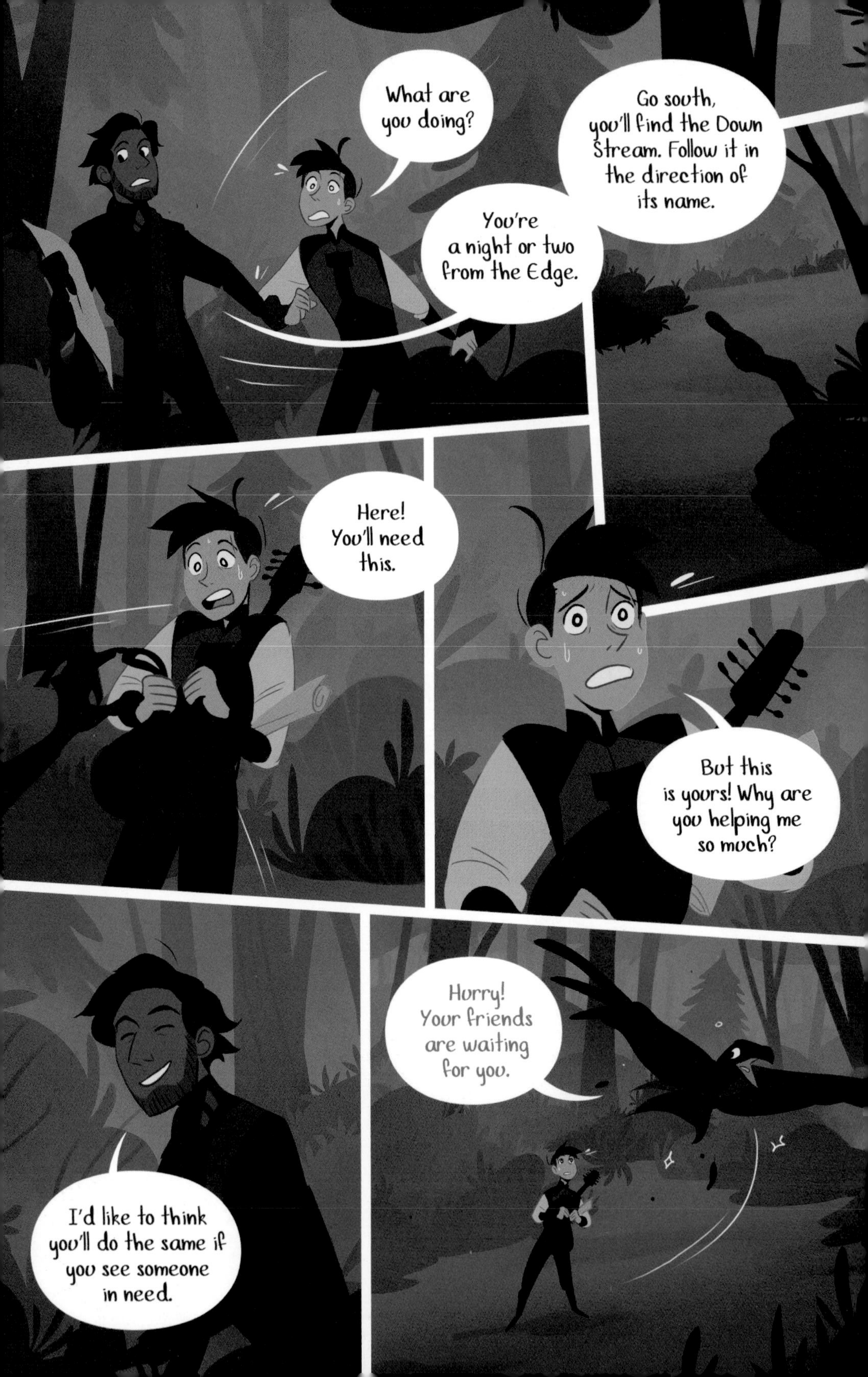
What are you doing?
Go south, you'll find the Down Stream. Follow it in the direction of its name.
You're a night or two from the Edge.
Here! You'll need this.
But this is yours! Why are you helping me so much?
I'd like to think you'll do the same if you see someone in need.
Hurry! Your friends are waiting for you.

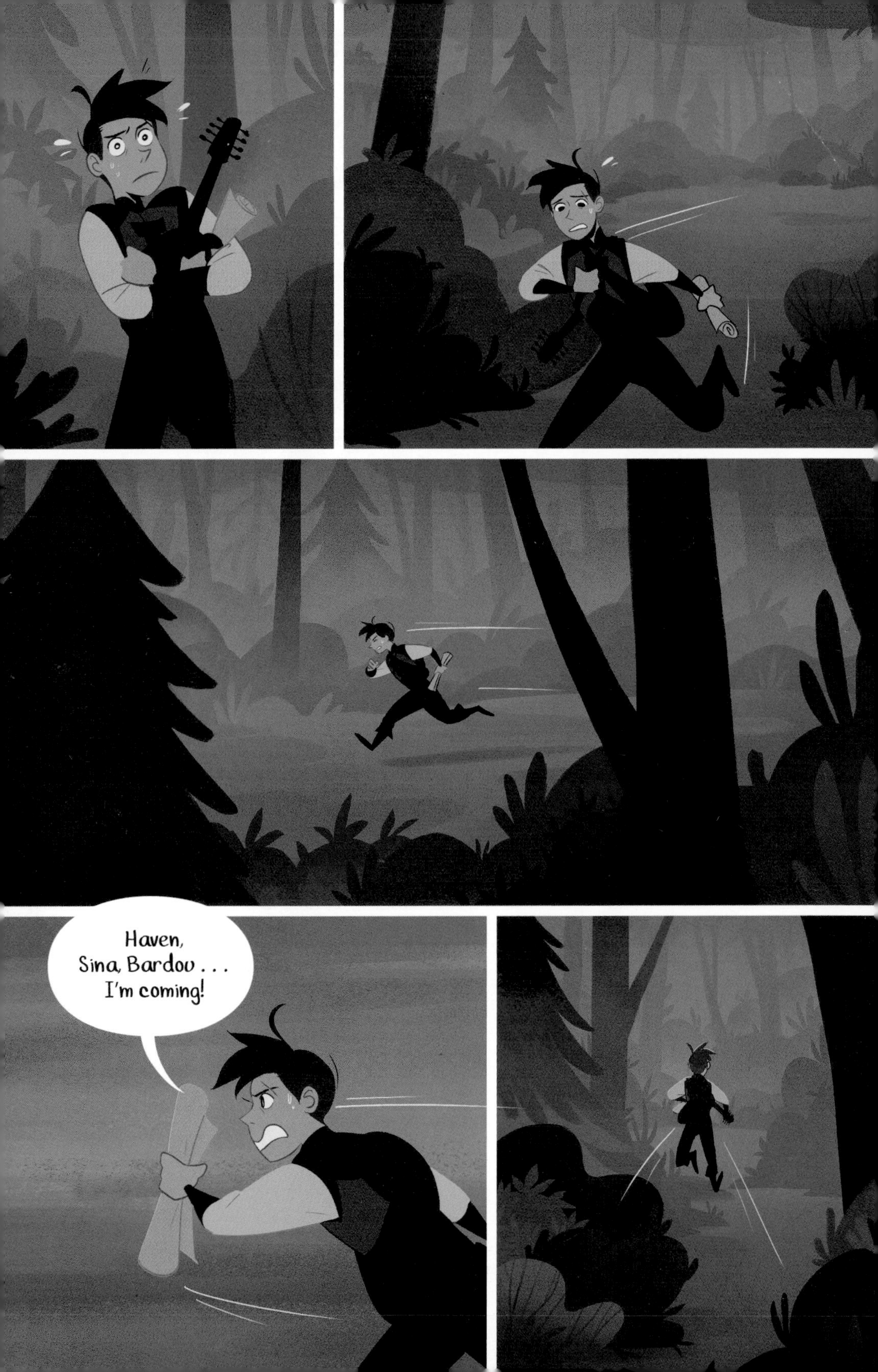
Haven, Sina, Bardou . . . I'm coming!

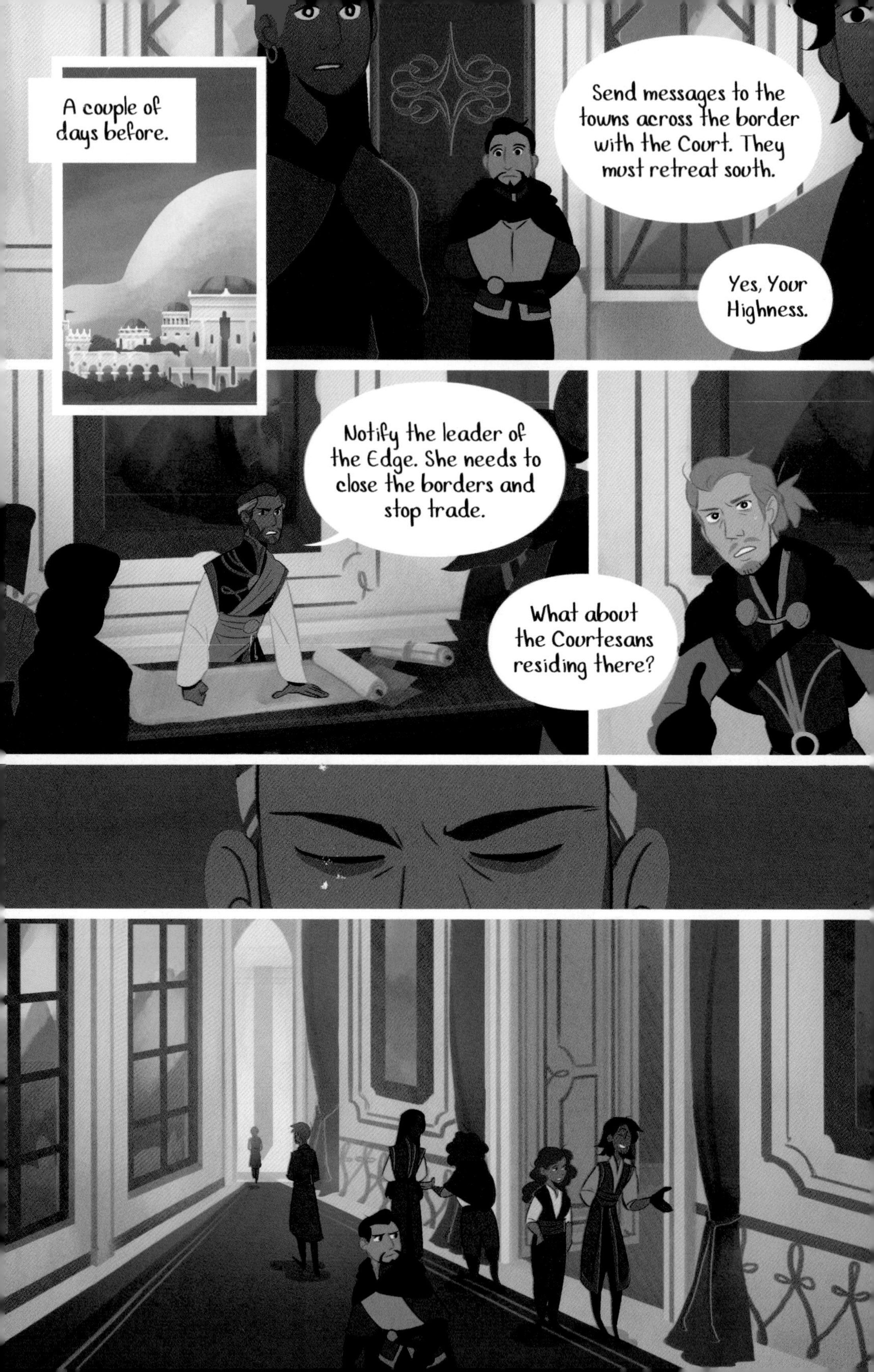
A couple of days before.
Send messages to the towns across the border with the Court. They must retreat south.
Yes, Your Highness.
Notify the leader of the Edge. She needs to close the borders and stop trade.
What about the Courtesans residing there?

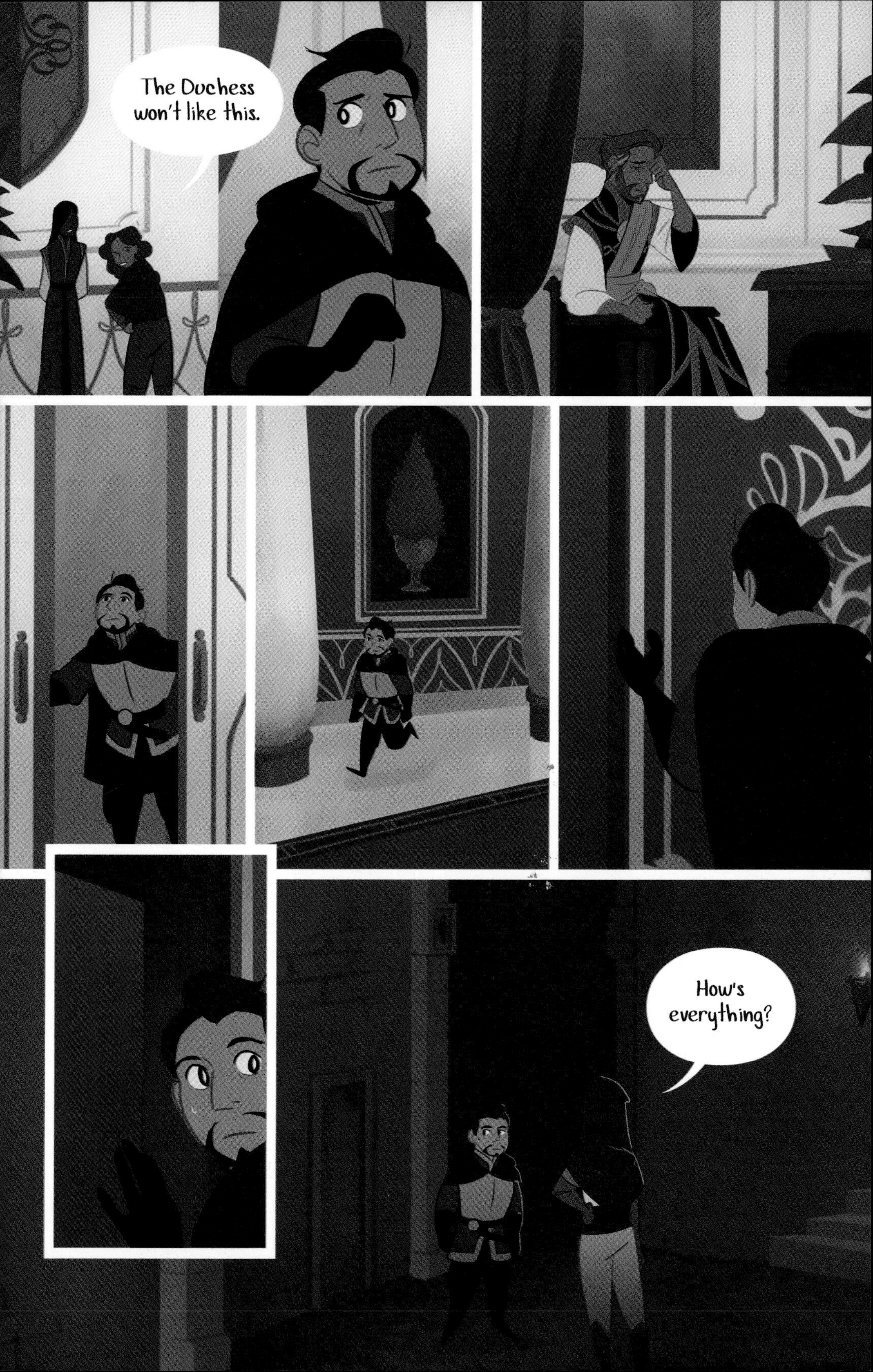
The Duchess won't like this.
How's everything?

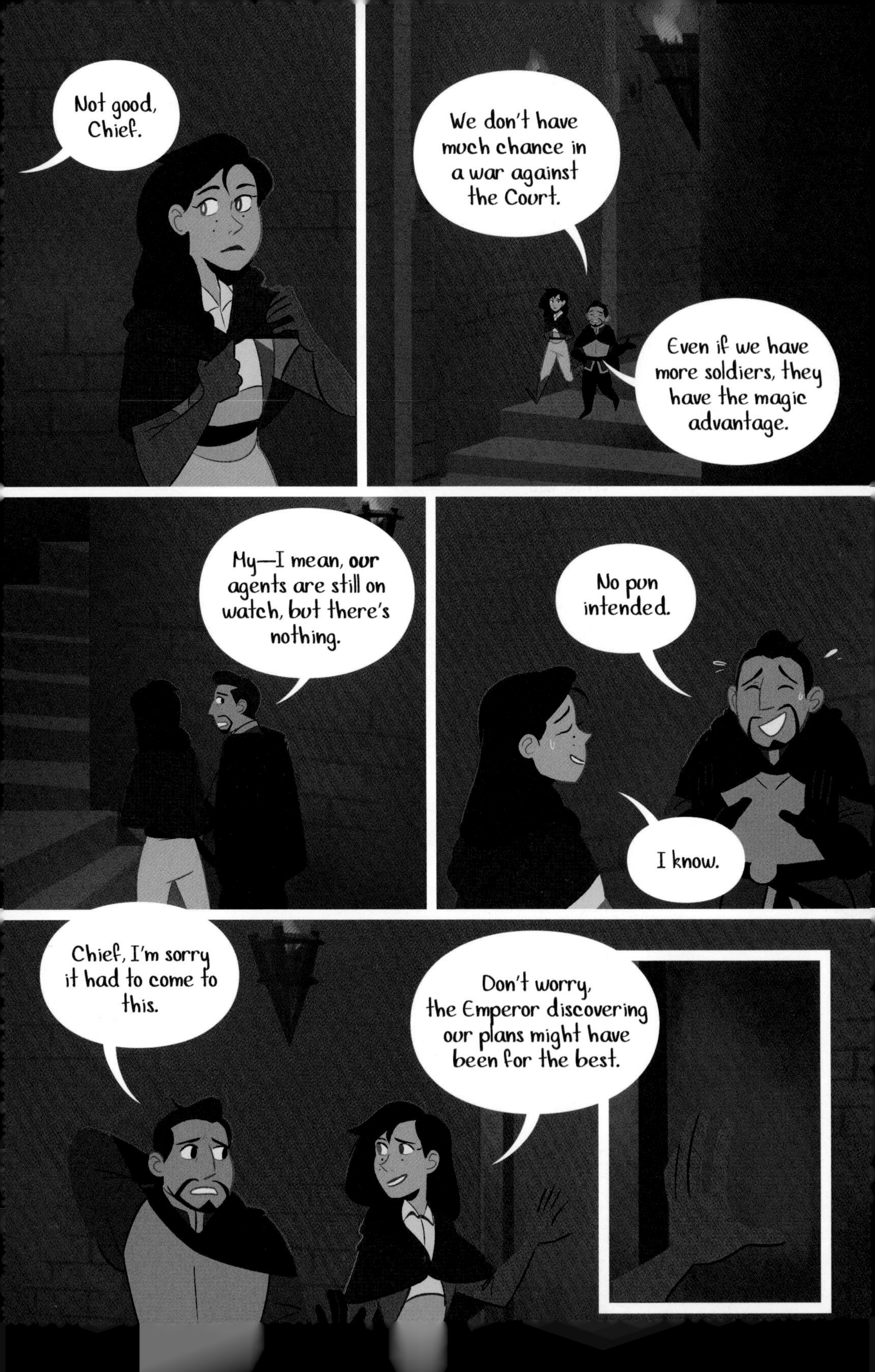
Not good, Chief.
We don't have much chance in a war against the Court.
Even if we have more soldiers, they have the magic advantage.
My—I mean, our agents are still on watch, but there's nothing.
No pun intended.
I know.
Chief, I'm sorry it had to come to this.
Don't worry, the Emperor discovering our plans might have been for the best.

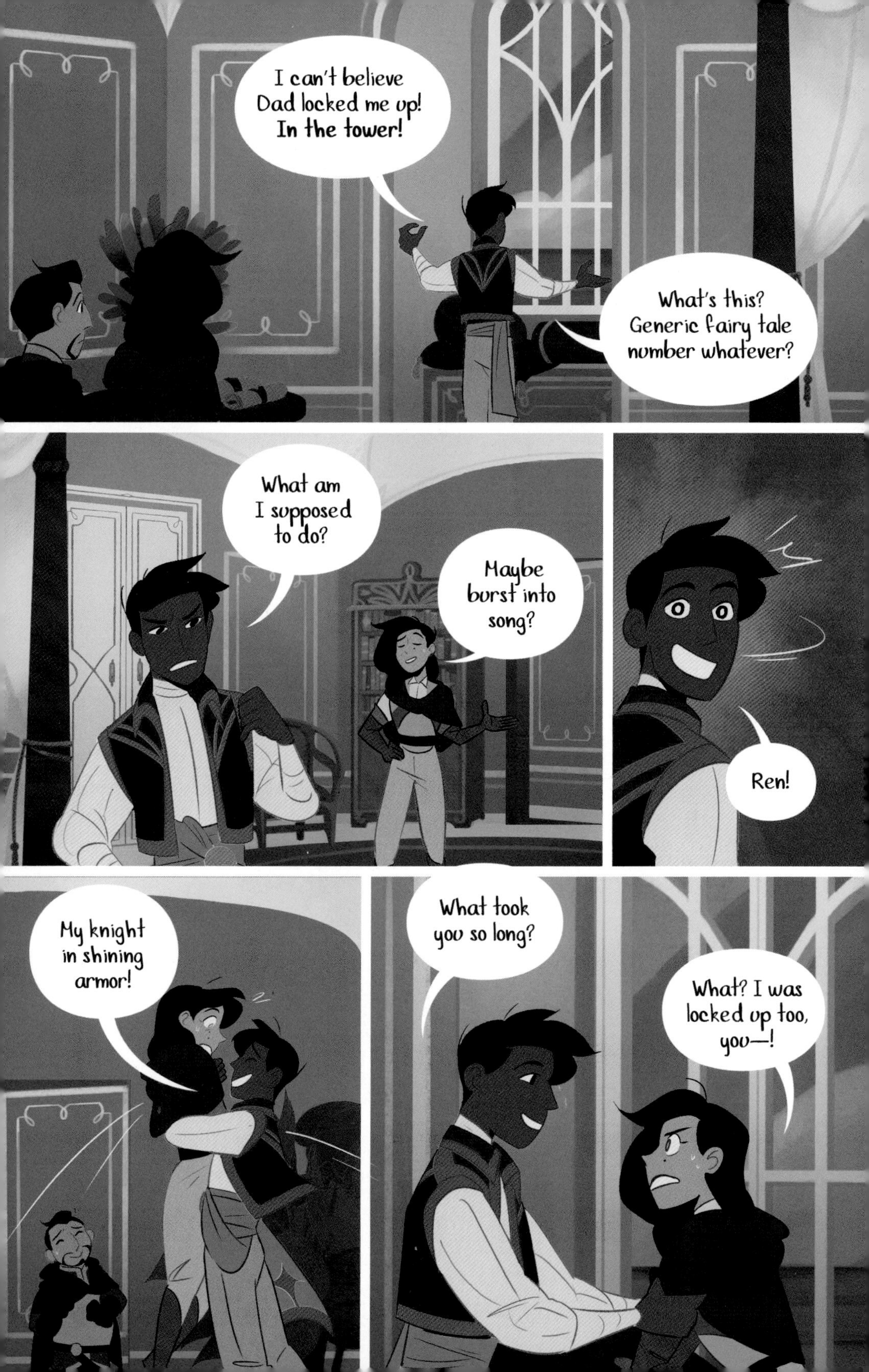
I can't believe Dad locked me up! In the tower!
What's this? Generic fairy tale number whatever?
What am I supposed to do?
Maybe burst into song?
Ren!
My knight in shining armor!
What took you so long?
What? I was locked up too, you—!

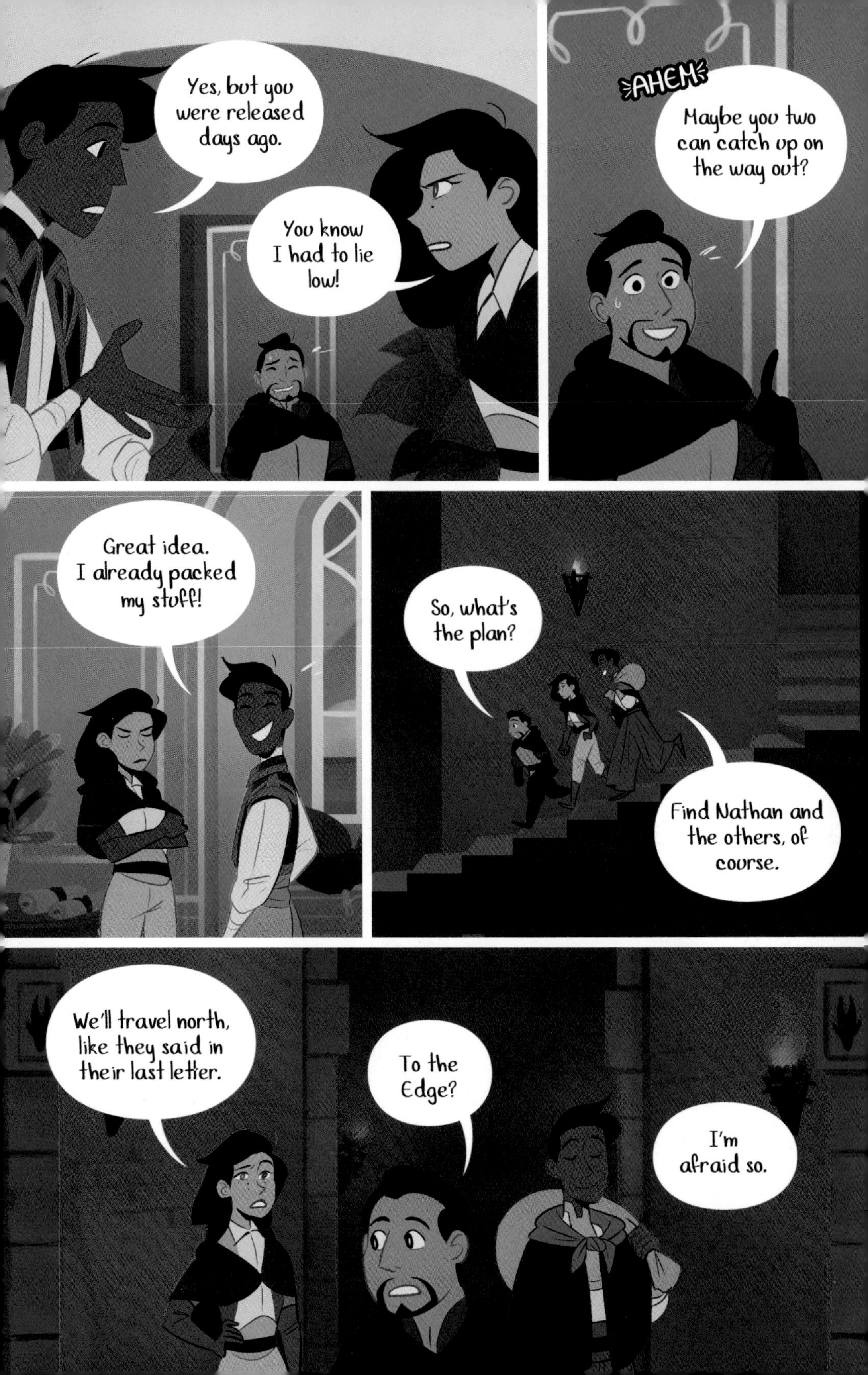
Yes, but you were released days ago.
You know I had to lie low!
AHEM
Maybe you two can catch up on the way out?
Great idea. I already packed my stuff!
So, what's the plan?
Find Nathan and the others, of course.
We'll travel north, like they said in their last letter.
To the Edge?
I'm afraid so.

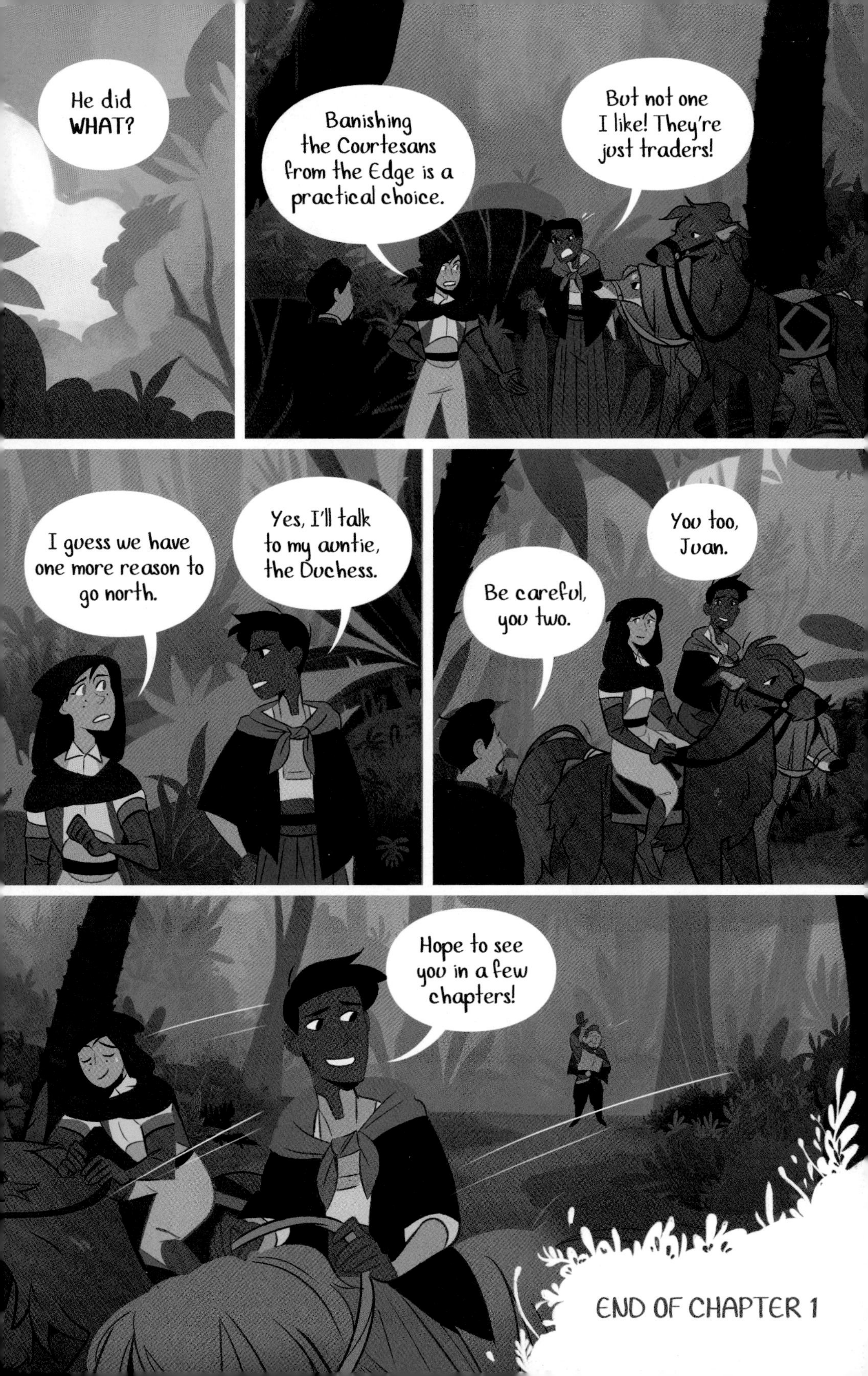
He did WHAT?
Banishing the Courtesans from the Edge is a practical choice.
But not one I like! They're just traders!
I guess we have one more reason to go north.
Yes, I'll talk to my auntie, the Duchess.
You too, Juan.
Be careful, you two.
Hope to see you in a few chapters!
END OF CHAPTER 1

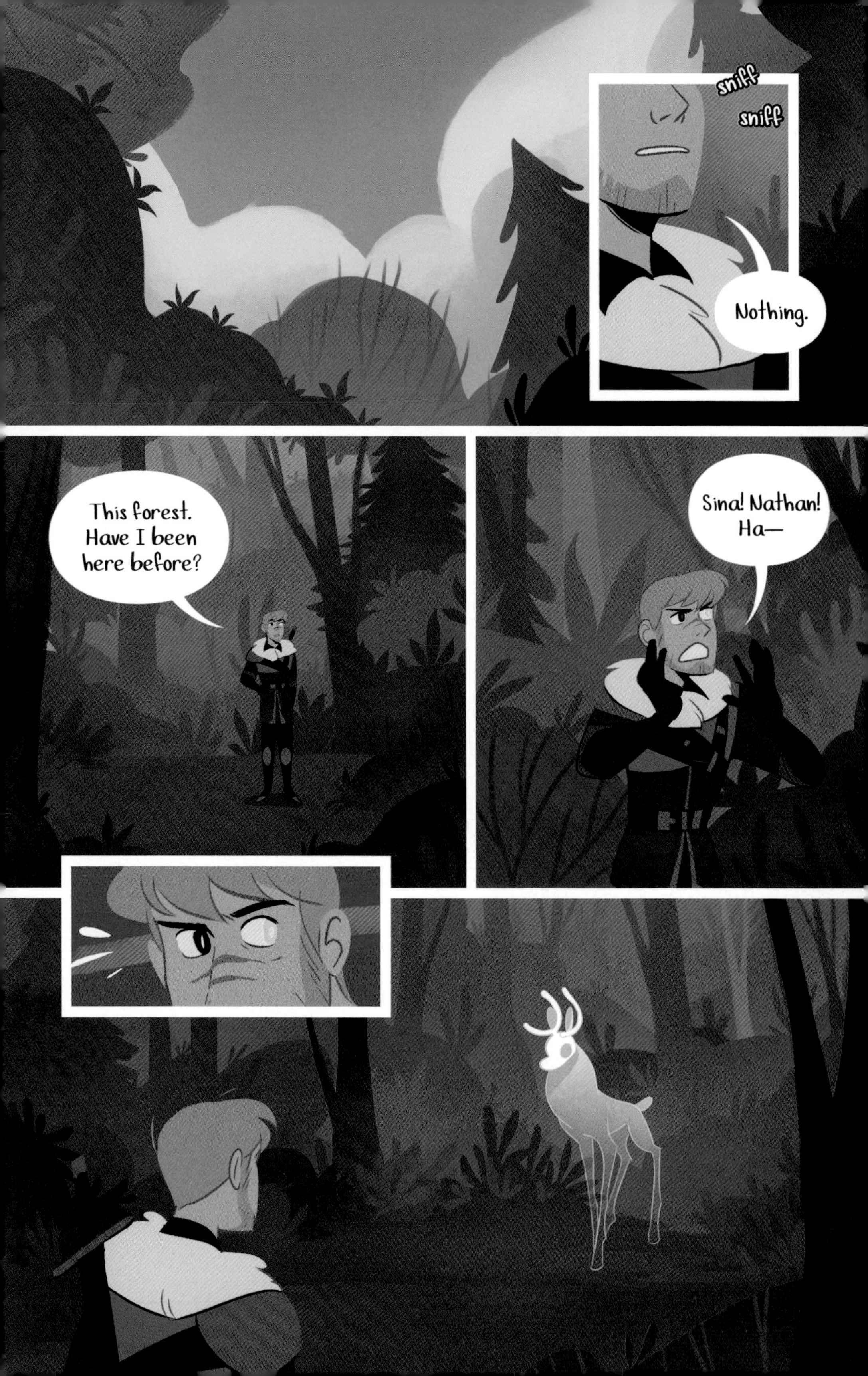
sniff
sniff
Nothing.
This forest. Have I been here before?
Sina! Nathan! Ha—

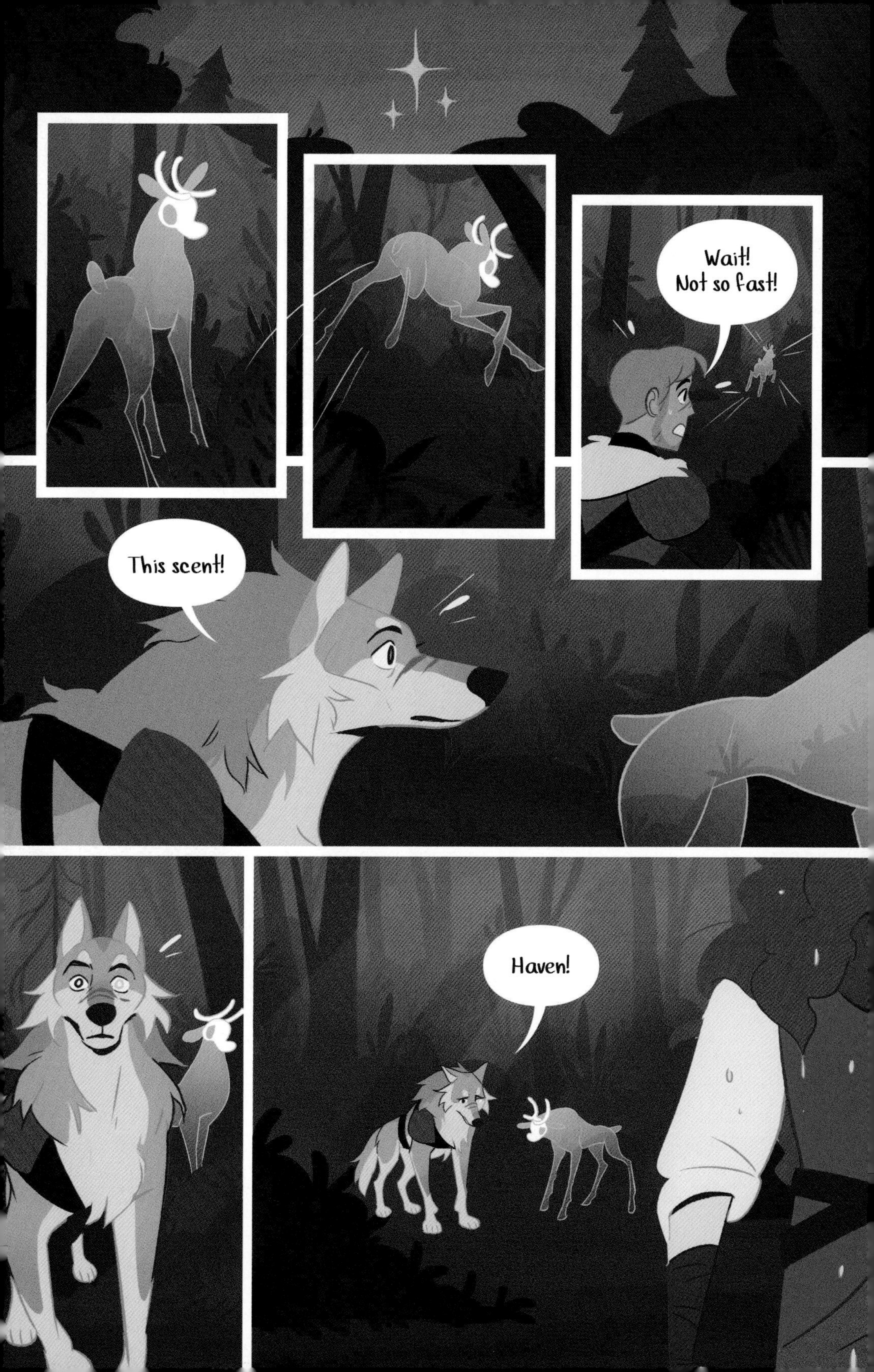
Wait! Not so fast!
This scent!
Haven!

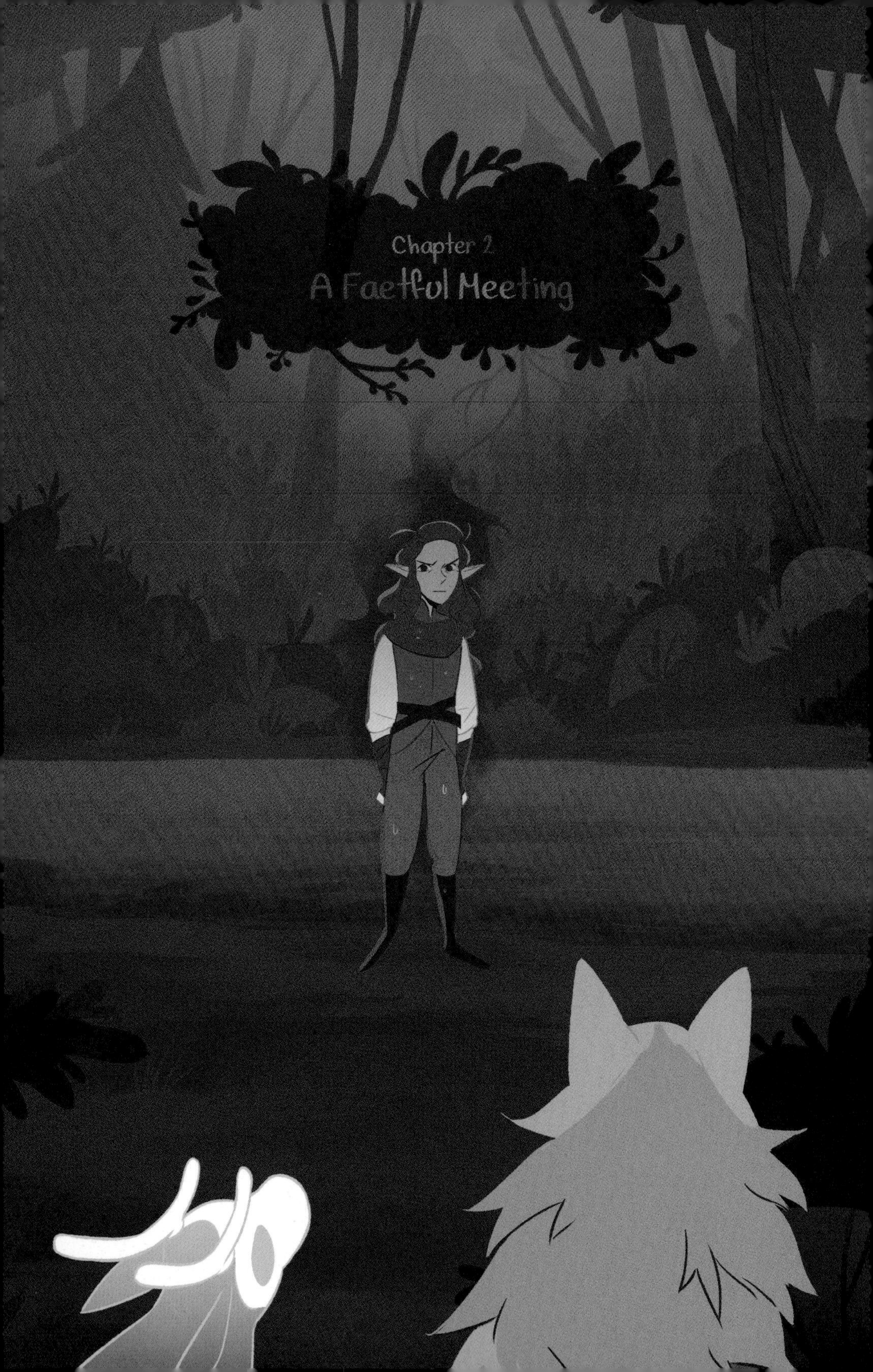
Chapter 2
A Faetful Meeting

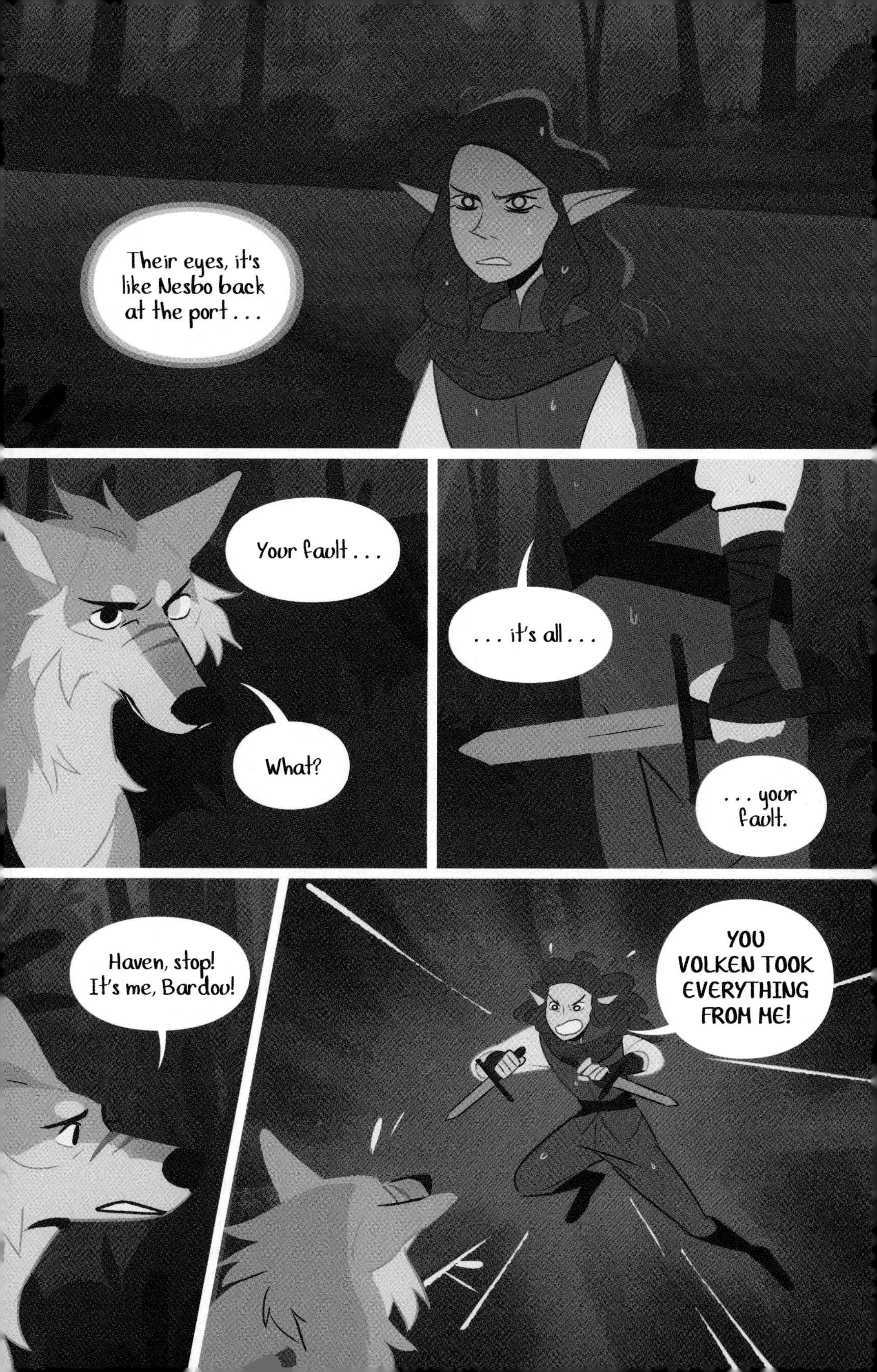
Their eyes, it's like Nesbo back at the port . . .
Your fault . . .
What?
. . . it's all . . .
. . . your fault.
Haven, stop! It's me, Bardou!
YOU VOLKEN TOOK EVERYTHING FROM ME!

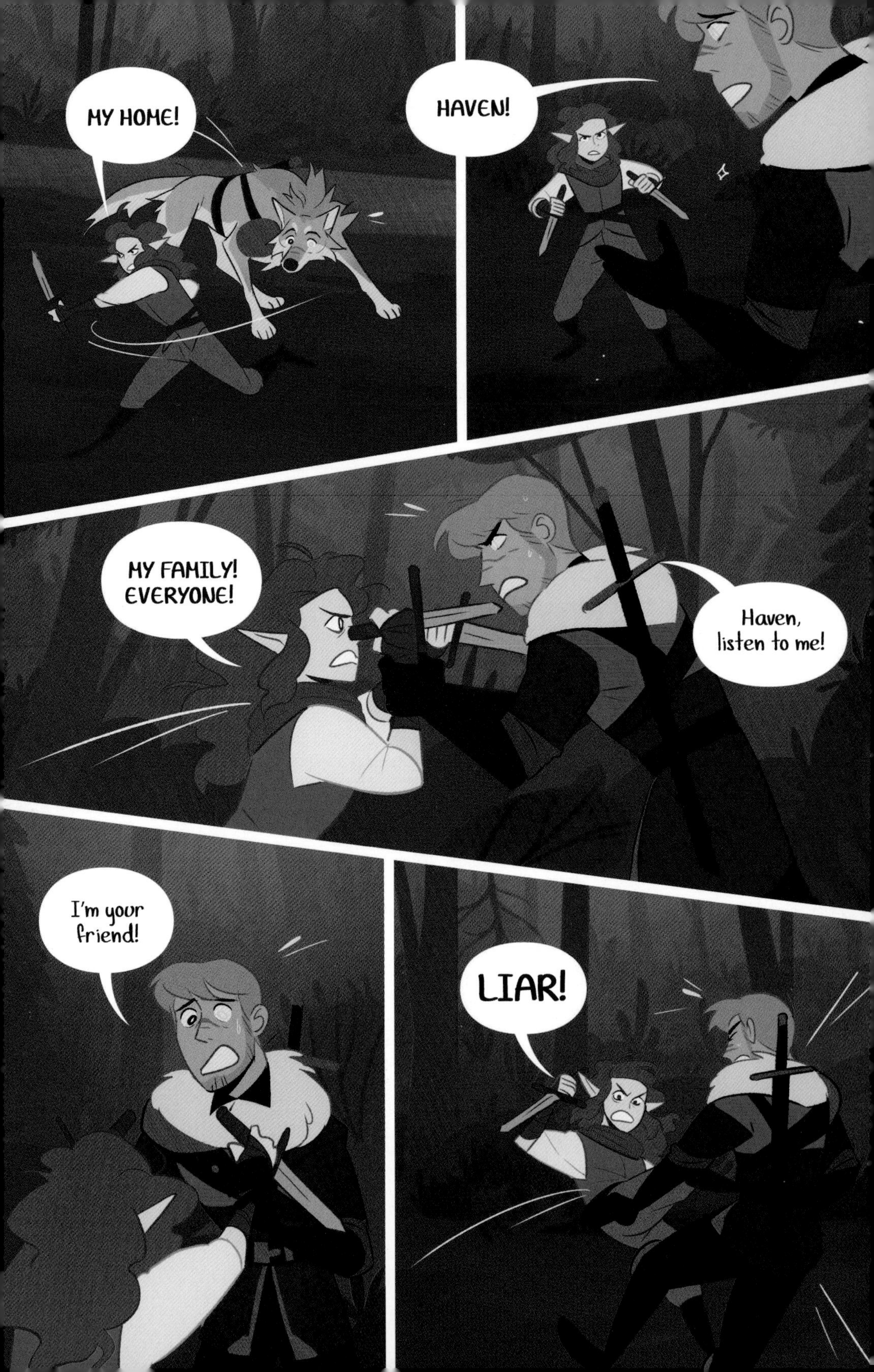
MY HOME!
HAVEN!
MY FAMILY! EVERYONE!
Haven, listen to me!
I'm your friend!
LIAR!

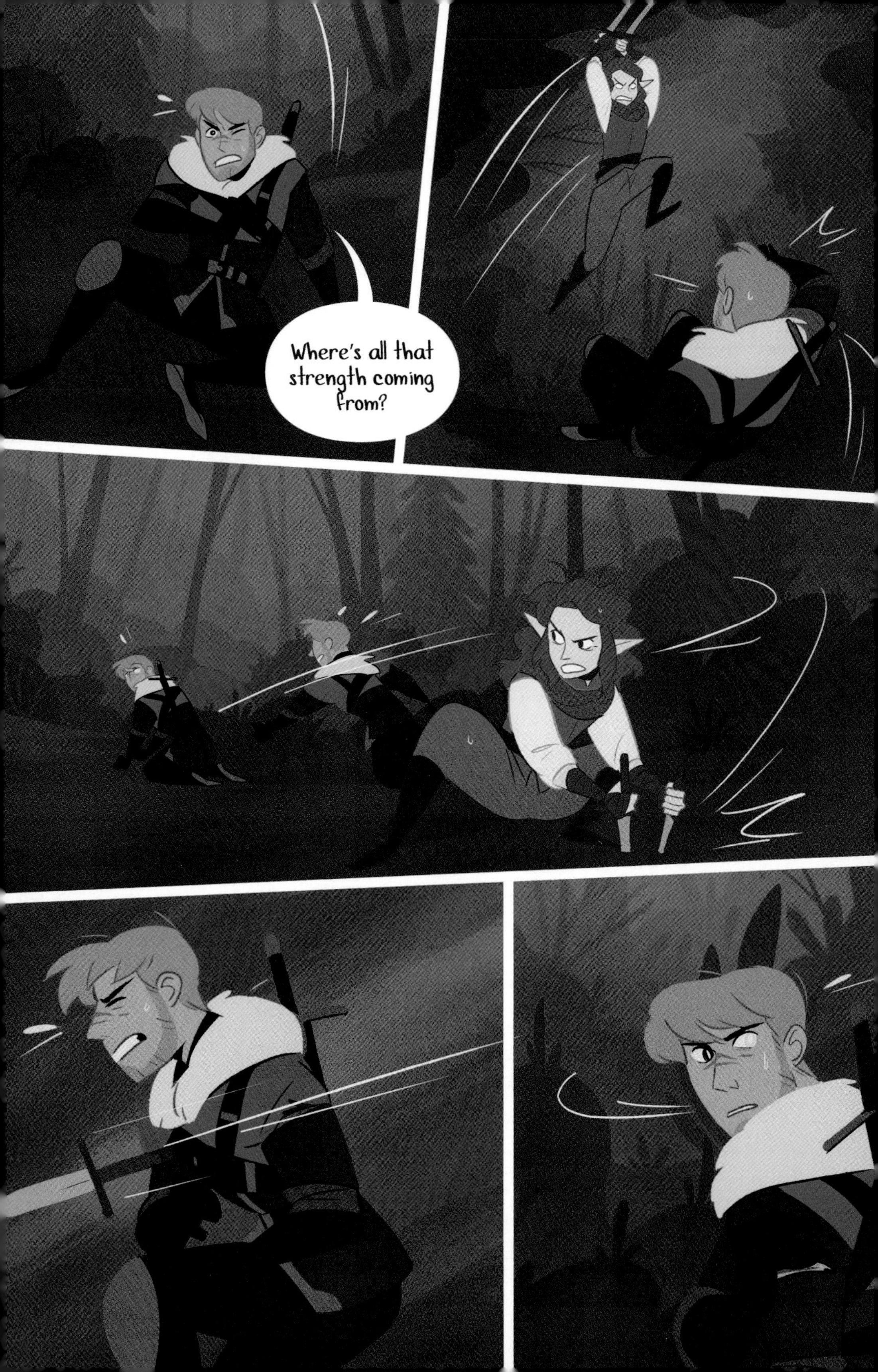
Where's all that strength coming from?

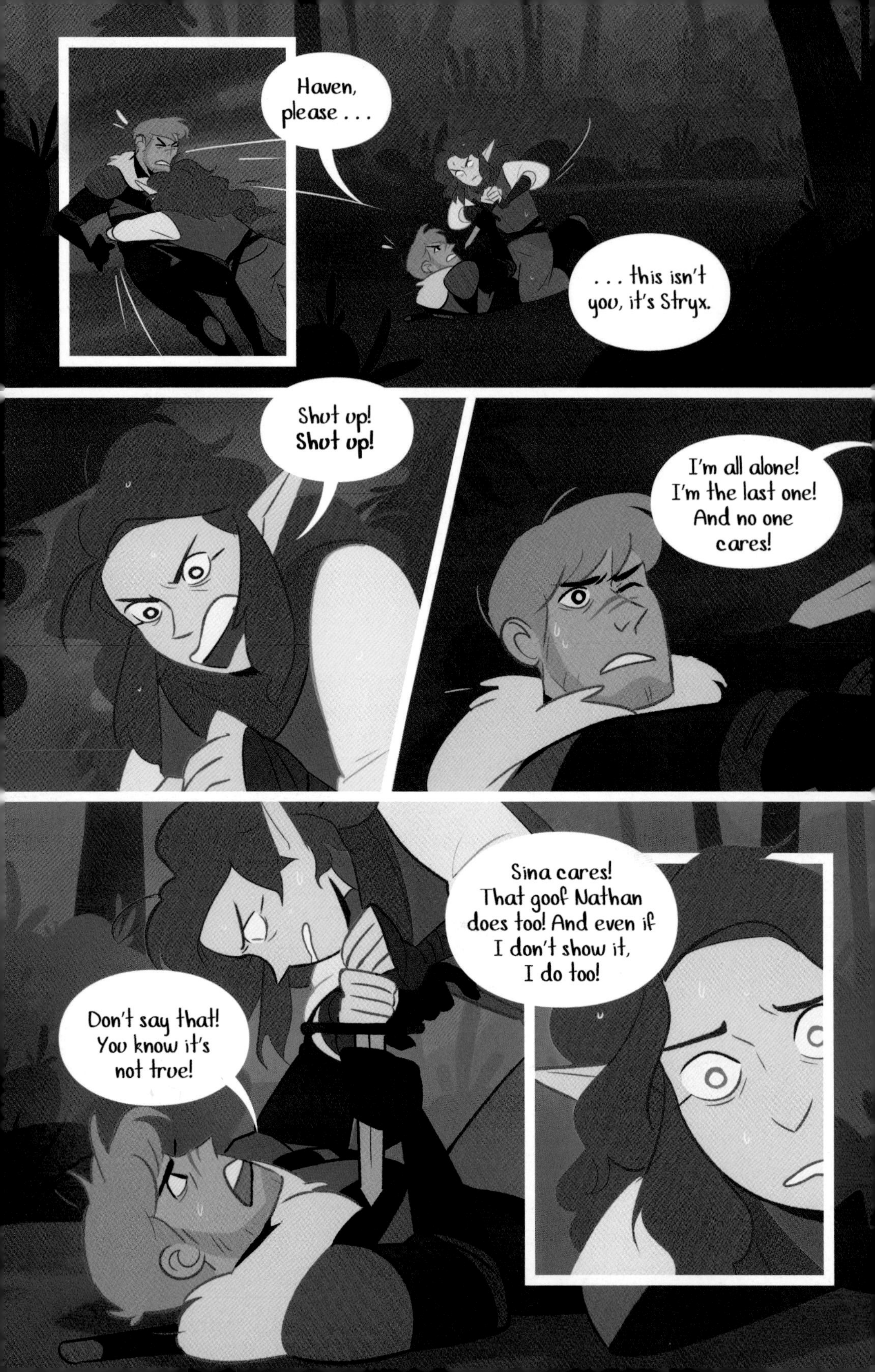
Haven, please . . .
. . . this isn't you, it's Stryx.
Shut up! Shut up!
I'm all alone! I'm the last one! And no one cares!
Sina cares! That goof Nathan does too! And even if I don't show it, I do too!
Don't say that! You know it's not true!

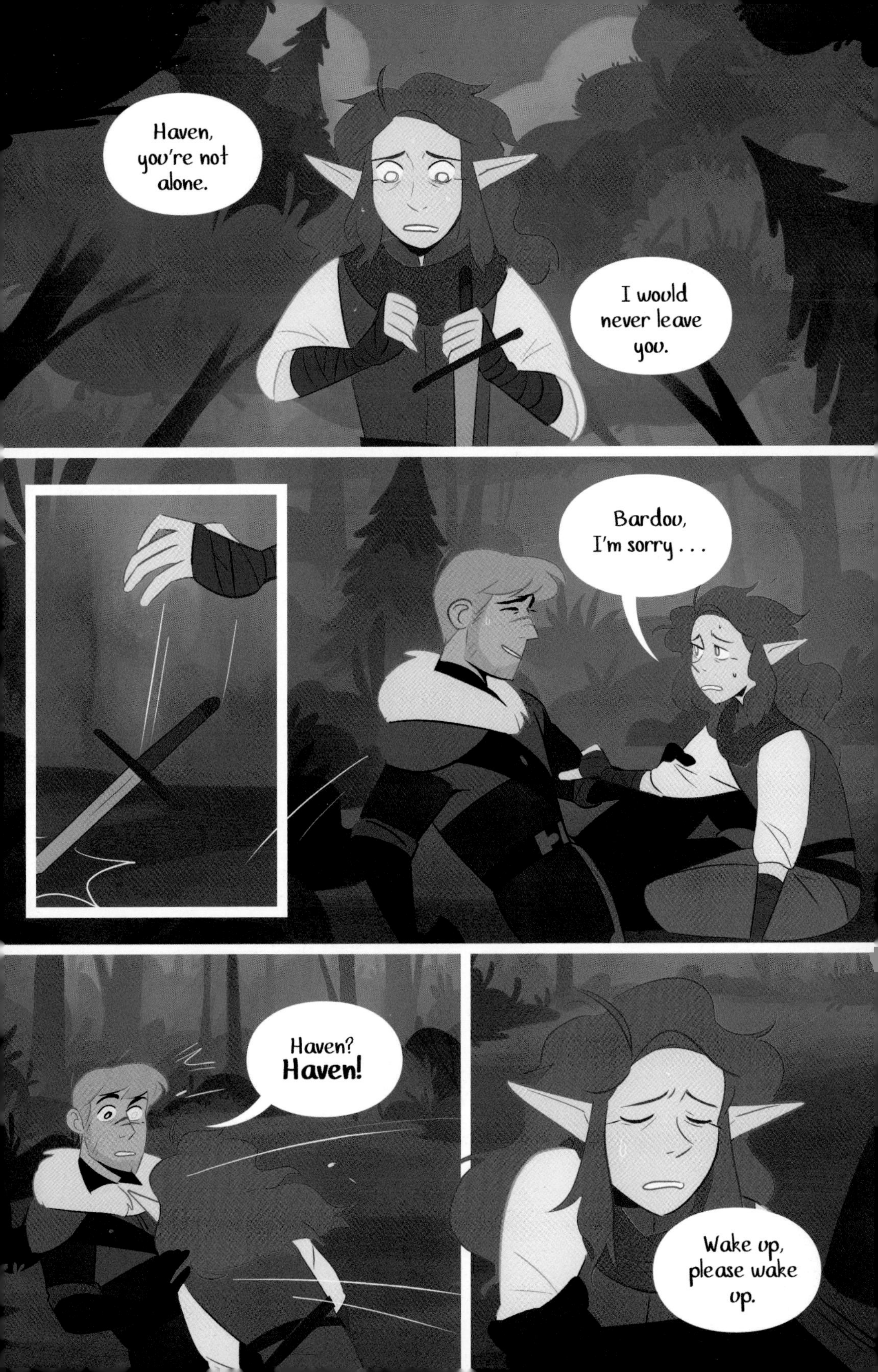
Haven, you're not alone.
I would never leave you.
Bardou, I'm sorry . . .
Haven? **Haven!**
Wake up, please wake up.

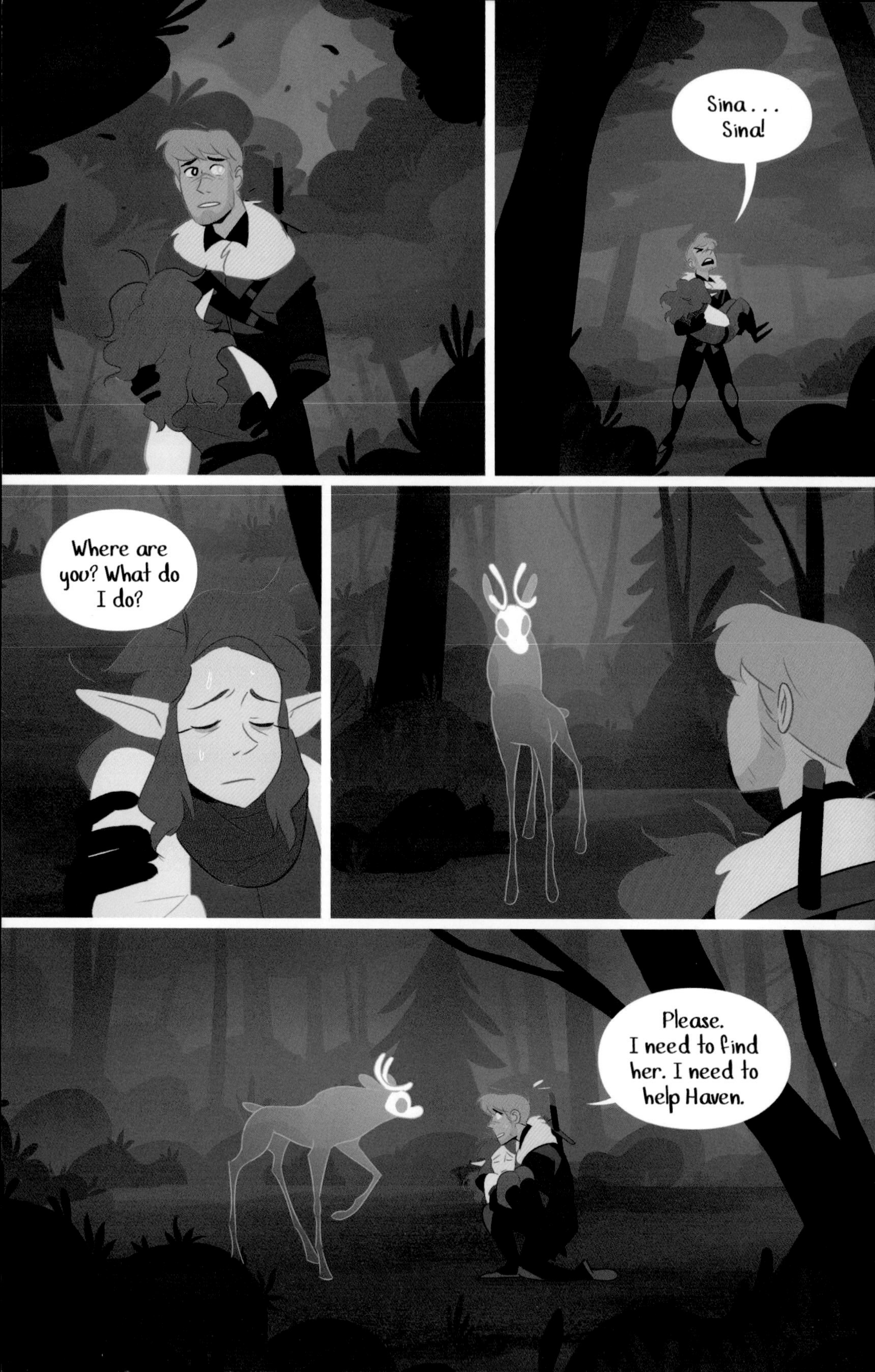
Sina . . .
Sina!
Where are you? What do I do?
Please. I need to find her. I need to help Haven.

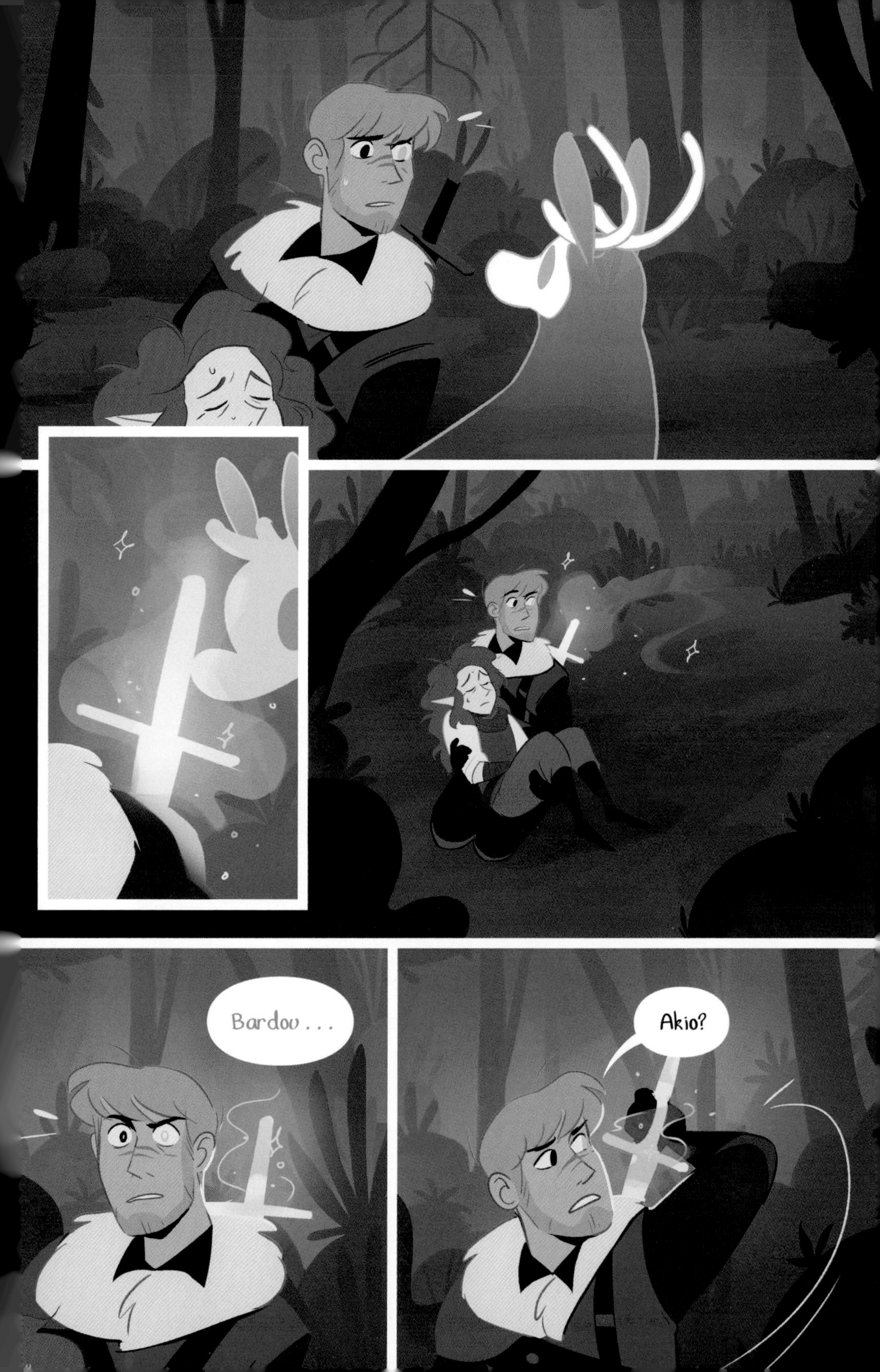
Bardou . . .
Akio?

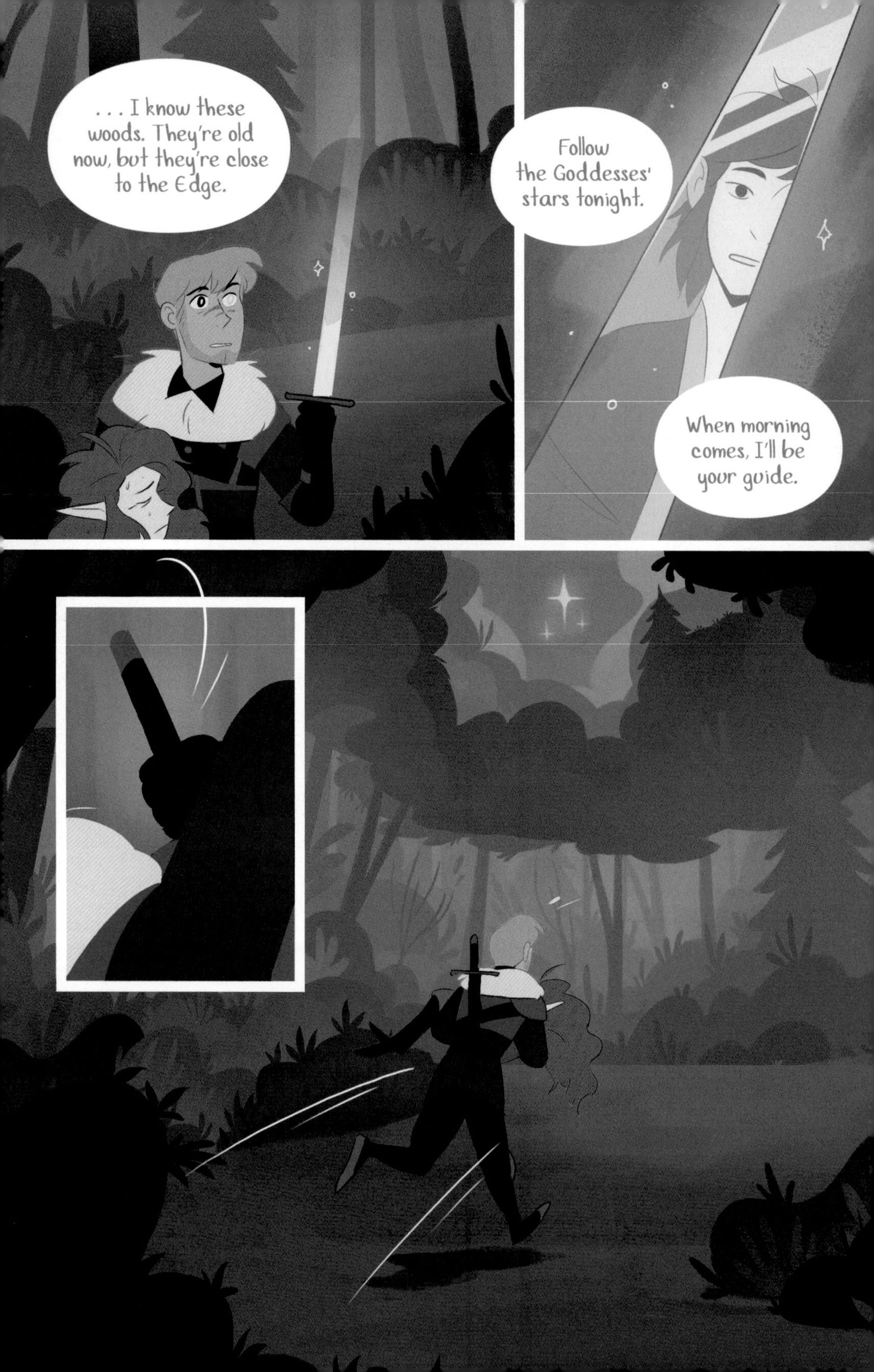
. . . I know these woods. They're old now, but they're close to the Edge.
Follow the Goddesses' stars tonight.
When morning comes, I'll be your guide.

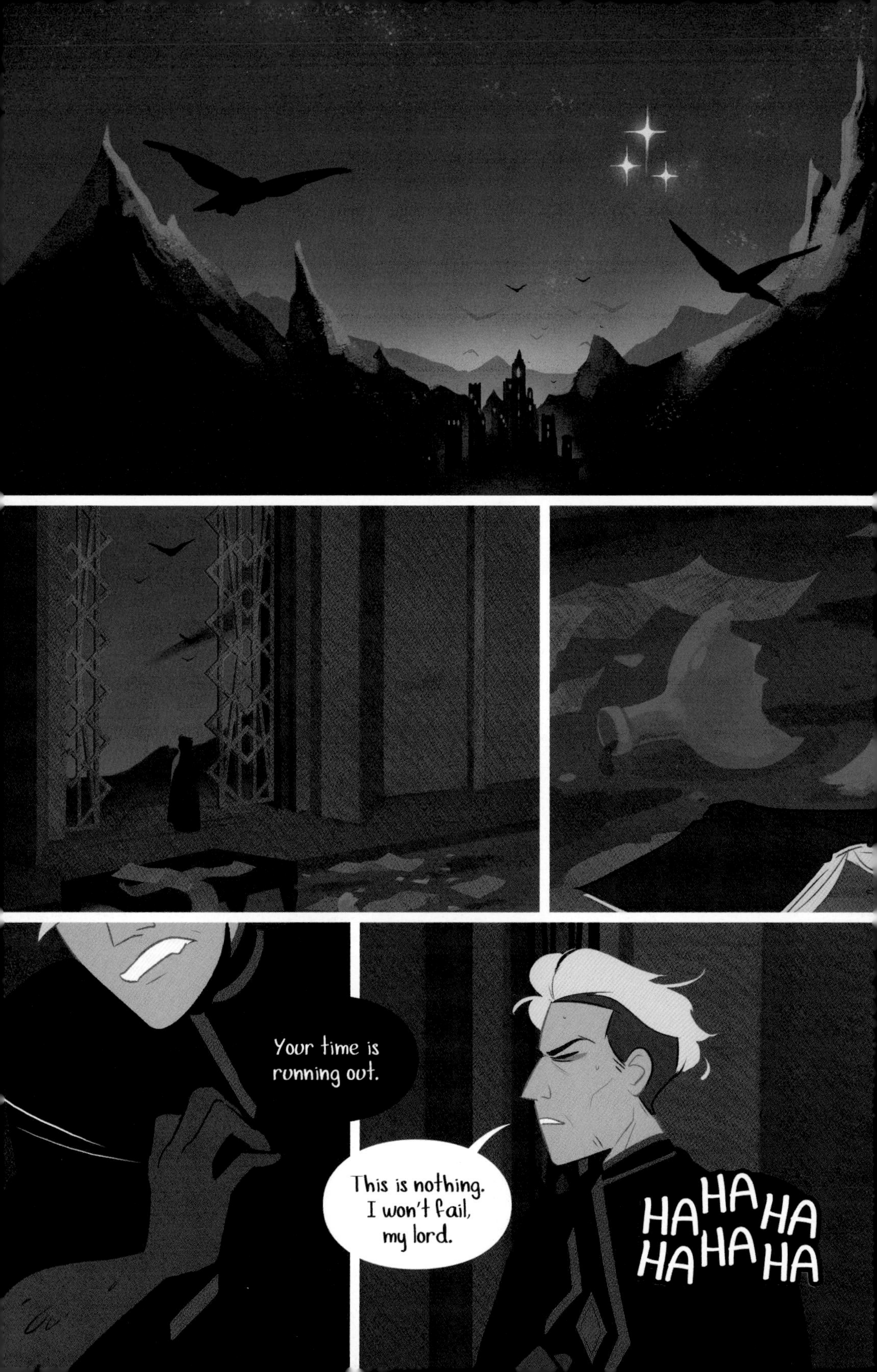
Your time is running out.
This is nothing. I won't fail, my lord.
HAHAHAHA
HAHAHAHA

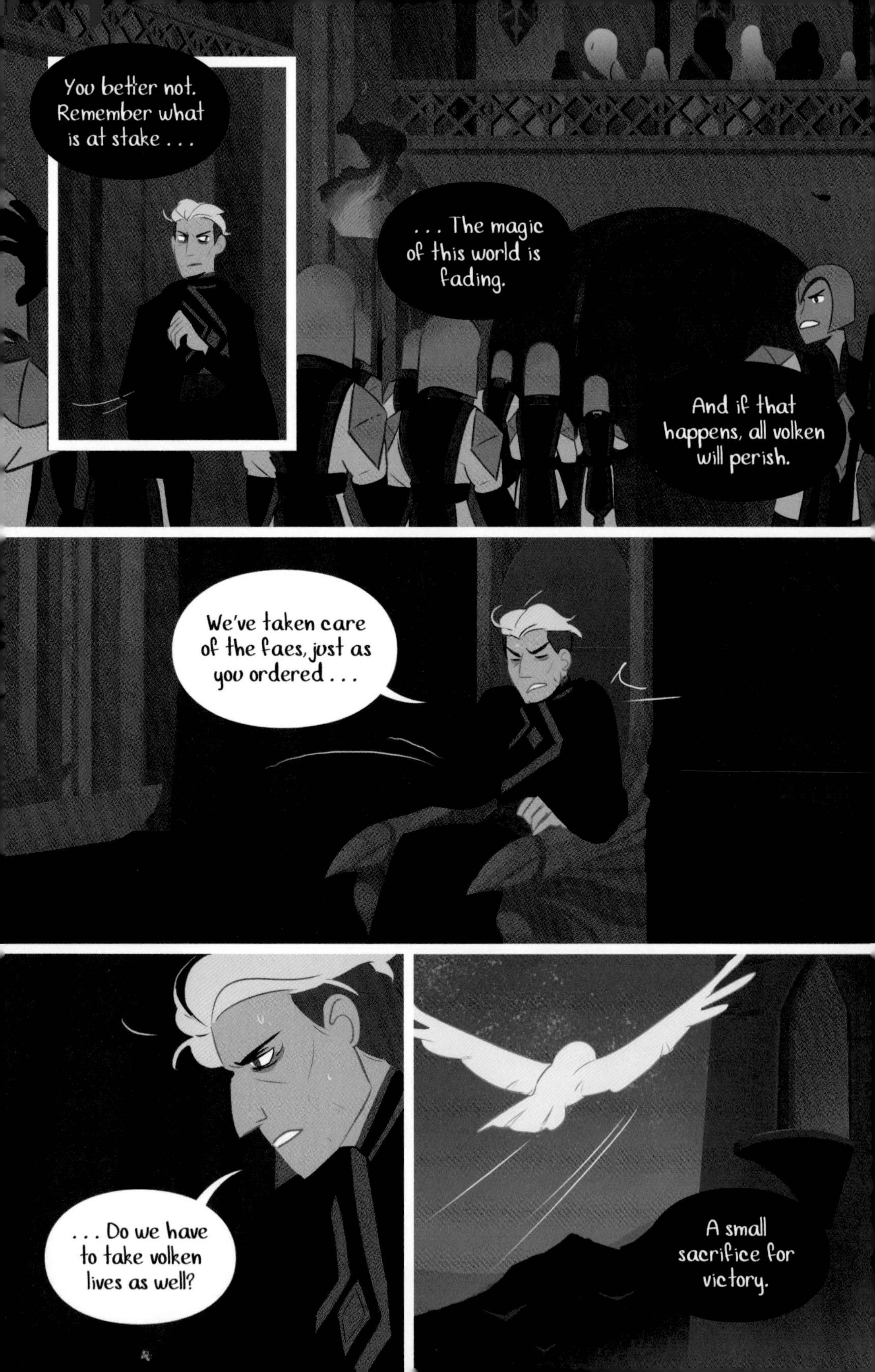
You better not. Remember what is at stake . . .
. . . The magic of this world is fading.
And if that happens, all volken will perish.
We've taken care of the faes, just as you ordered . . .
. . . Do we have to take volken lives as well?
A small sacrifice for victory.

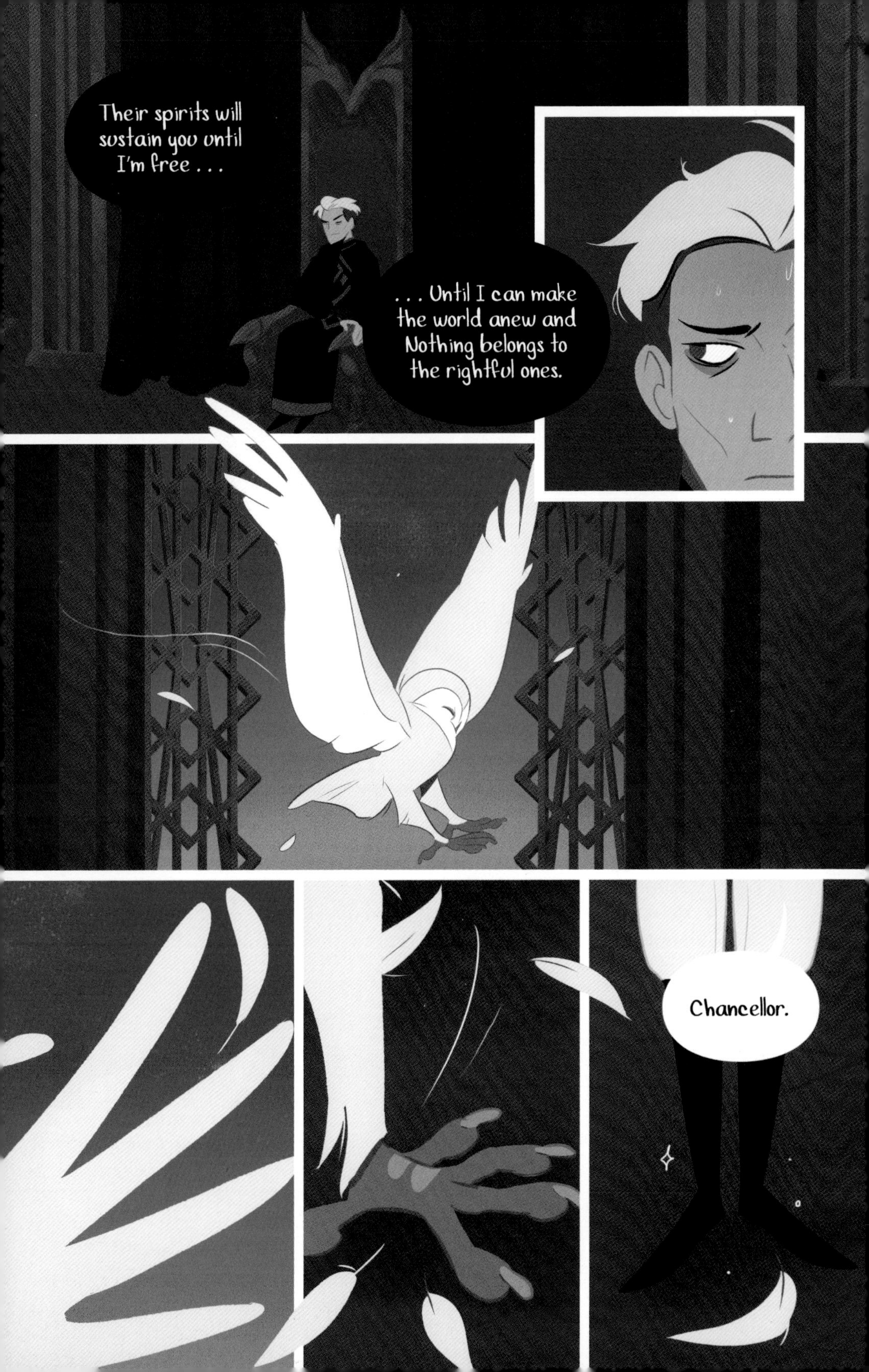
Their spirits will sustain you until I'm free . . .
. . . Until I can make the world anew and Nothing belongs to the rightful ones.
Chancellor.

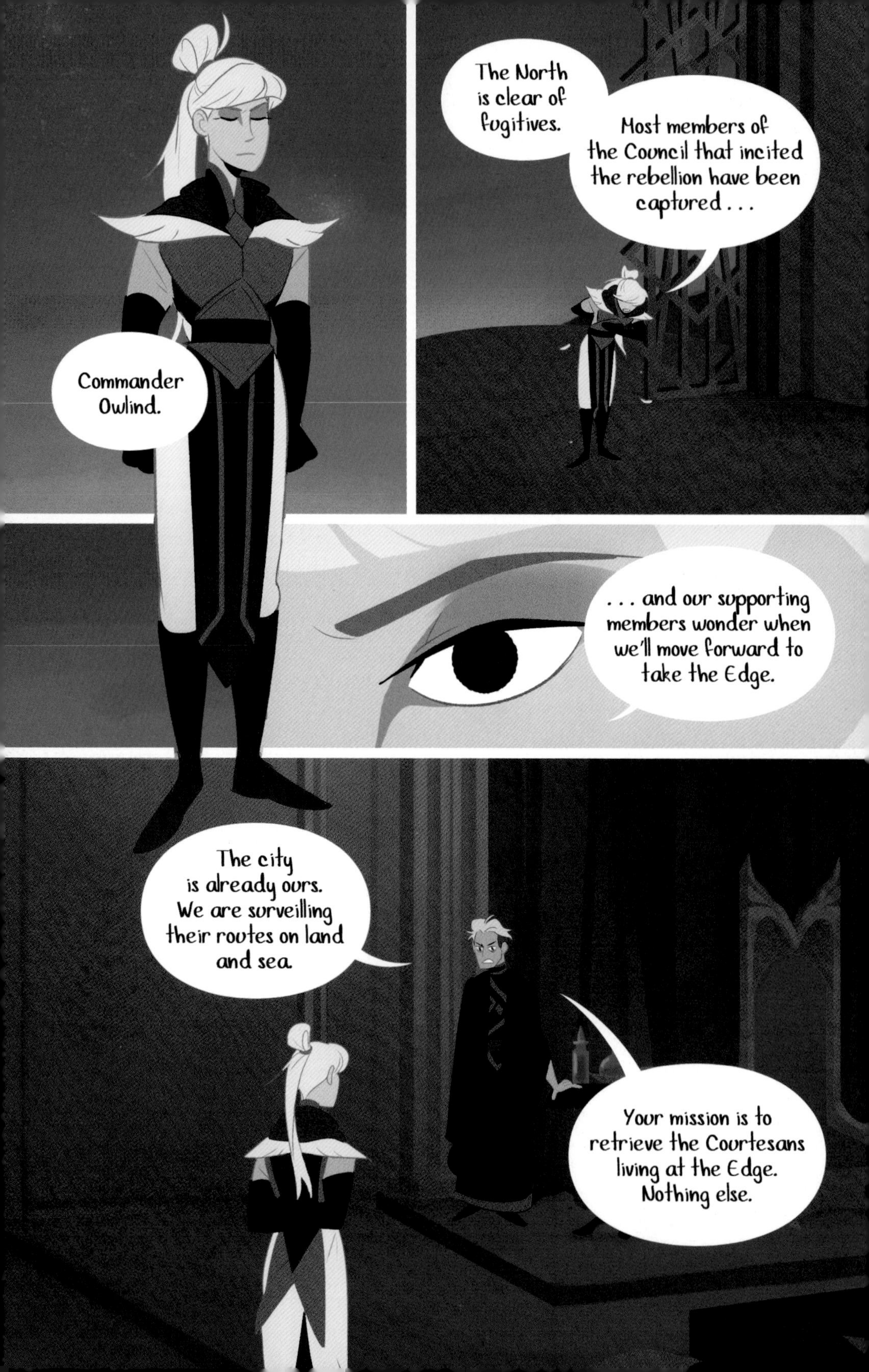
Commander Owlind.
The North is clear of fugitives.
Most members of the Council that incited the rebellion have been captured . . .
. . . and our supporting members wonder when we'll move forward to take the Edge.
The city is already ours. We are surveilling their routes on land and sea.
Your mission is to retrieve the Courtesans living at the Edge. Nothing else.

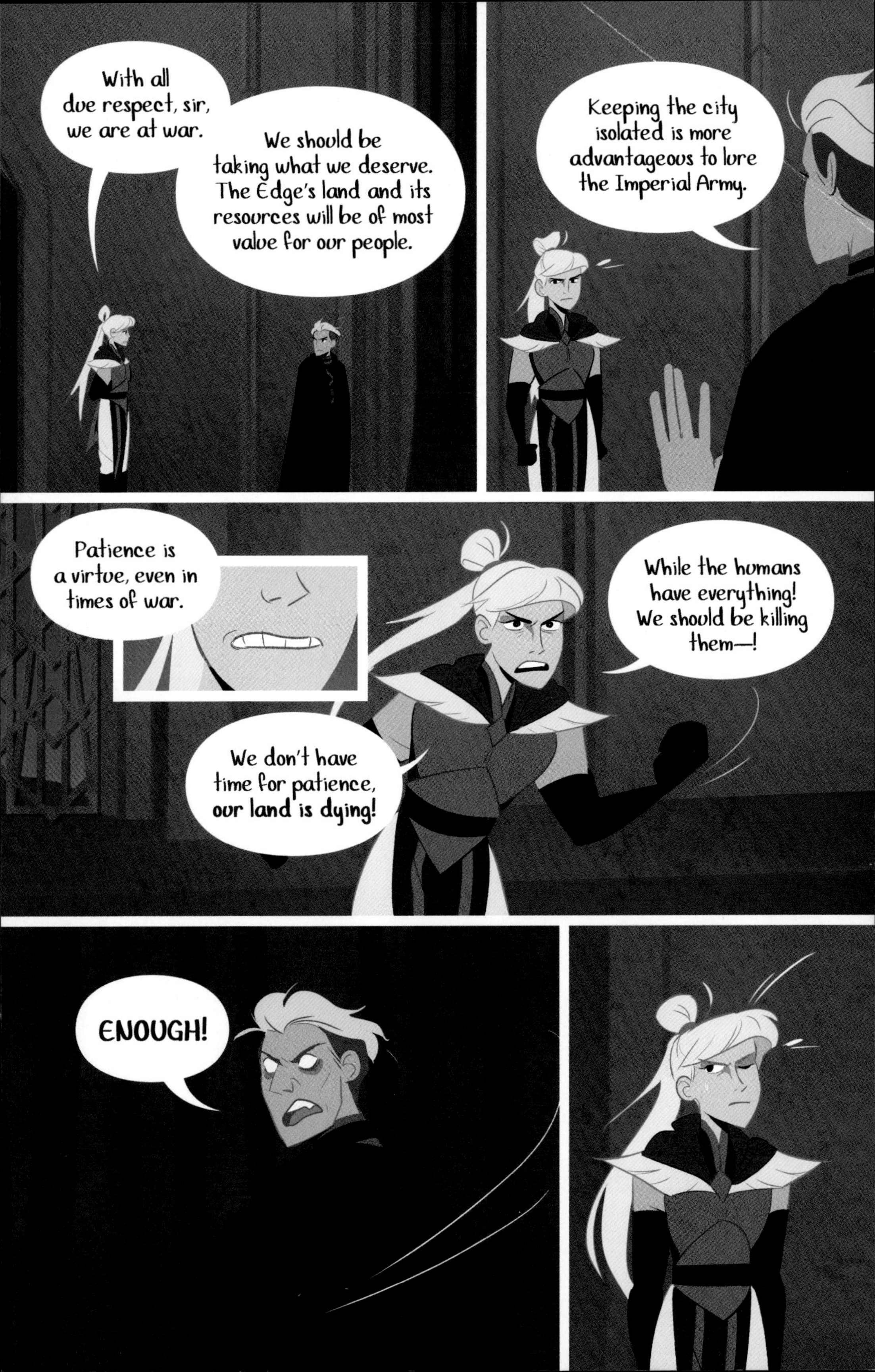
With all due respect, sir, we are at war.
We should be taking what we deserve. The Edge's land and its resources will be of most value for our people.
Keeping the city isolated is more advantageous to lure the Imperial Army.
Patience is a virtue, even in times of war.
While the humans have everything! We should be killing them—!
We don't have time for patience, our land is dying!
ENOUGH!

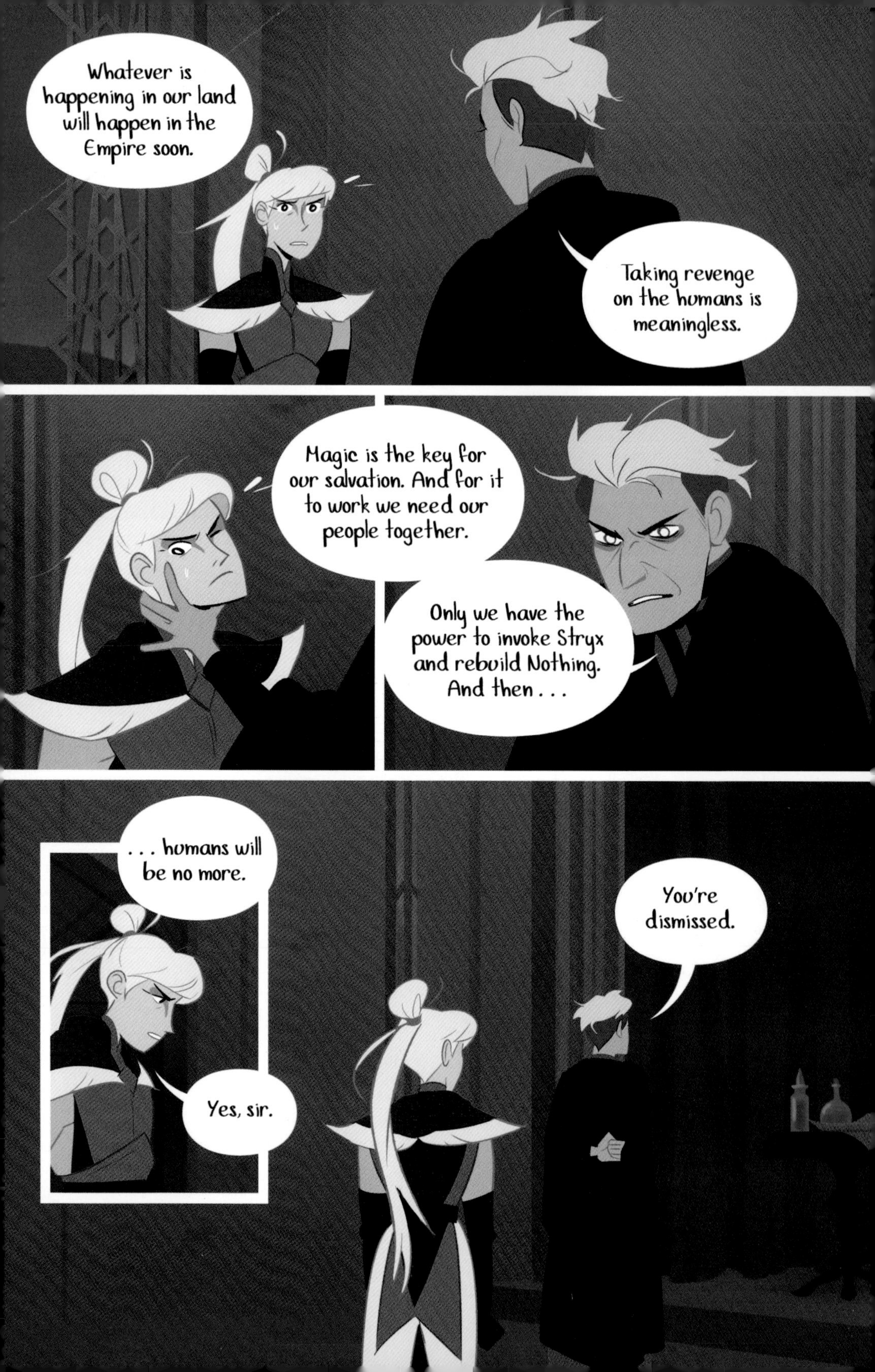
Whatever is happening in our land will happen in the Empire soon.
Taking revenge on the humans is meaningless.
Magic is the key for our salvation. And for it to work we need our people together.
Only we have the power to invoke Stryx and rebuild Nothing. And then . . .
. . . humans will be no more.
Yes, sir.
You're dismissed.

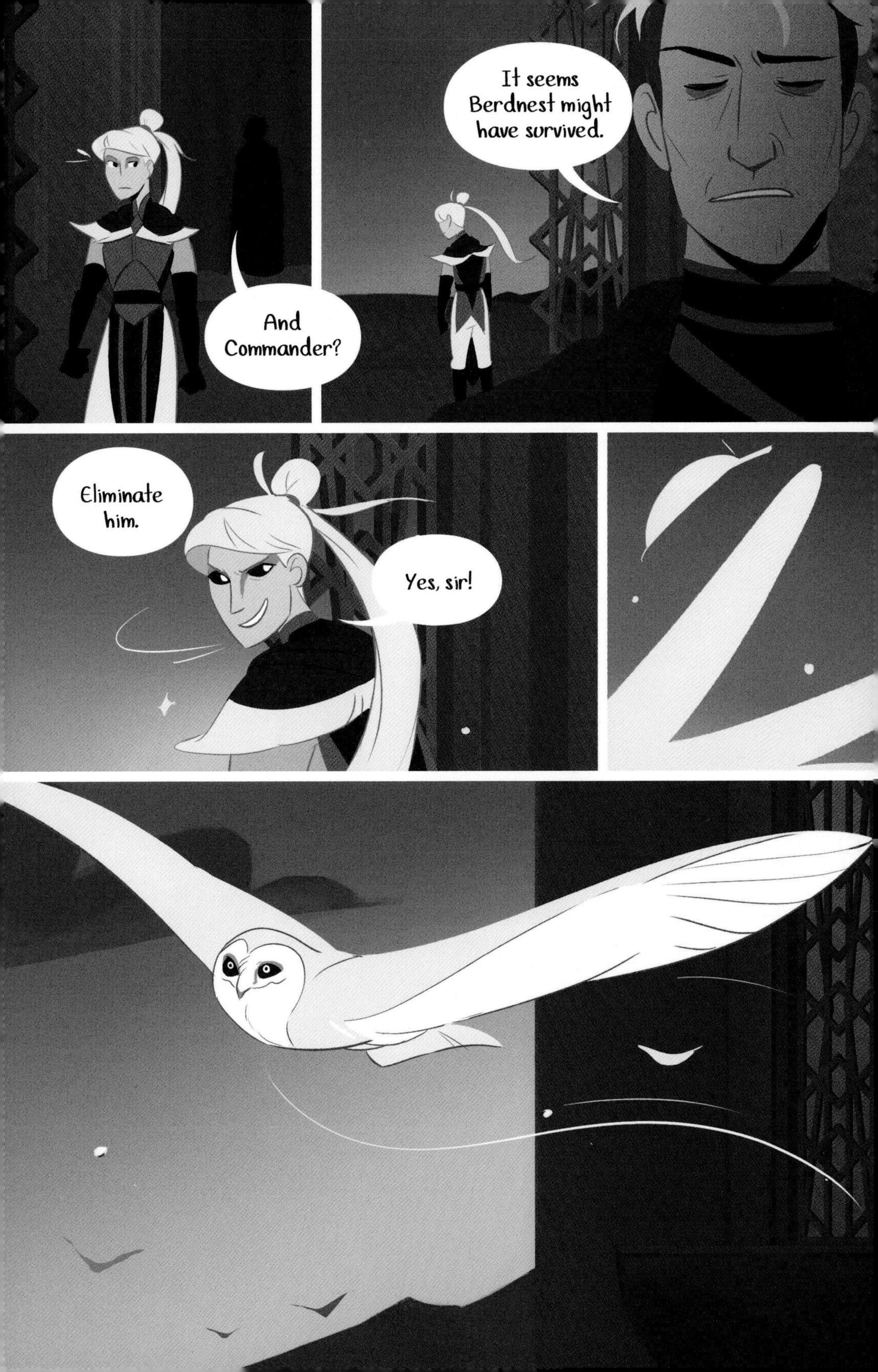
It seems Berdnest might have survived.
And Commander?
Eliminate him.
Yes, sir!

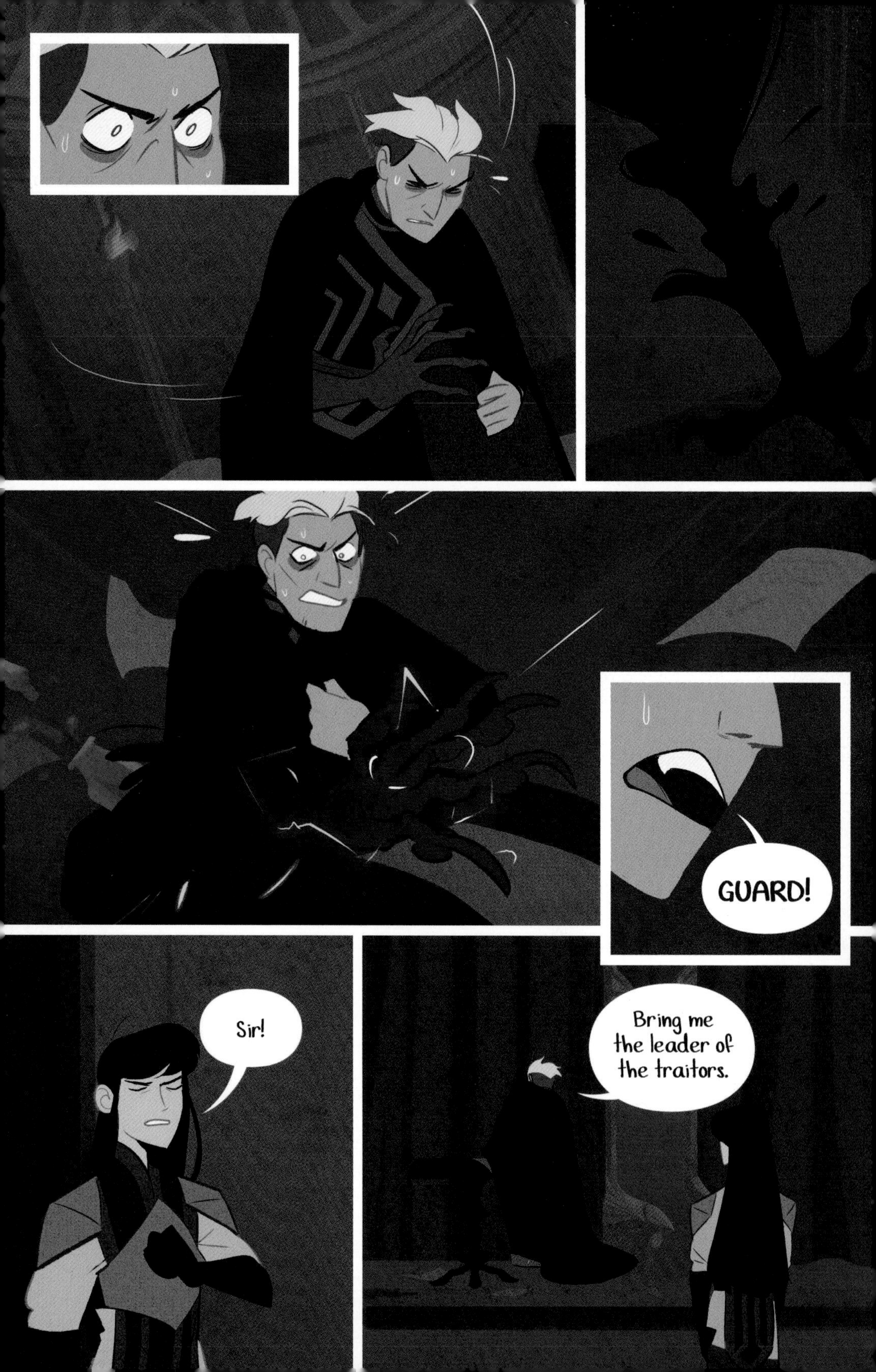
GUARD!
Sir!
Bring me the leader of the traitors.

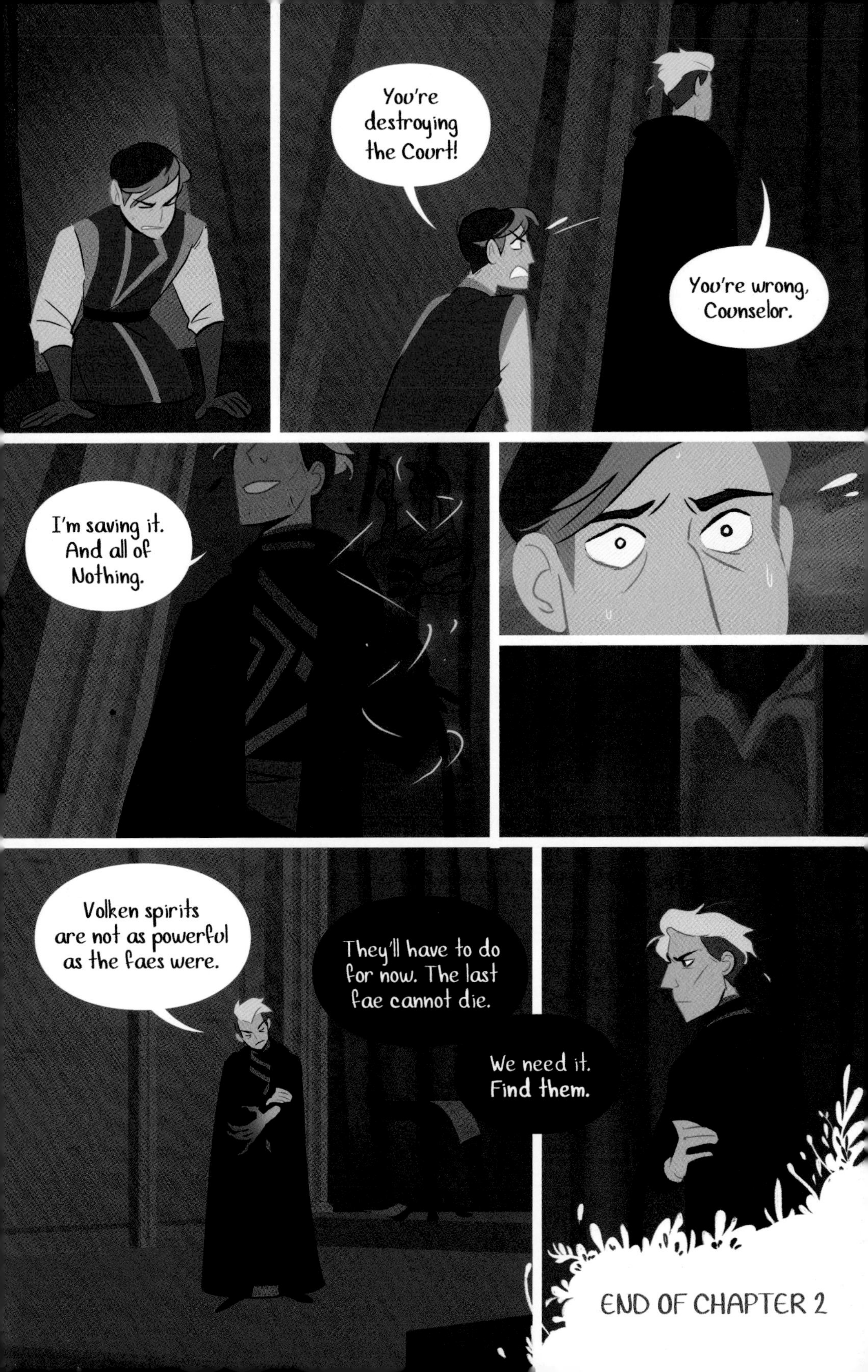
You're destroying the Court!
You're wrong, Counselor.
I'm saving it. And all of Nothing.
Volken spirits are not as powerful as the faes were.
They'll have to do for now. The last fae cannot die.
We need it. Find them.
END OF CHAPTER 2

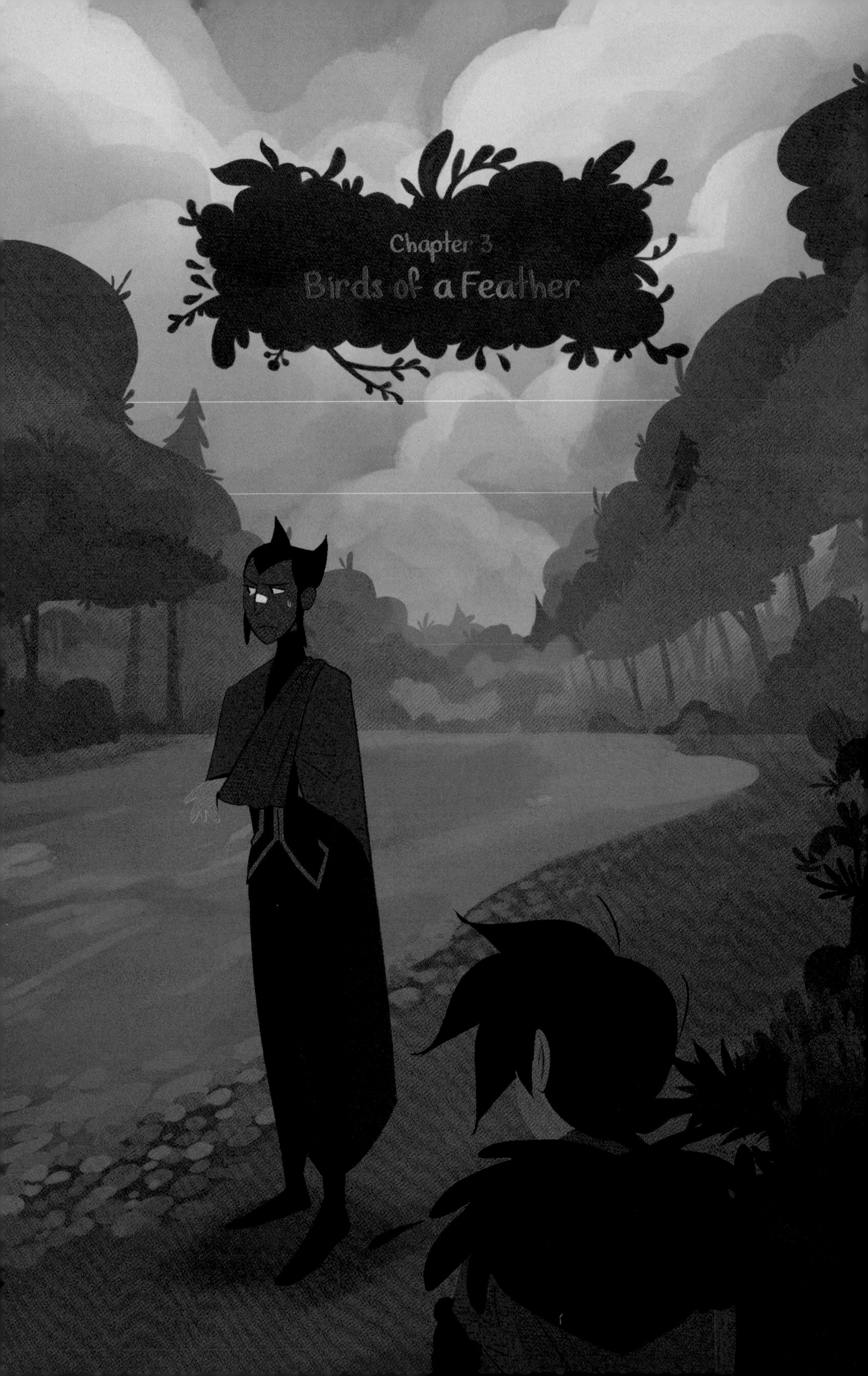
Chapter 3
Birds of a Feather

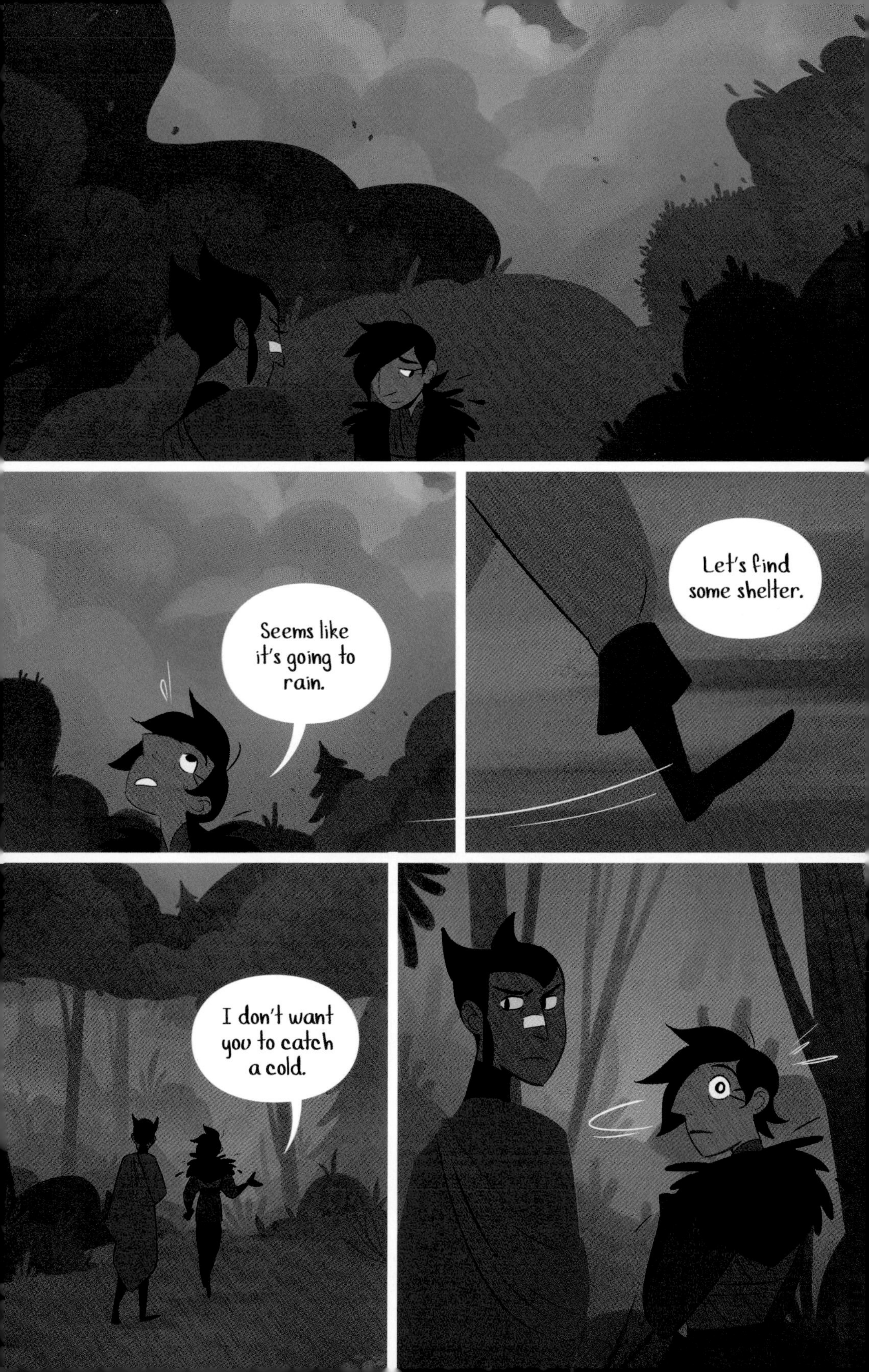
Seems like it's going to rain.
Let's find some shelter.
I don't want you to catch a cold.

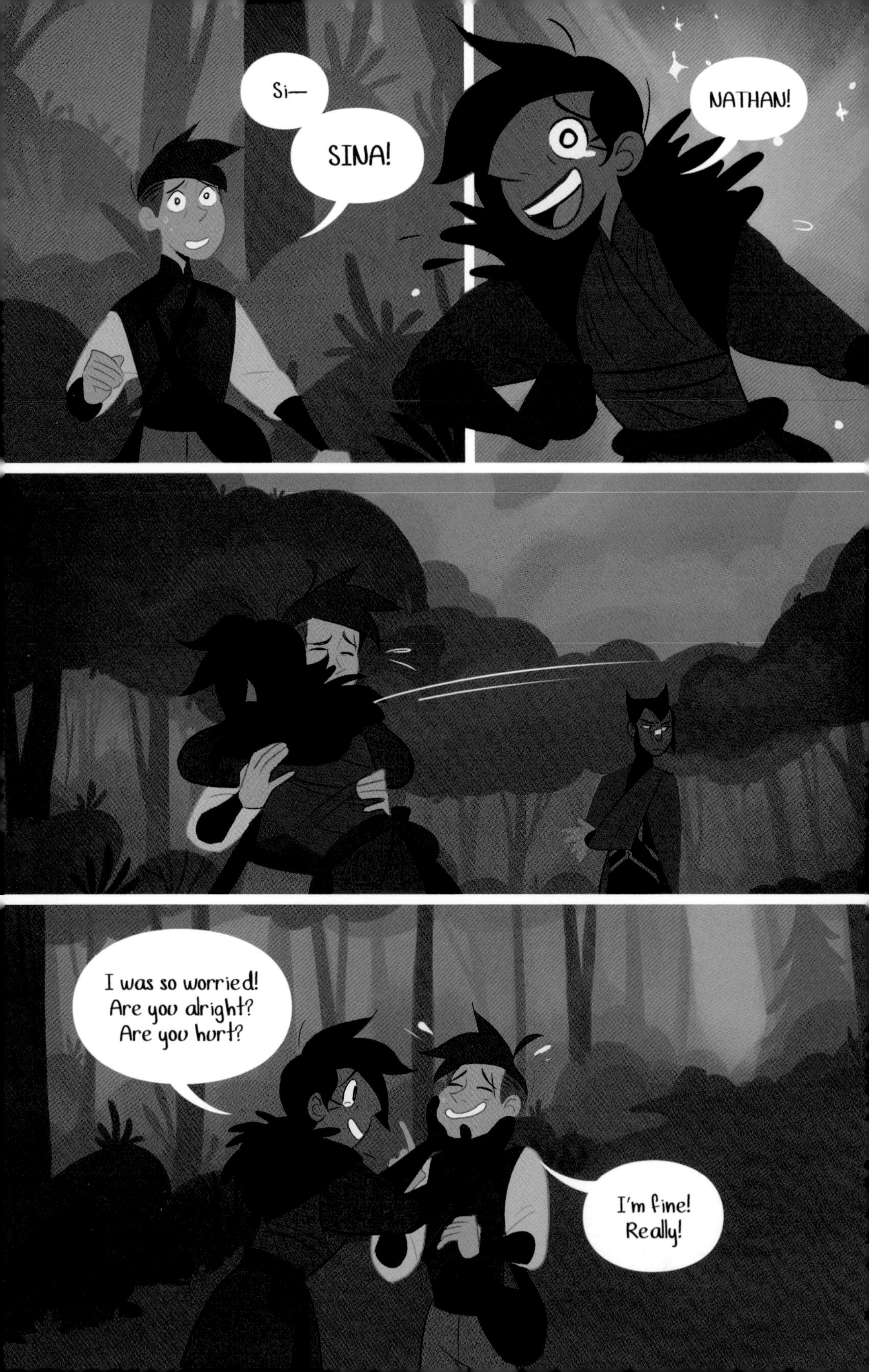
Si—
SINA!
NATHAN!
I was so worried! Are you alright? Are you hurt?
I'm fine! Really!

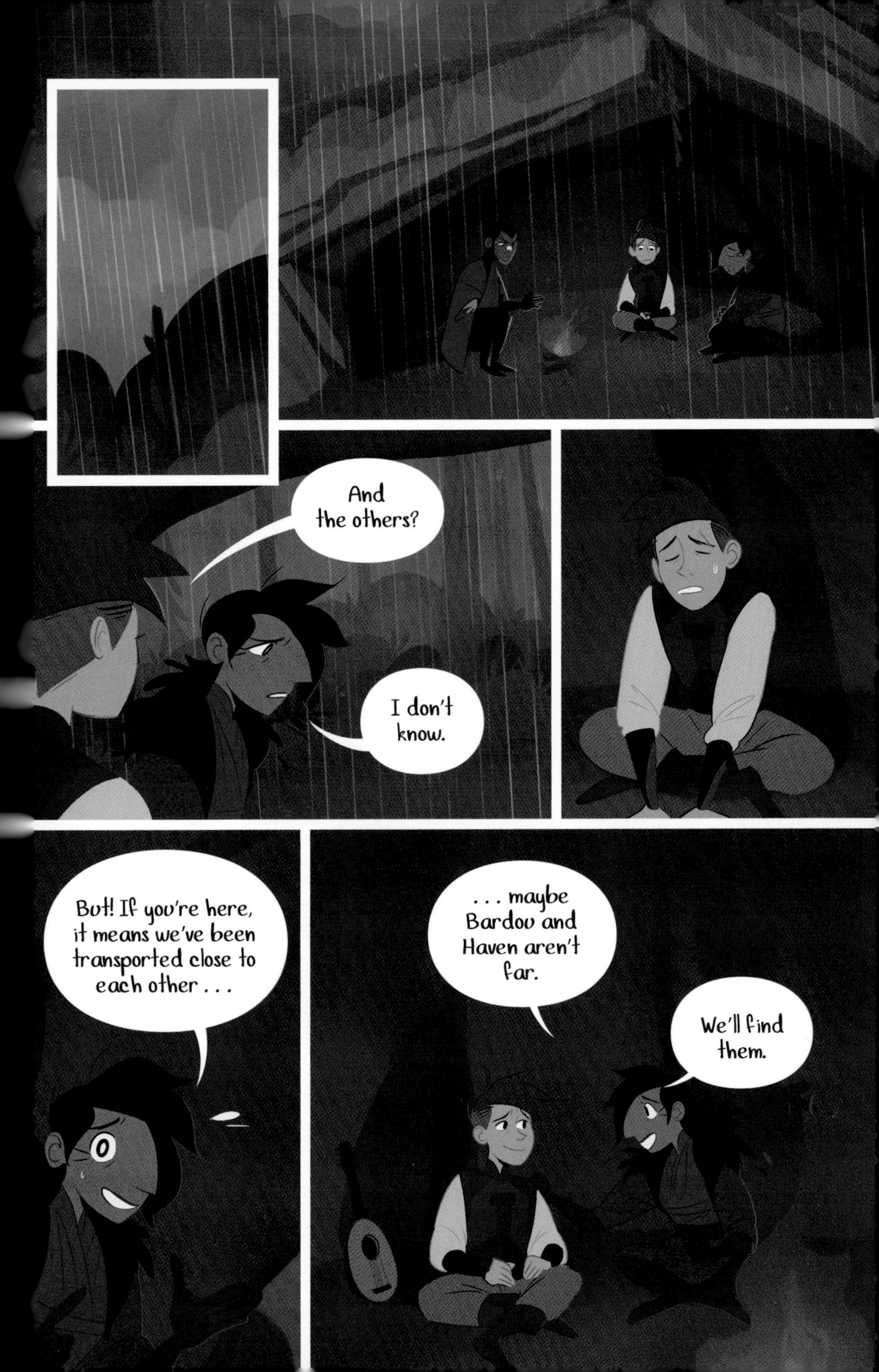
And the others?
I don't know.
But! If you're here, it means we've been transported close to each other . . .
. . . maybe Bardou and Haven aren't far.
We'll find them.

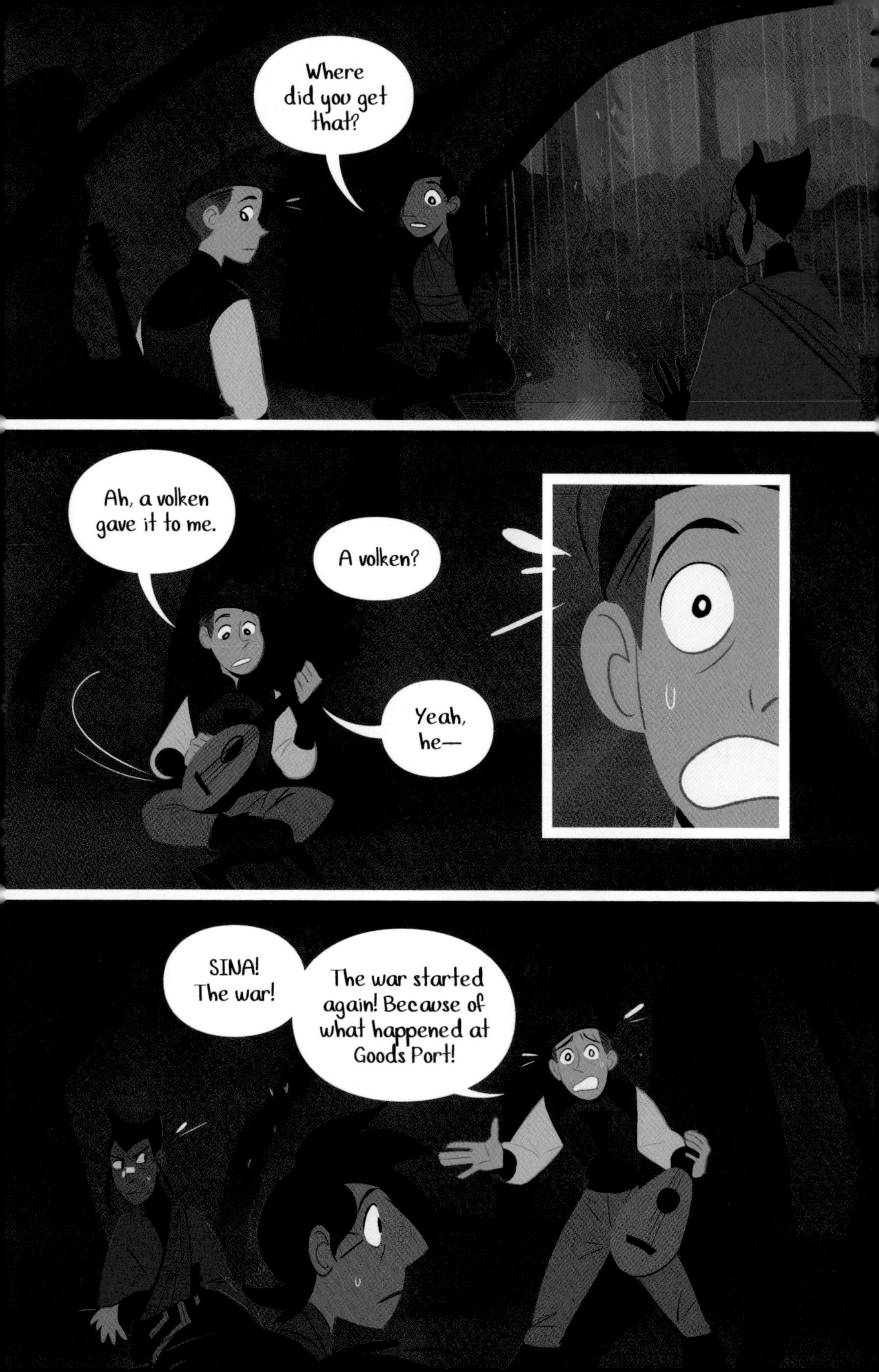
Where did you get that?
Ah, a volken gave it to me.
A volken?
Yeah, he—
SINA! The war!
The war started again! Because of what happened at Goods Port!

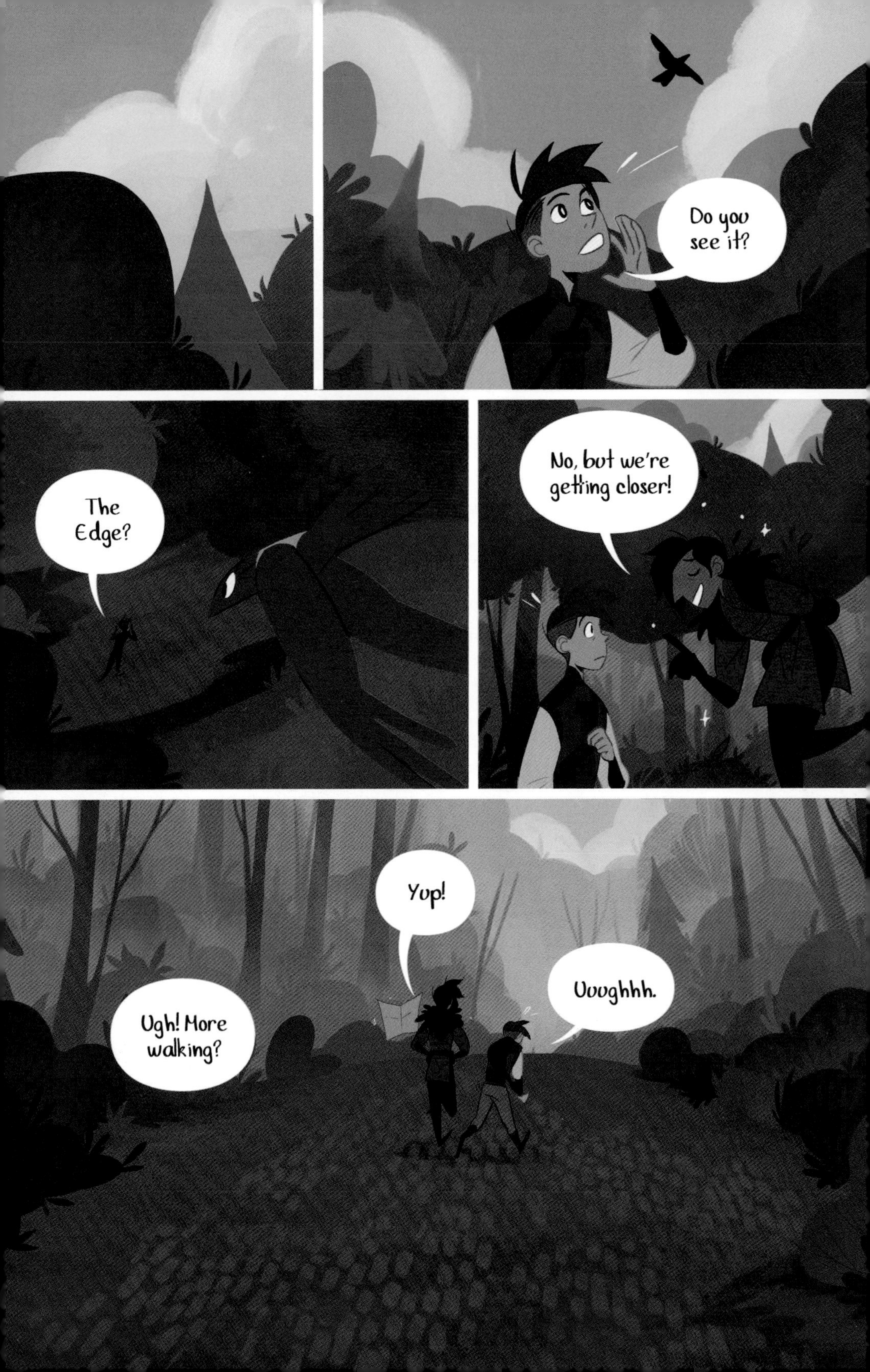
Do you see it?
The Edge?
No, but we're getting closer!
Yup!
Ugh! More walking?
Uuughhh.

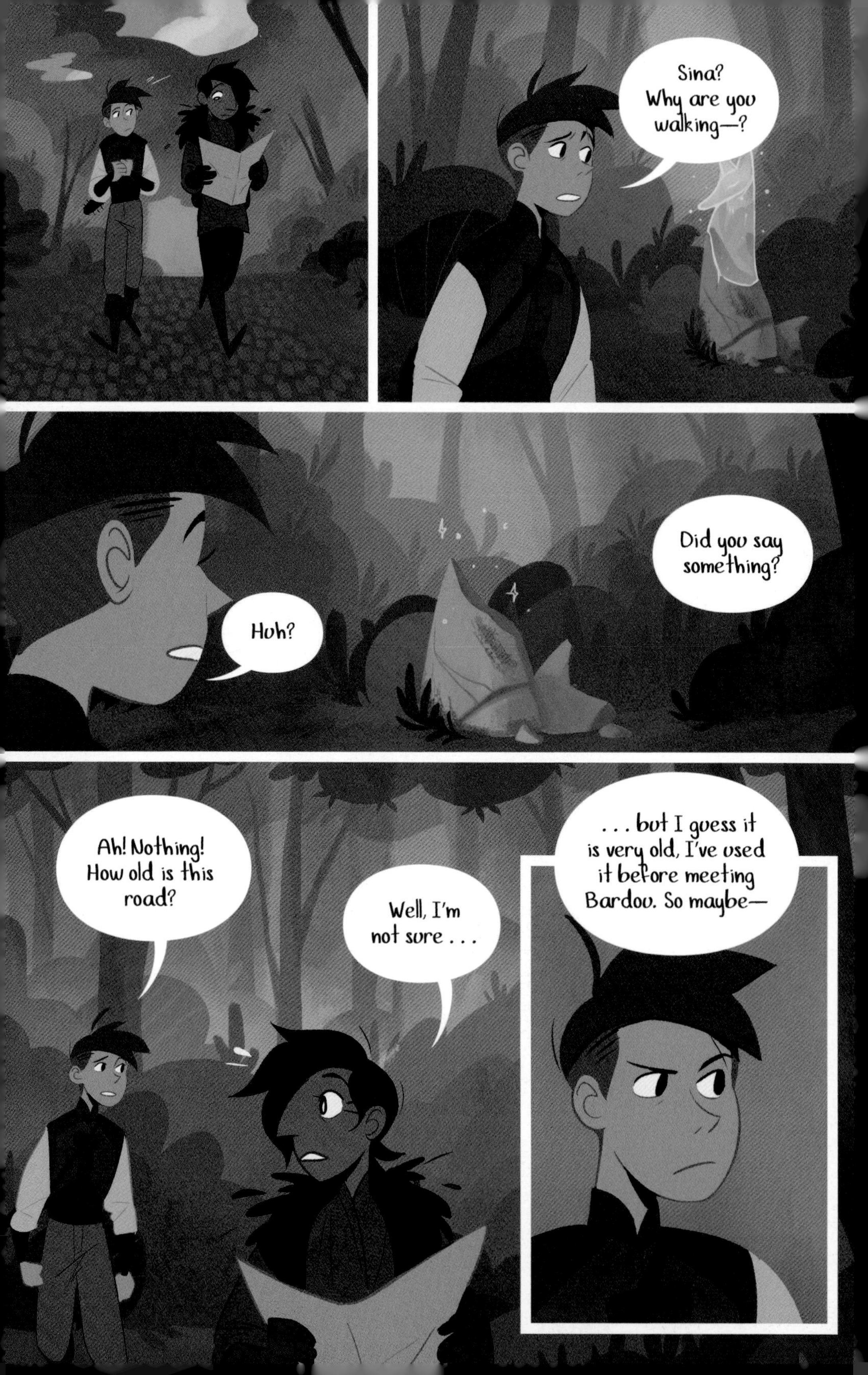
Sina? Why are you walking—?
Did you say something?
Huh?
Ah! Nothing! How old is this road?
Well, I'm not sure . . .
. . . but I guess it is very old, I've used it before meeting Bardou. So maybe—

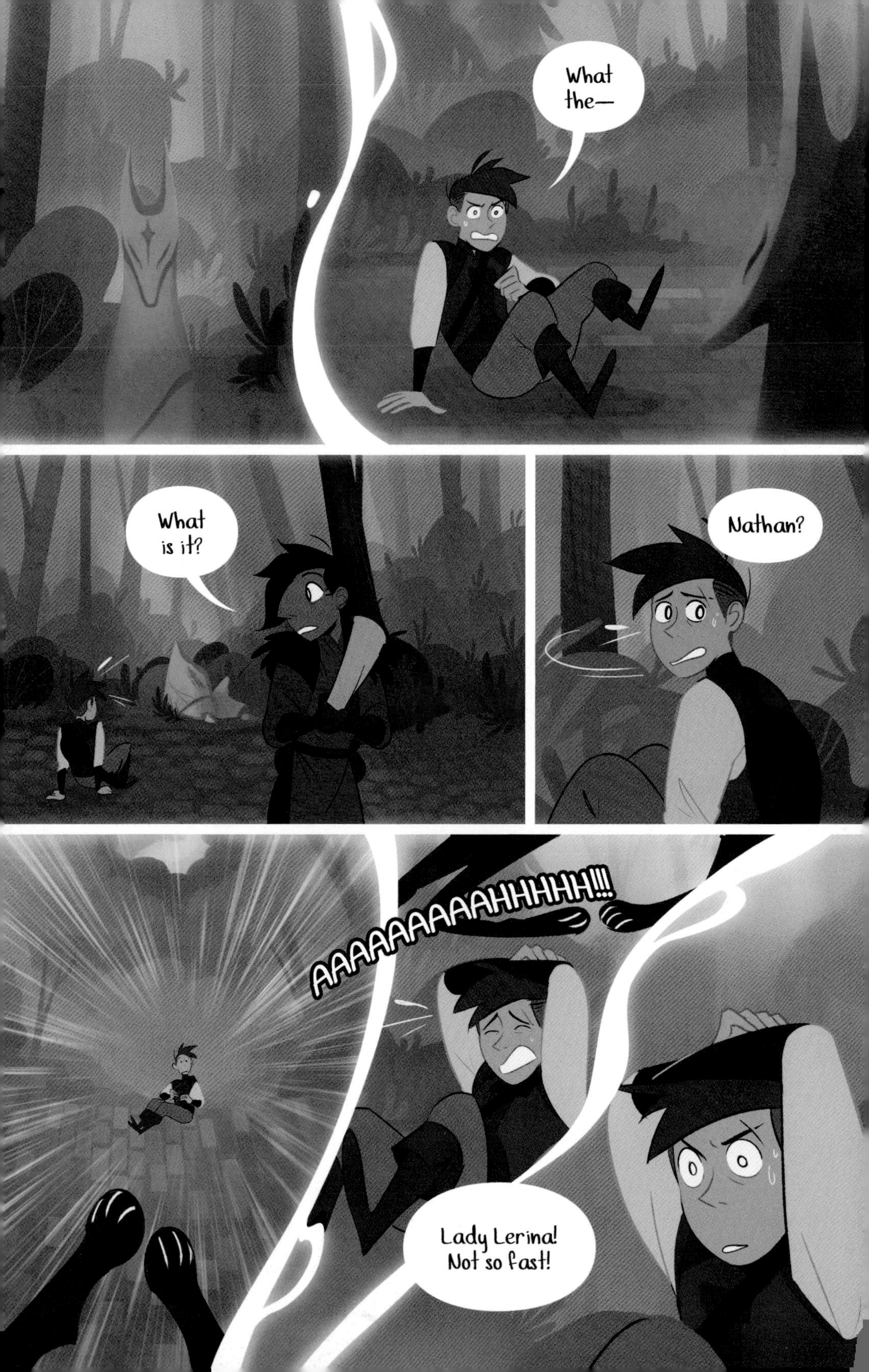
What the—
What is it?
Nathan?
AAAAAAAAAHHHHHH!!!
Lady Lerina! Not so fast!

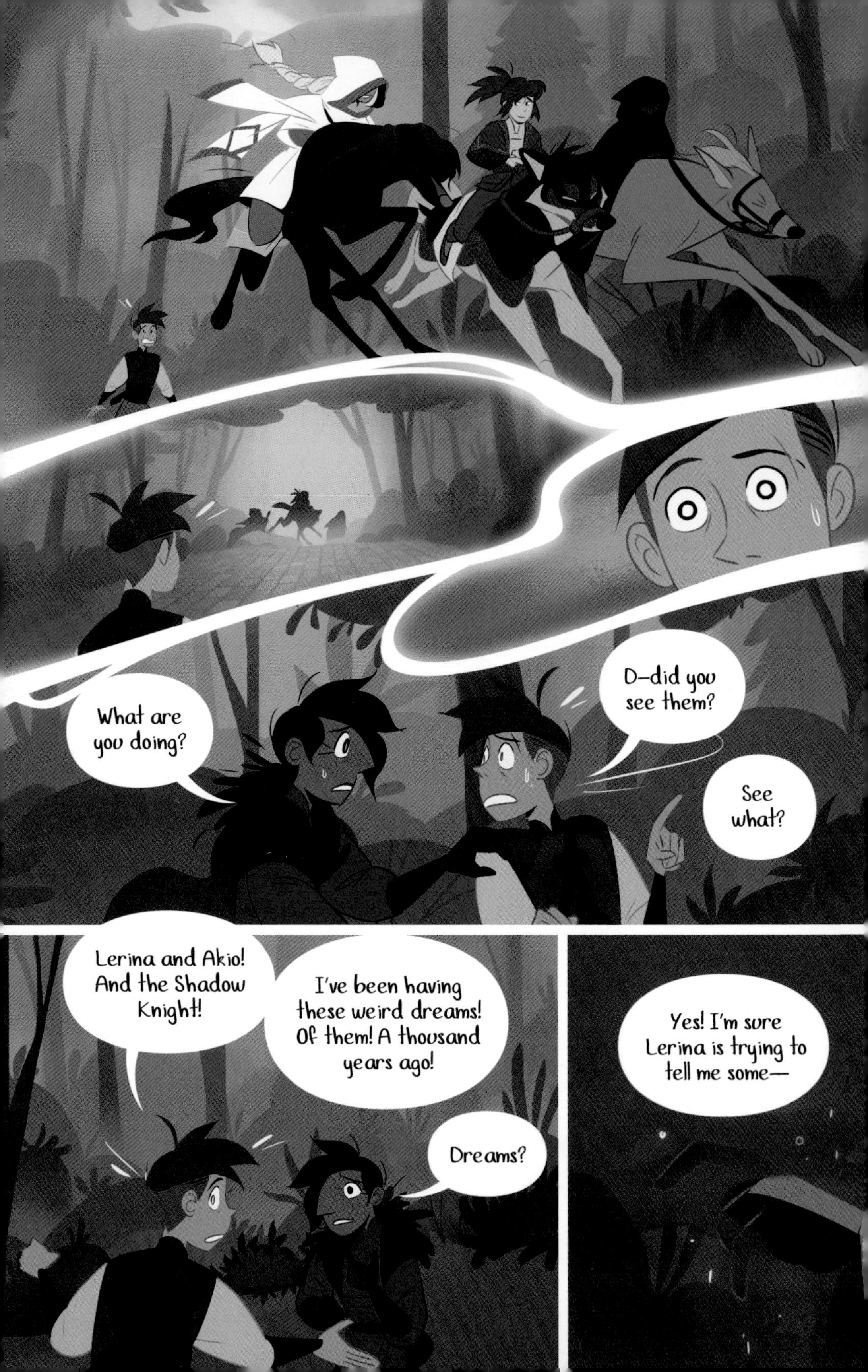
What are you doing?
D-did you see them?
See what?
Lerina and Akio! And the Shadow Knight!
I've been having these weird dreams! Of them! A thousand years ago!
Dreams?
Yes! I'm sure Lerina is trying to tell me some—

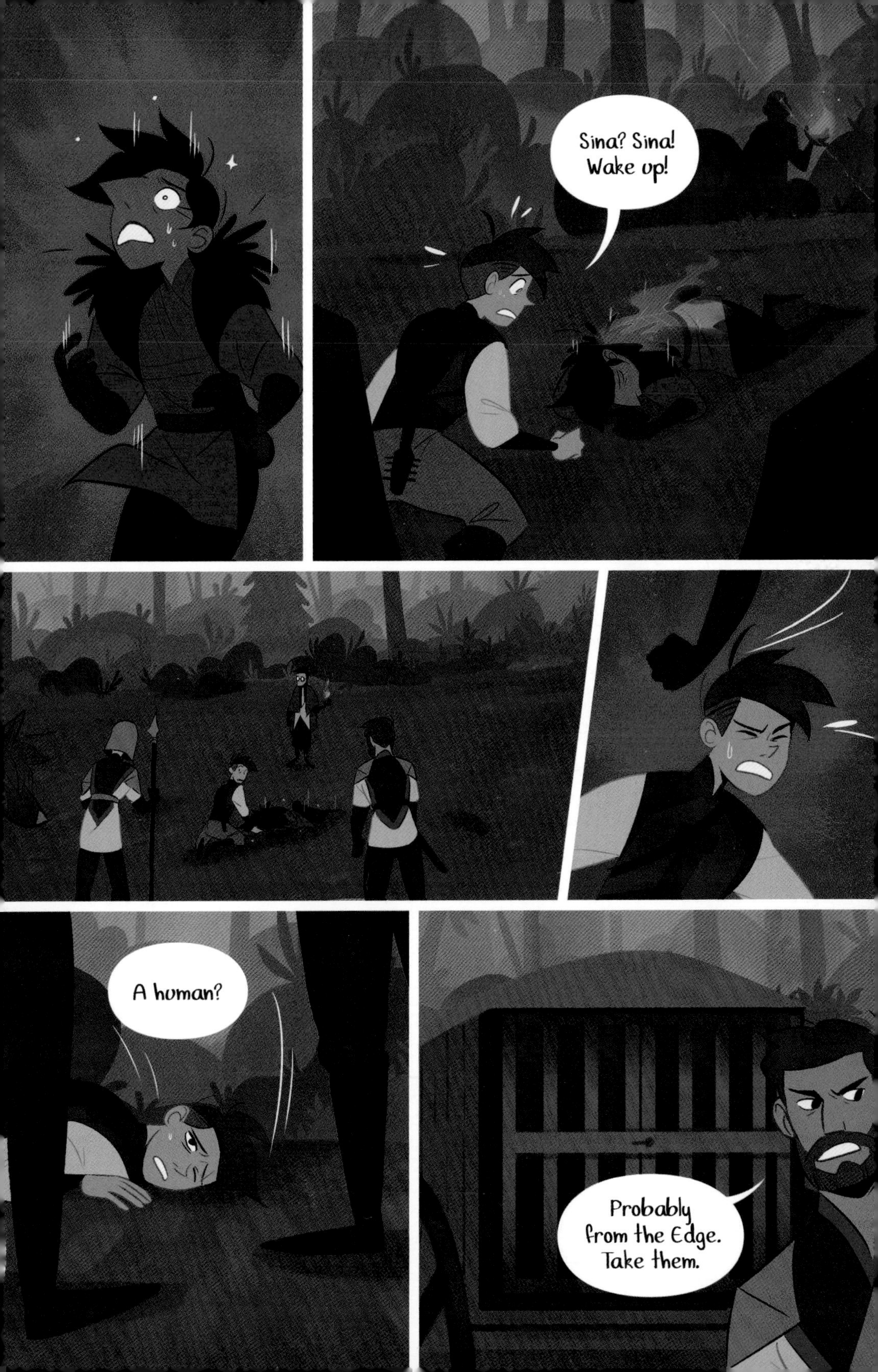
Sina? Sina! Wake up!
A human?
Probably from the Edge. Take them.

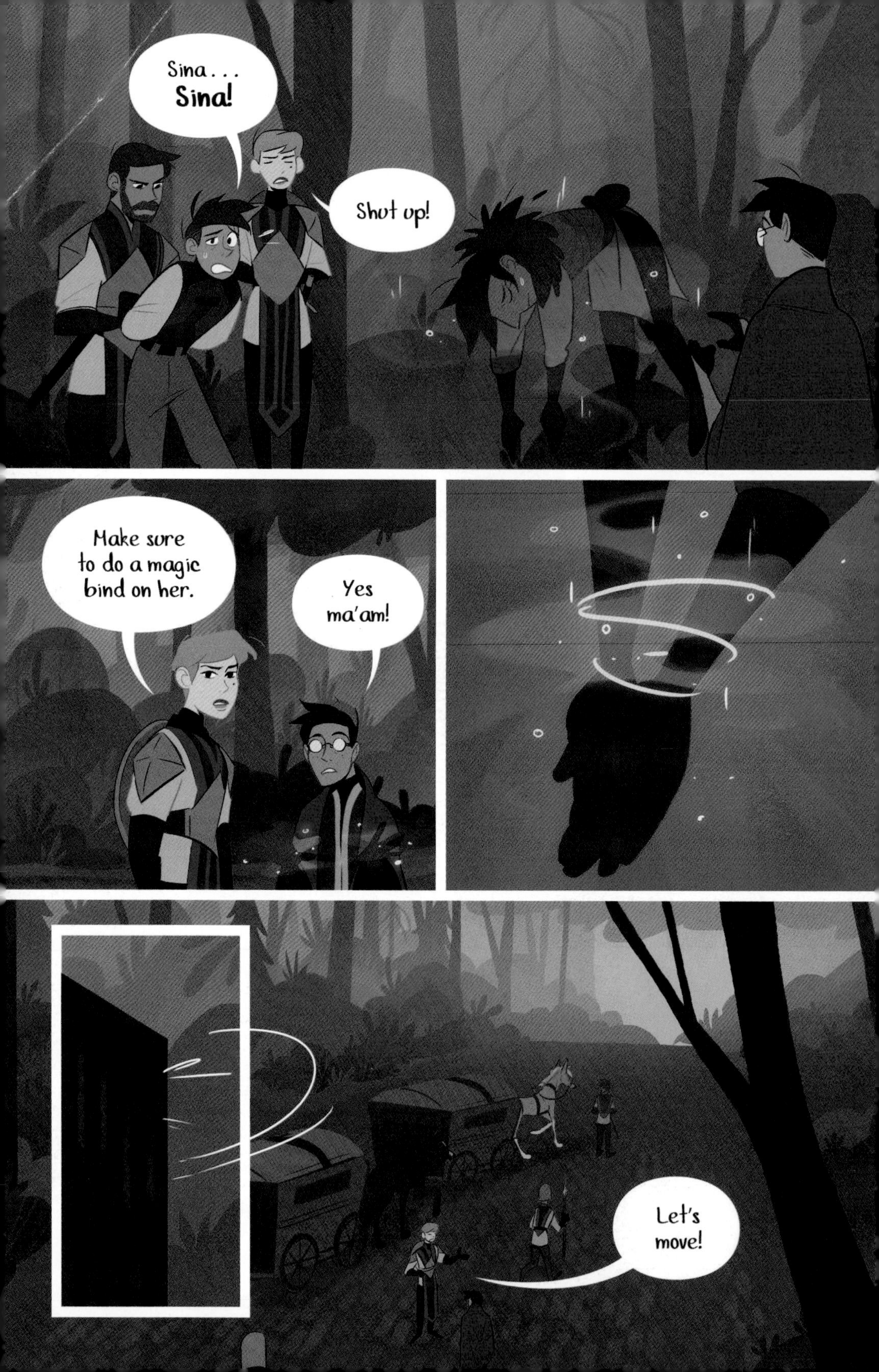
Sina . . .
Sina!
Shut up!
Make sure to do a magic bind on her.
Yes ma'am!
Let's move!

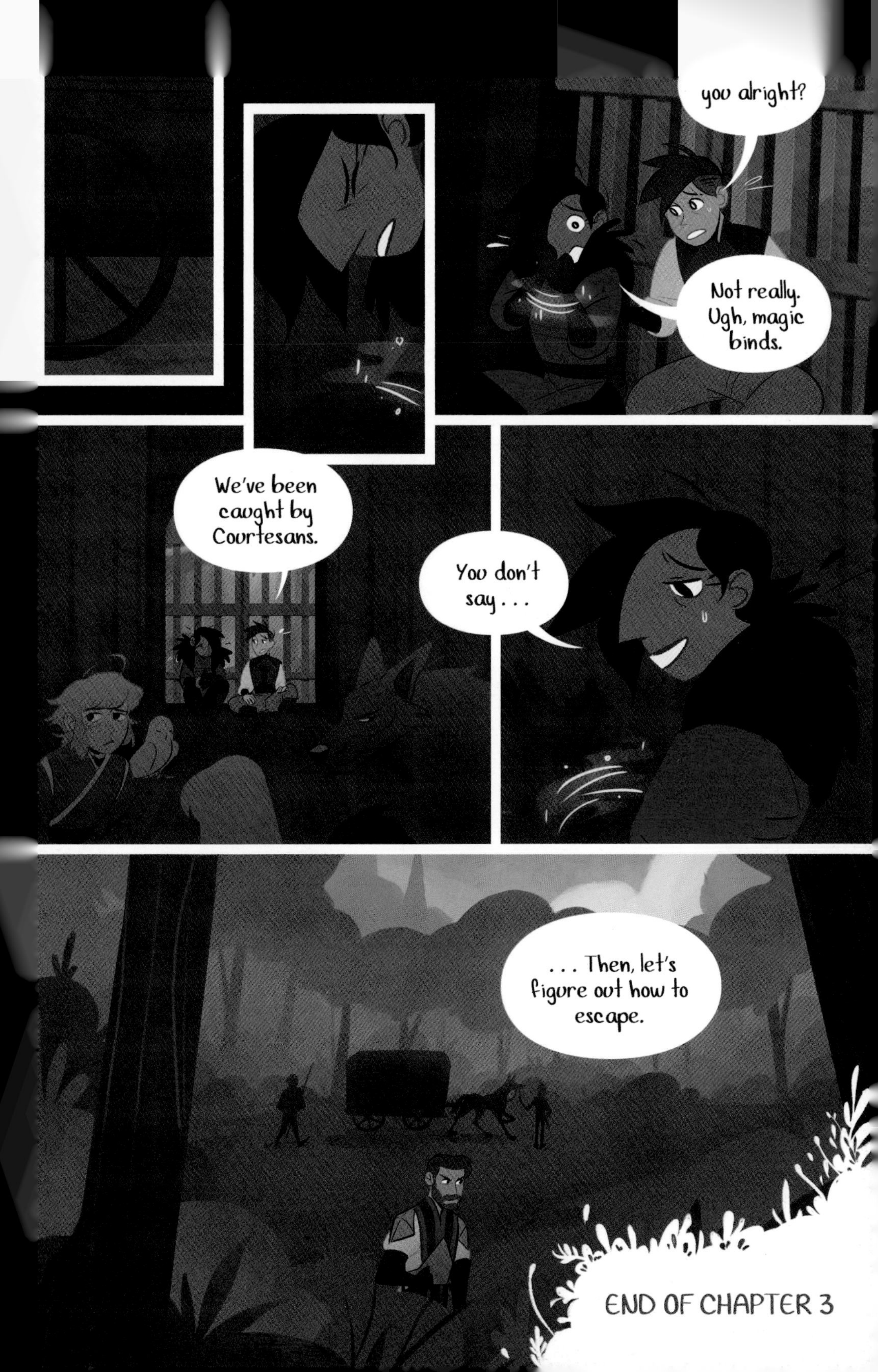

you alright?
Not really. Ugh, magic binds.
We've been caught by Courtesans.
You don't say . . .
. . . Then, let's figure out how to escape.
END OF CHAPTER 3

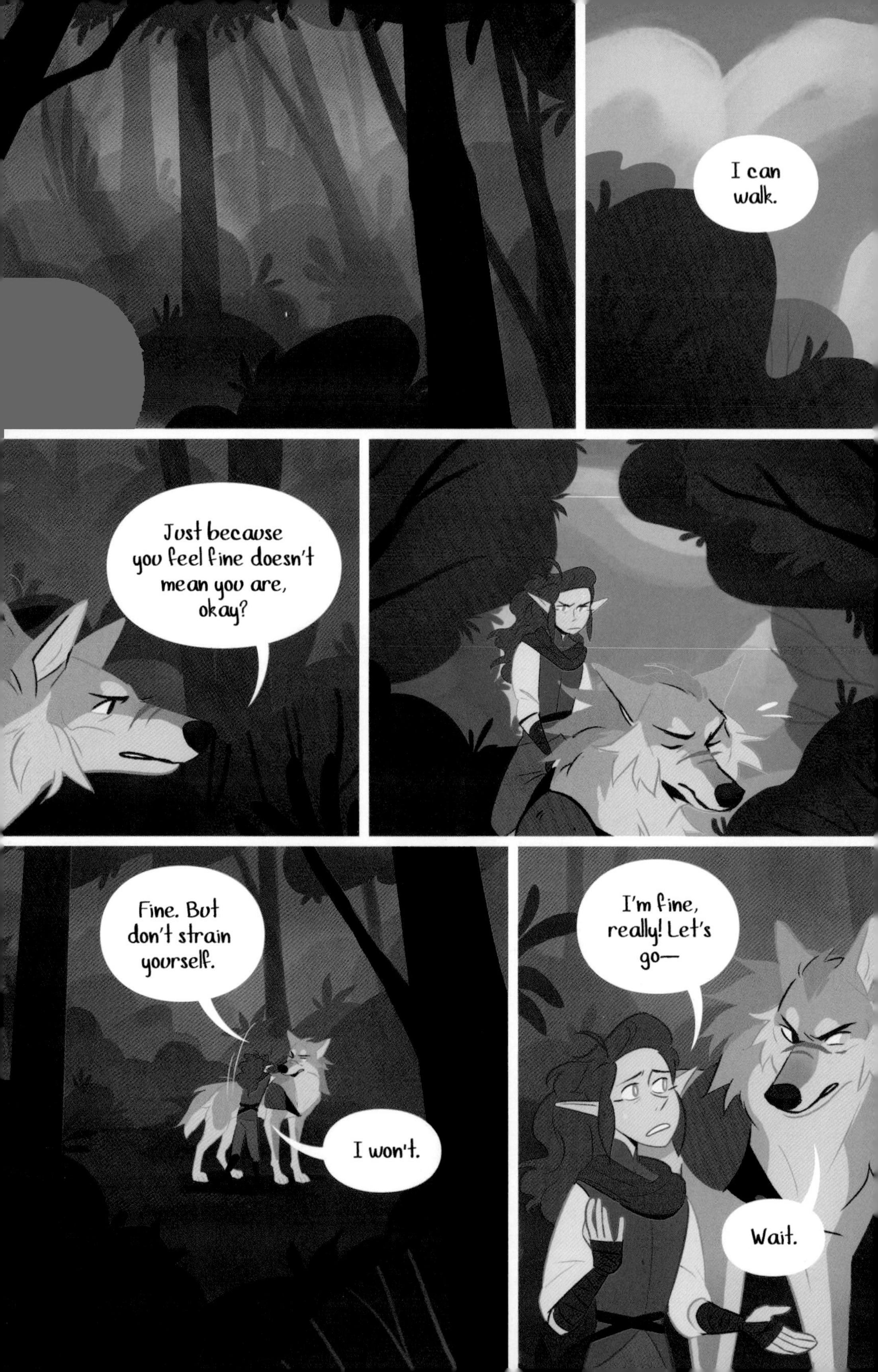
I can walk.
Just because you feel fine doesn't mean you are, okay?
Fine. But don't strain yourself.
I won't.
I'm fine, really! Let's go—
Wait.

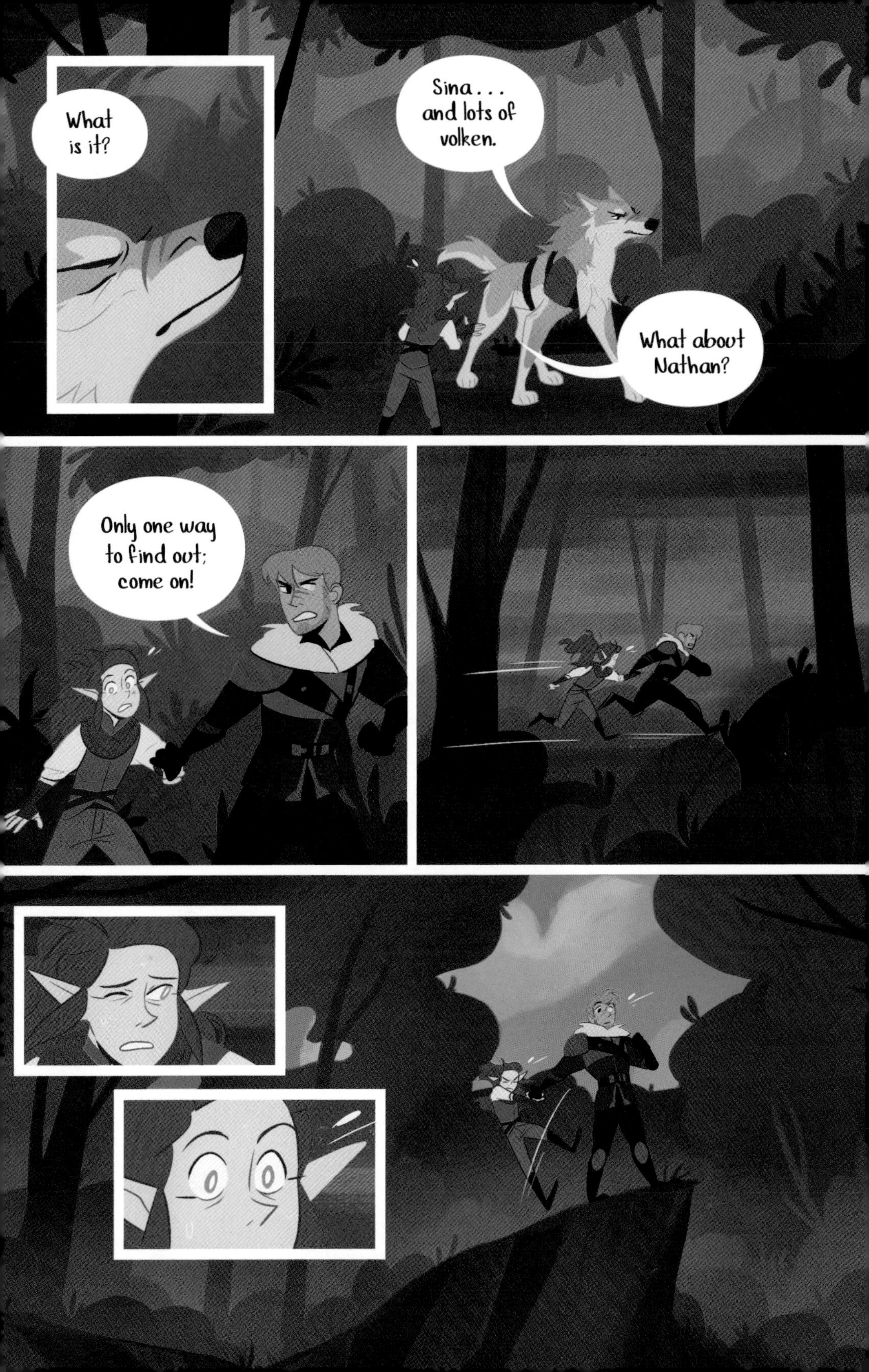
What is it?
Sina . . . and lots of volken.
What about Nathan?
Only one way to find out; come on!

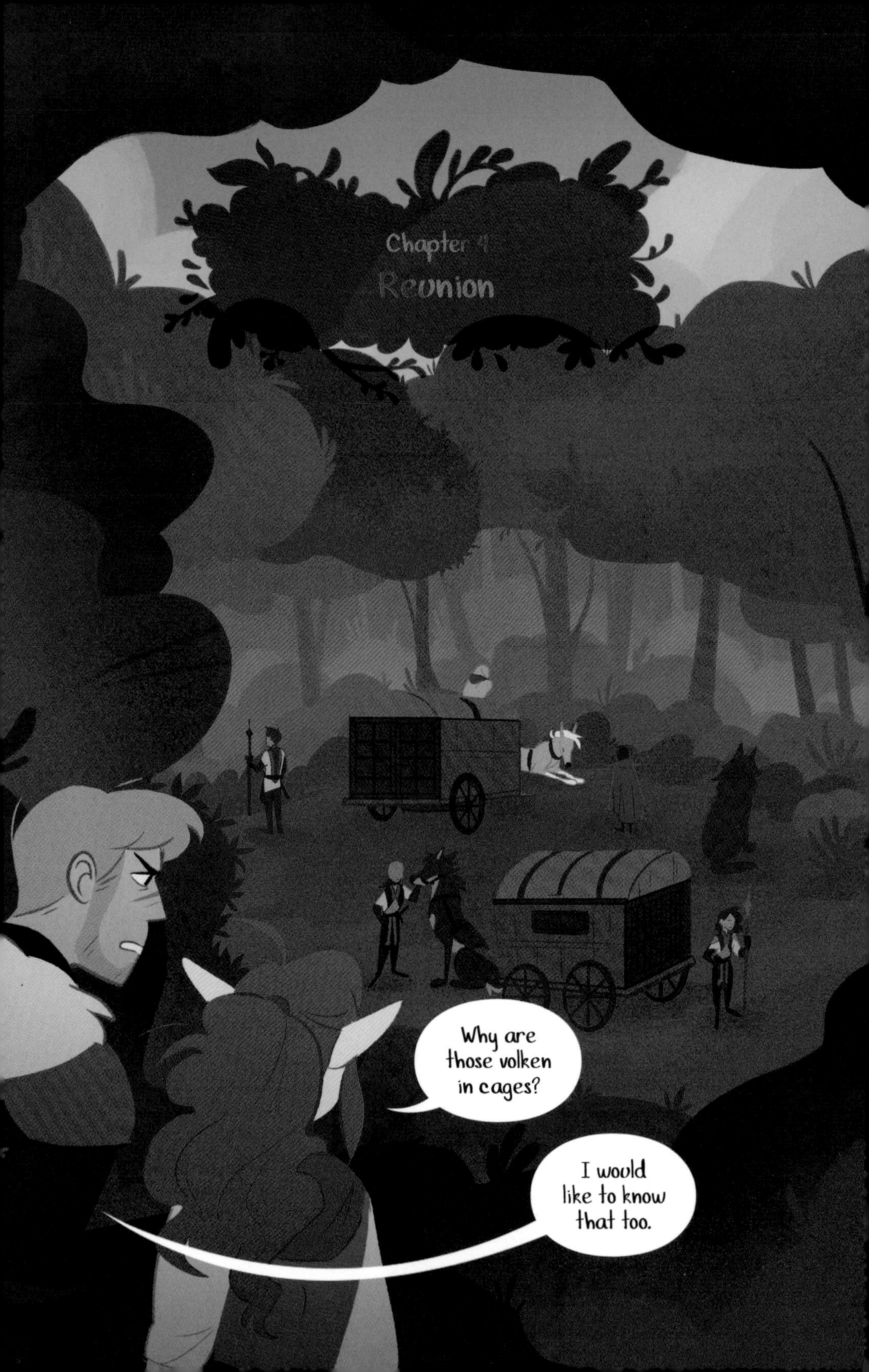
Chapter 4
Reunion
Why are those volken in cages?
I would like to know that too.

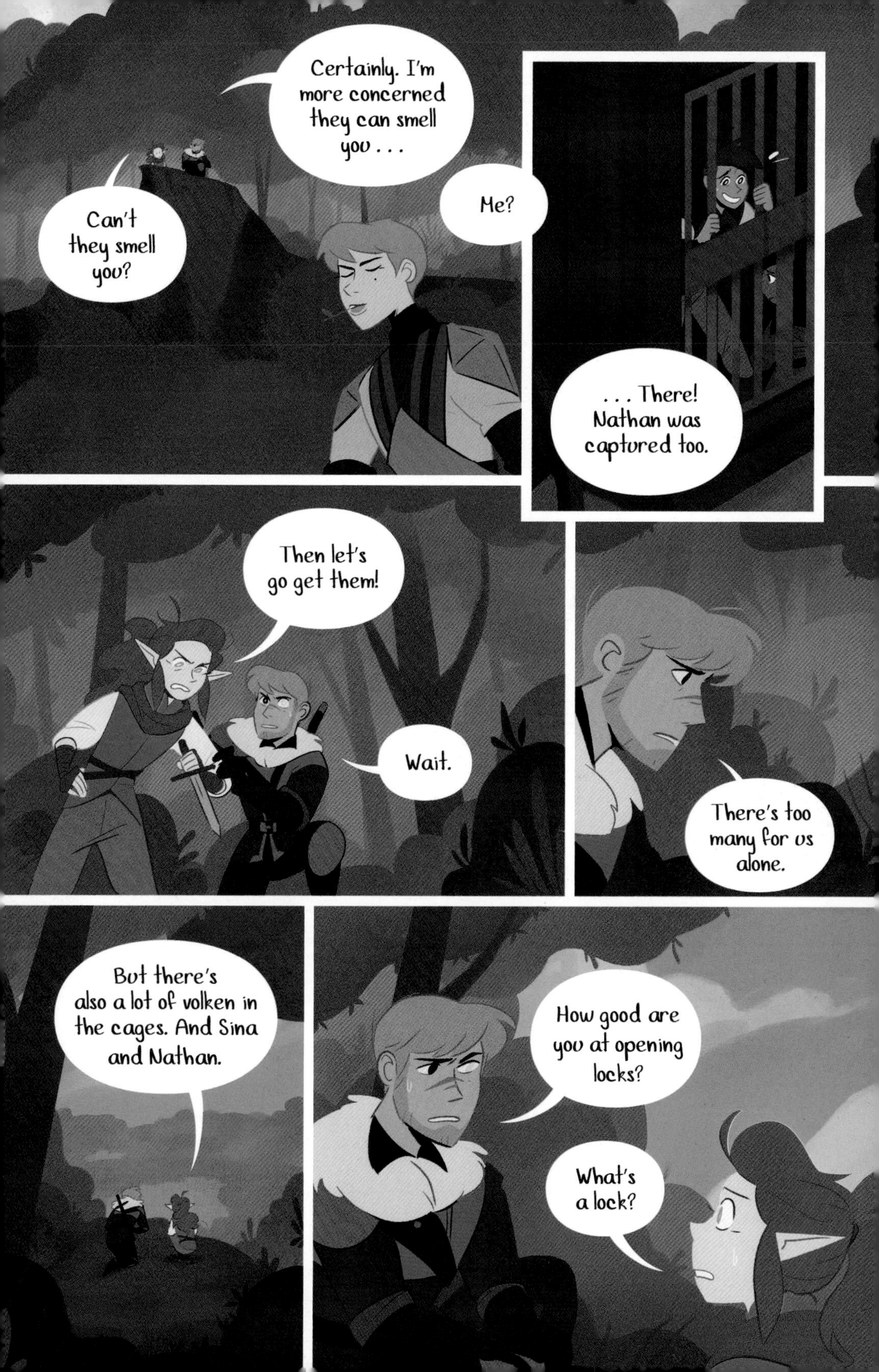
Can't they smell you?
Certainly. I'm more concerned they can smell you . . .
Me?
. . . There! Nathan was captured too.
Then let's go get them!
Wait.
There's too many for us alone.
But there's also a lot of volken in the cages. And Sina and Nathan.
How good are you at opening locks?
What's a lock?

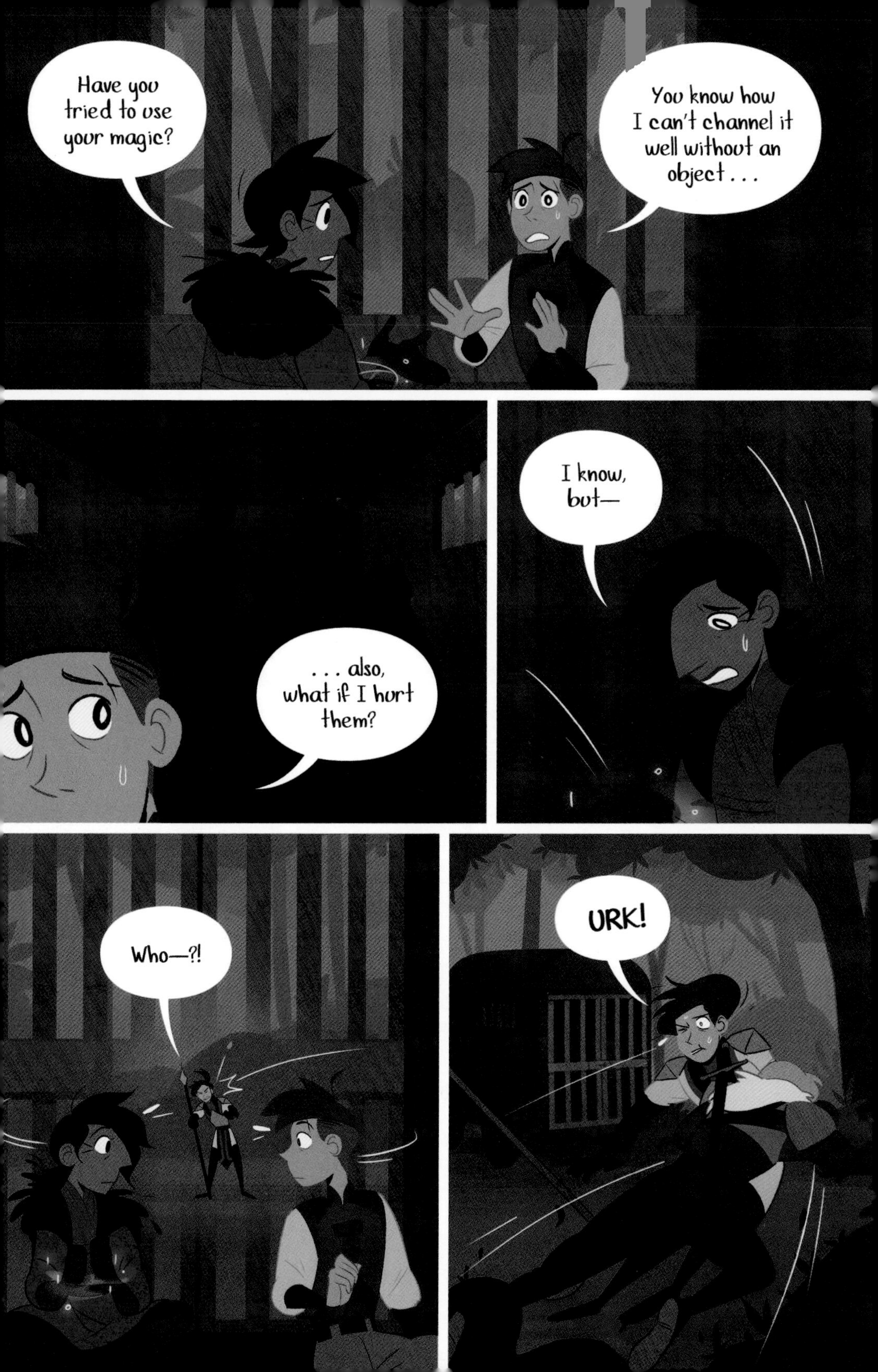
Have you tried to use your magic?
You know how I can't channel it well without an object . . .
. . . also, what if I hurt them?
I know, but—
Who—?!
URK!

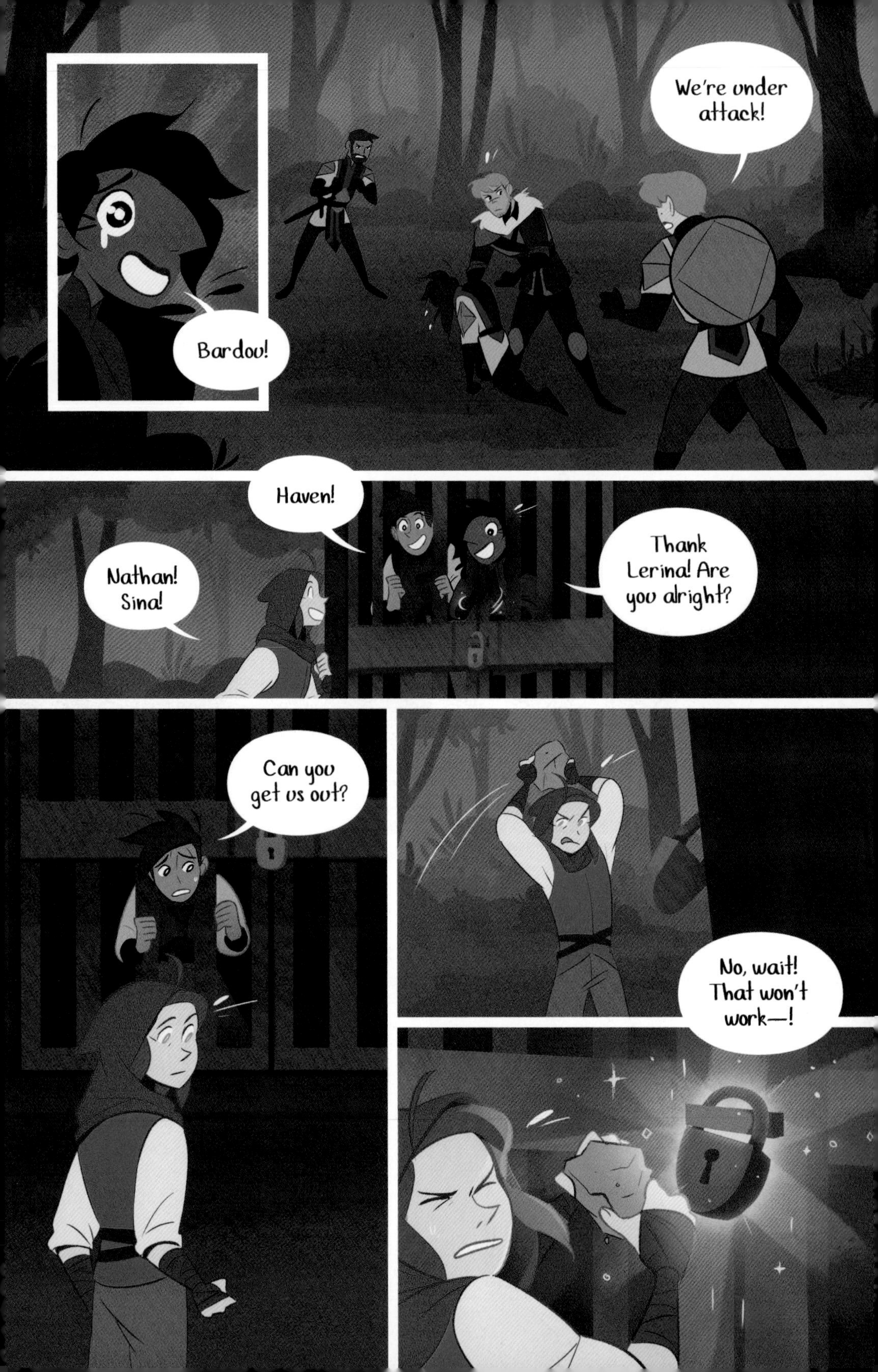
Bardou!
We're under attack!
Haven!
Nathan! Sina!
Thank Lerina! Are you alright?
Can you get us out?
No, wait! That won't work—!

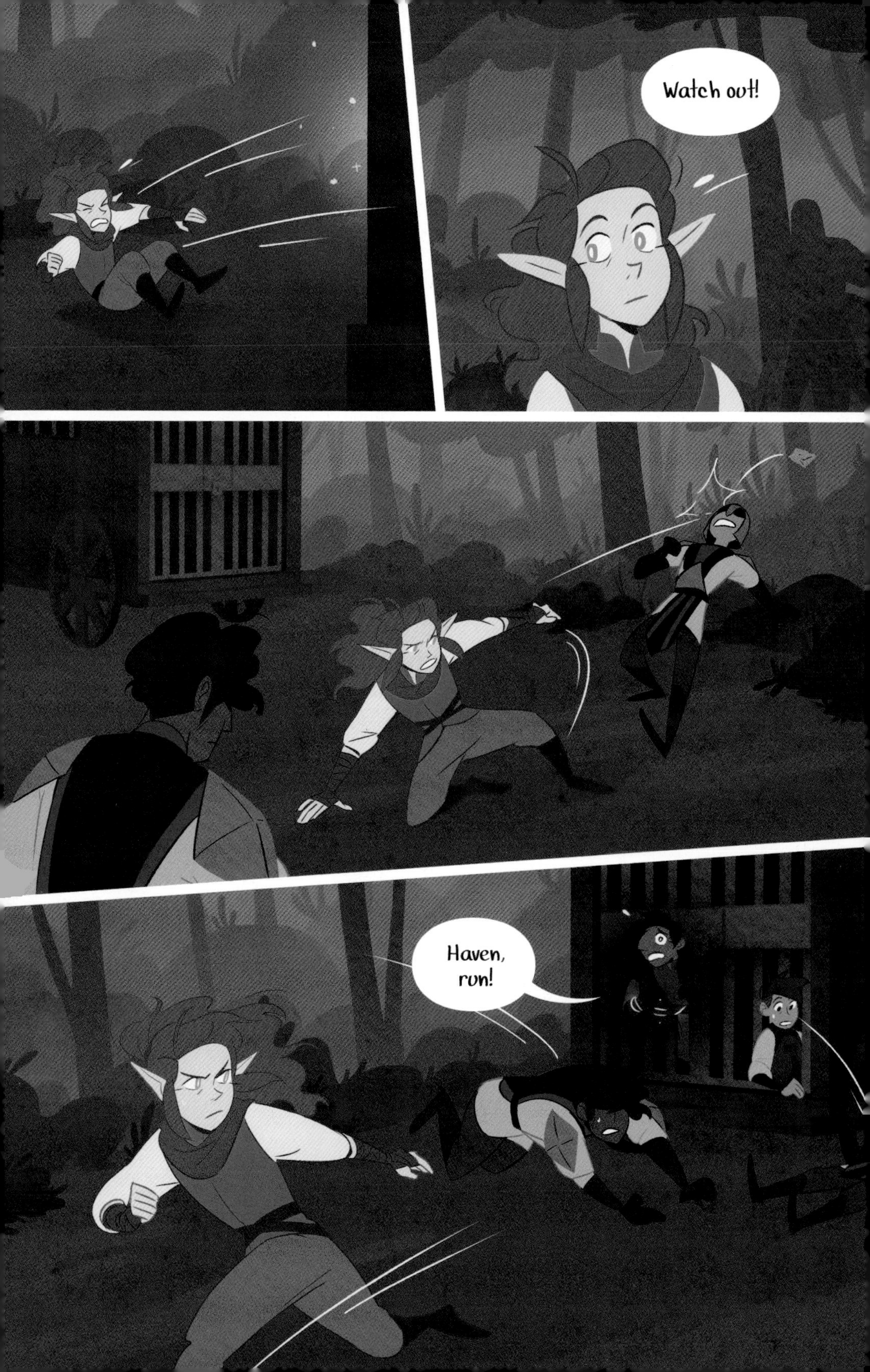
Watch out!
Haven, run!

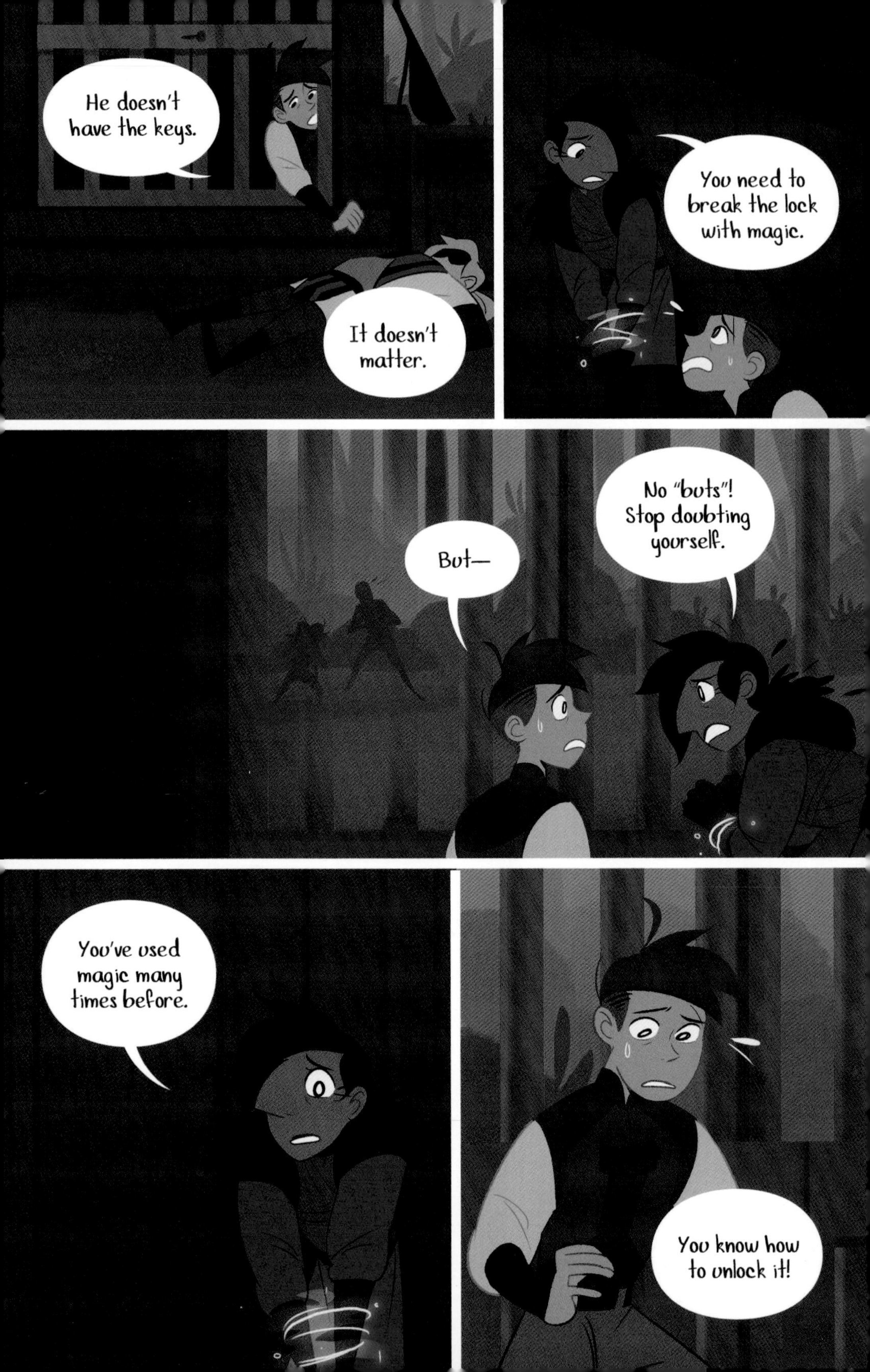
He doesn't have the keys.
It doesn't matter.
You need to break the lock with magic.
But—
No "buts"! Stop doubting yourself.
You've used magic many times before.
You know how to unlock it!

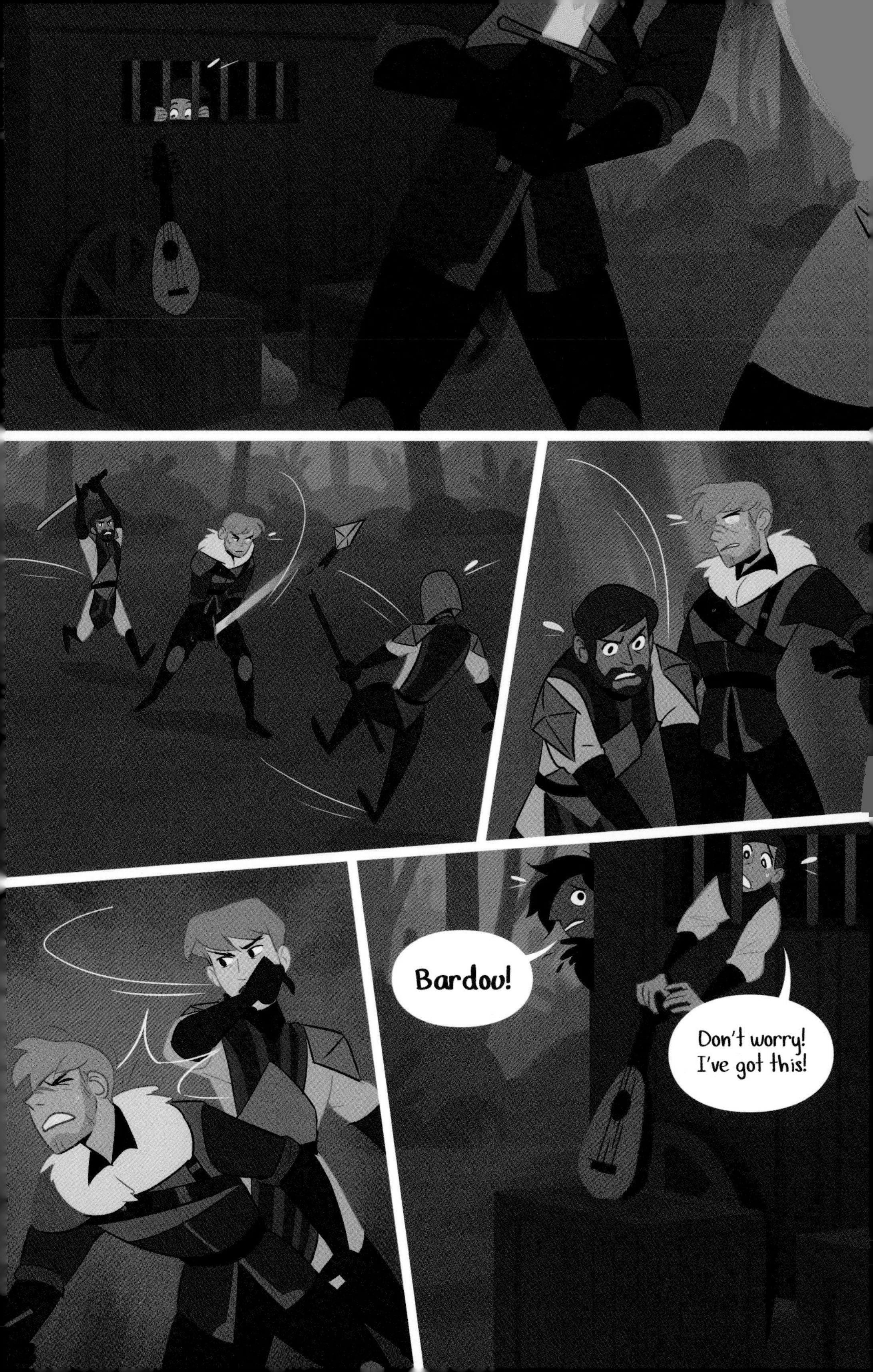

Bardou!
Don't worry! I've got this!

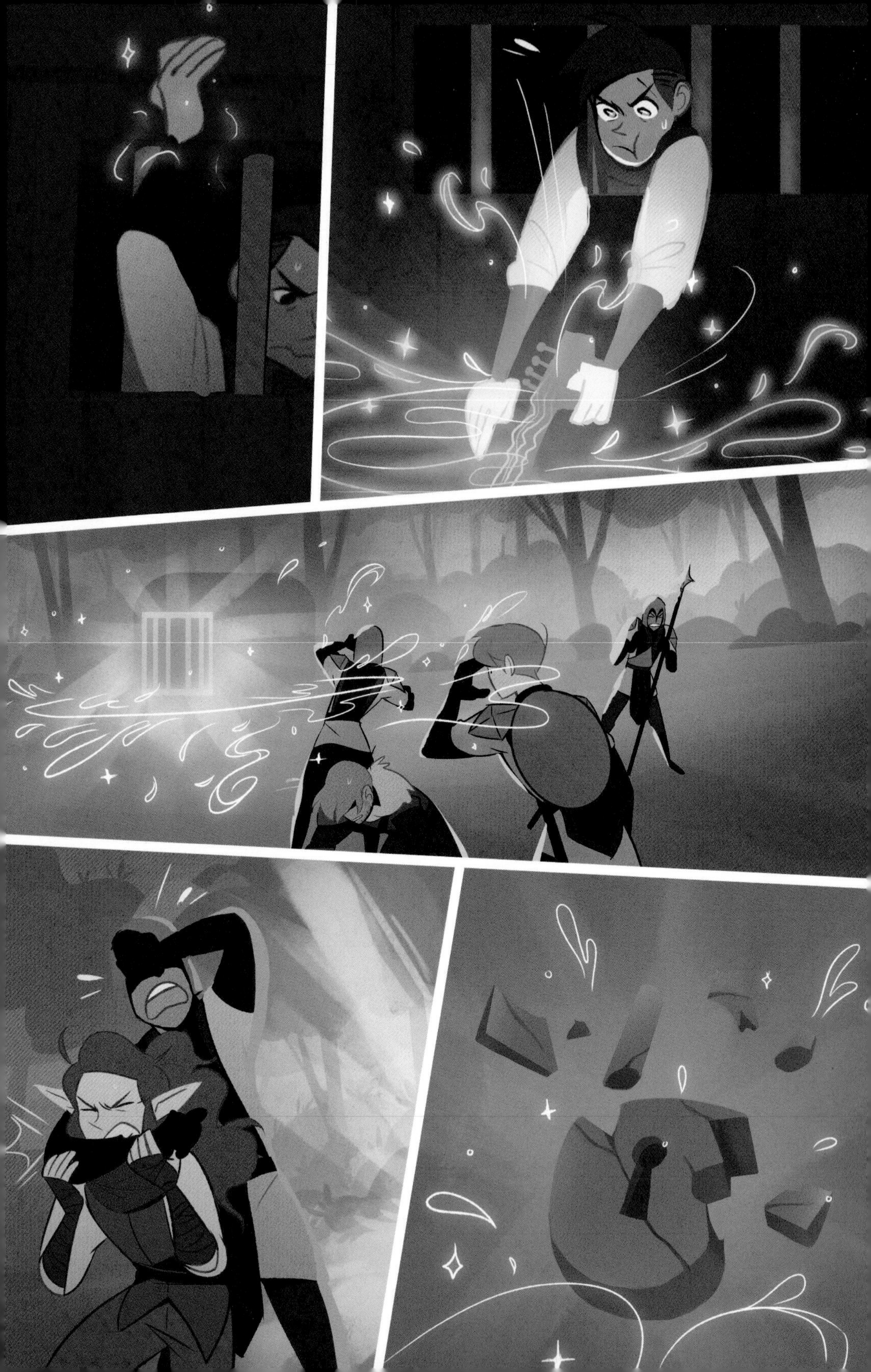

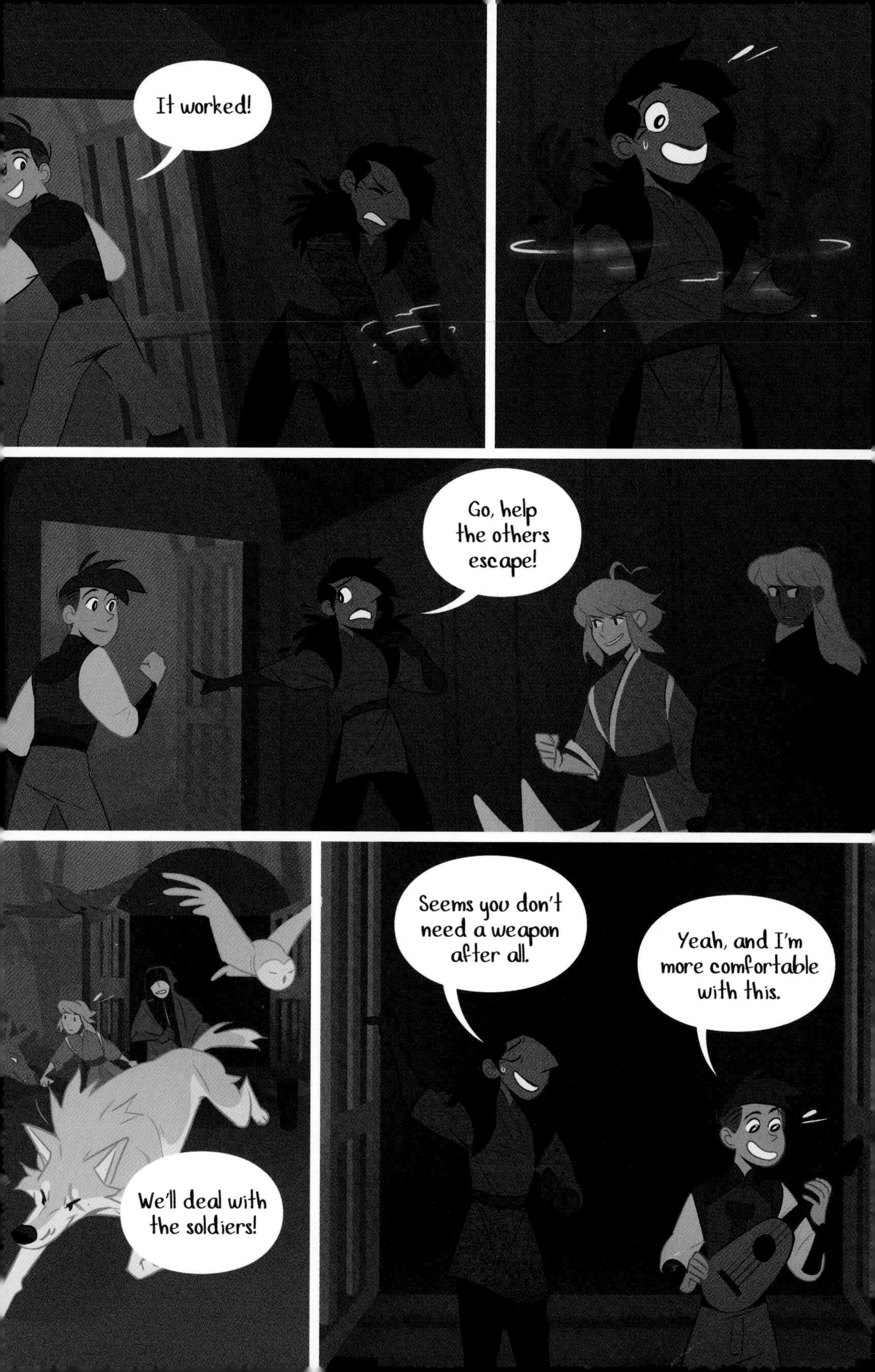
It worked!
Go, help the others escape!
We'll deal with the soldiers!
Seems you don't need a weapon after all.
Yeah, and I'm more comfortable with this.

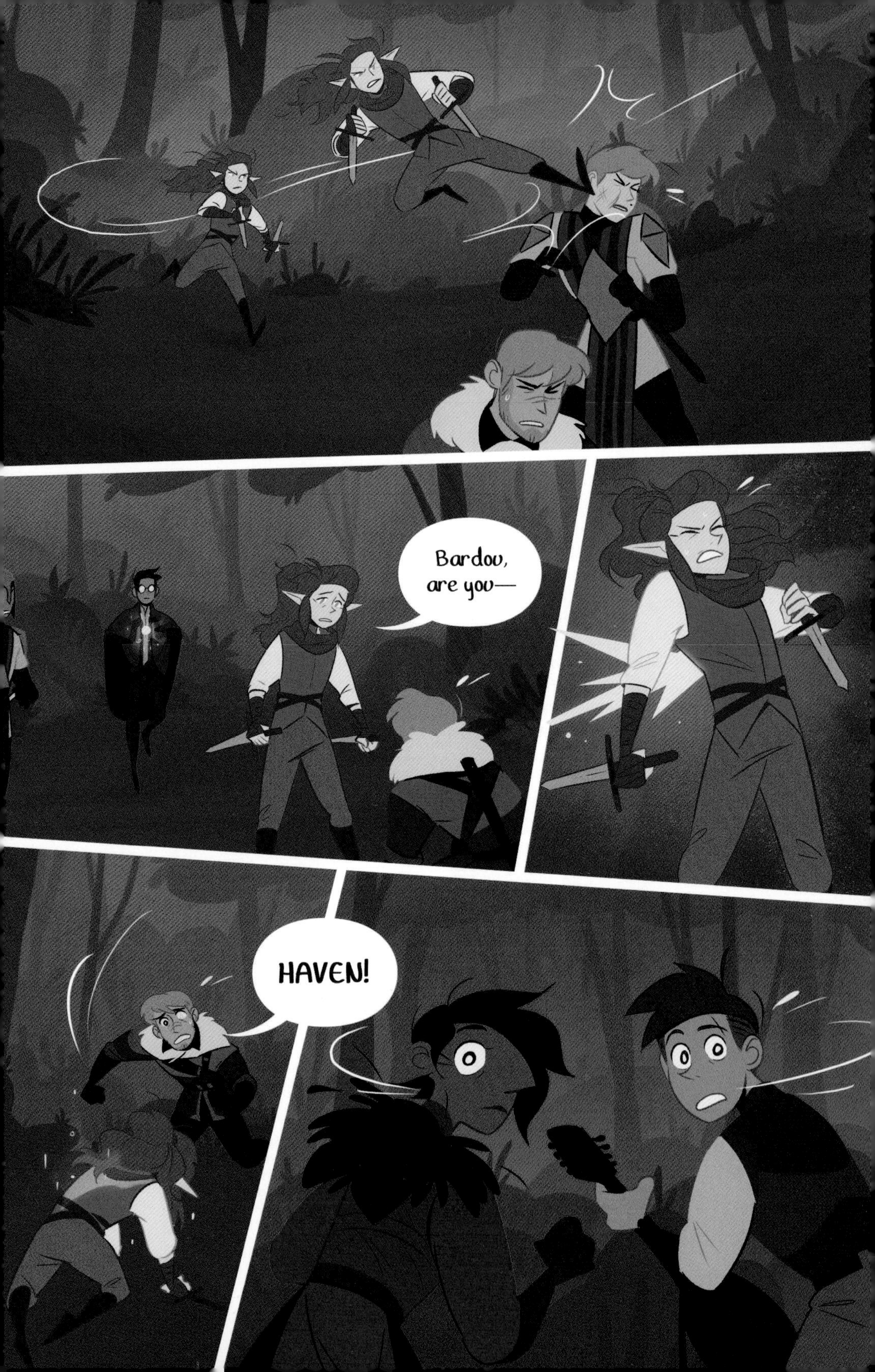
Bardou,
are you—
HAVEN!

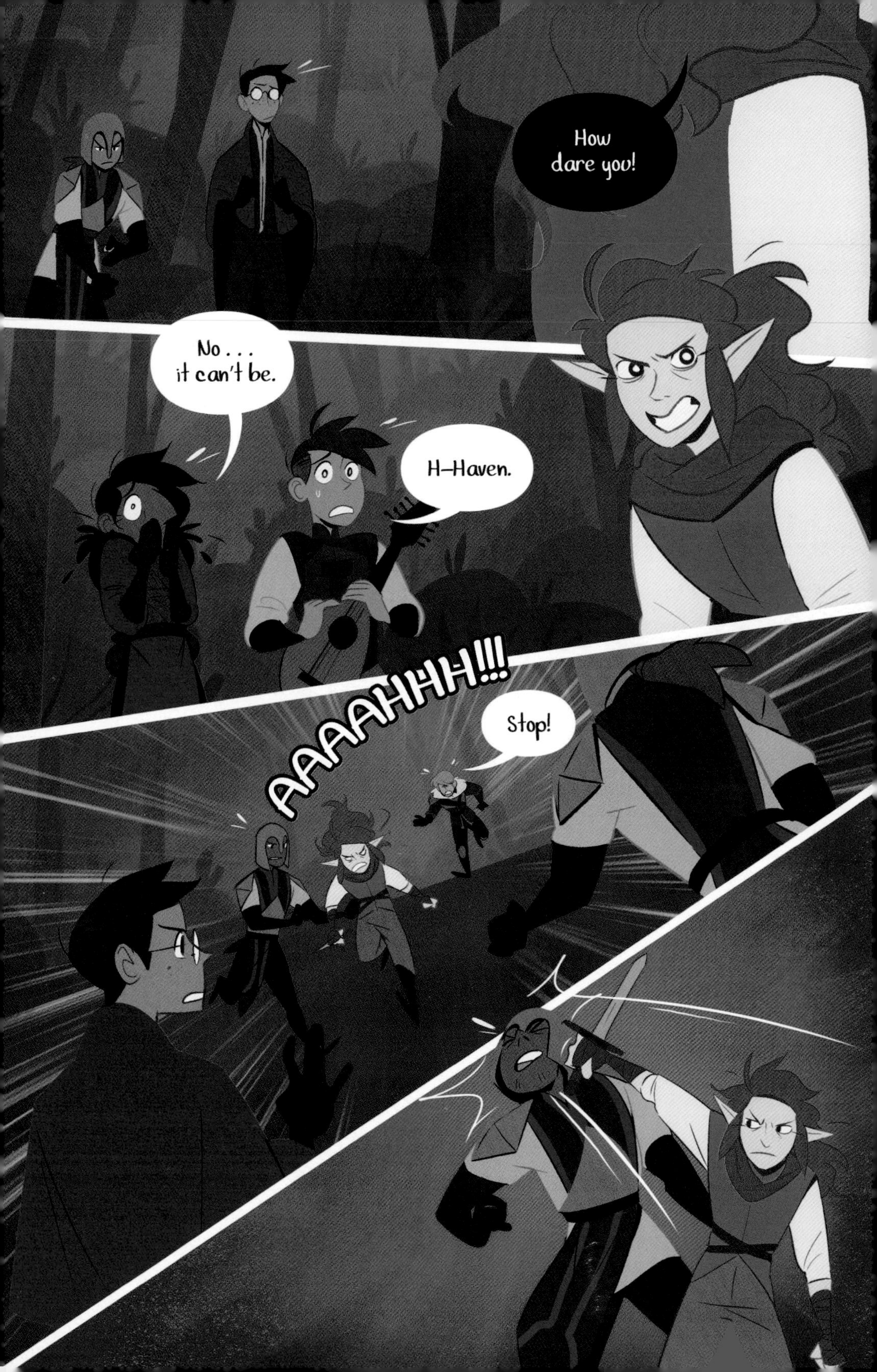
How dare you!
No . . . it can't be.
H—Haven.
AAAAHHH!!!
Stop!

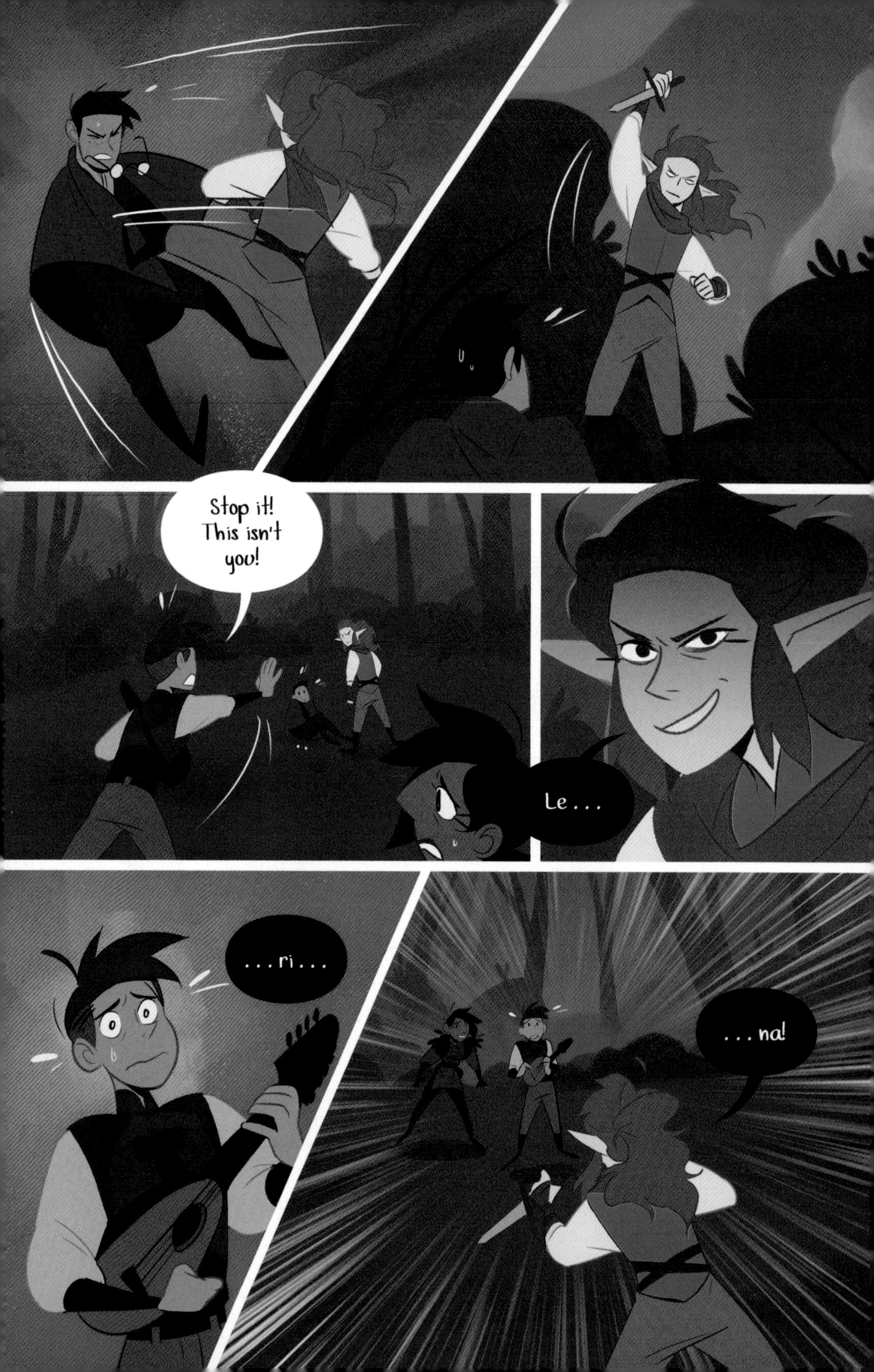
Stop it! This isn't you!
Le . . .
. . . ri . . .
. . . na!

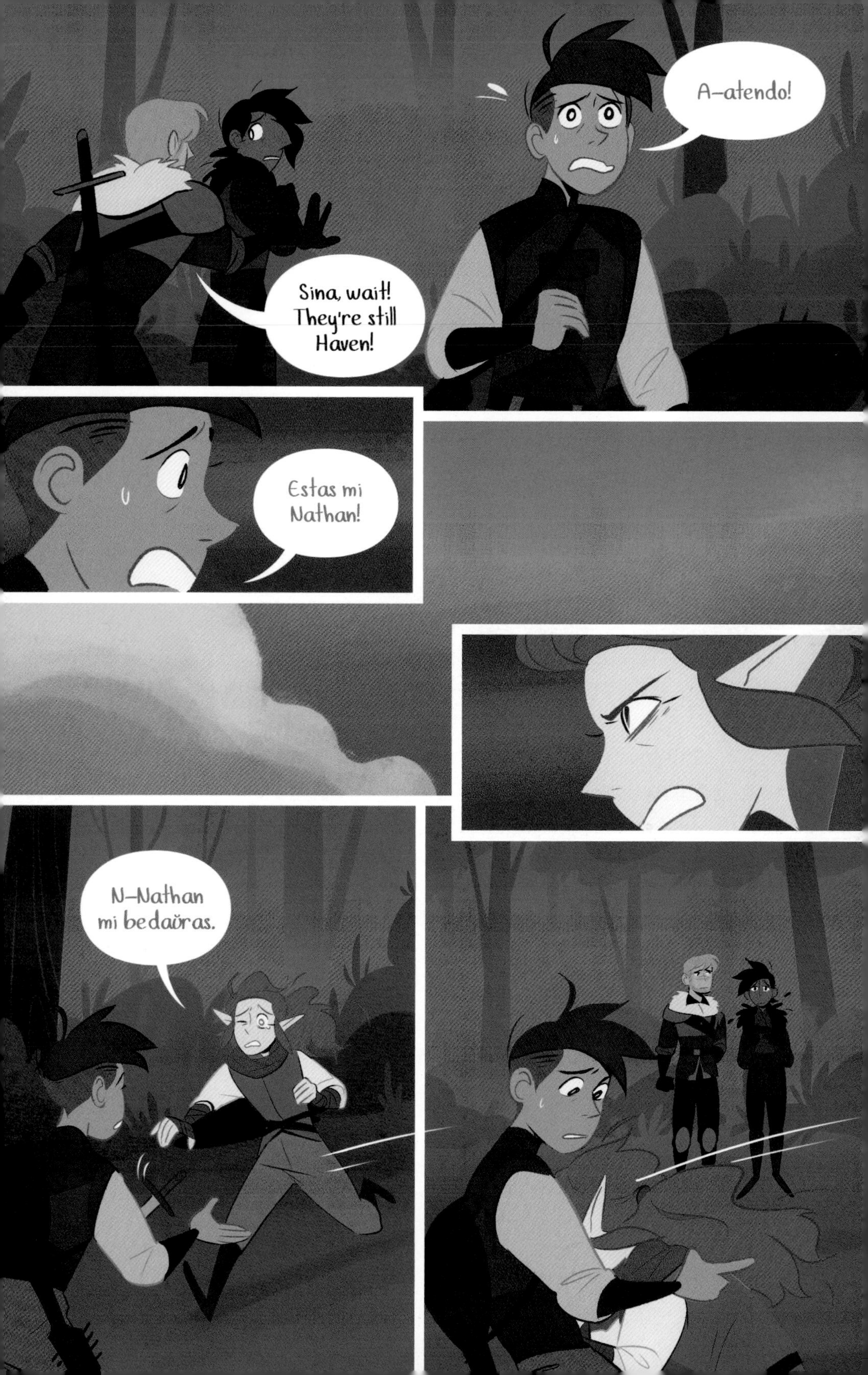
Sina, wait! They're still Haven!
A-atendo!
Estas mi Nathan!
N-Nathan mi bedaŭras.

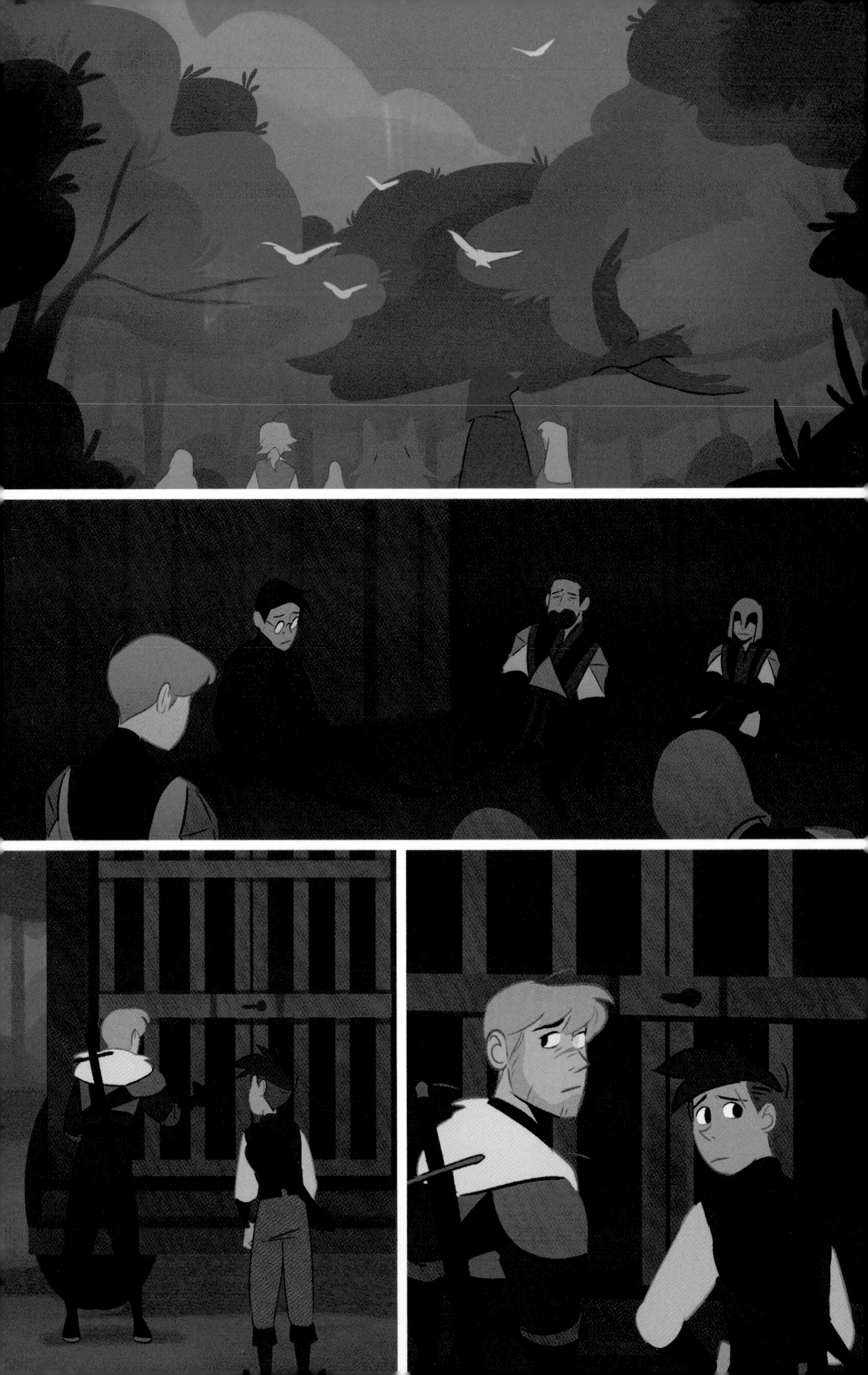

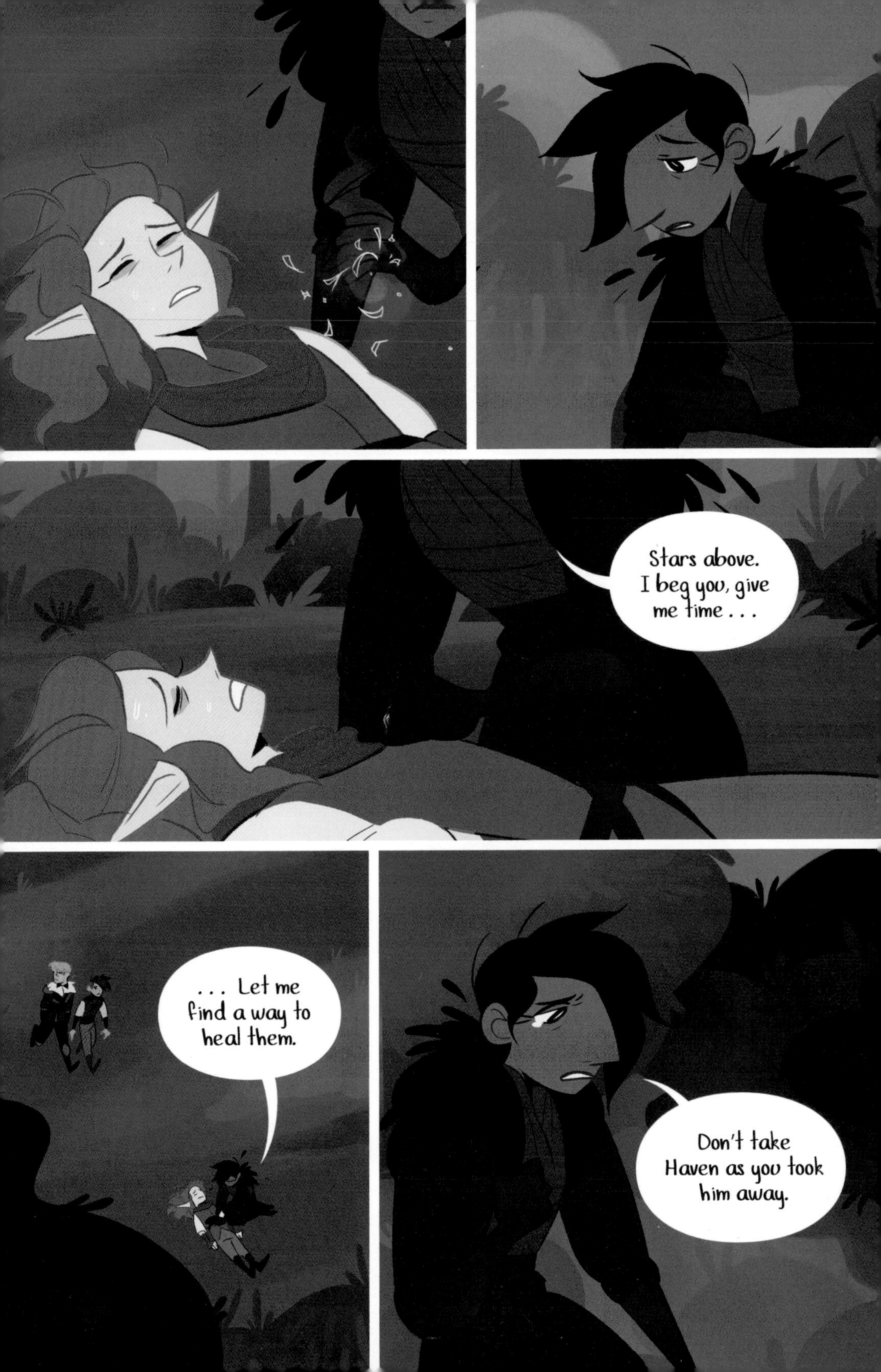
Stars above. I beg you, give me time . . .
. . . Let me find a way to heal them.
Don't take Haven as you took him away.

END OF CHAPTER 4

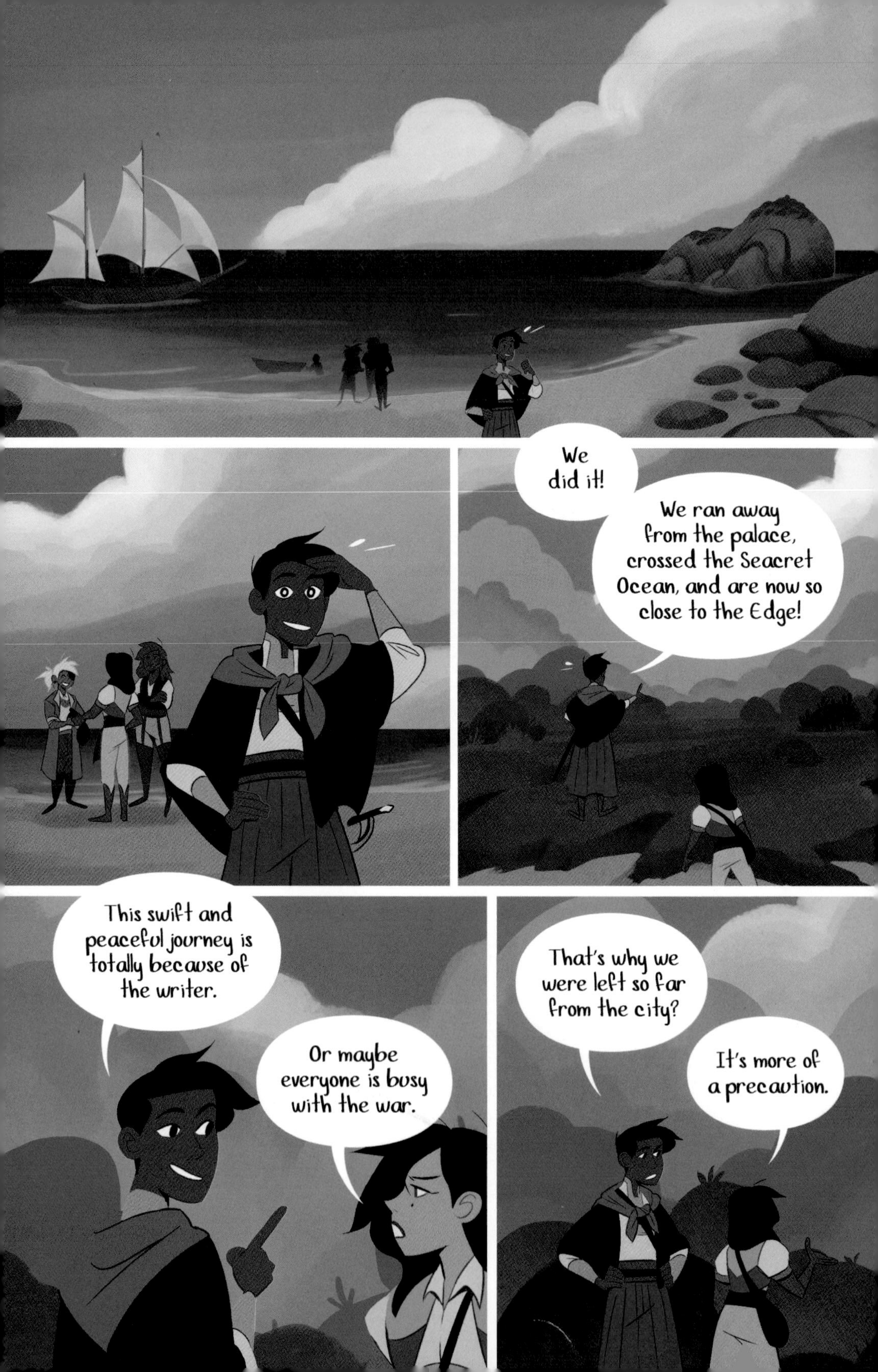
We did it!
We ran away from the palace, crossed the Seacret Ocean, and are now so close to the Edge!
This swift and peaceful journey is totally because of the writer.
Or maybe everyone is busy with the war.
That's why we were left so far from the city?
It's more of a precaution.

Chapter 5
Icy Volken
. . . You're very far from home, Imperial Highness.

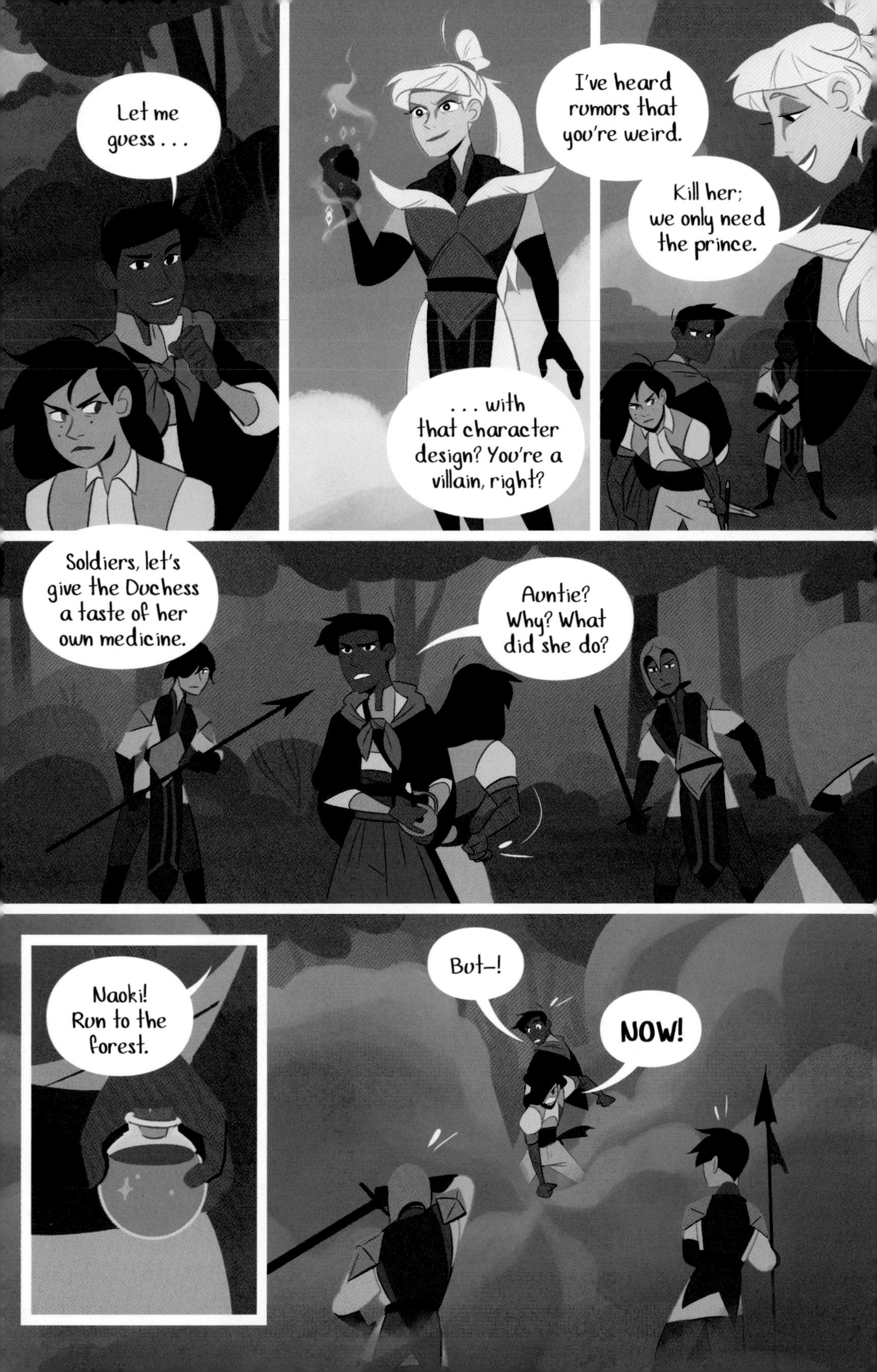
Let me guess . . .
. . . with that character design? You're a villain, right?
I've heard rumors that you're weird.
Kill her; we only need the prince.
Soldiers, let's give the Duchess a taste of her own medicine.
Auntie? Why? What did she do?
Naoki! Run to the forest.
But–!
NOW!

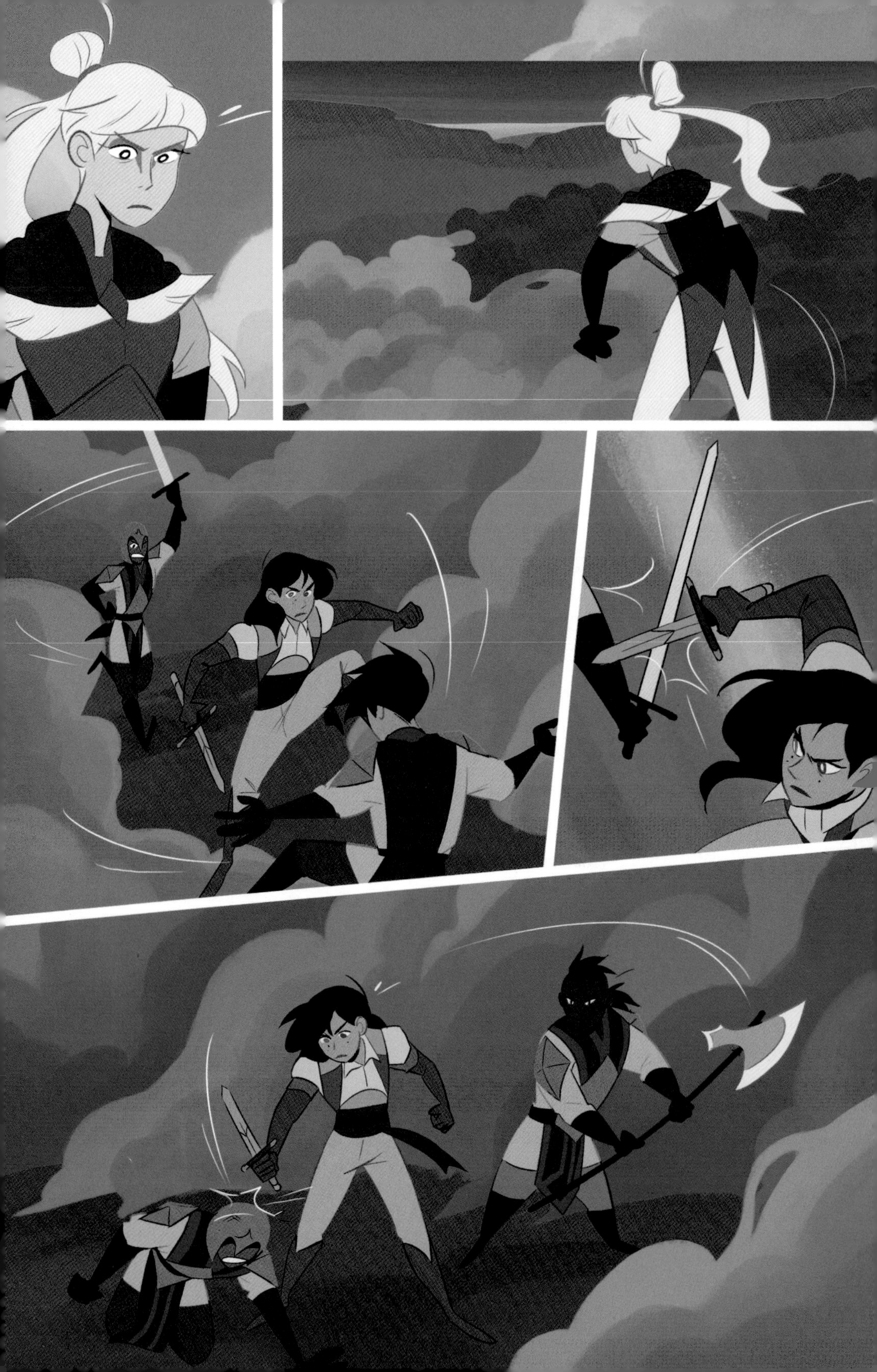

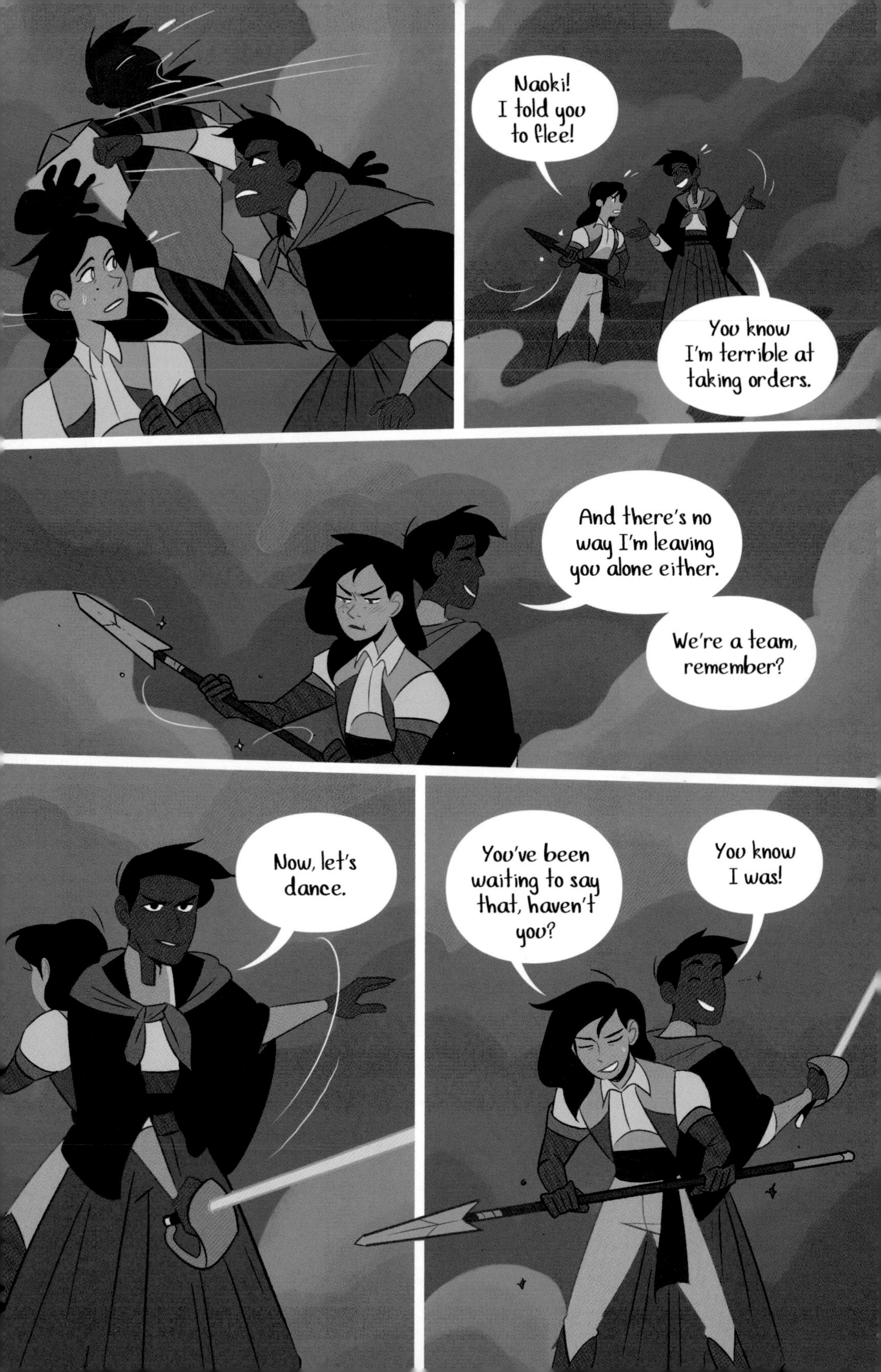
Naoki! I told you to flee!
You know I'm terrible at taking orders.
And there's no way I'm leaving you alone either.
We're a team, remember?
Now, let's dance.
You've been waiting to say that, haven't you?
You know I was!

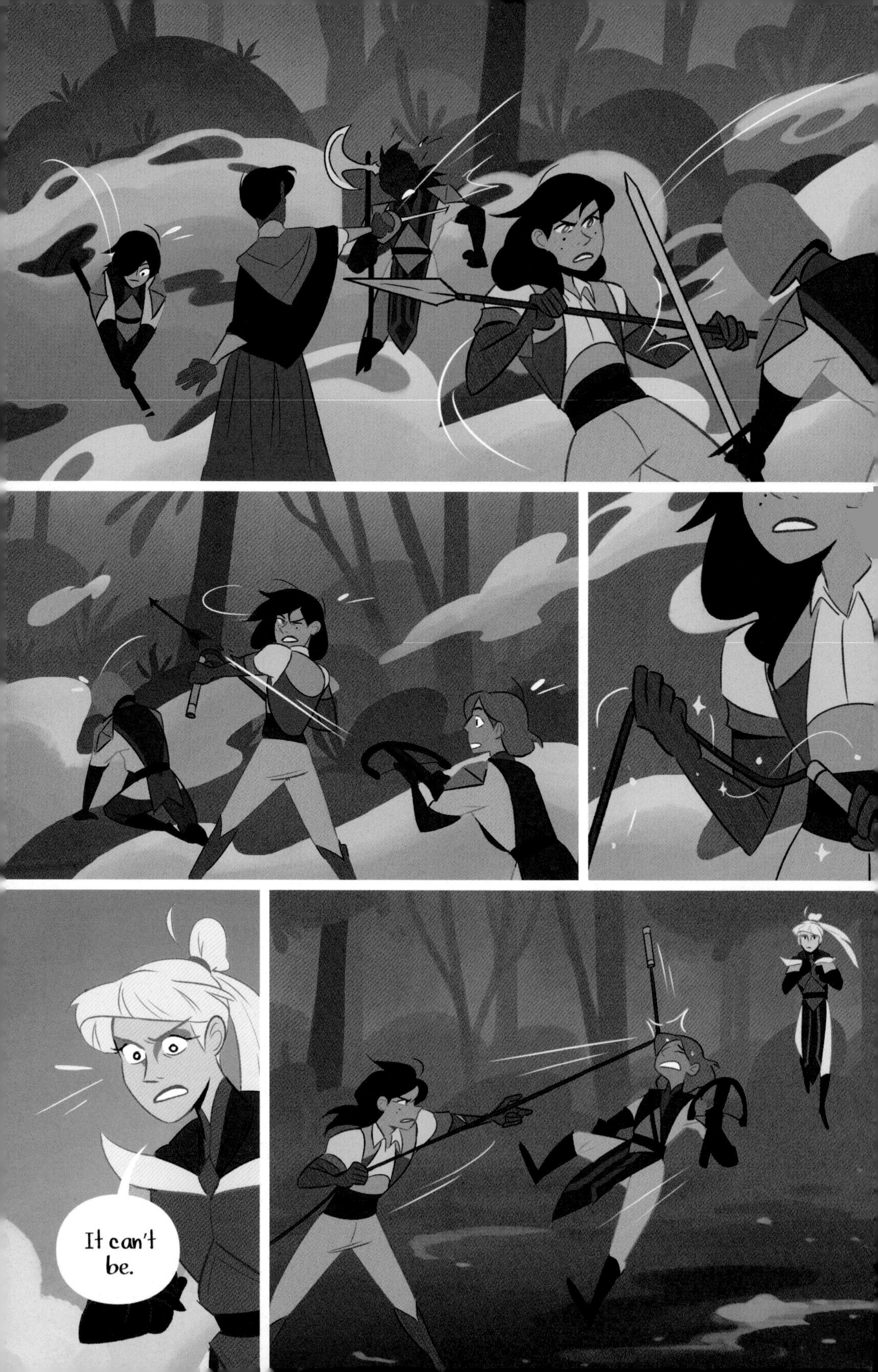
It can't be.

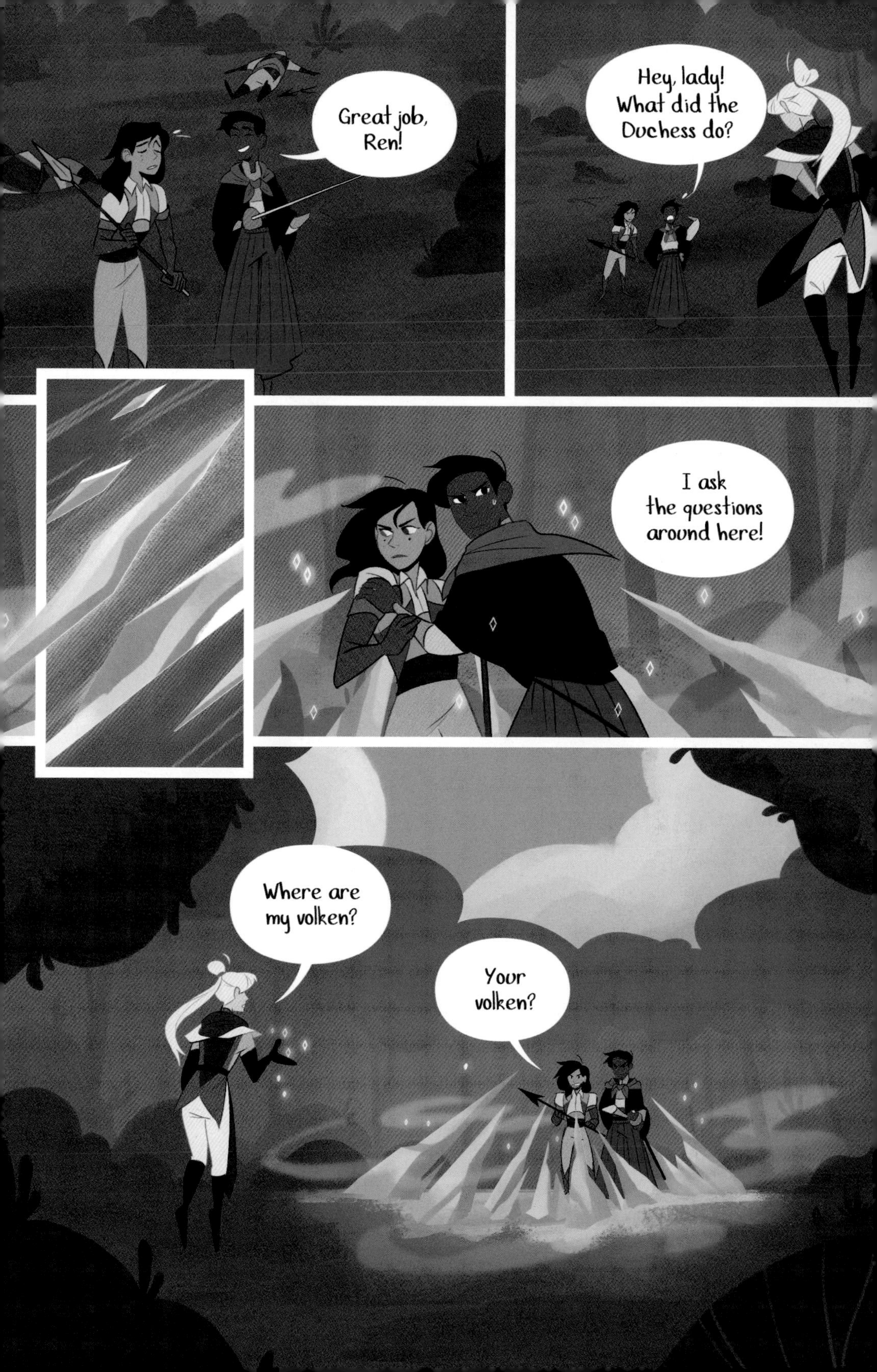
Great job, Ren!
Hey, lady! What did the Duchess do?
I ask the questions around here!
Where are my volken?
Your volken?

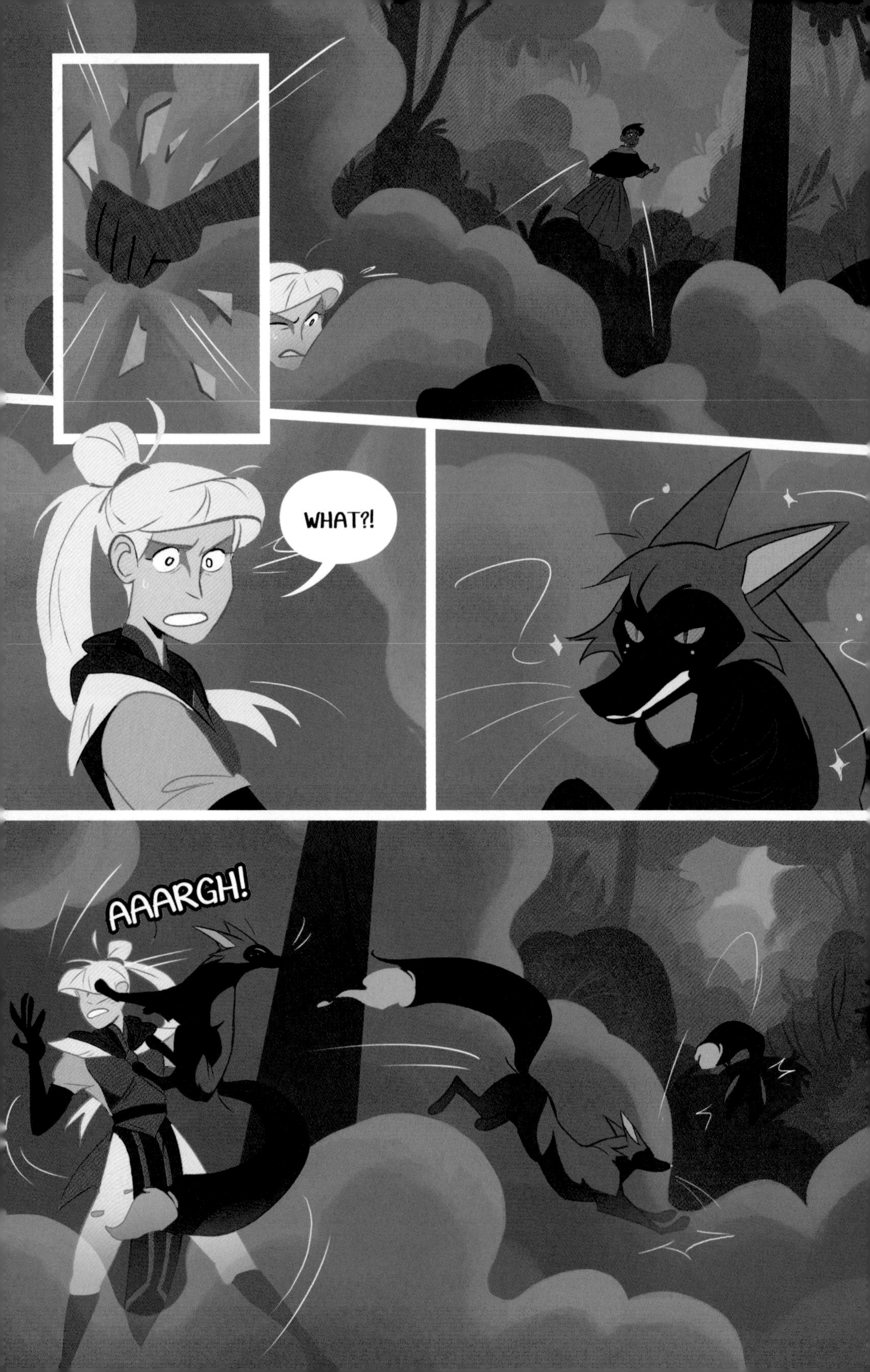
WHAT?!
AAARGH!

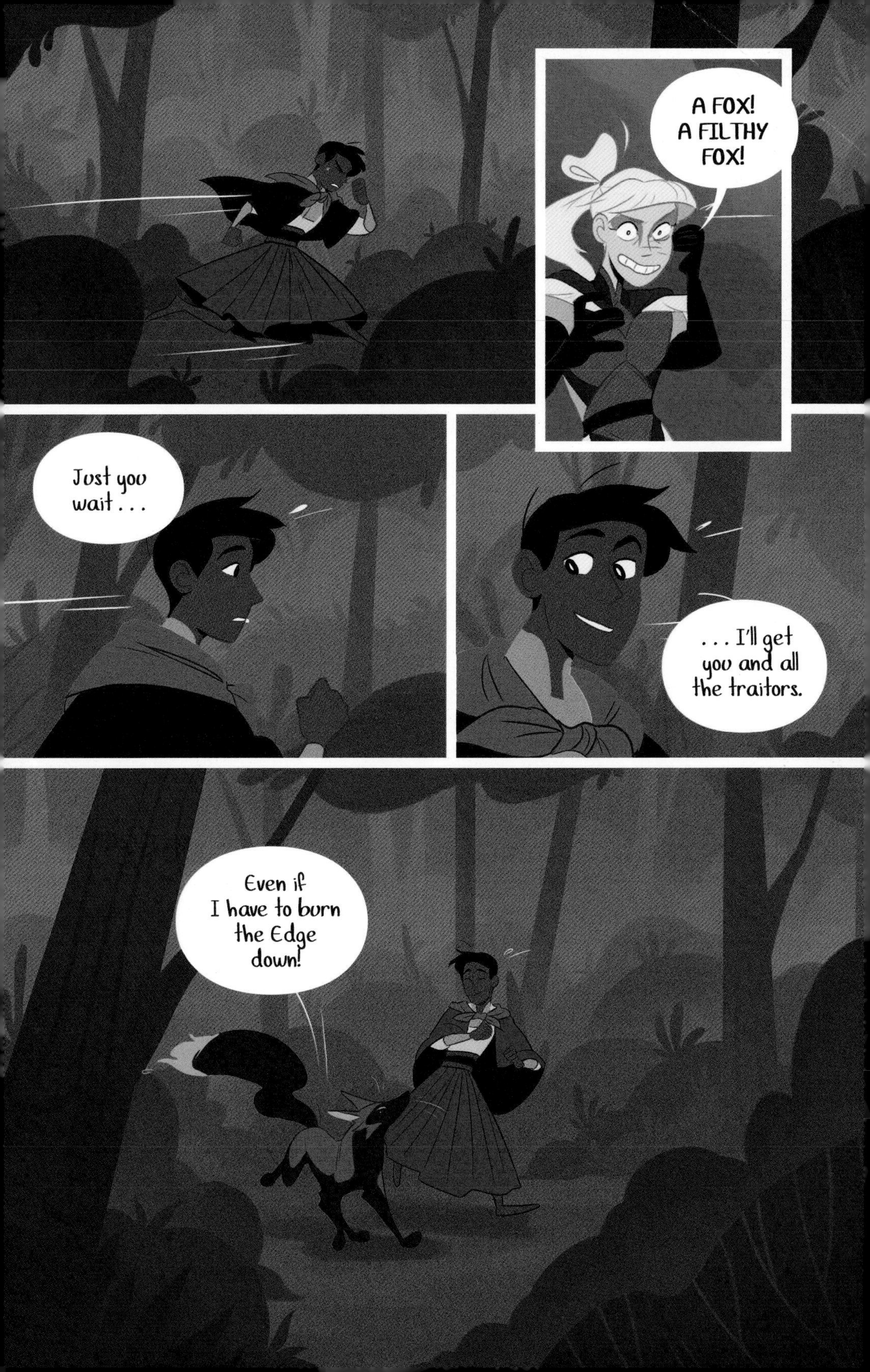
A FOX! A FILTHY FOX!
Just you wait . . .
. . . I'll get you and all the traitors.
Even if I have to burn the Edge down!

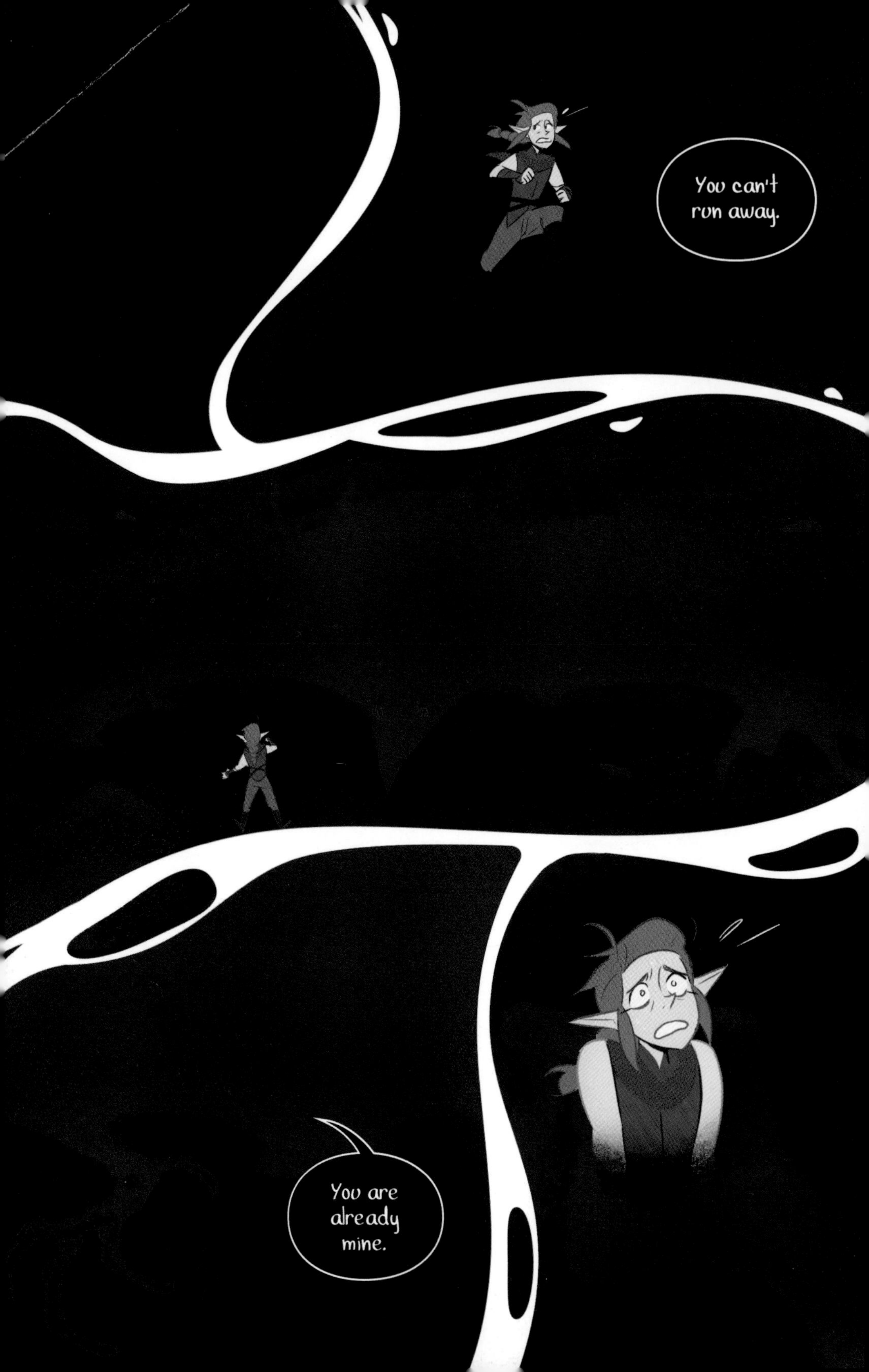
You can't run away.
You are already mine.

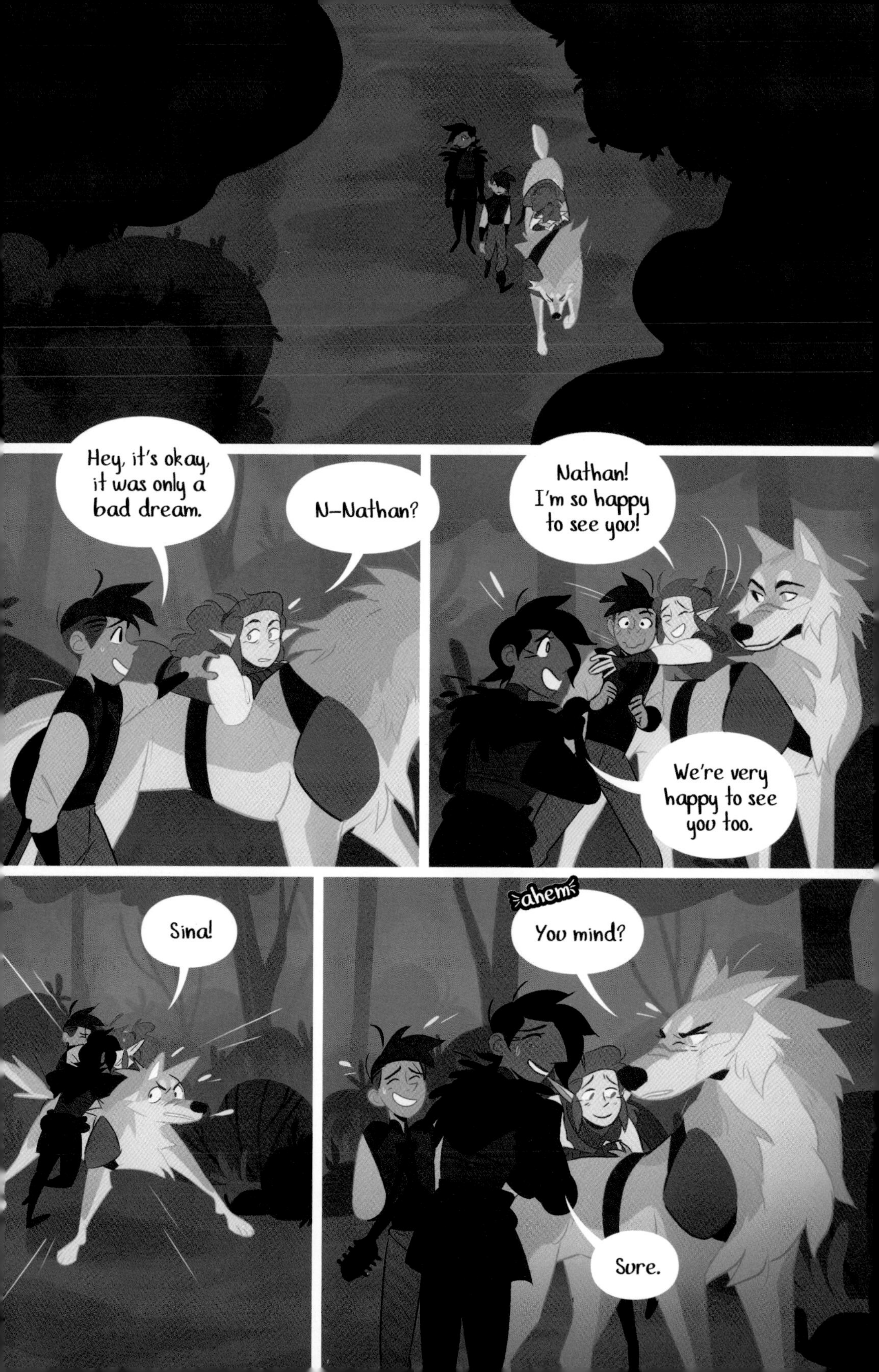
Hey, it's okay, it was only a bad dream.
N–Nathan?
Nathan! I'm so happy to see you!
We're very happy to see you too.
Sina!
ahem
You mind?
Sure.

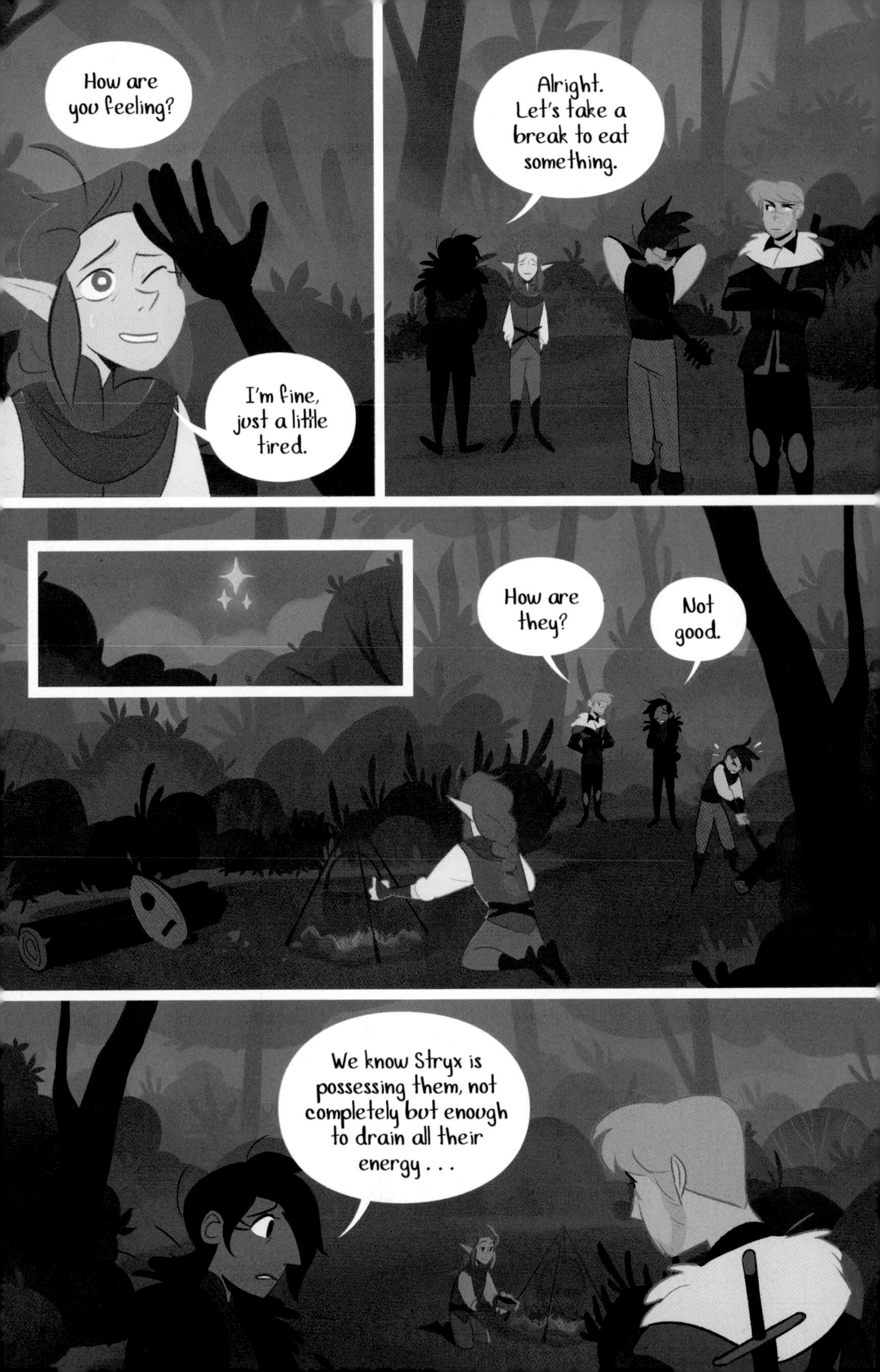
How are you feeling?
I'm fine, just a little tired.
Alright. Let's take a break to eat something.
How are they?
Not good.
We know Stryx is possessing them, not completely but enough to drain all their energy . . .

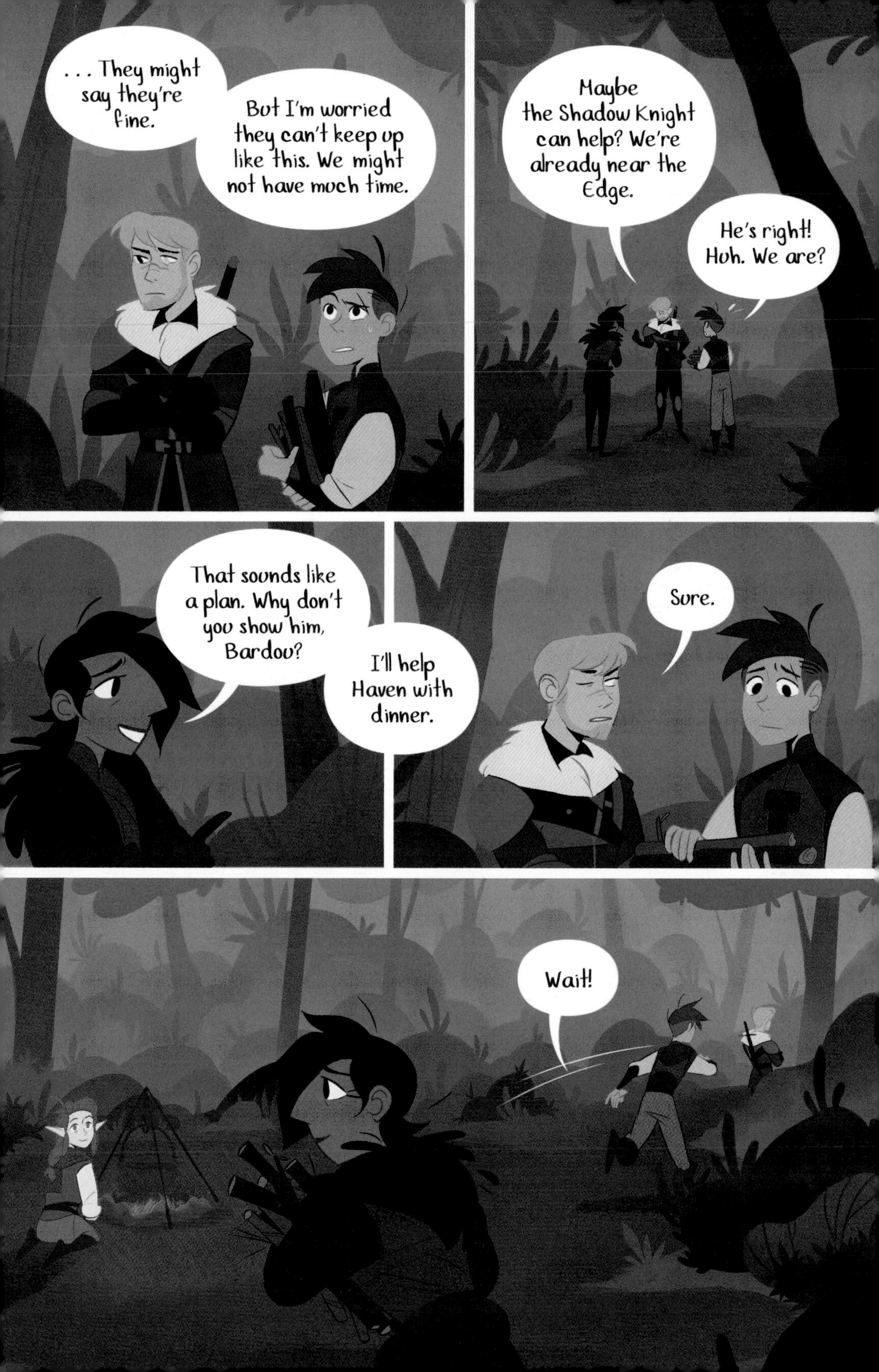
. . . They might say they're fine.
But I'm worried they can't keep up like this. We might not have much time.
Maybe the Shadow Knight can help? We're already near the Edge.
He's right! Huh. We are?
That sounds like a plan. Why don't you show him, Bardou?
I'll help Haven with dinner.
Sure.
Wait!

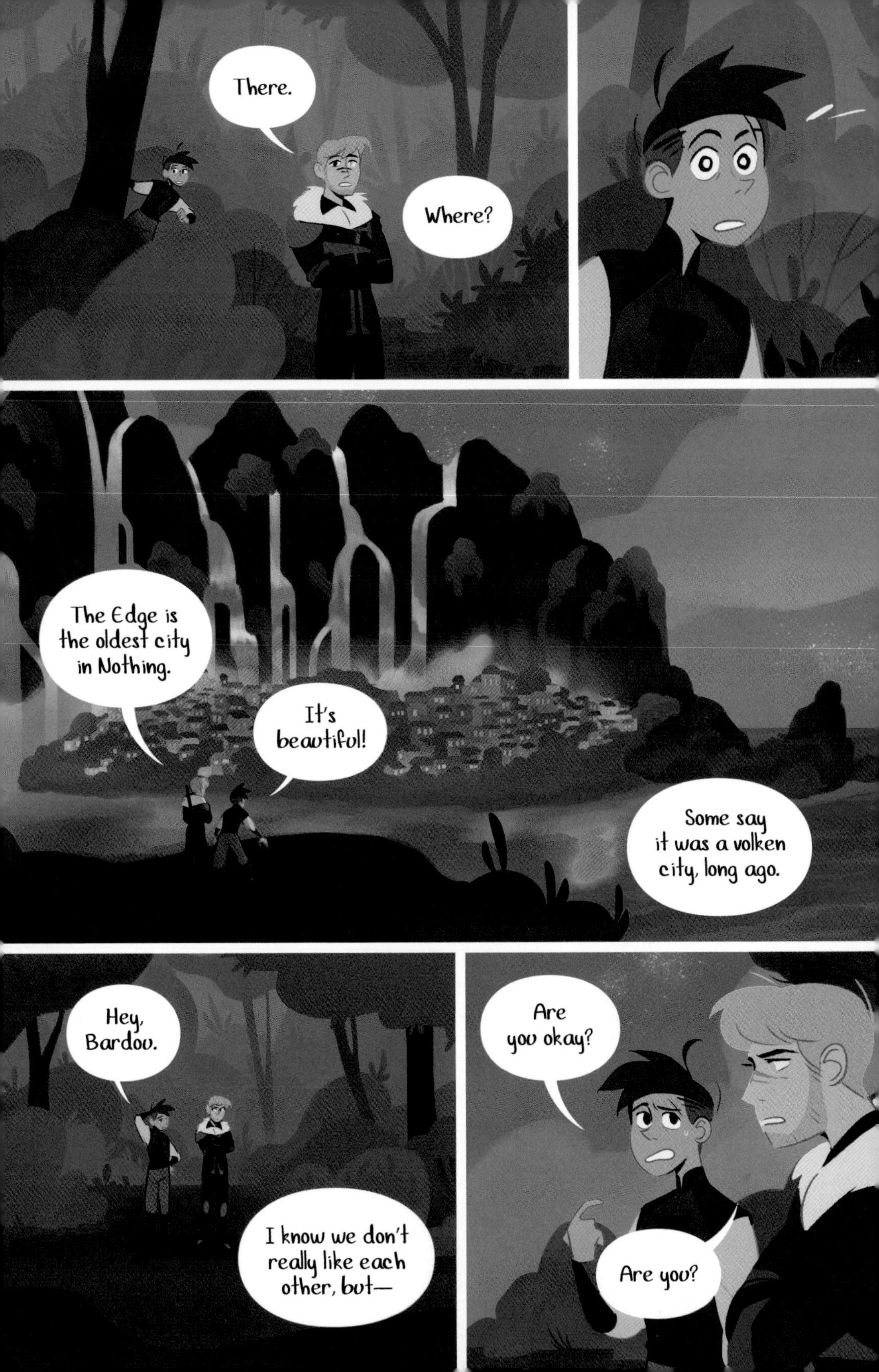
There.
Where?
The Edge is the oldest city in Nothing.
It's beautiful!
Some say it was a volken city, long ago.
Hey, Bardou.
I know we don't really like each other, but—
Are you okay?
Are you?

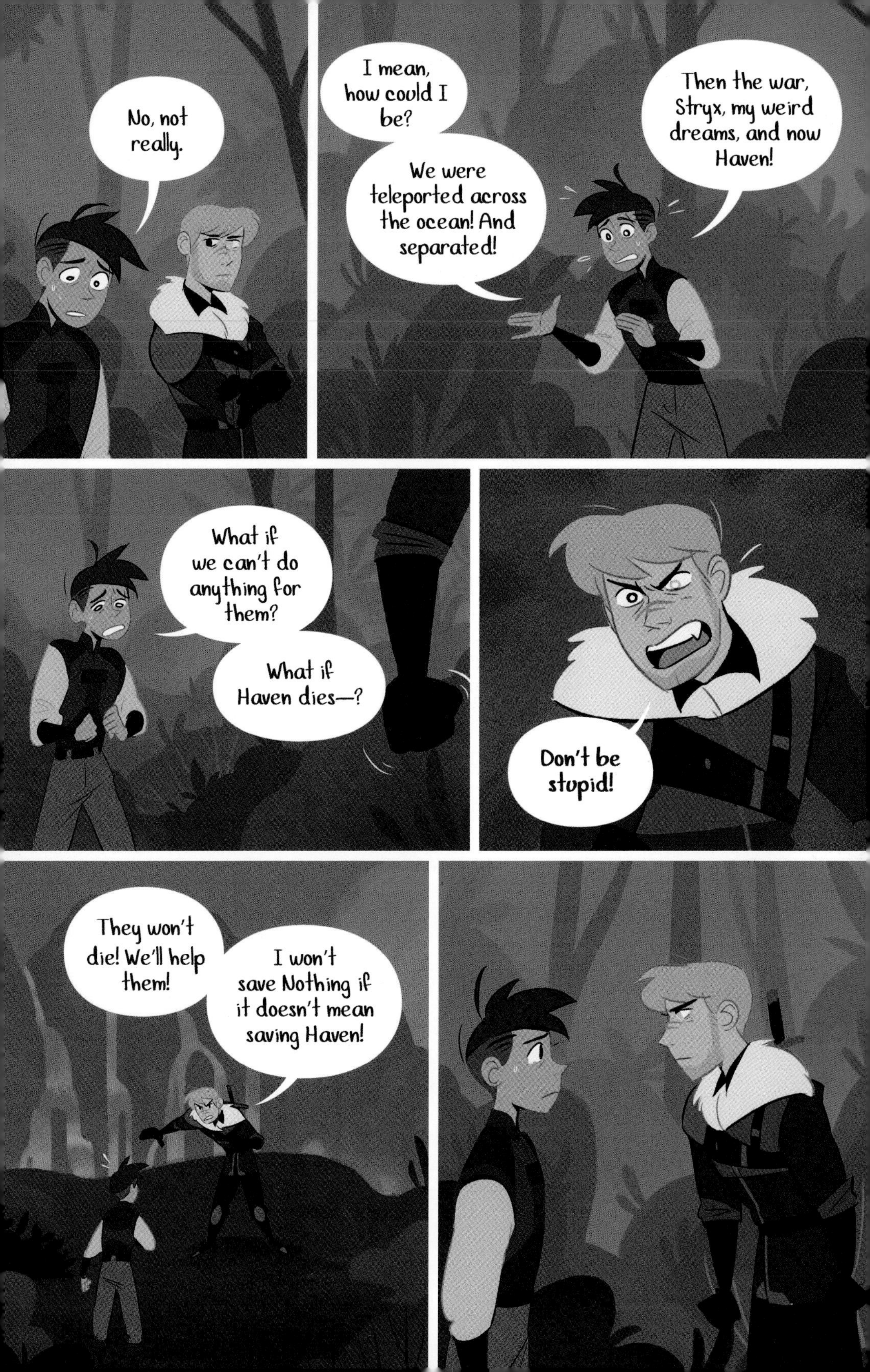
No, not really.
I mean, how could I be?
We were teleported across the ocean! And separated!
Then the war, Stryx, my weird dreams, and now Haven!
What if we can't do anything for them?
What if Haven dies—?
Don't be stupid!
They won't die! We'll help them!
I won't save Nothing if it doesn't mean saving Haven!

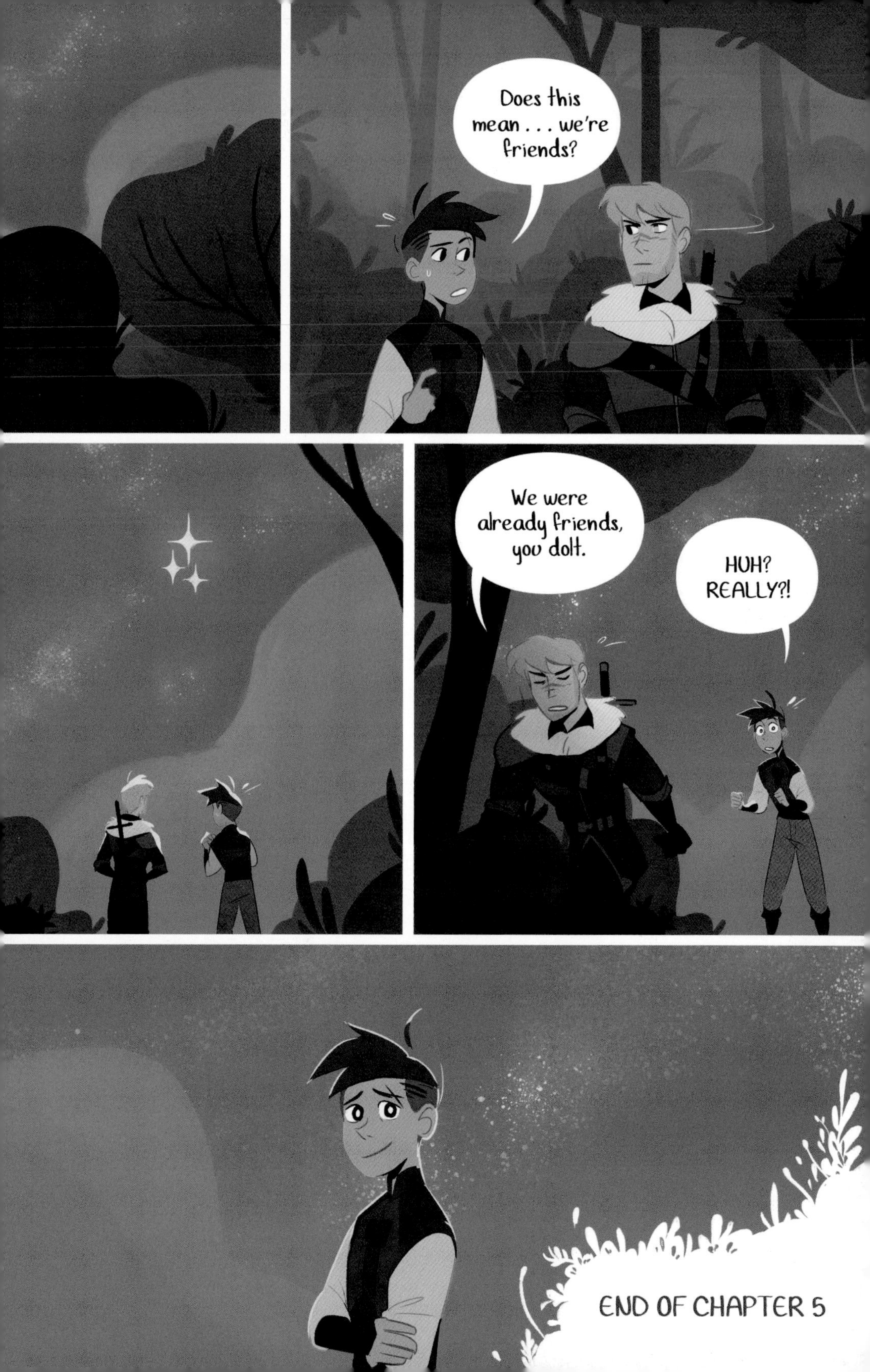
Does this mean . . . we're friends?
We were already friends, you dolt.
HUH? REALLY?!
END OF CHAPTER 5

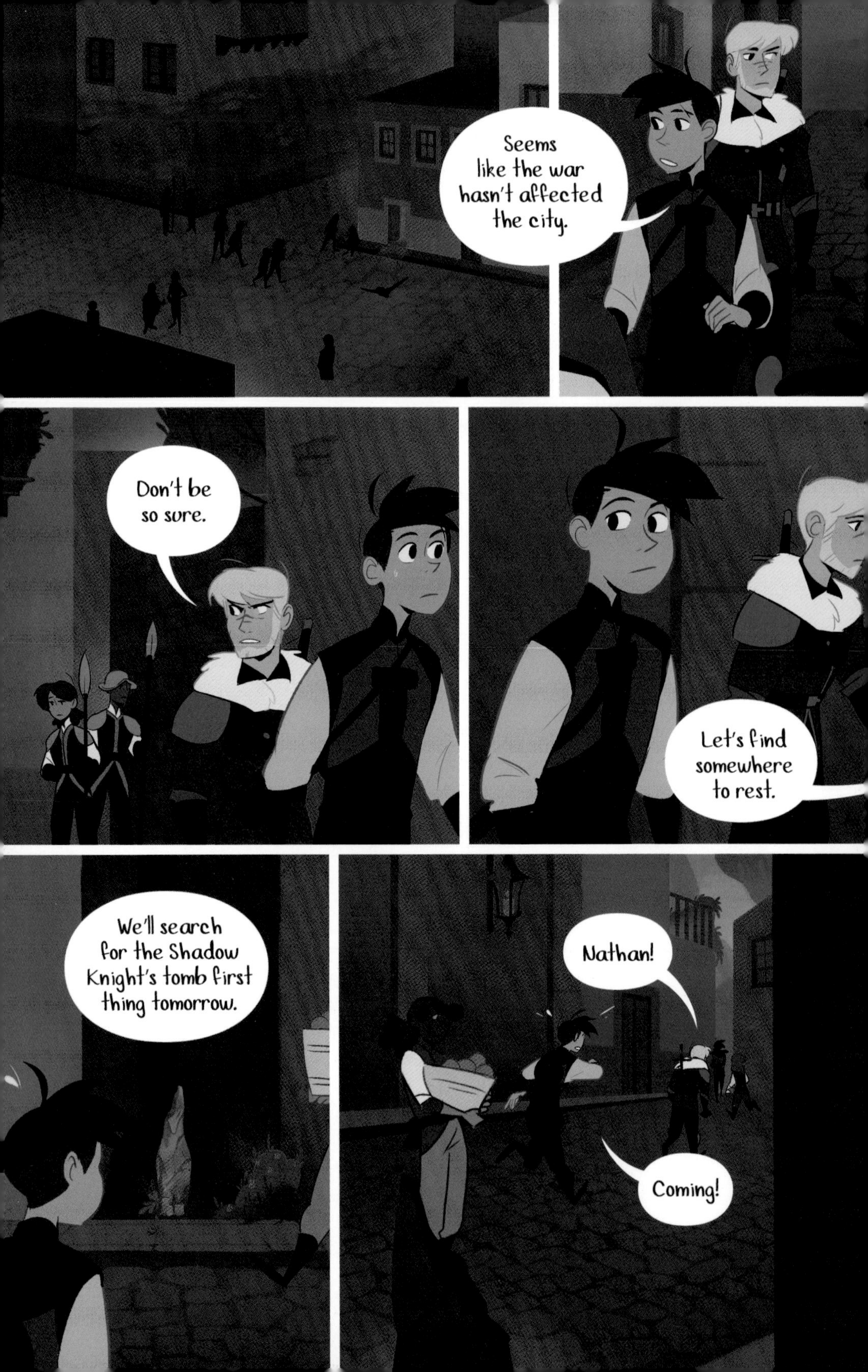
Seems like the war hasn't affected the city.
Don't be so sure.
Let's find somewhere to rest.
We'll search for the Shadow Knight's tomb first thing tomorrow.
Nathan!
Coming!

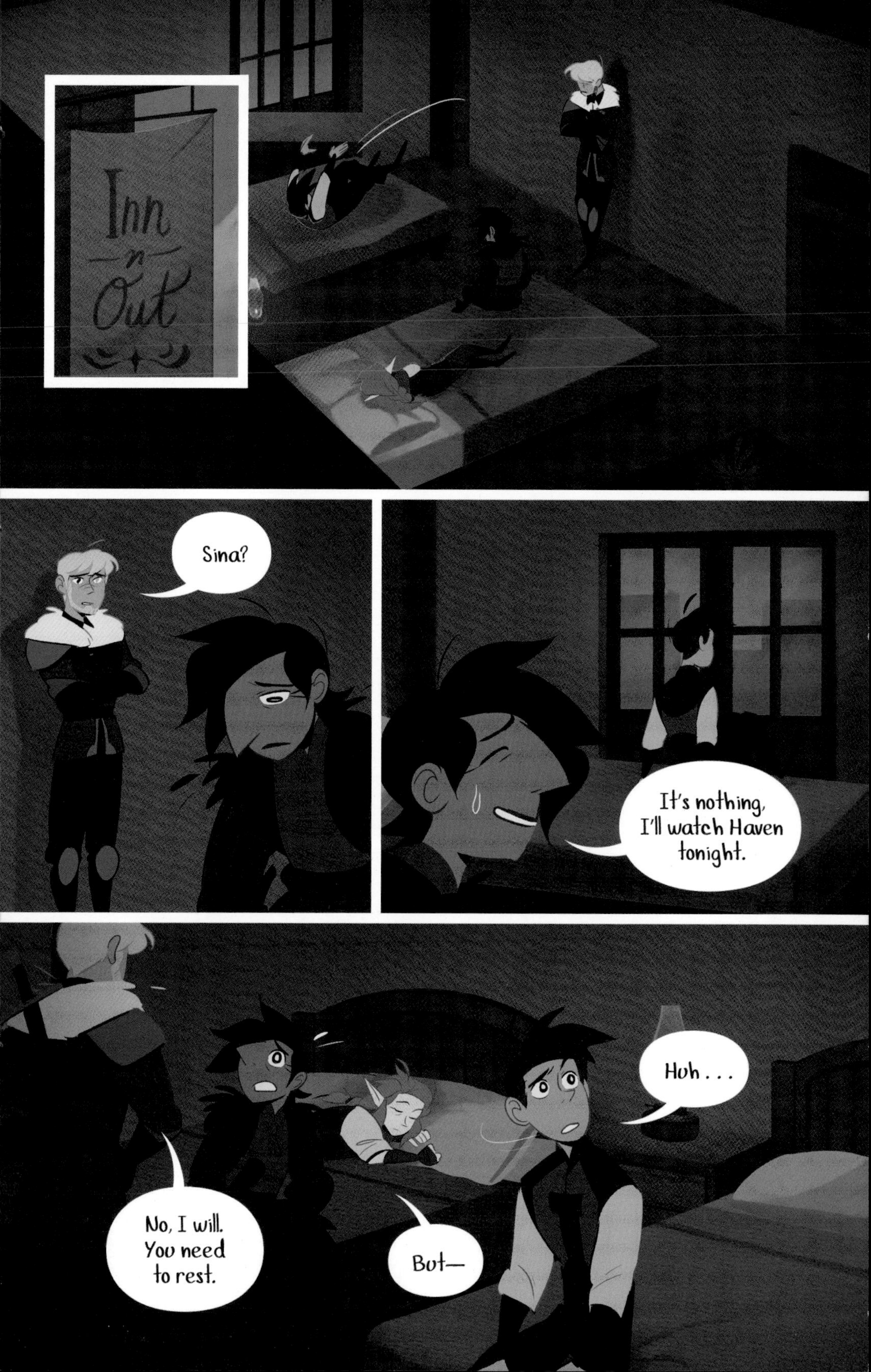
Inn
n
Out
Sina?
It's nothing, I'll watch Haven tonight.
Huh . . .
No, I will. You need to rest.
But—

Chapter 6
Edge of the Empire
. . . People here sure like doggorses.
Those weird statues are everywhere.

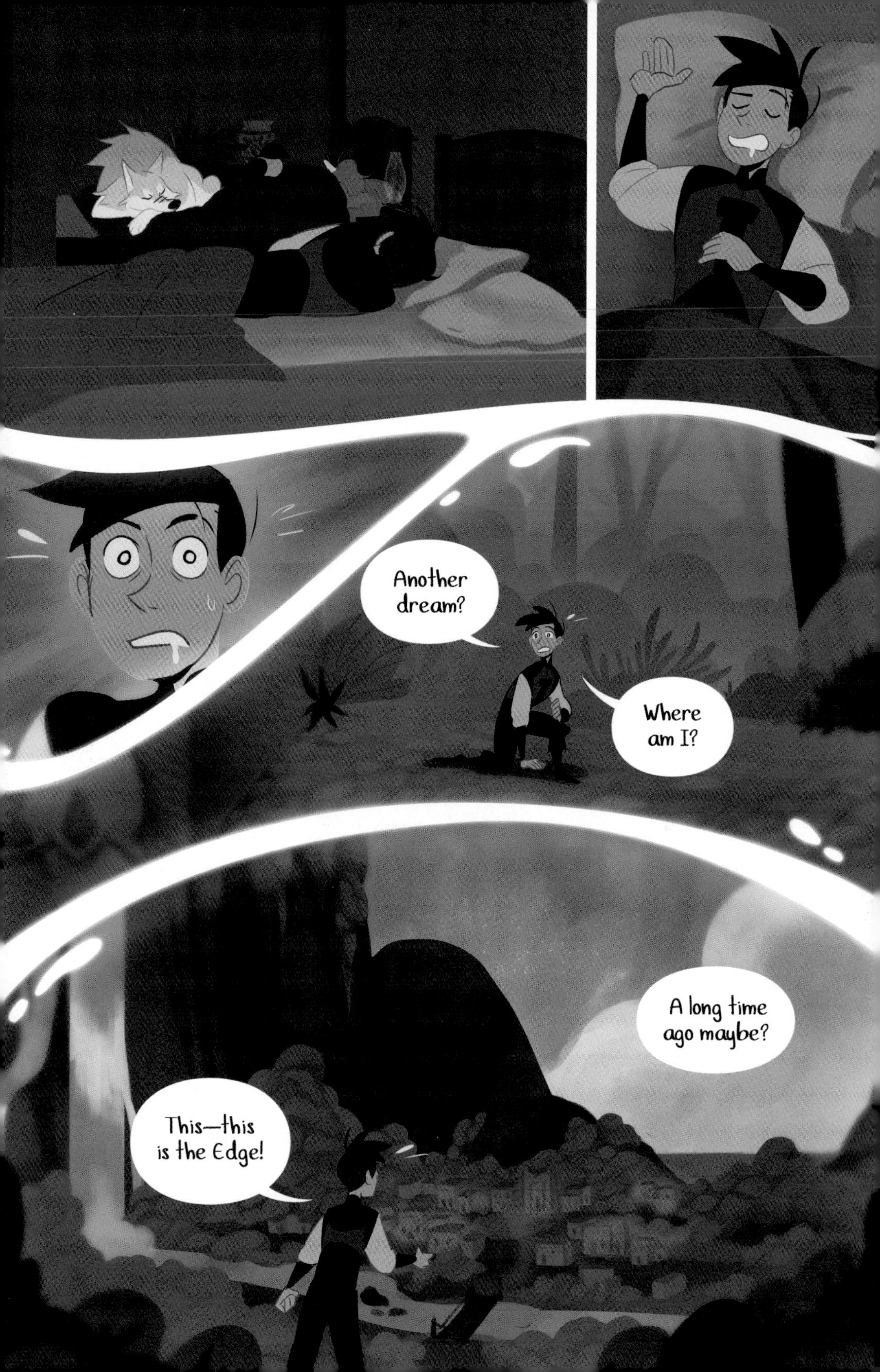
Another dream?
Where am I?
A long time ago maybe?
This—this is the Edge!

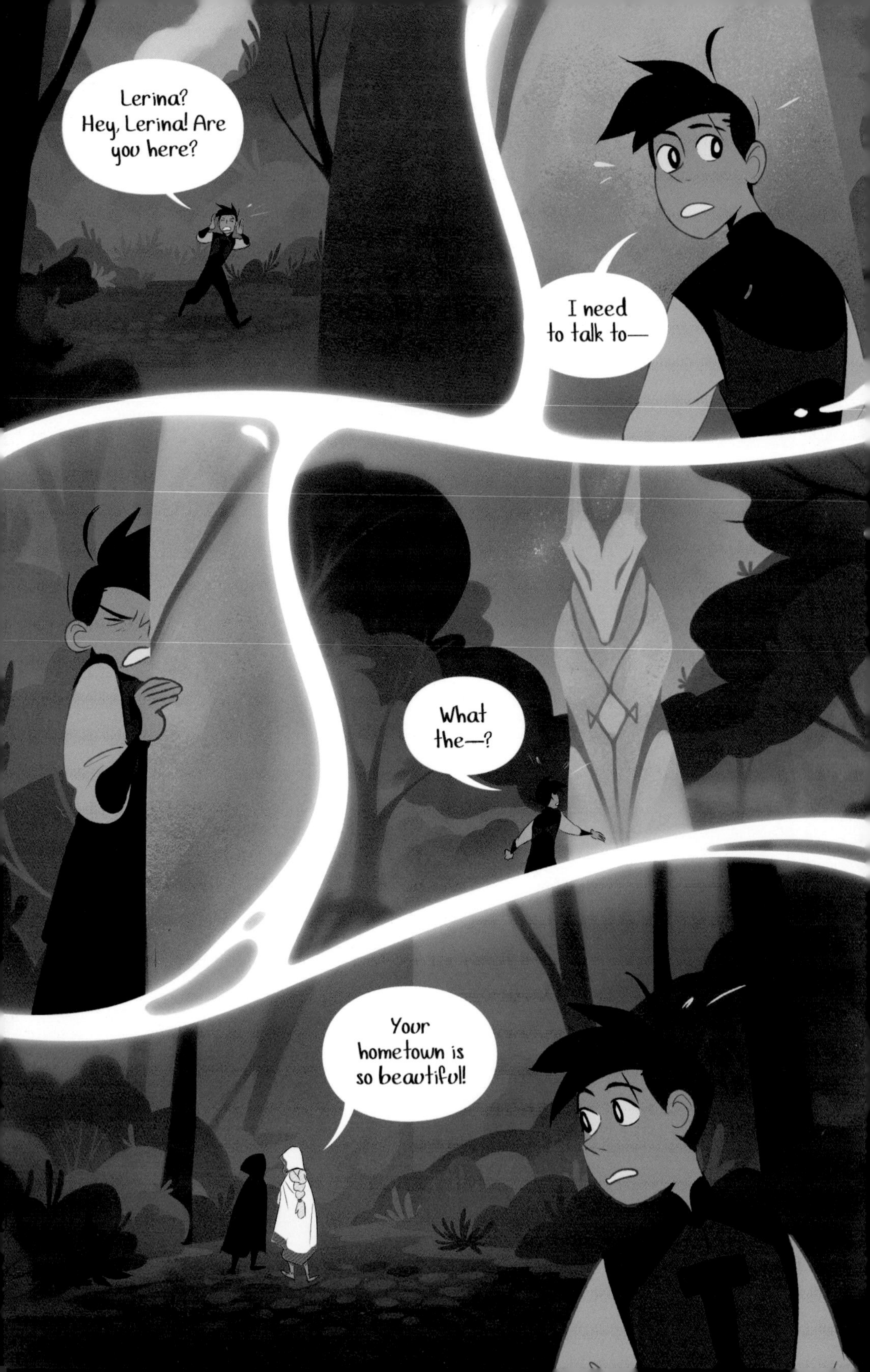
Lerina?
Hey, Lerina! Are you here?
I need to talk to—
What the—?
Your hometown is so beautiful!

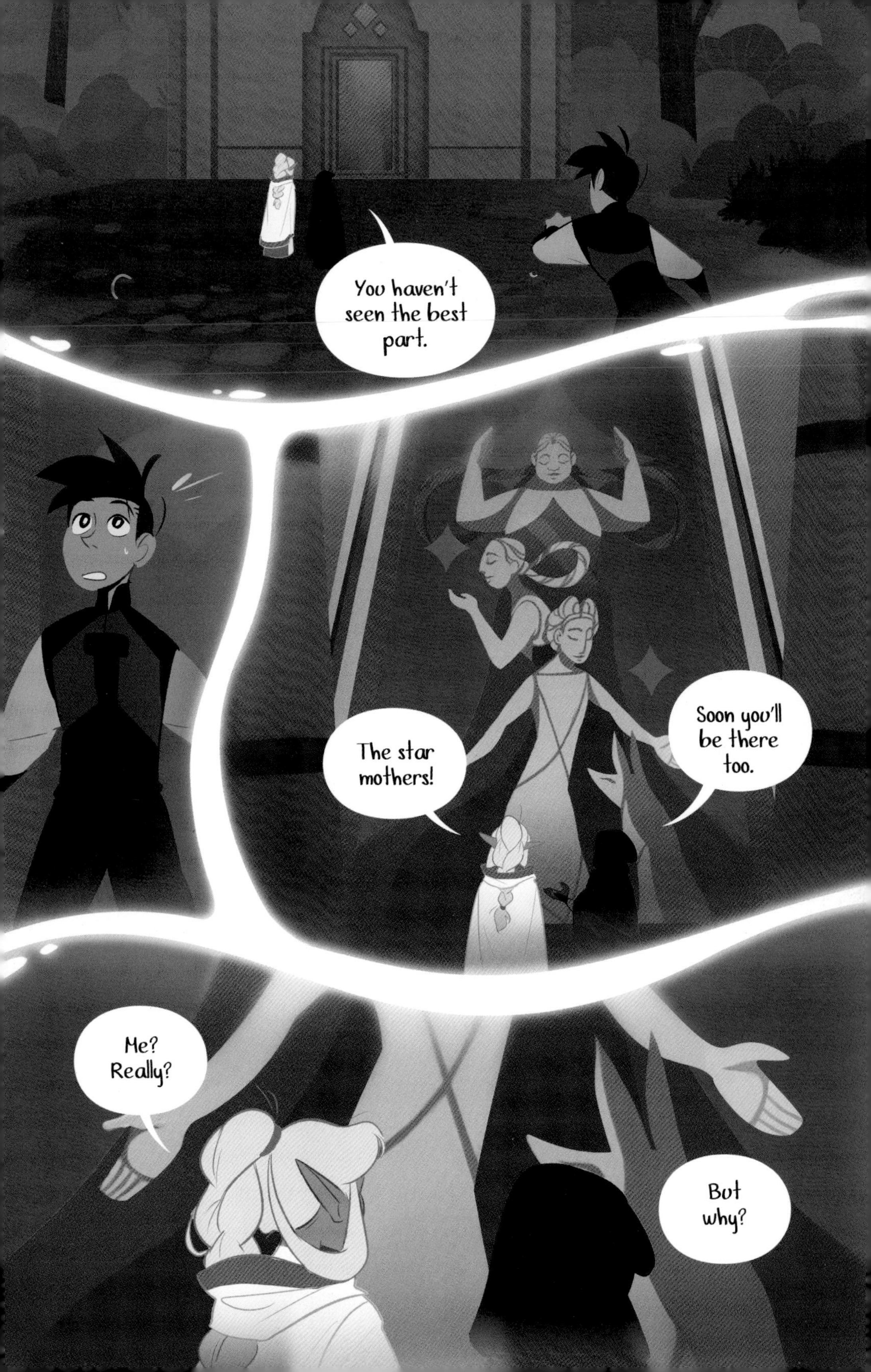
You haven't seen the best part.
The star mothers!
Soon you'll be there too.
Me? Really?
But why?

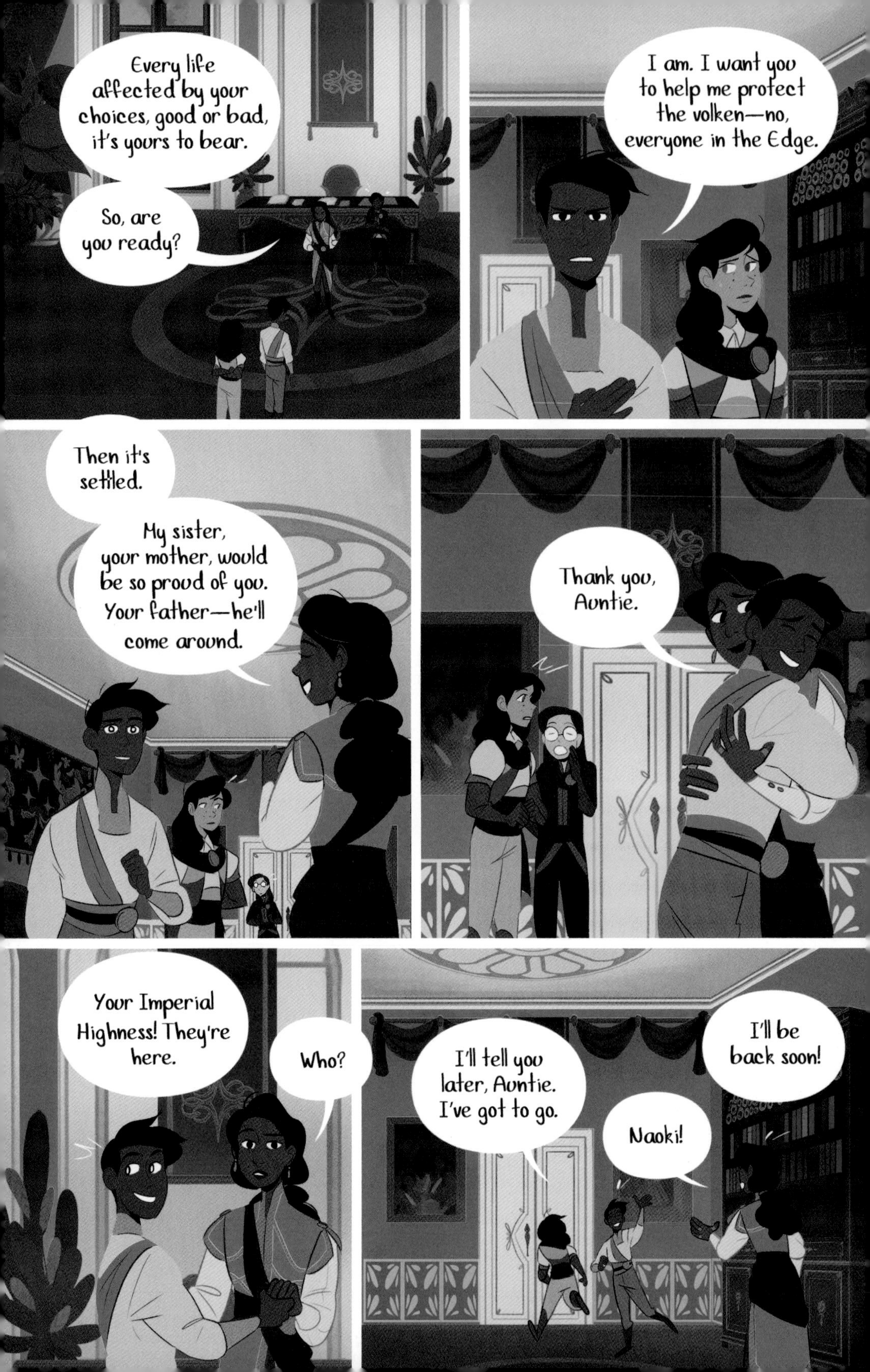
Every life affected by your choices, good or bad, it's yours to bear.
So, are you ready?
I am. I want you to help me protect the volken—no, everyone in the Edge.
Then it's settled.
My sister, your mother, would be so proud of you. Your father—he'll come around.
Thank you, Auntie.
Your Imperial Highness! They're here.
Who?
I'll tell you later, Auntie. I've got to go.
I'll be back soon!
Naoki!

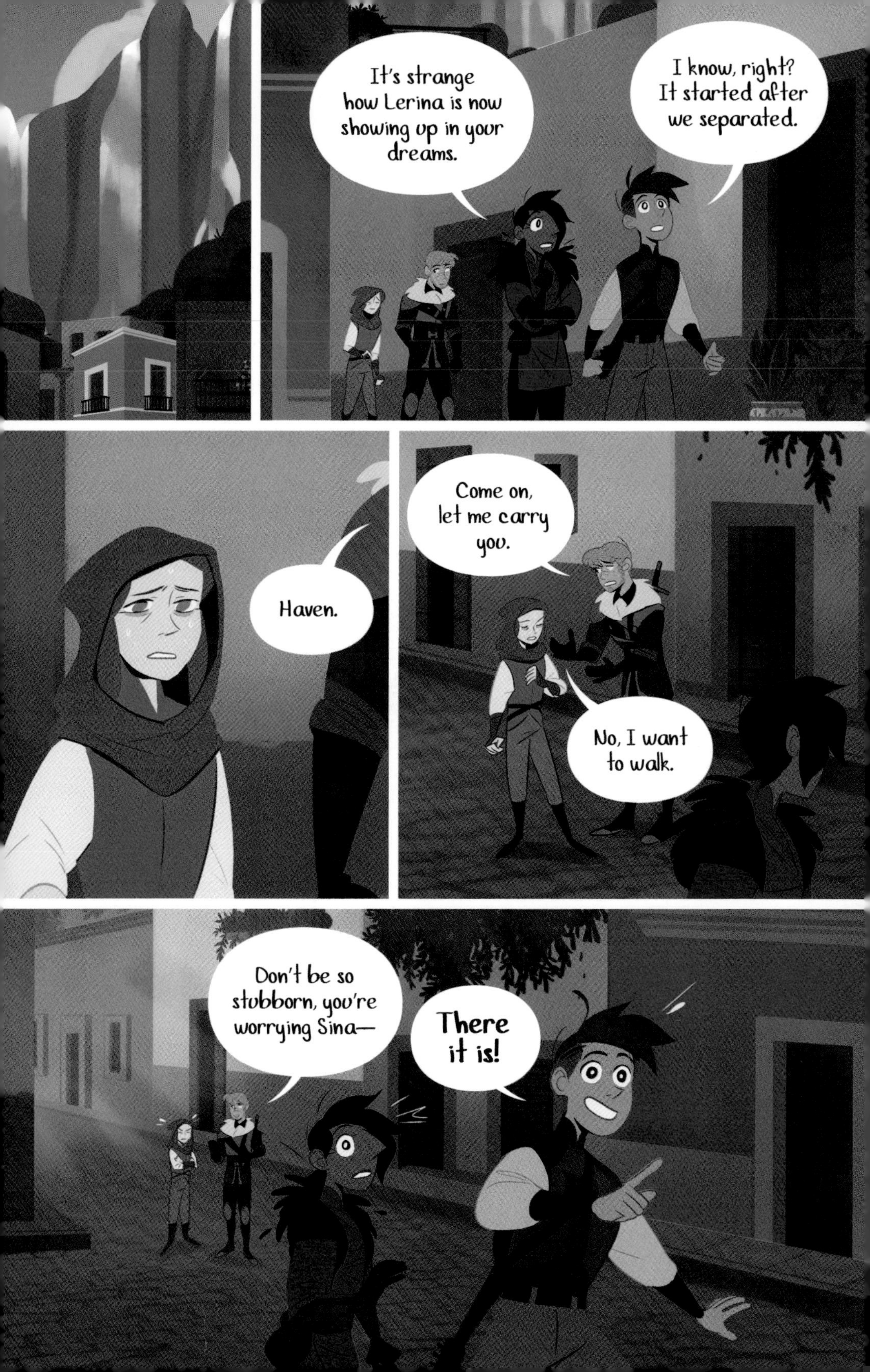
It's strange how Lerina is now showing up in your dreams.
I know, right? It started after we separated.
Haven.
Come on, let me carry you.
No, I want to walk.
Don't be so stubborn, you're worrying Sina—
There it is!

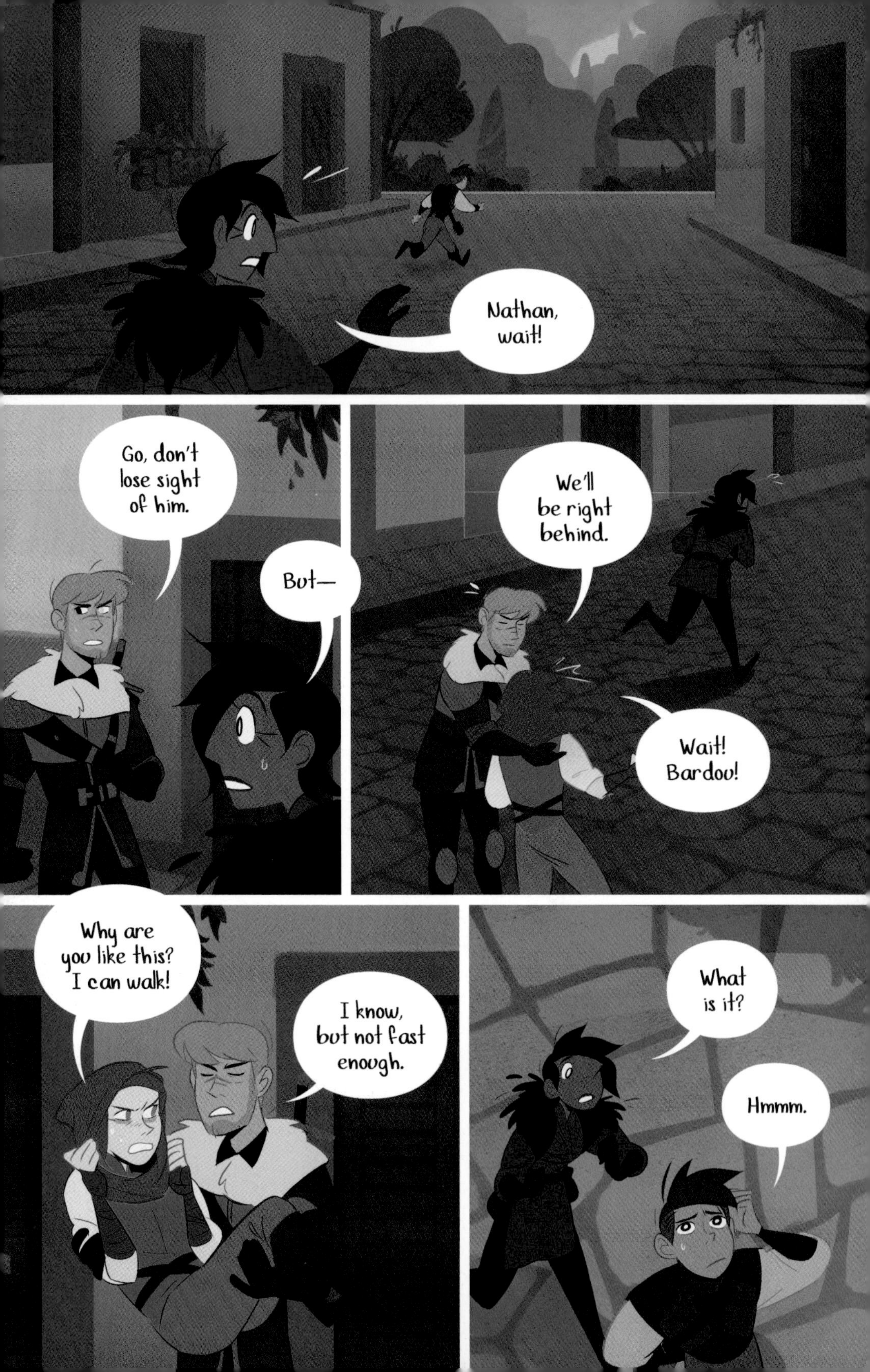

Nathan, wait!
Go, don't lose sight of him.
But—
We'll be right behind.
Wait! Bardou!
Why are you like this? I can walk!
I know, but not fast enough.
What is it?
Hmmm.

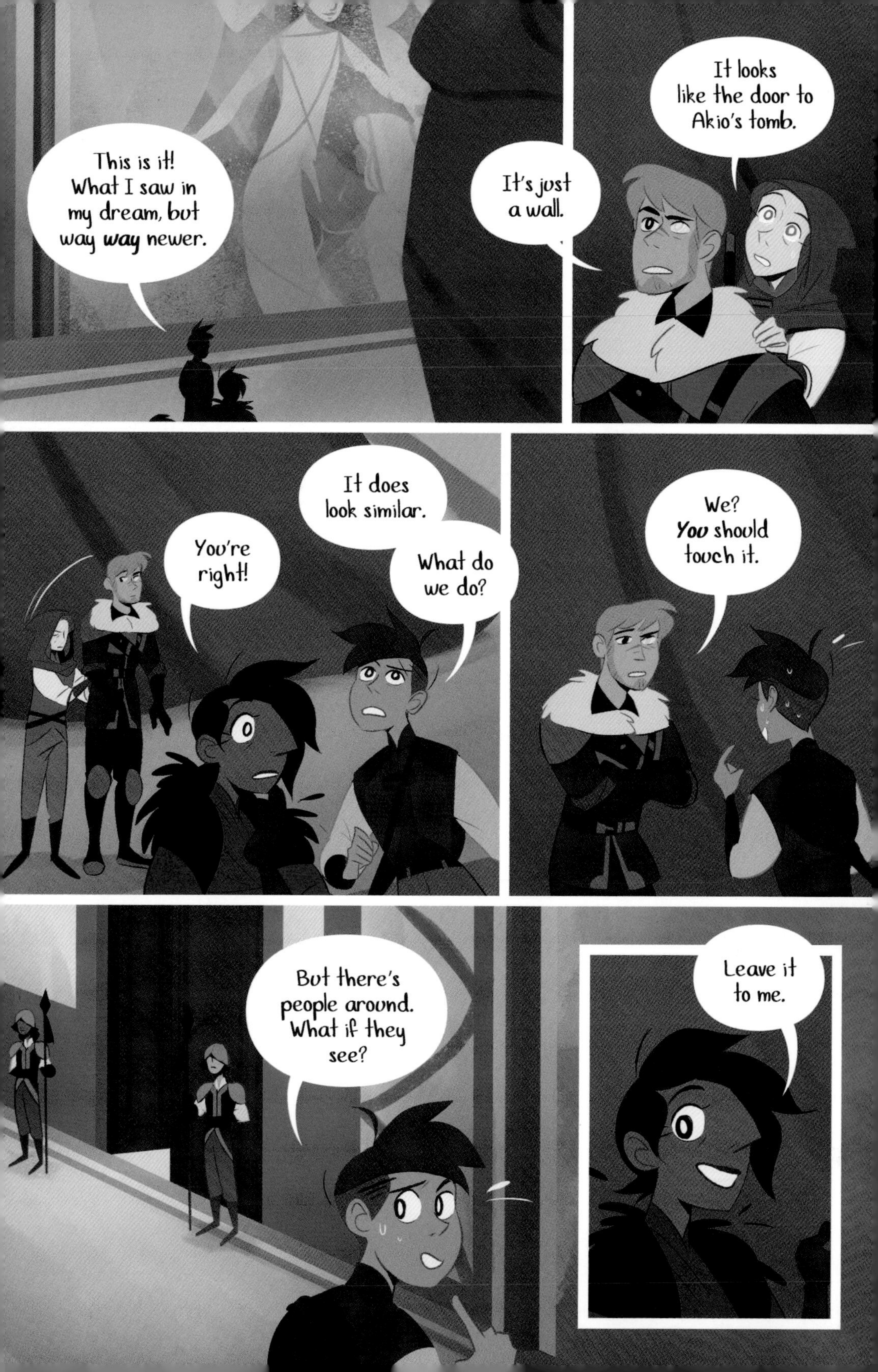
This is it! What I saw in my dream, but way **way** newer.
It's just a wall.
It looks like the door to Akio's tomb.
You're right!
It does look similar.
What do we do?
We? ***You*** should touch it.
But there's people around. What if they see?
Leave it to me.

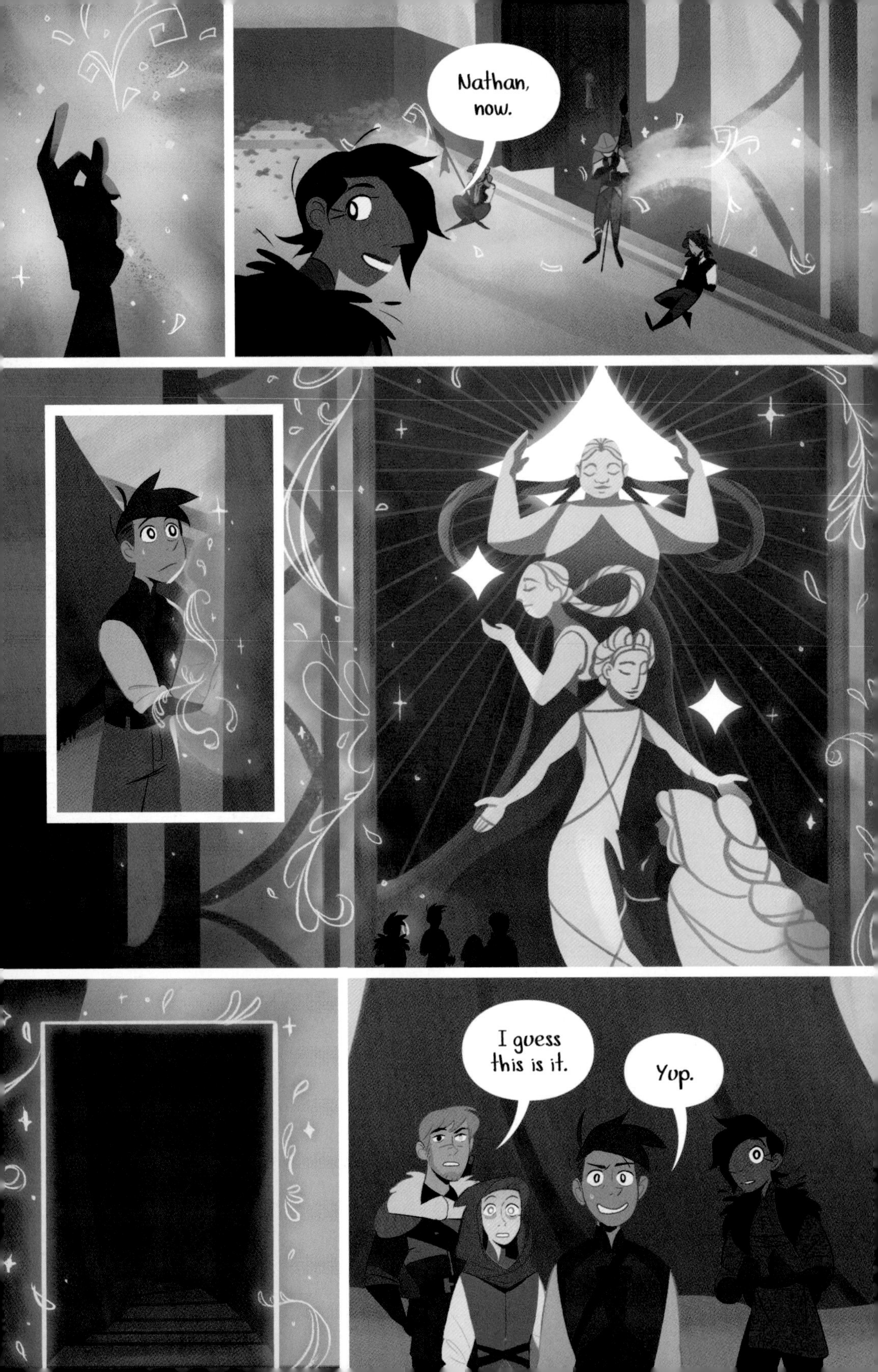
Nathan, now.
I guess this is it.
Yup.

END OF CHAPTER 6

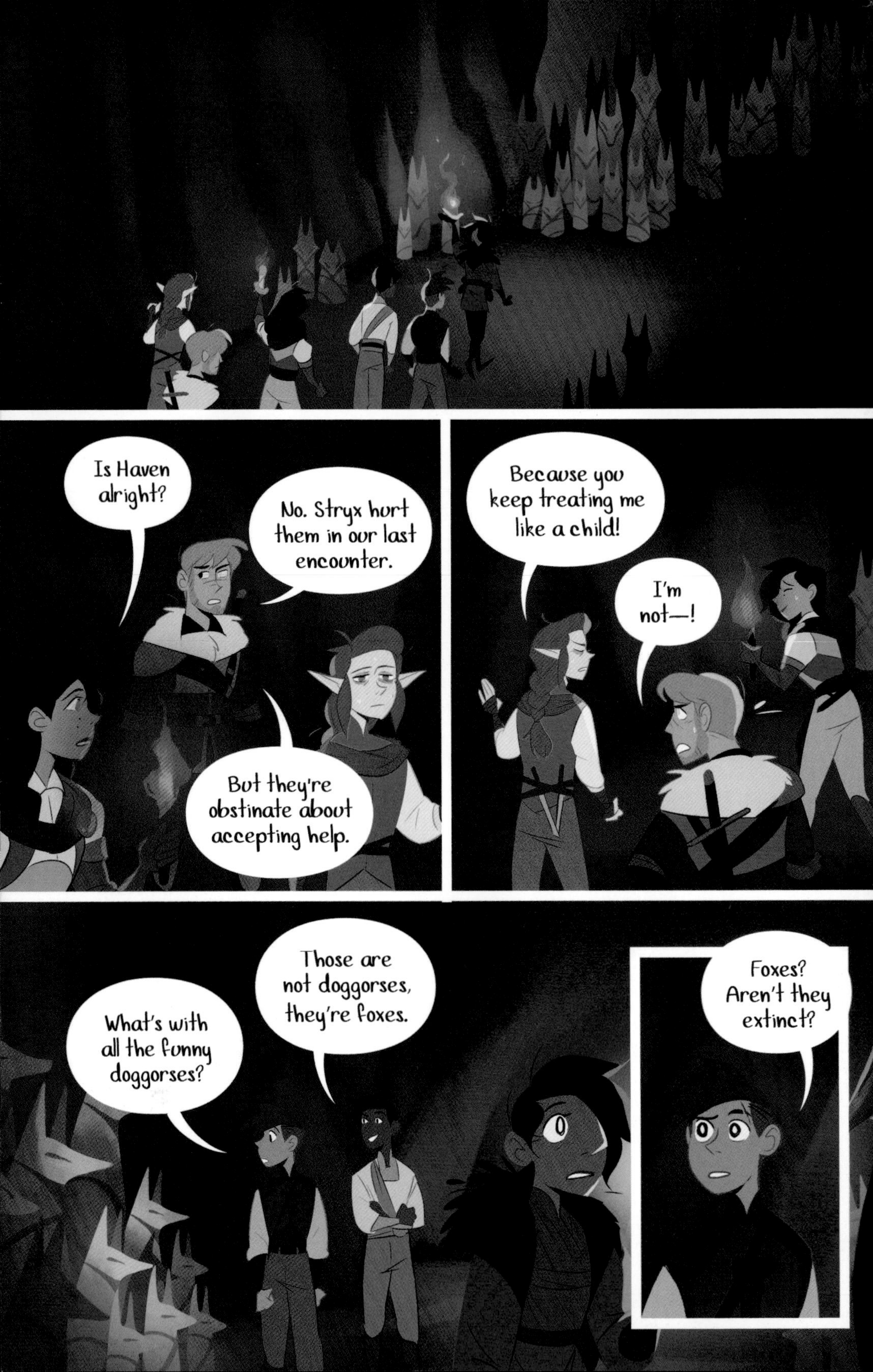
Is Haven alright?
No. Stryx hurt them in our last encounter.
But they're obstinate about accepting help.
Because you keep treating me like a child!
I'm not—!
What's with all the funny doggorses?
Those are not doggorses, they're foxes.
Foxes? Aren't they extinct?

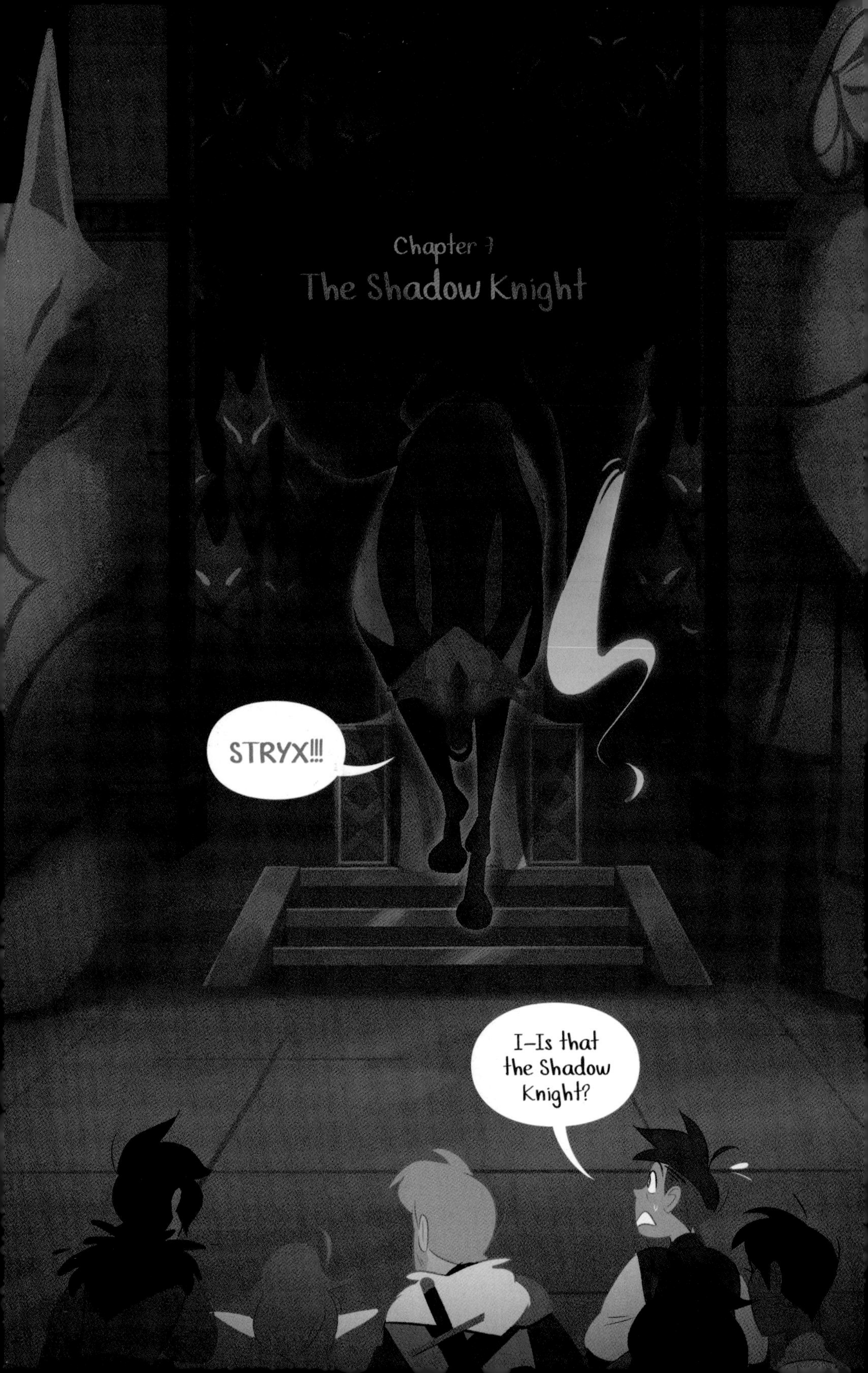
Chapter 7
The Shadow Knight
STRYX!!!
I–Is that the Shadow Knight?

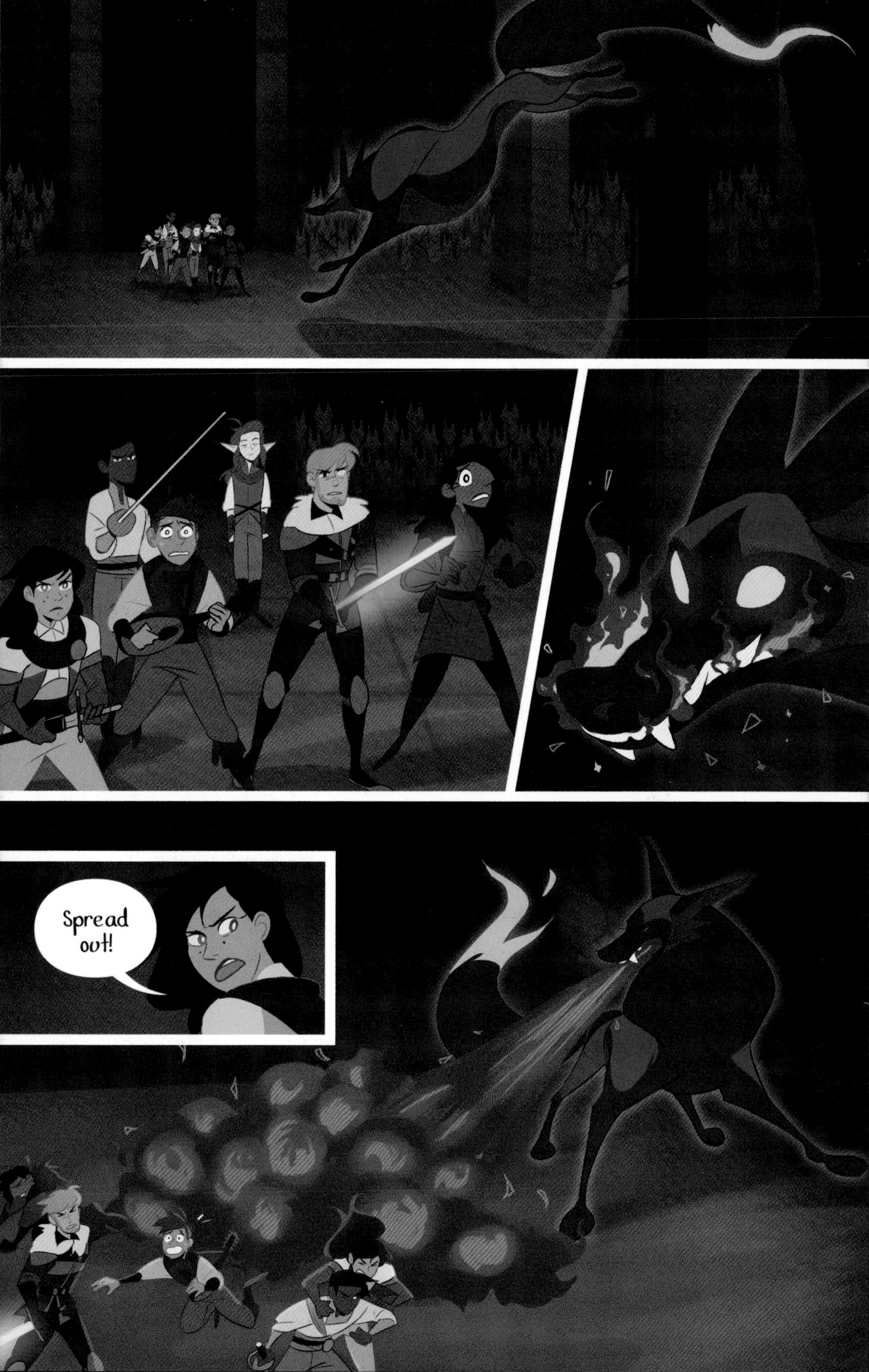
Spread out!

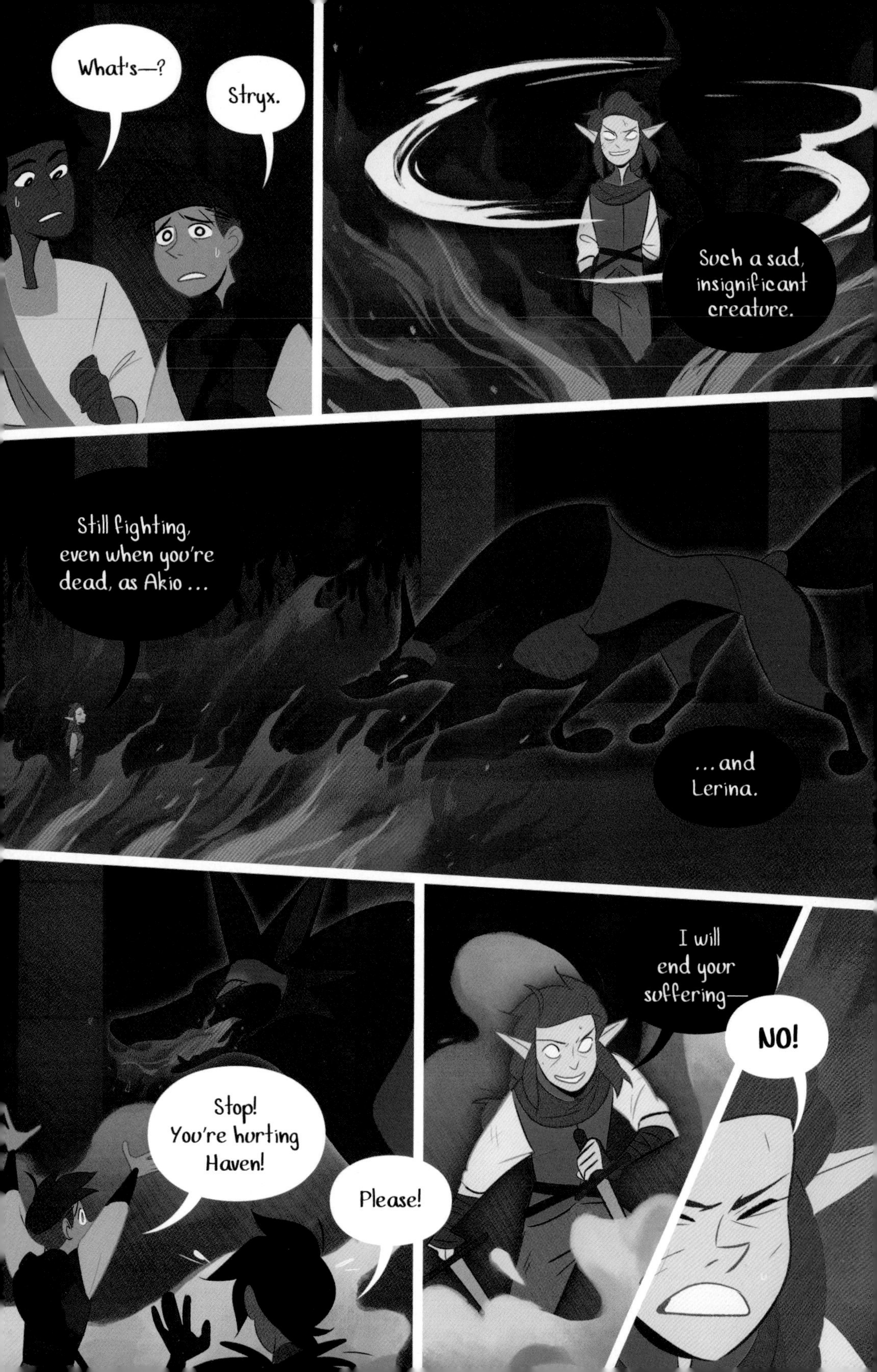
What's—?
Stryx.
Such a sad, insignificant creature.
Still fighting, even when you're dead, as Akio …
… and Lerina.
Stop! You're hurting Haven!
Please!
I will end your suffering—
NO!

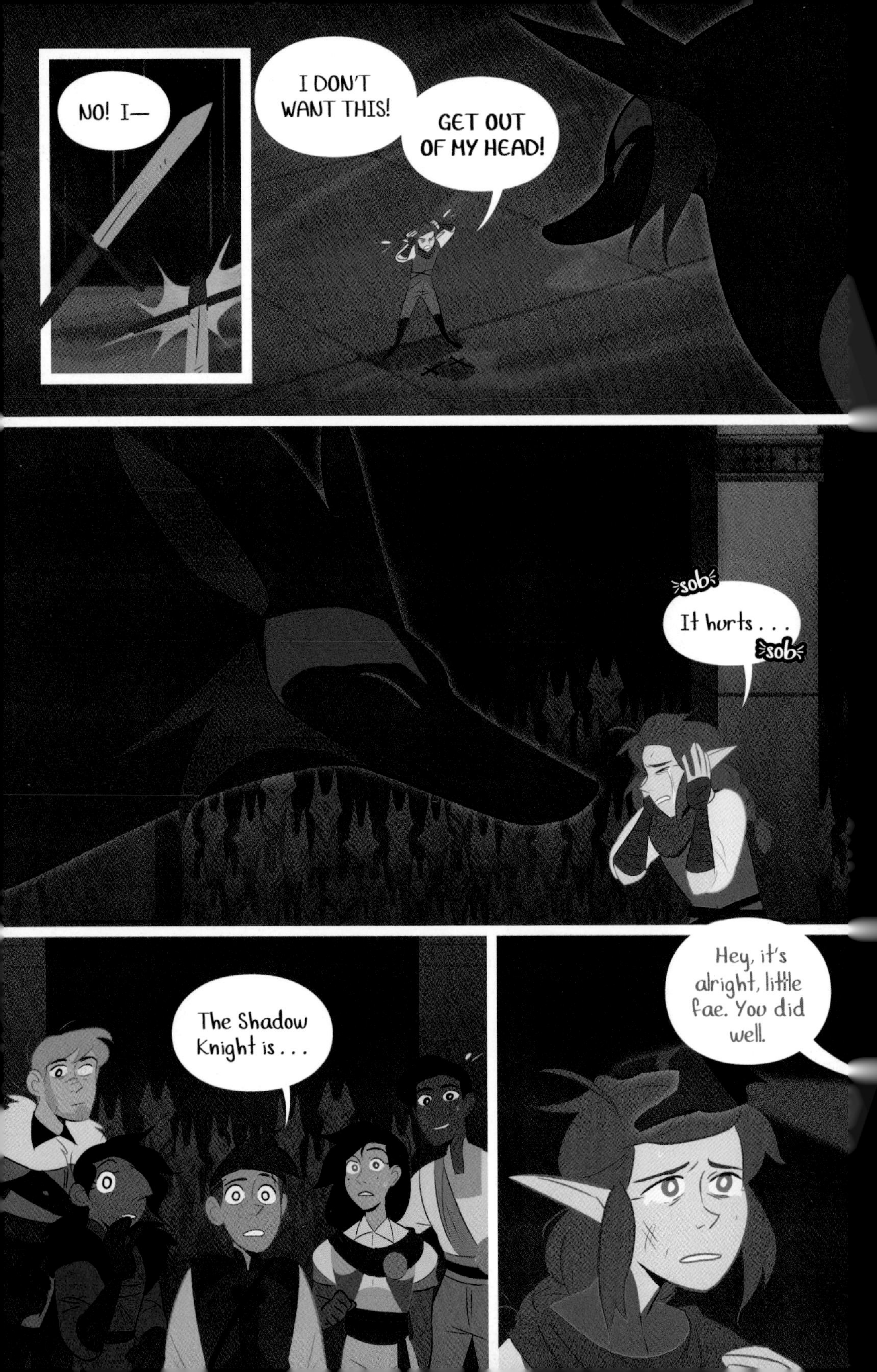
NO! I—
I DON'T WANT THIS!
GET OUT OF MY HEAD!
sob
It hurts . . .
sob
The Shadow Knight is . . .
Hey, it's alright, little fae. You did well.

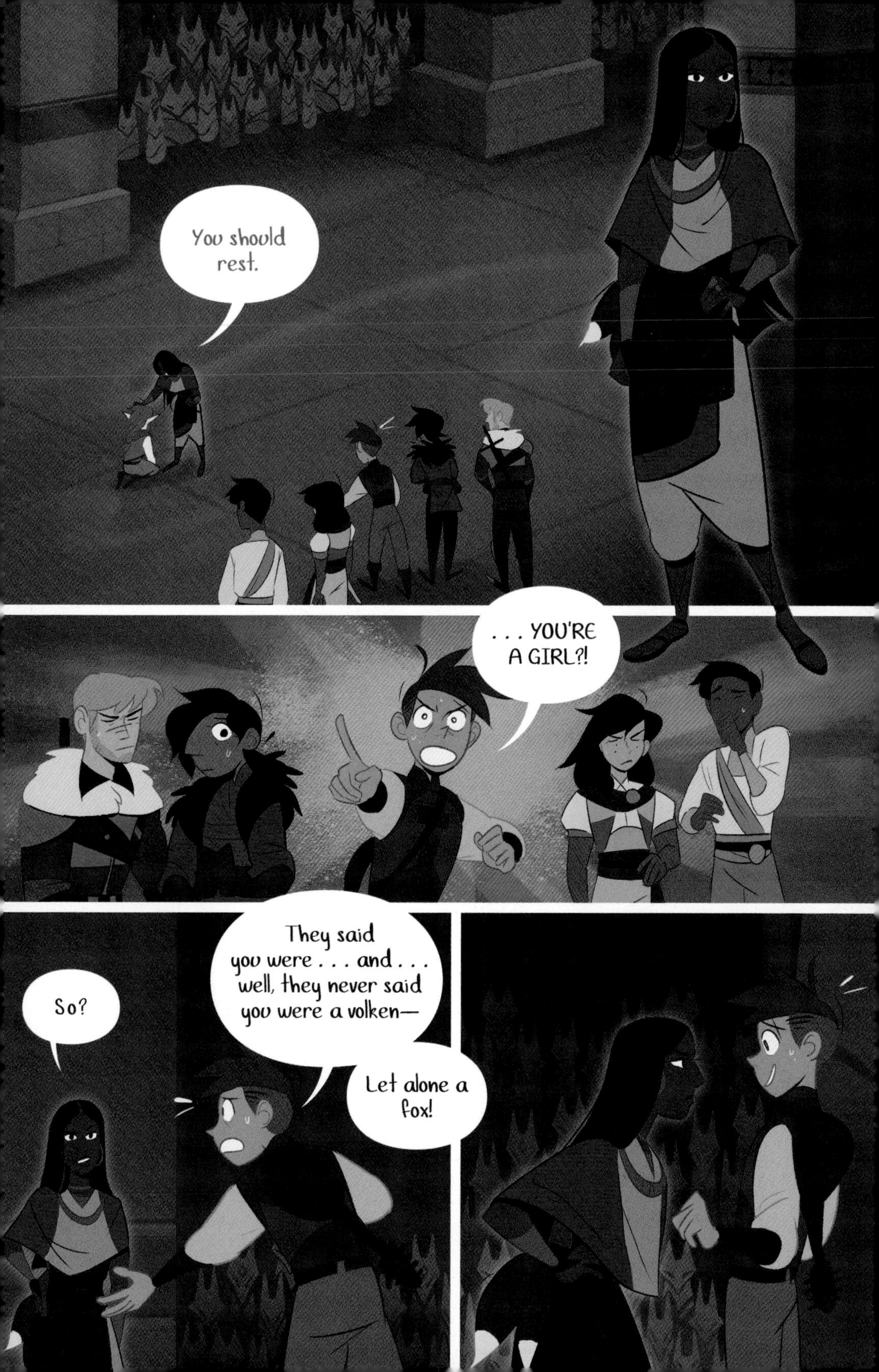
You should rest.
. . . YOU'RE A GIRL?!
So?
They said you were . . . and . . . well, they never said you were a volken—
Let alone a fox!

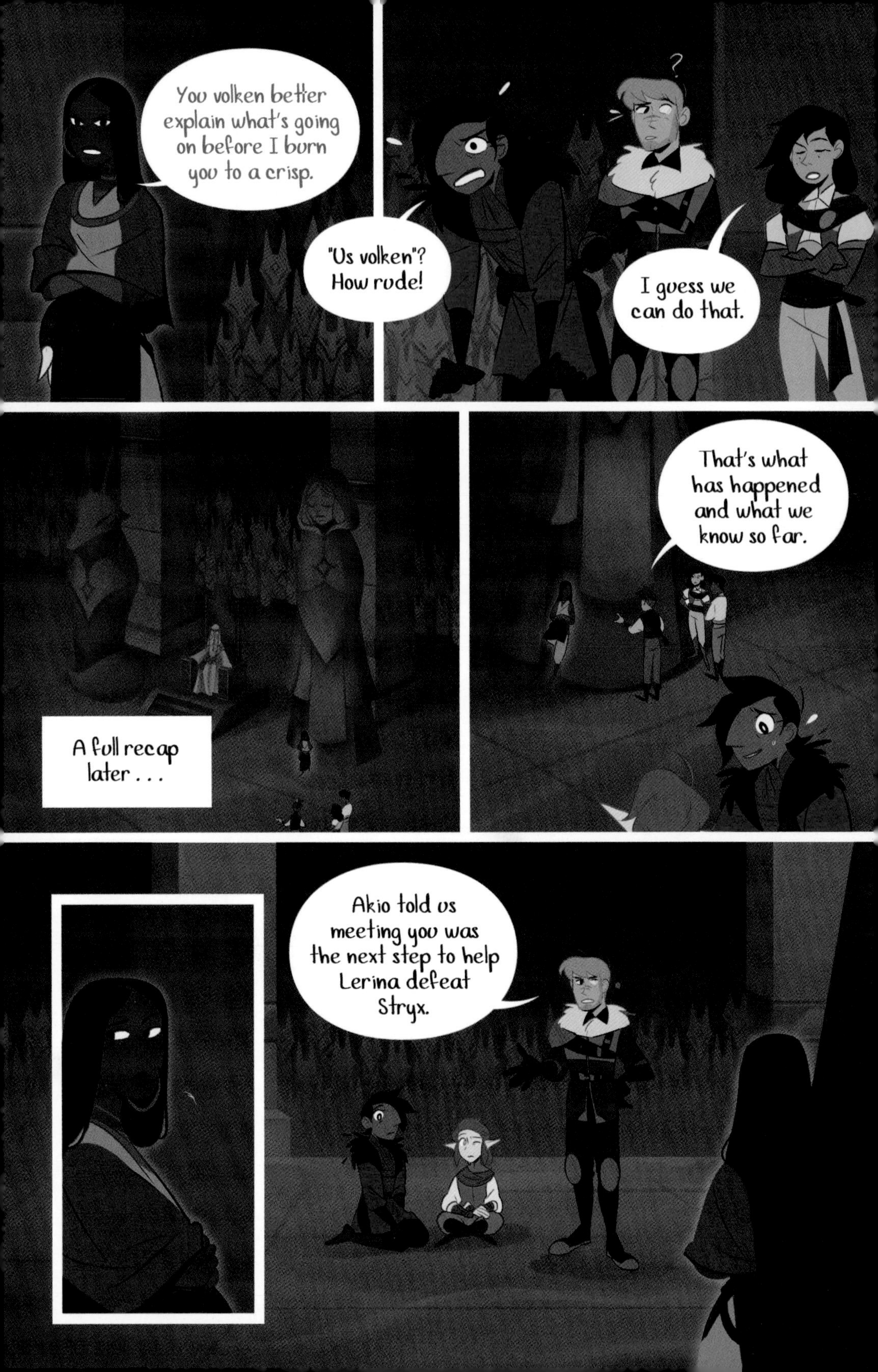
You volken better explain what's going on before I burn you to a crisp.
"Us volken"? How rude!
I guess we can do that.
A full recap later . . .
That's what has happened and what we know so far.
Akio told us meeting you was the next step to help Lerina defeat Stryx.

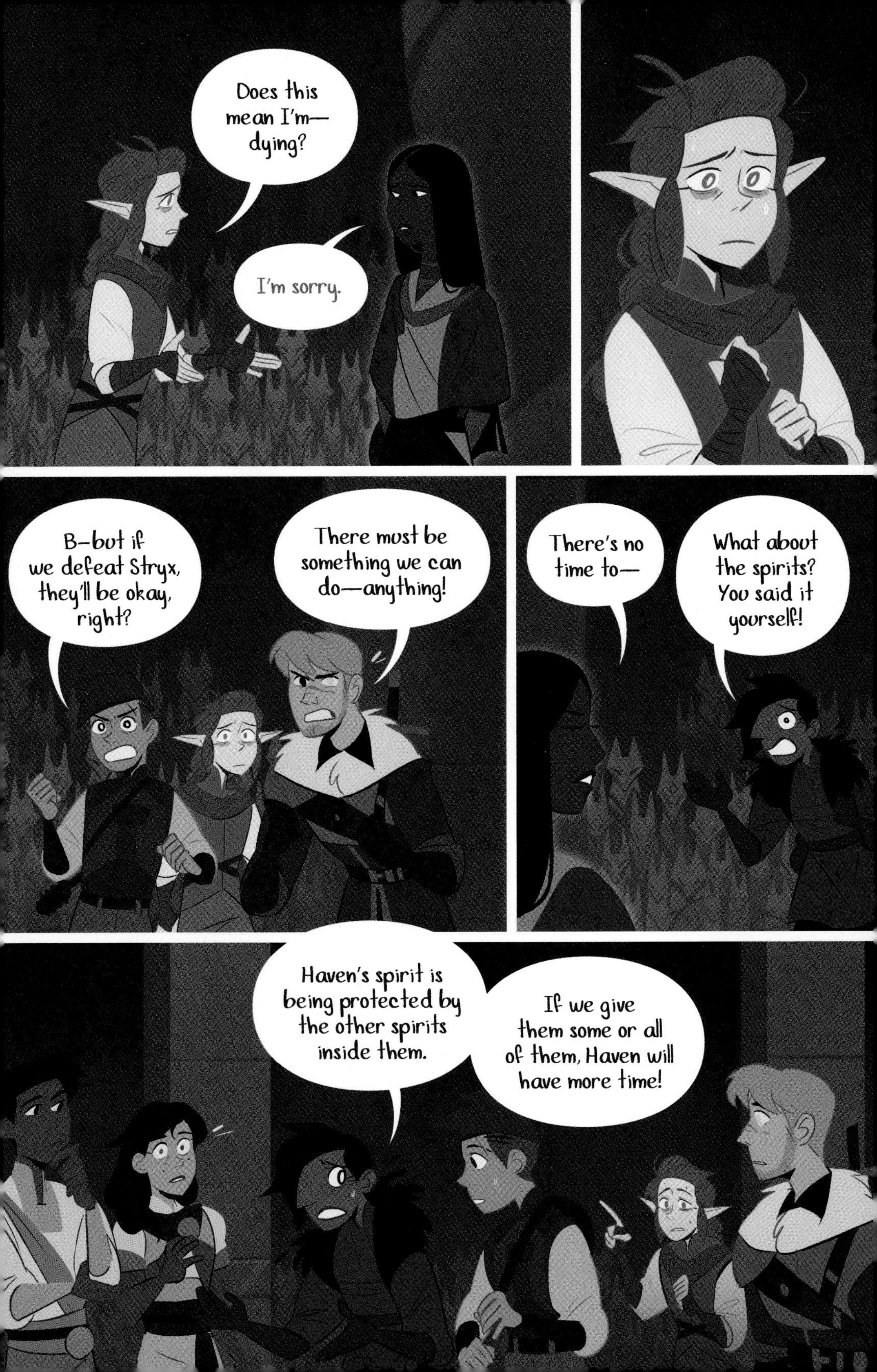
Does this mean I'm— dying?
I'm sorry.
B-but if we defeat Stryx, they'll be okay, right?
There must be something we can do—anything!
There's no time to—
What about the spirits? You said it yourself!
Haven's spirit is being protected by the other spirits inside them.
If we give them some or all of them, Haven will have more time!

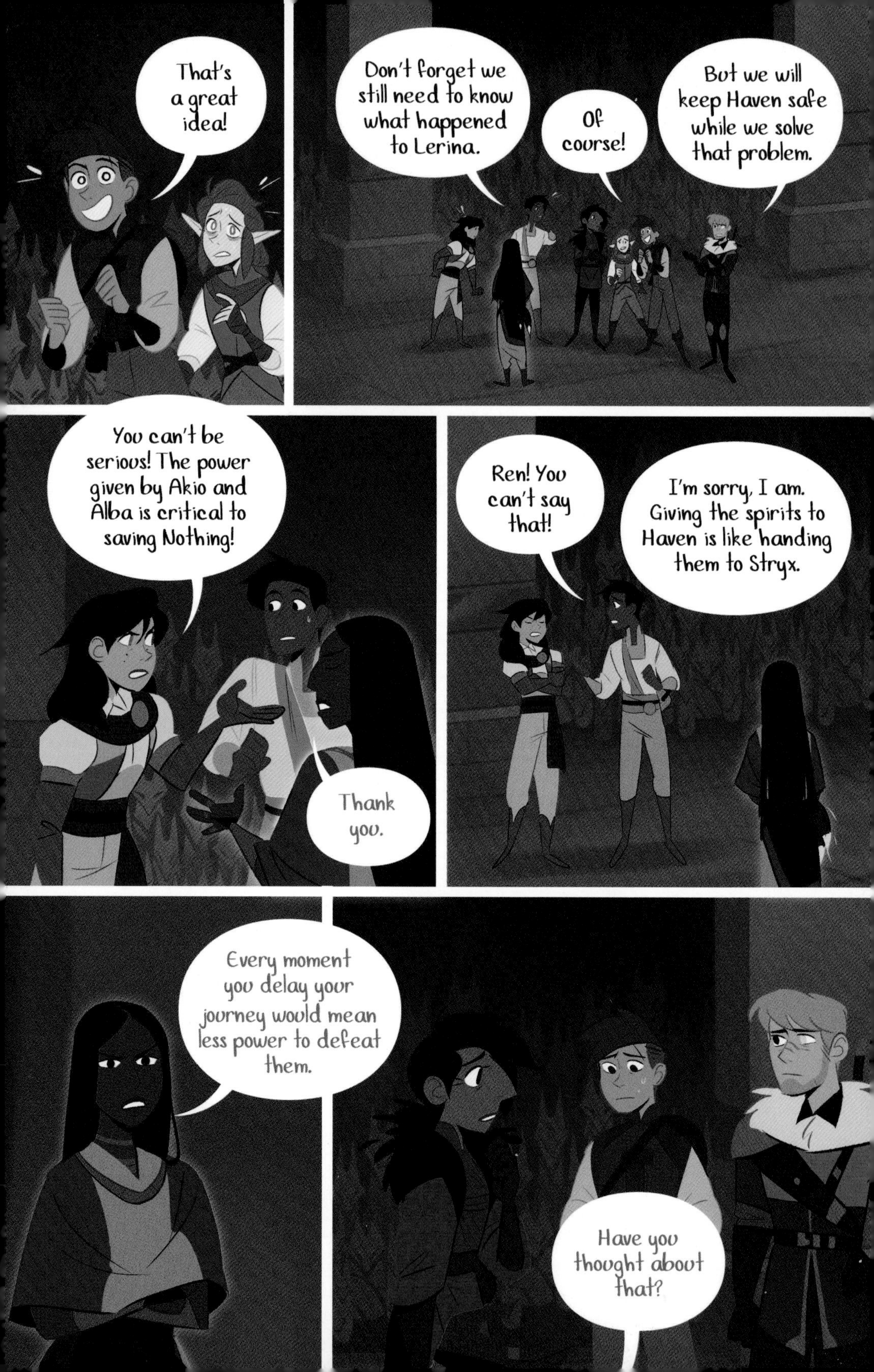
That's a great idea!
Don't forget we still need to know what happened to Lerina.
Of course!
But we will keep Haven safe while we solve that problem.
You can't be serious! The power given by Akio and Alba is critical to saving Nothing!
Thank you.
Ren! You can't say that!
I'm sorry, I am. Giving the spirits to Haven is like handing them to Stryx.
Every moment you delay your journey would mean less power to defeat them.
Have you thought about that?

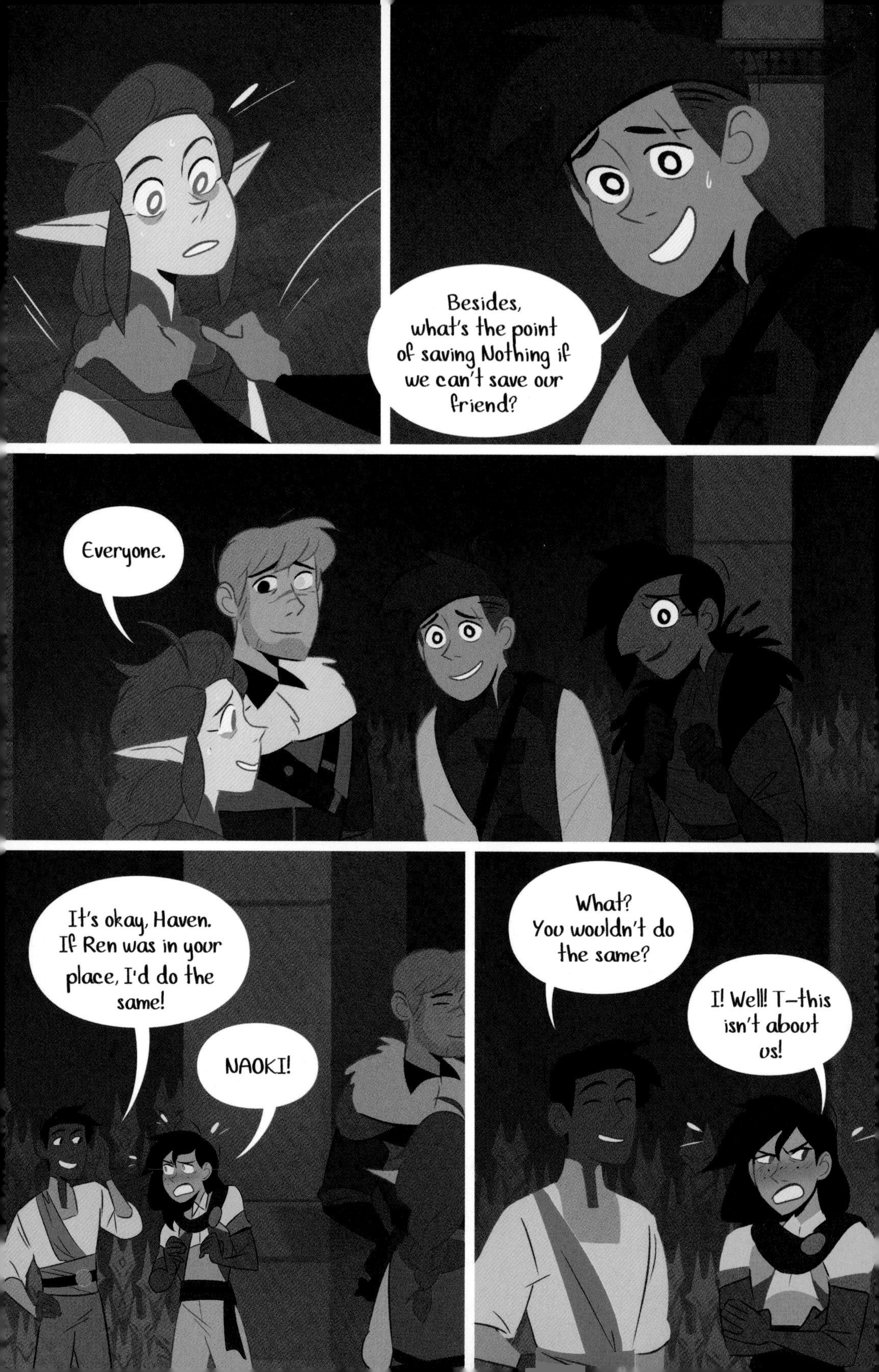
Besides, what's the point of saving Nothing if we can't save our friend?
Everyone.
It's okay, Haven. If Ren was in your place, I'd do the same!
NAOKI!
What? You wouldn't do the same?
I! Well! T–this isn't about us!

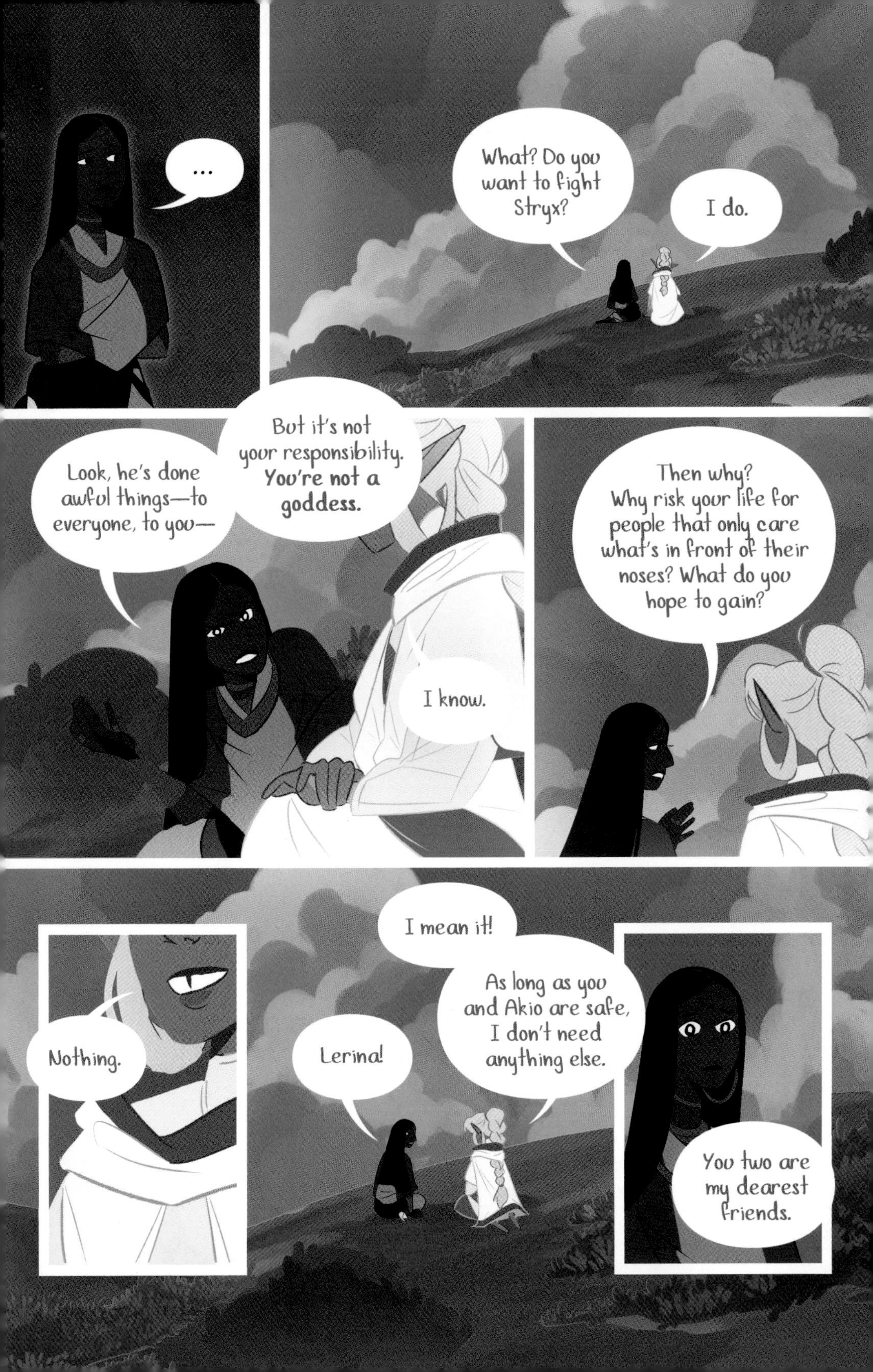
...
What? Do you want to fight Stryx?
I do.
Look, he's done awful things—to everyone, to you—
But it's not your responsibility. **You're not a goddess.**
I know.
Then why? Why risk your life for people that only care what's in front of their noses? What do you hope to gain?
Nothing.
Lerina!
I mean it!
As long as you and Akio are safe, I don't need anything else.
You two are my dearest friends.

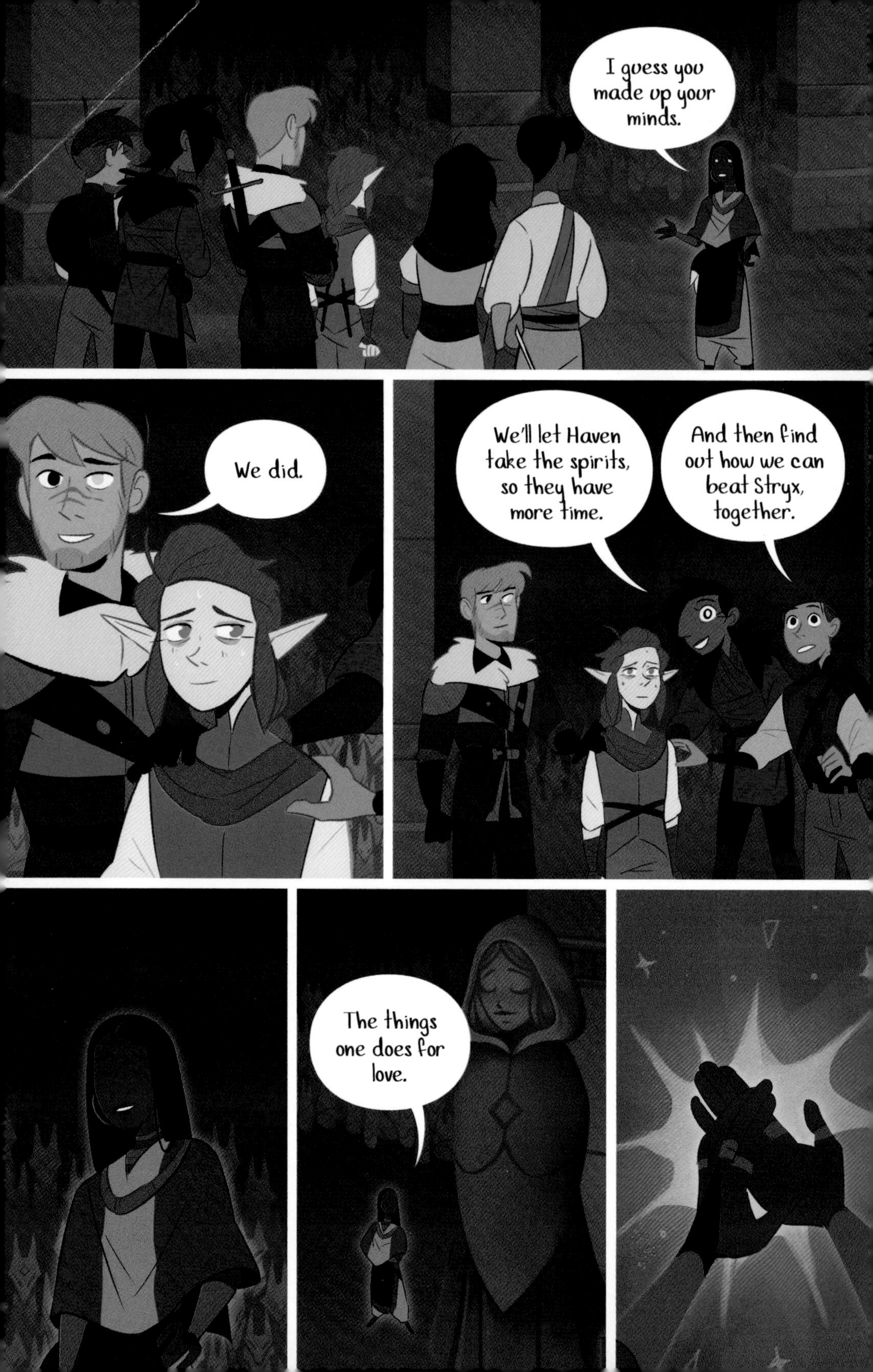
I guess you made up your minds.
We did.
We'll let Haven take the spirits, so they have more time.
And then find out how we can beat Stryx, together.
The things one does for love.

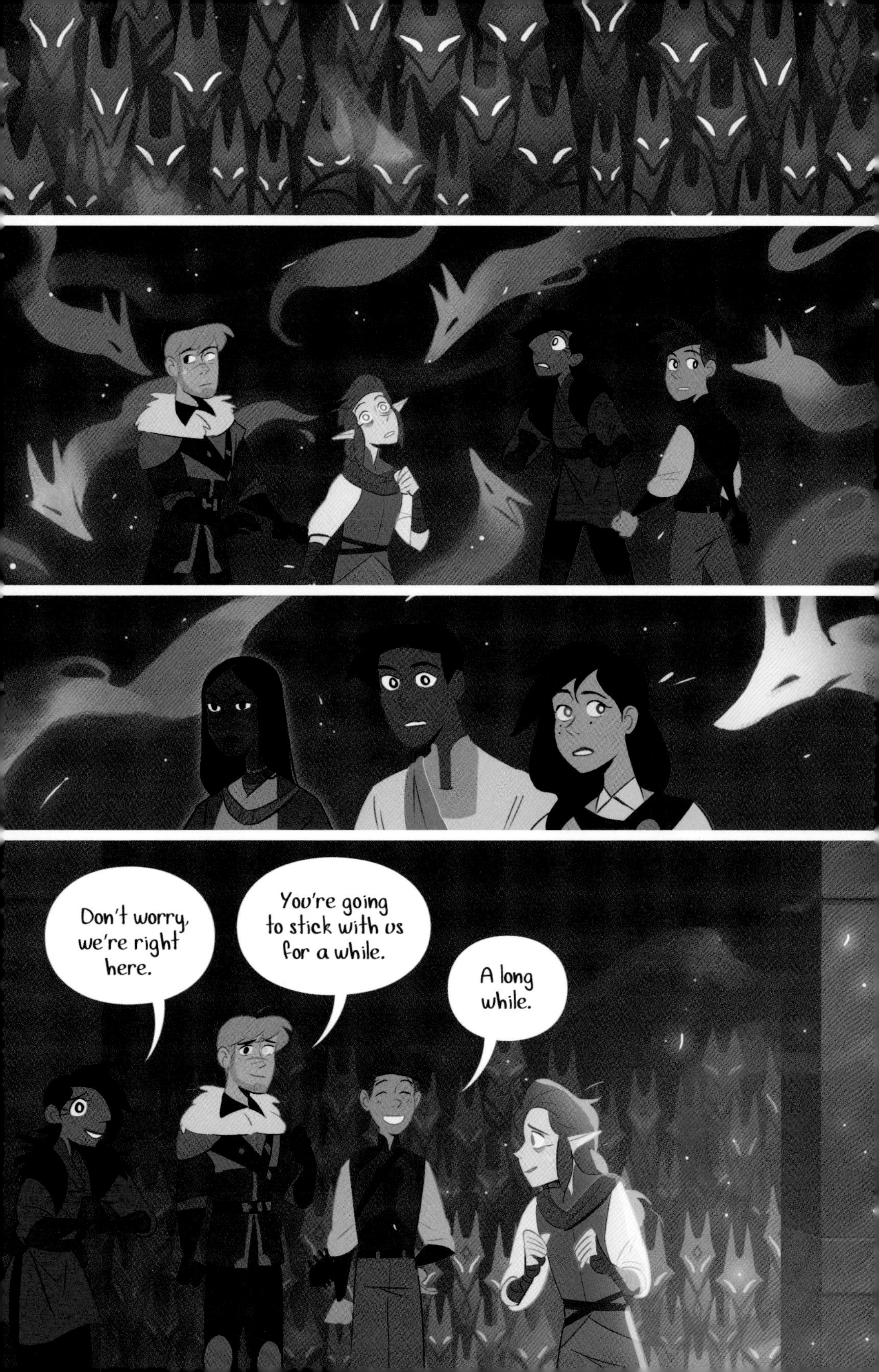
Don't worry, we're right here.
You're going to stick with us for a while.
A long while.

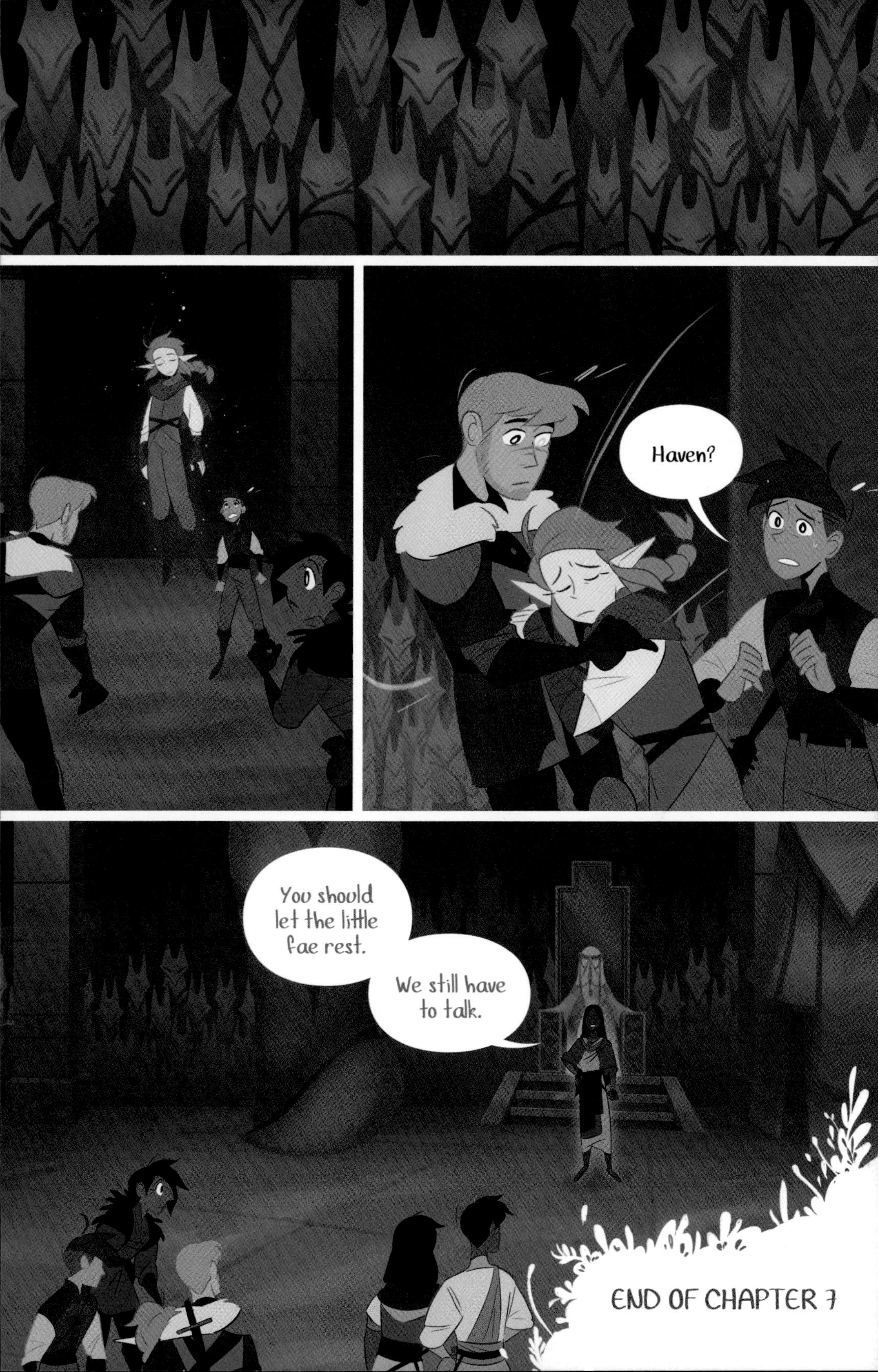
Haven?
You should let the little fae rest.
We still have to talk.
END OF CHAPTER 7

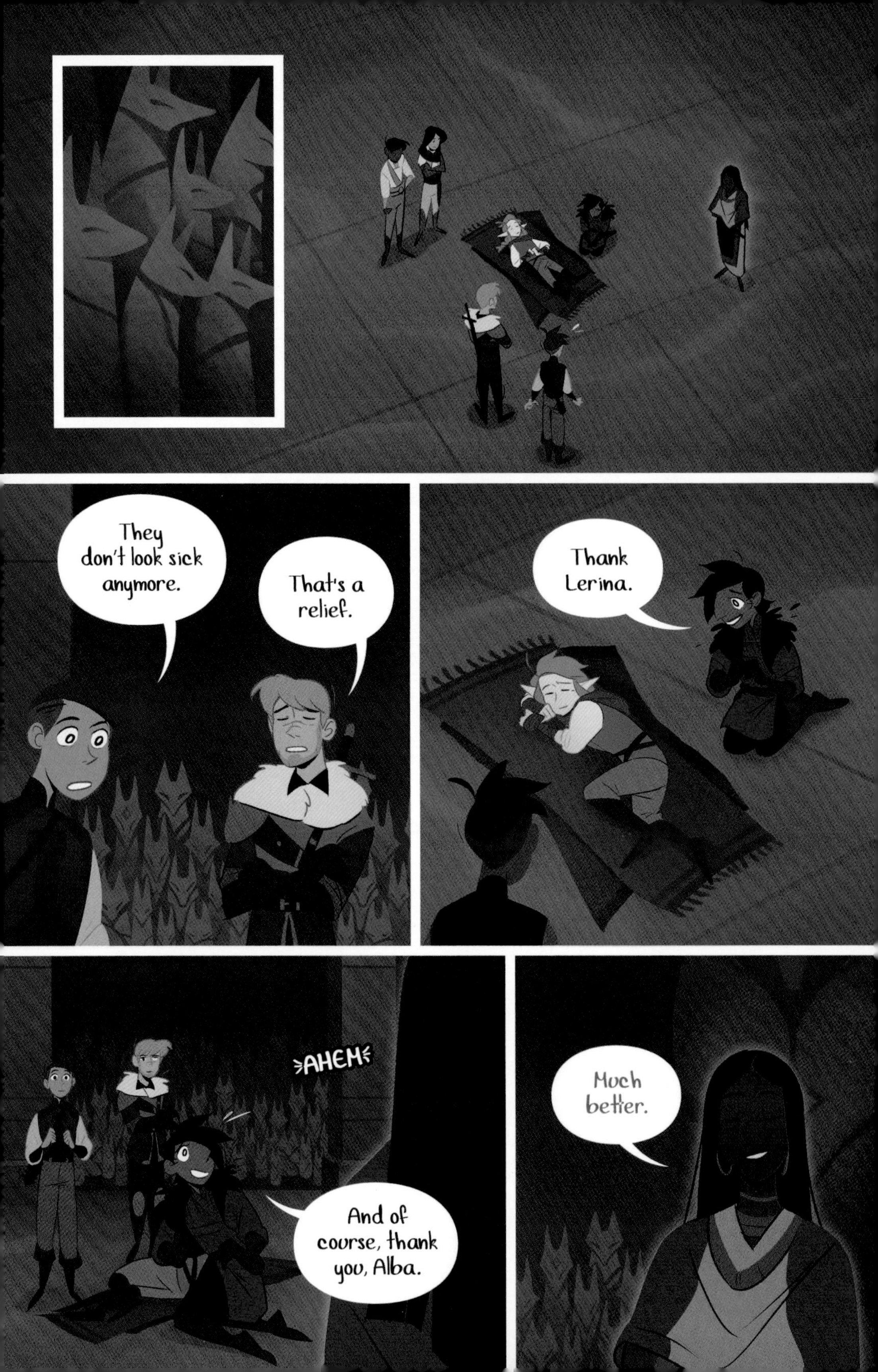
They don't look sick anymore.
That's a relief.
Thank Lerina.
AHEM
And of course, thank you, Alba.
Much better.

Chapter 8
The Fox-gotten

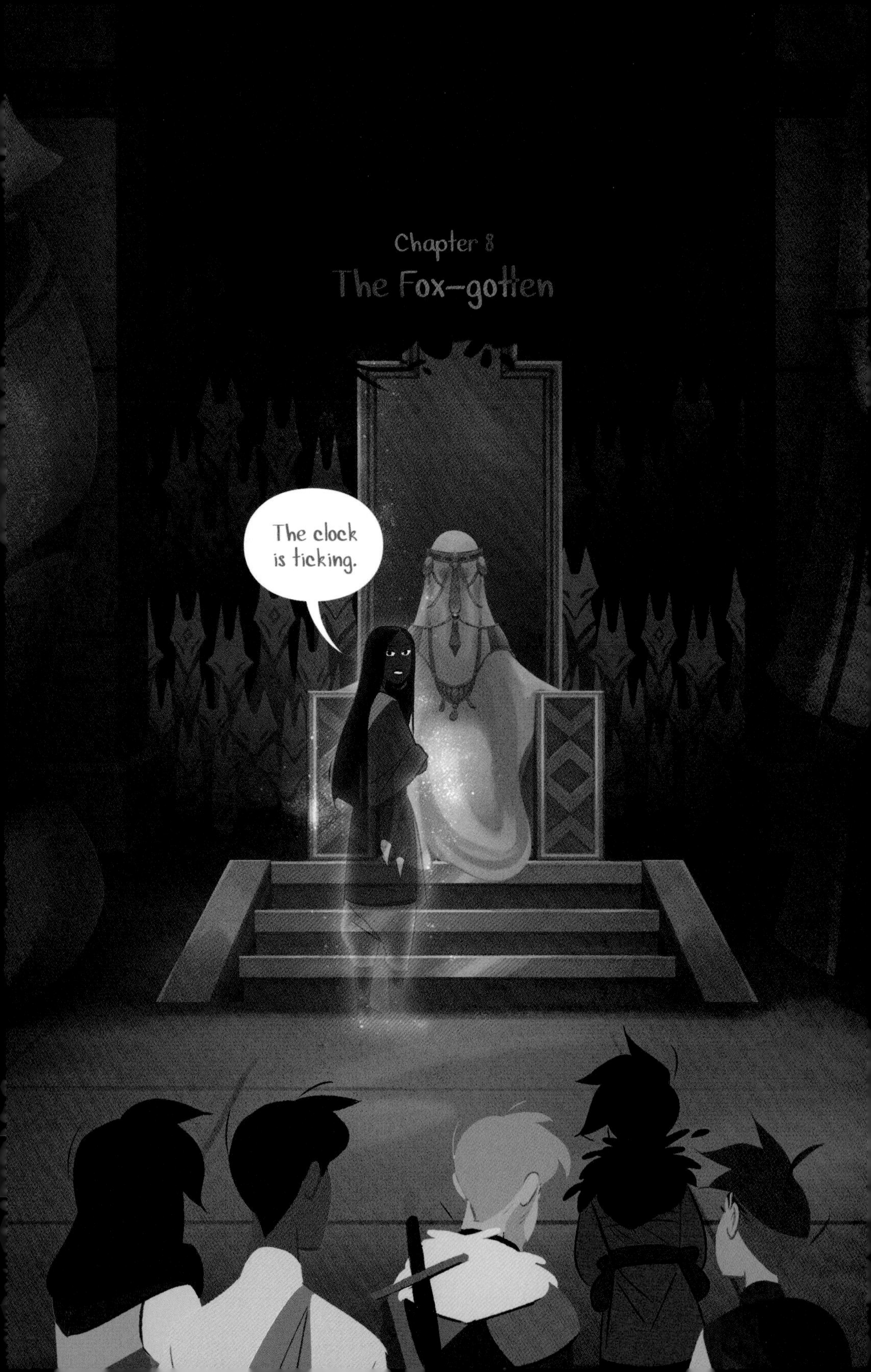

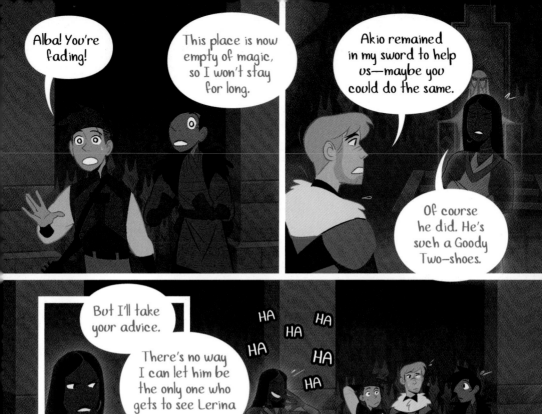

Alba! You're fading!

This place is now empty of magic, so I won't stay for long.

Akio remained in my sword to help us—maybe you could do the same.

Of course he did. He's such a Goody Two-shoes.

But I'll take your advice.

There's no way I can let him be the only one who gets to see Lerina again.

HA HA HA HA HA HA HA

Okay, so! You said we need to find Lerina.

That's right, you should go to That City.

What cit—

Don't!

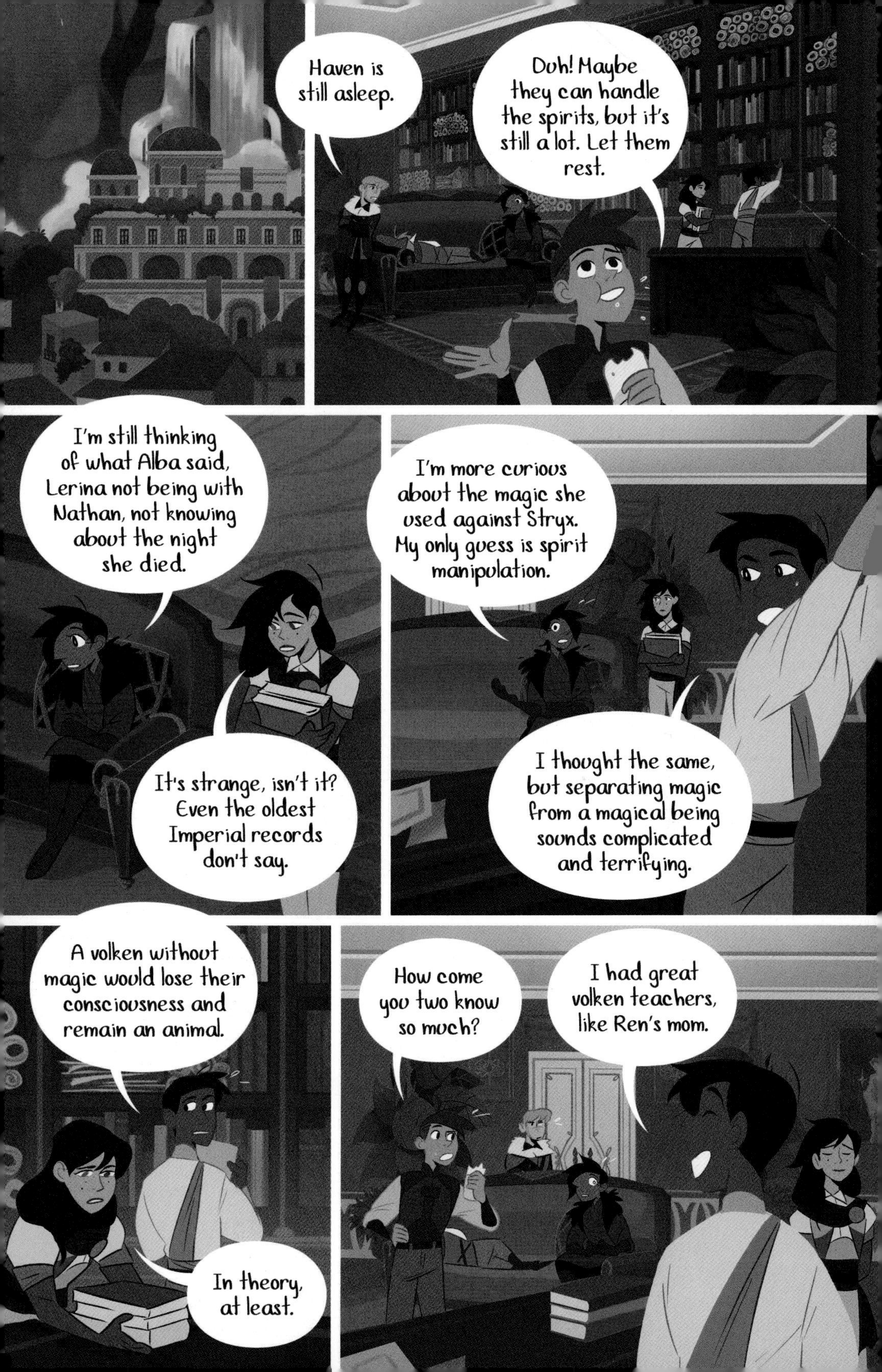
Haven is still asleep.
Duh! Maybe they can handle the spirits, but it's still a lot. Let them rest.
I'm still thinking of what Alba said, Lerina not being with Nathan, not knowing about the night she died.
It's strange, isn't it? Even the oldest Imperial records don't say.
I'm more curious about the magic she used against Stryx. My only guess is spirit manipulation.
I thought the same, but separating magic from a magical being sounds complicated and terrifying.
A volken without magic would lose their consciousness and remain an animal.
In theory, at least.
How come you two know so much?
I had great volken teachers, like Ren's mom.

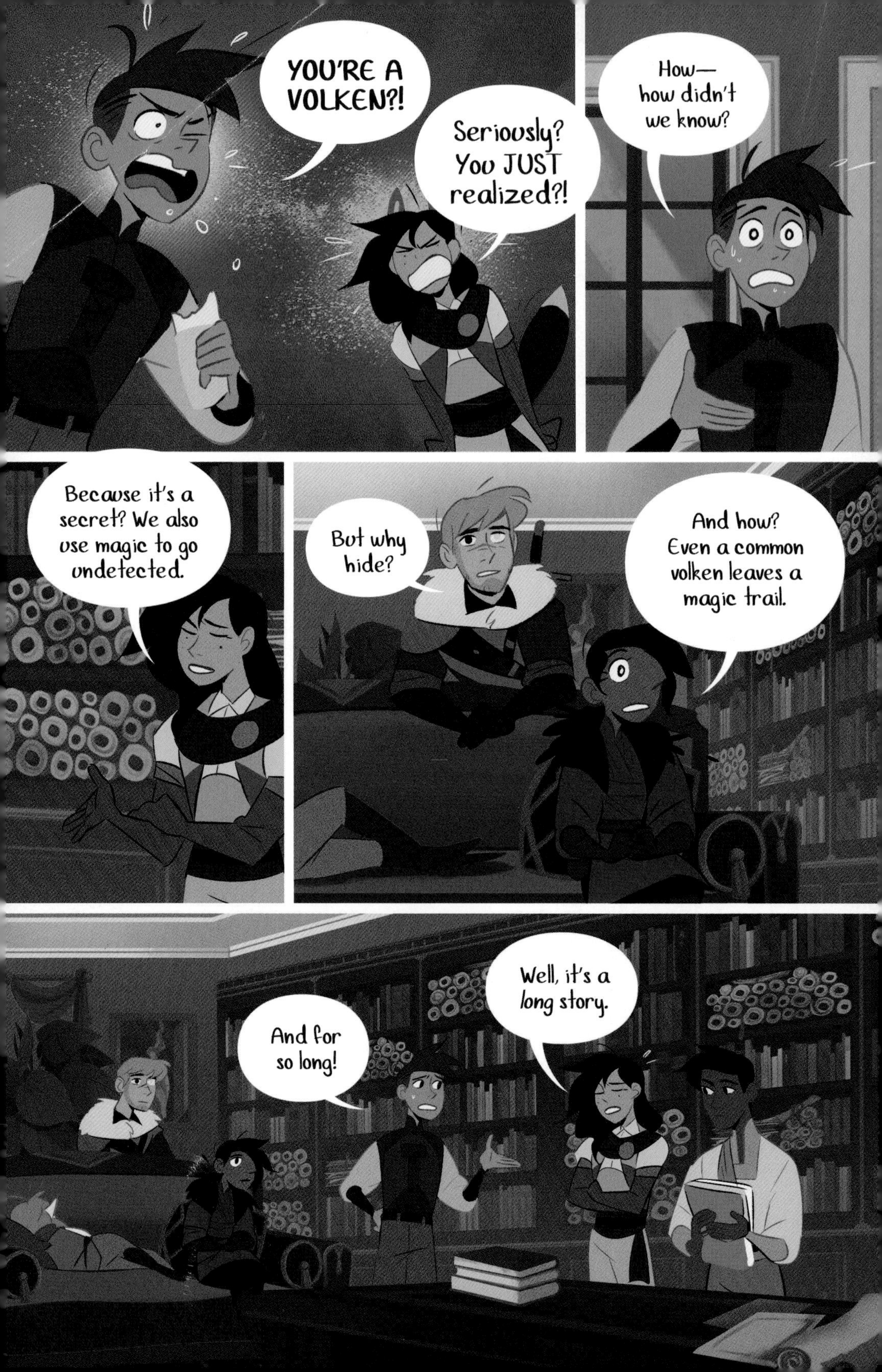
YOU'RE A VOLKEN?!
Seriously? You JUST realized?!
How— how didn't we know?
Because it's a secret? We also use magic to go undetected.
But why hide?
And how? Even a common volken leaves a magic trail.
And for so long!
Well, it's a long story.

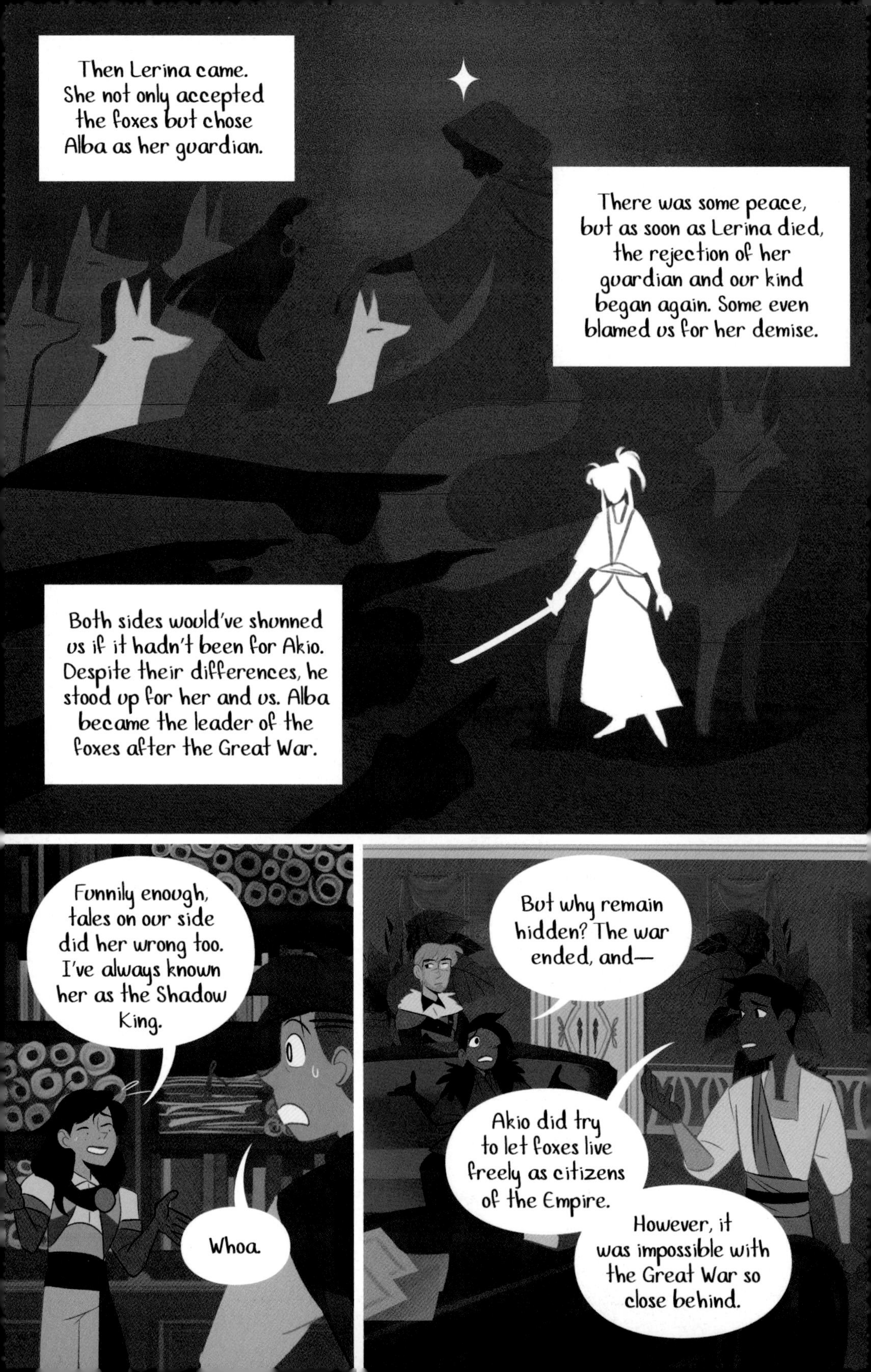
Then Lerina came. She not only accepted the foxes but chose Alba as her guardian.
There was some peace, but as soon as Lerina died, the rejection of her guardian and our kind began again. Some even blamed us for her demise.
Both sides would've shunned us if it hadn't been for Akio. Despite their differences, he stood up for her and us. Alba became the leader of the foxes after the Great War.
Funnily enough, tales on our side did her wrong too. I've always known her as the Shadow King.
Whoa.
But why remain hidden? The war ended, and—
Akio did try to let foxes live freely as citizens of the Empire.
However, it was impossible with the Great War so close behind.

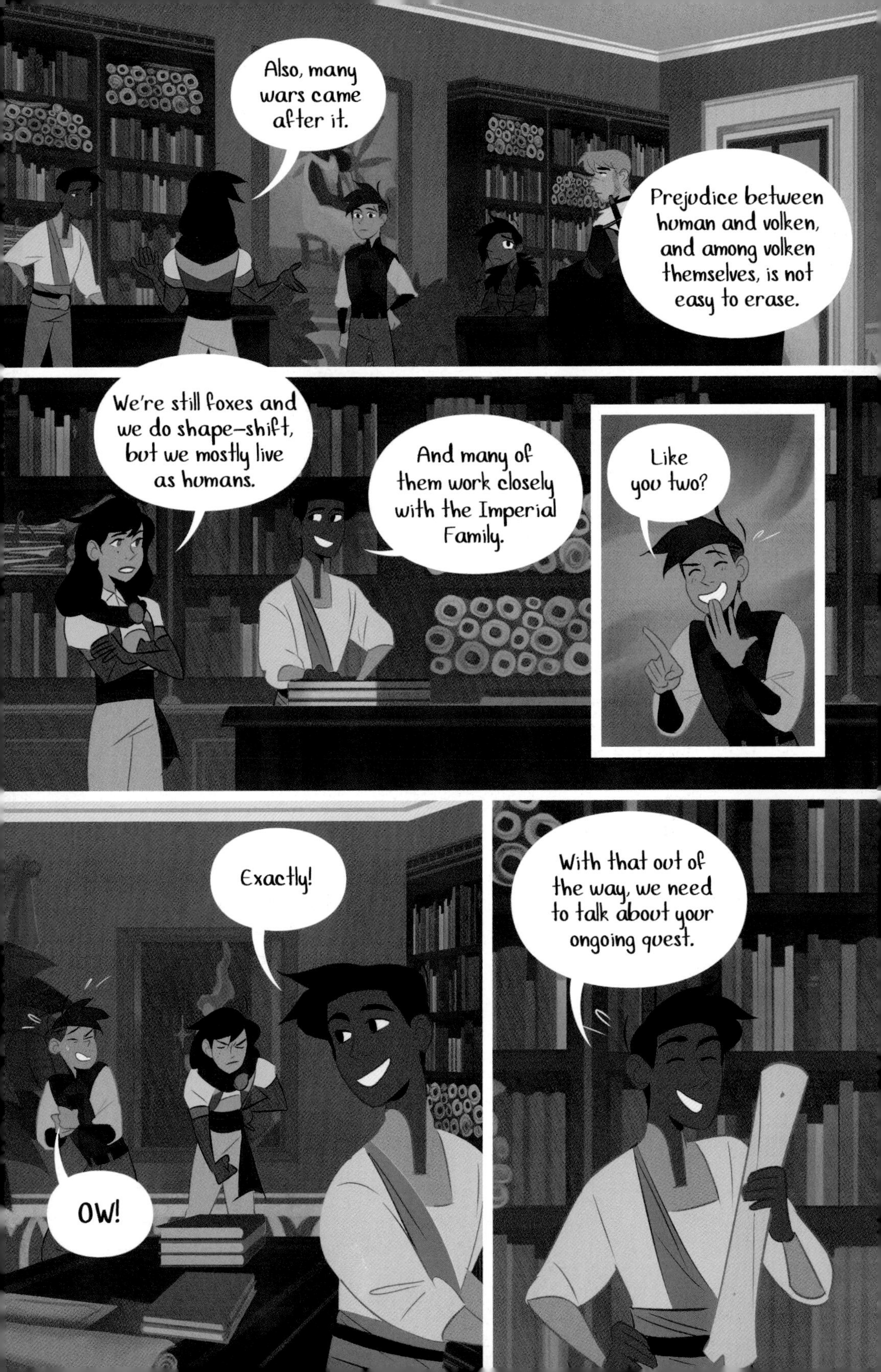
Also, many wars came after it.
Prejudice between human and volken, and among volken themselves, is not easy to erase.
We're still foxes and we do shape-shift, but we mostly live as humans.
And many of them work closely with the Imperial Family.
Like you two?
Exactly!
OW!
With that out of the way, we need to talk about your ongoing quest.

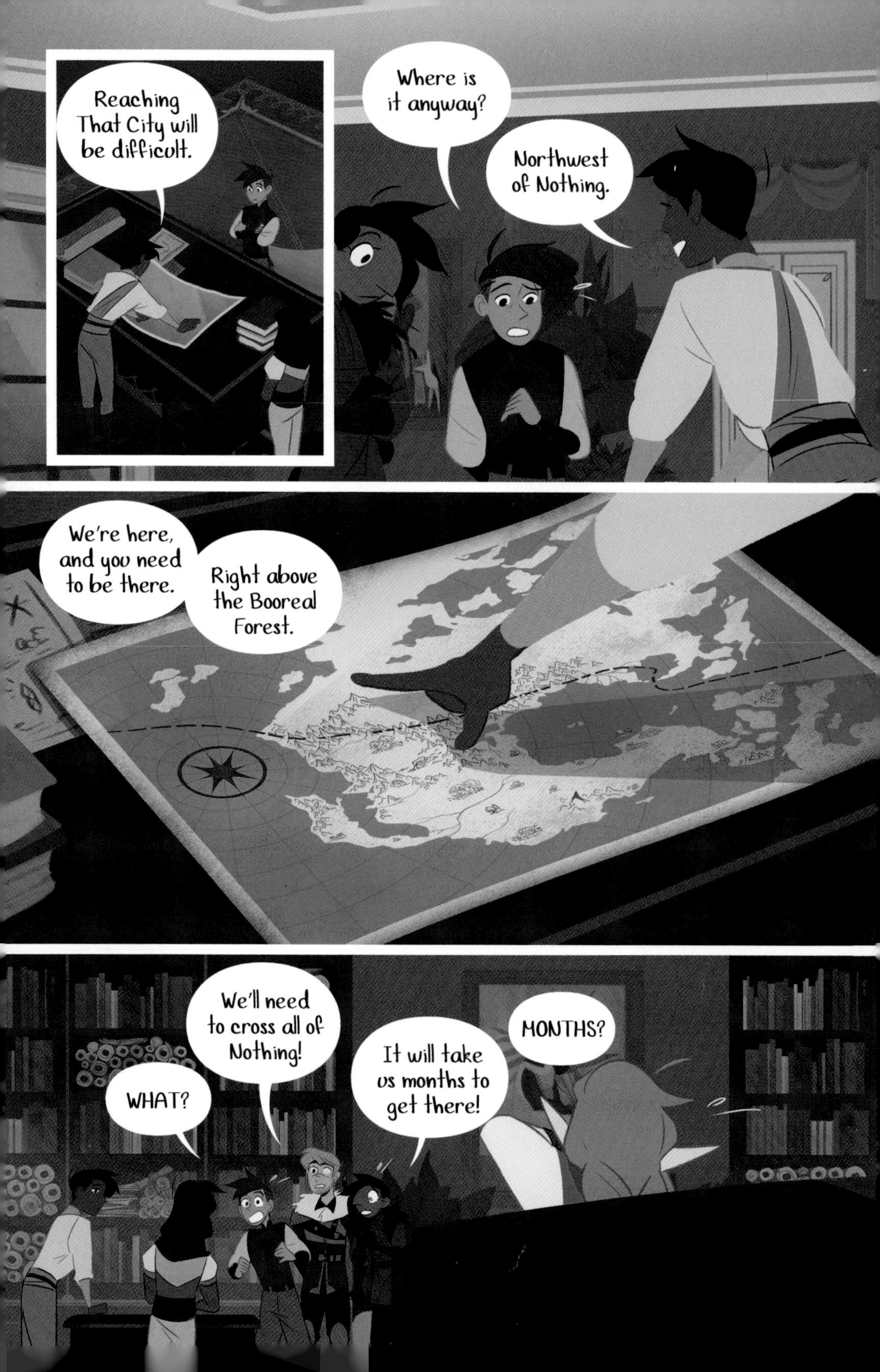
Reaching That City will be difficult.
Where is it anyway?
Northwest of Nothing.
We're here, and you need to be there.
Right above the Booreal Forest.
We'll need to cross all of Nothing!
WHAT?
It will take us months to get there!
MONTHS?

END OF CHAPTER 8

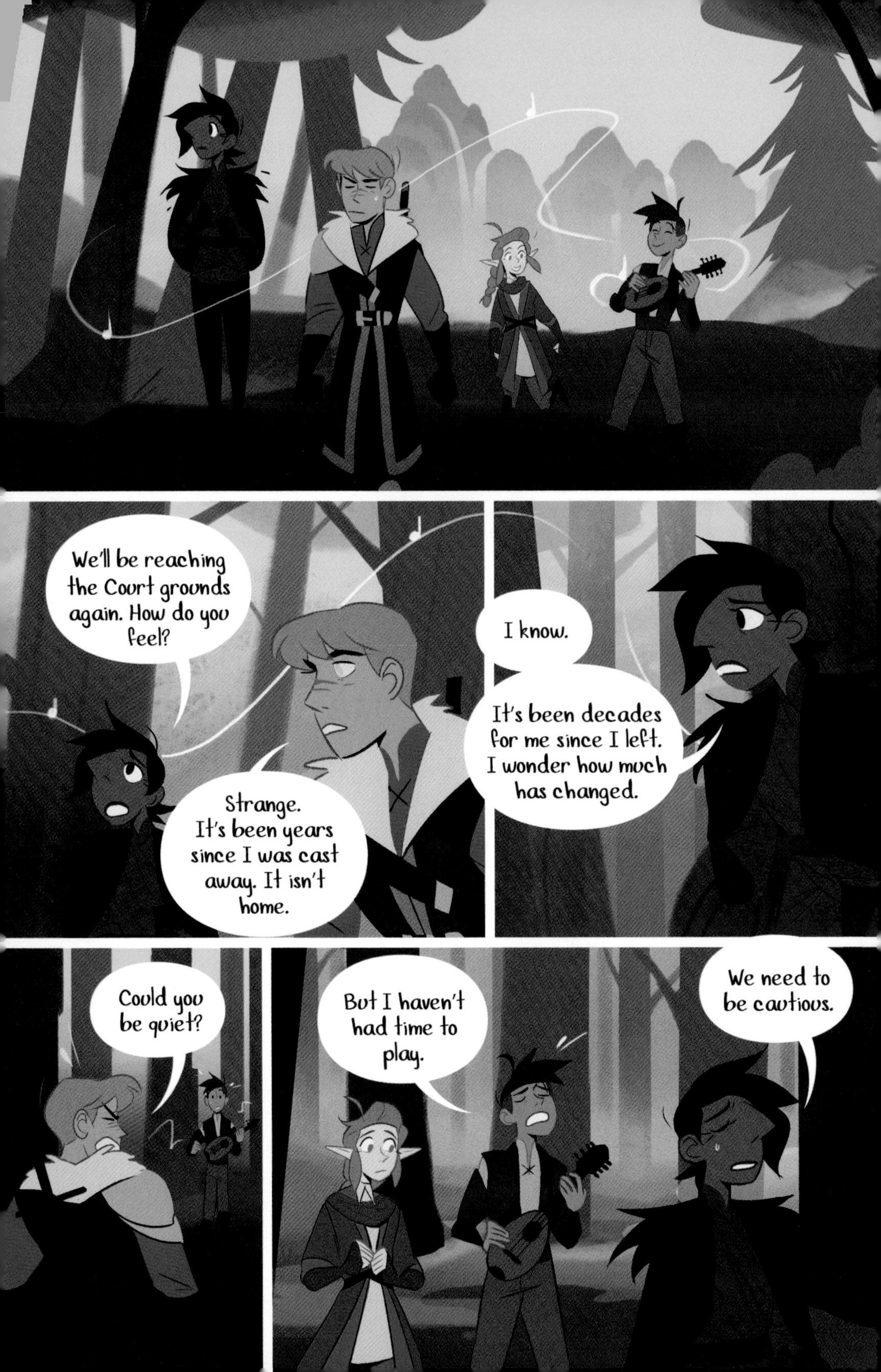
We'll be reaching the Court grounds again. How do you feel?
Strange. It's been years since I was cast away. It isn't home.
I know.
It's been decades for me since I left. I wonder how much has changed.
Could you be quiet?
But I haven't had time to play.
We need to be cautious.

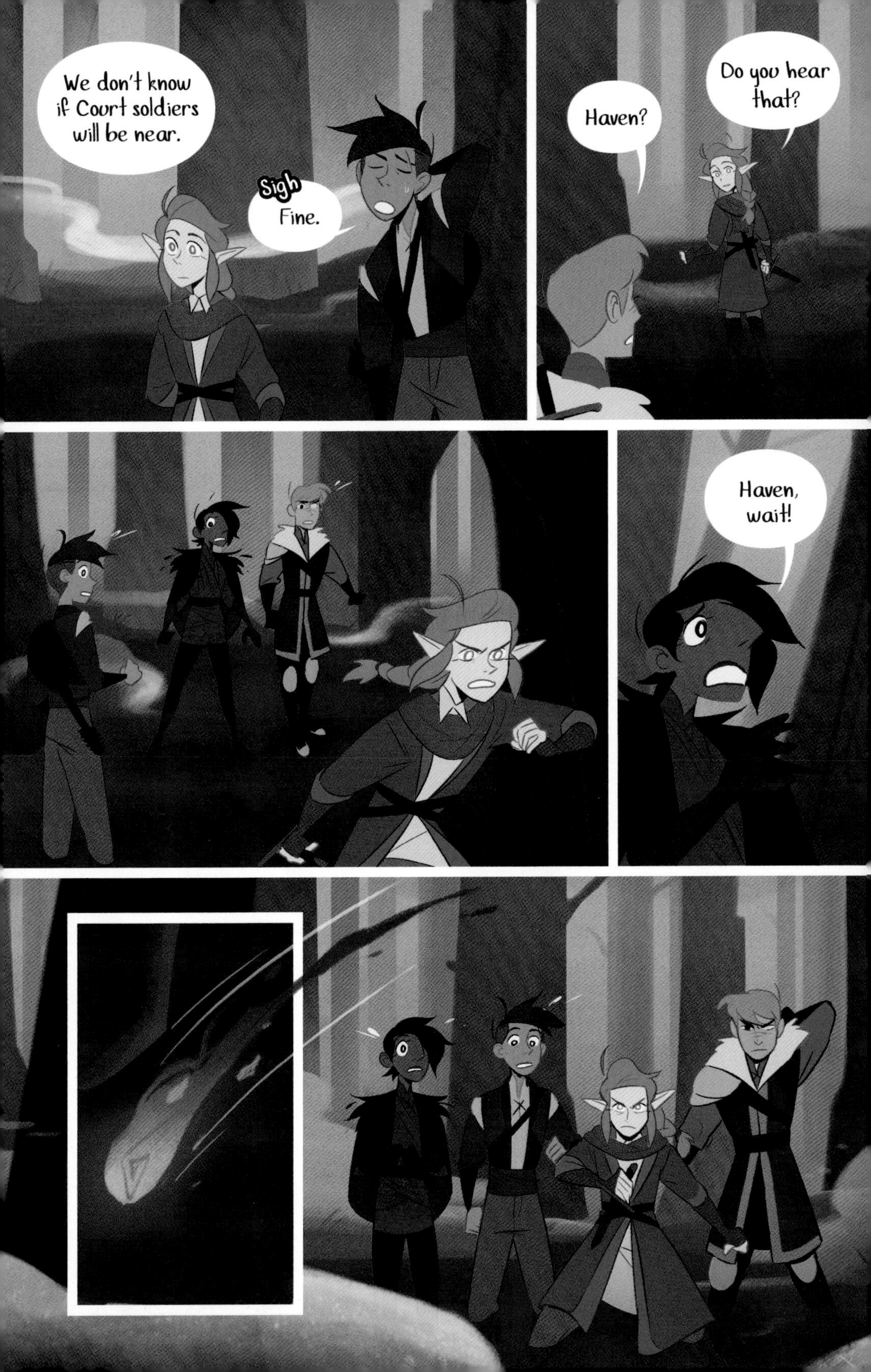
We don't know if Court soldiers will be near.
Sigh
Fine.
Haven?
Do you hear that?
Haven, wait!

Chapter 9
Crowsroads
What are you lot doing here?
We could ask you the same thing!

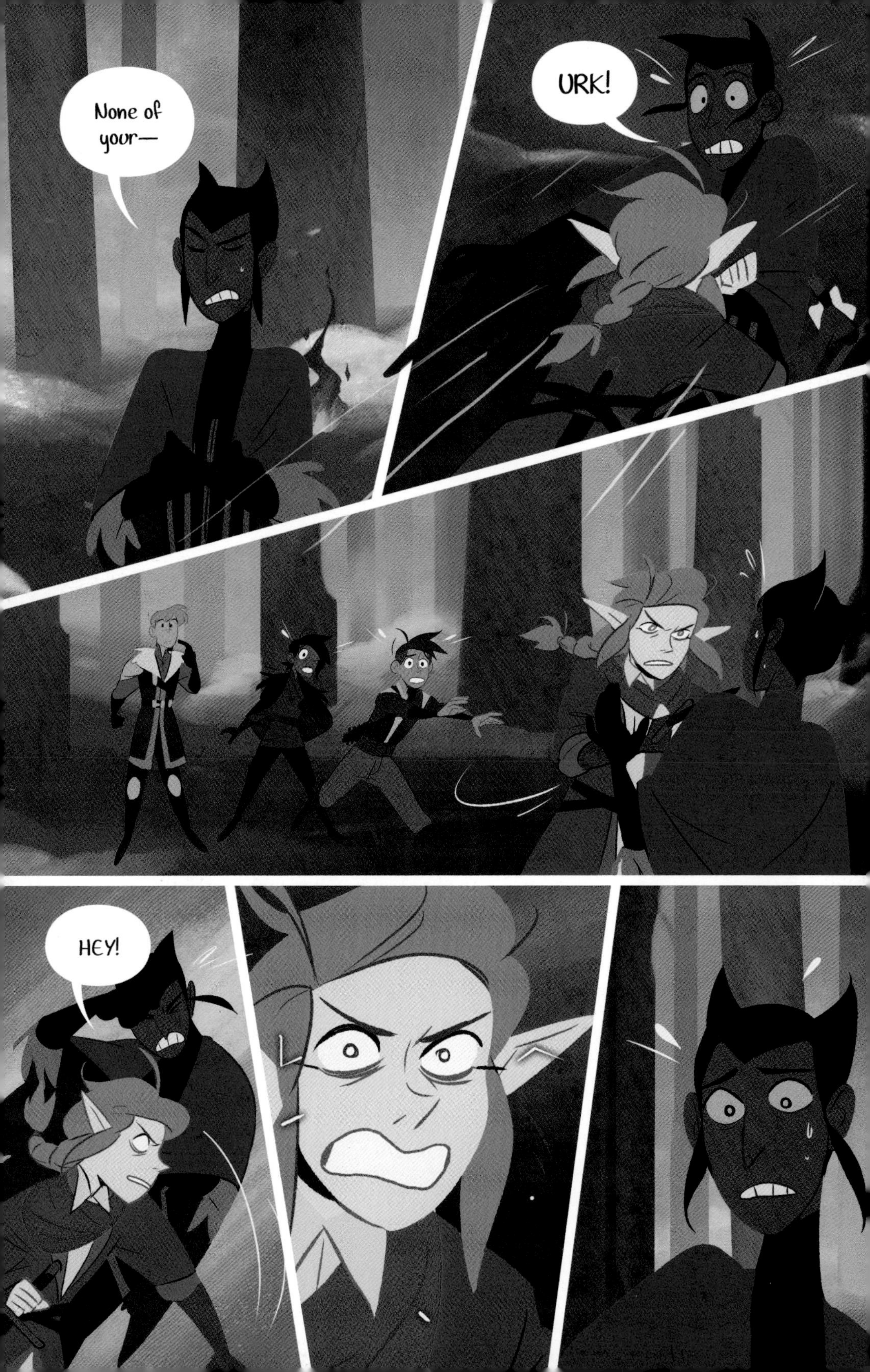
None of your—
URK!
HEY!

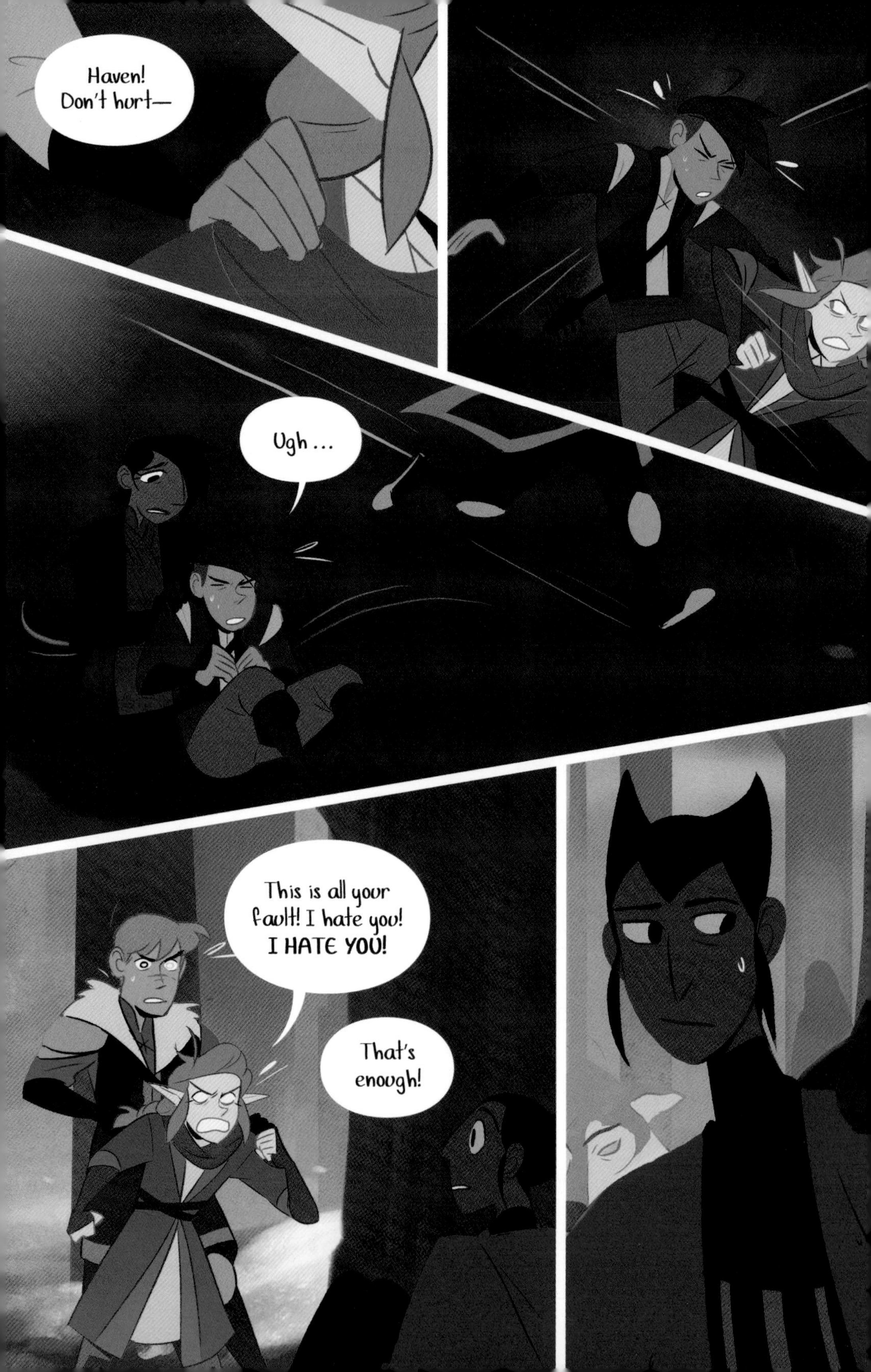
Haven! Don't hurt—
Ugh ...
This is all your fault! I hate you! I HATE YOU!
That's enough!

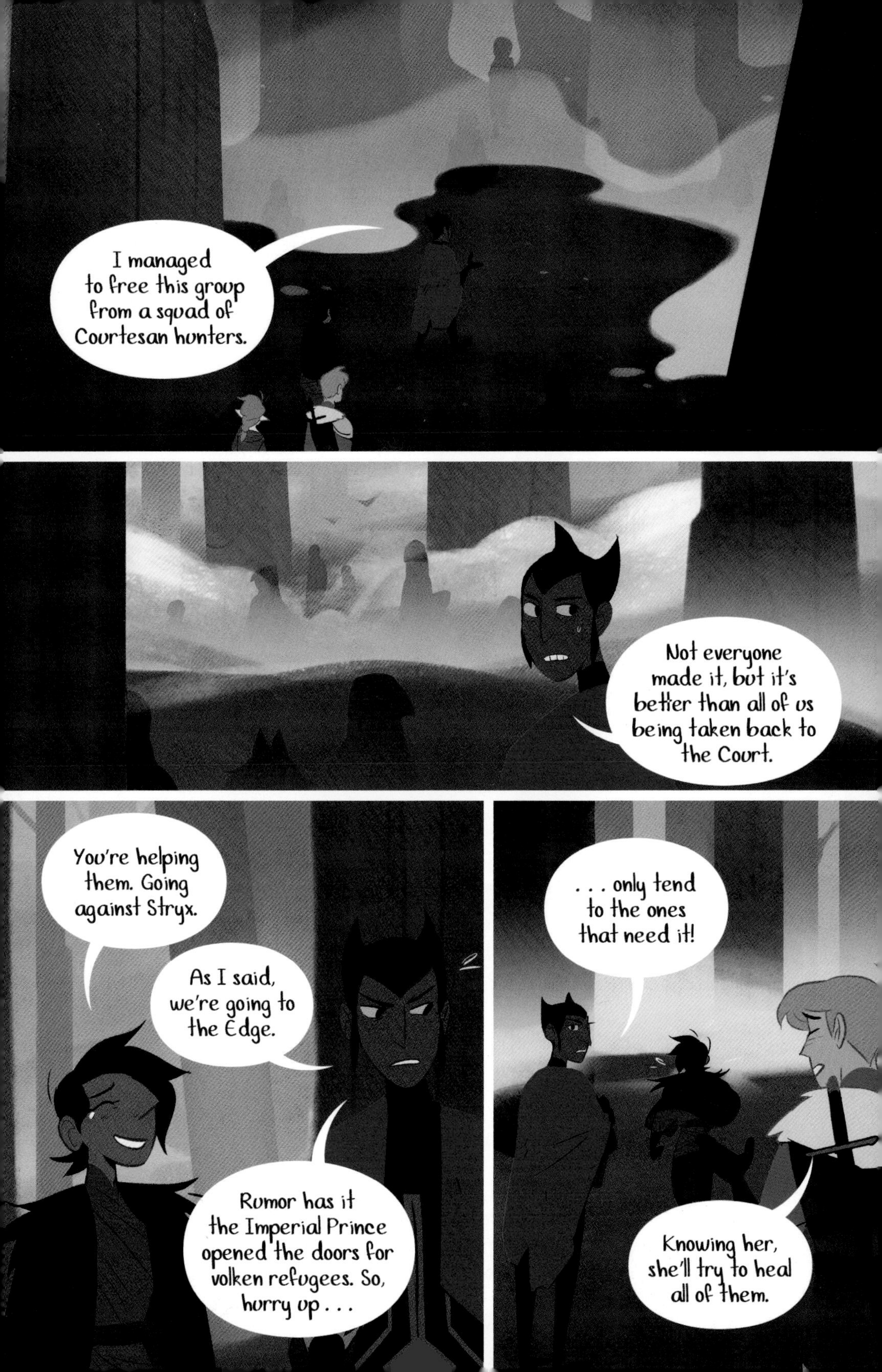
I managed to free this group from a squad of Courtesan hunters.
Not everyone made it, but it's better than all of us being taken back to the Court.
You're helping them. Going against Stryx.
As I said, we're going to the Edge.
Rumor has it the Imperial Prince opened the doors for volken refugees. So, hurry up . . .
. . . only tend to the ones that need it!
Knowing her, she'll try to heal all of them.

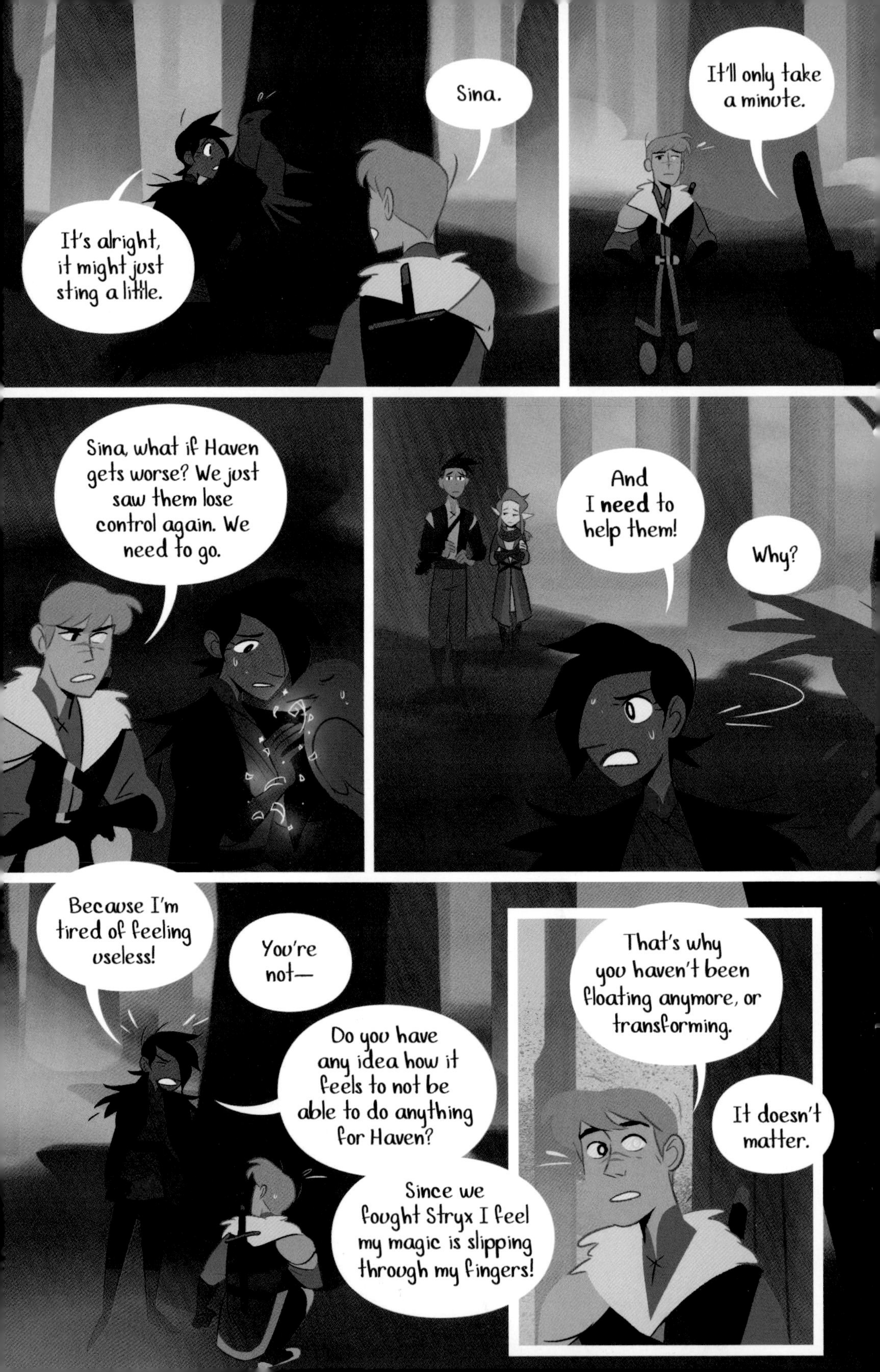
Sina.
It's alright, it might just sting a little.
It'll only take a minute.
Sina, what if Haven gets worse? We just saw them lose control again. We need to go.
And I **need** to help them!
Why?
Because I'm tired of feeling useless!
You're not—
Do you have any idea how it feels to not be able to do anything for Haven?
Since we fought Stryx I feel my magic is slipping through my fingers!
That's why you haven't been floating anymore, or transforming.
It doesn't matter.

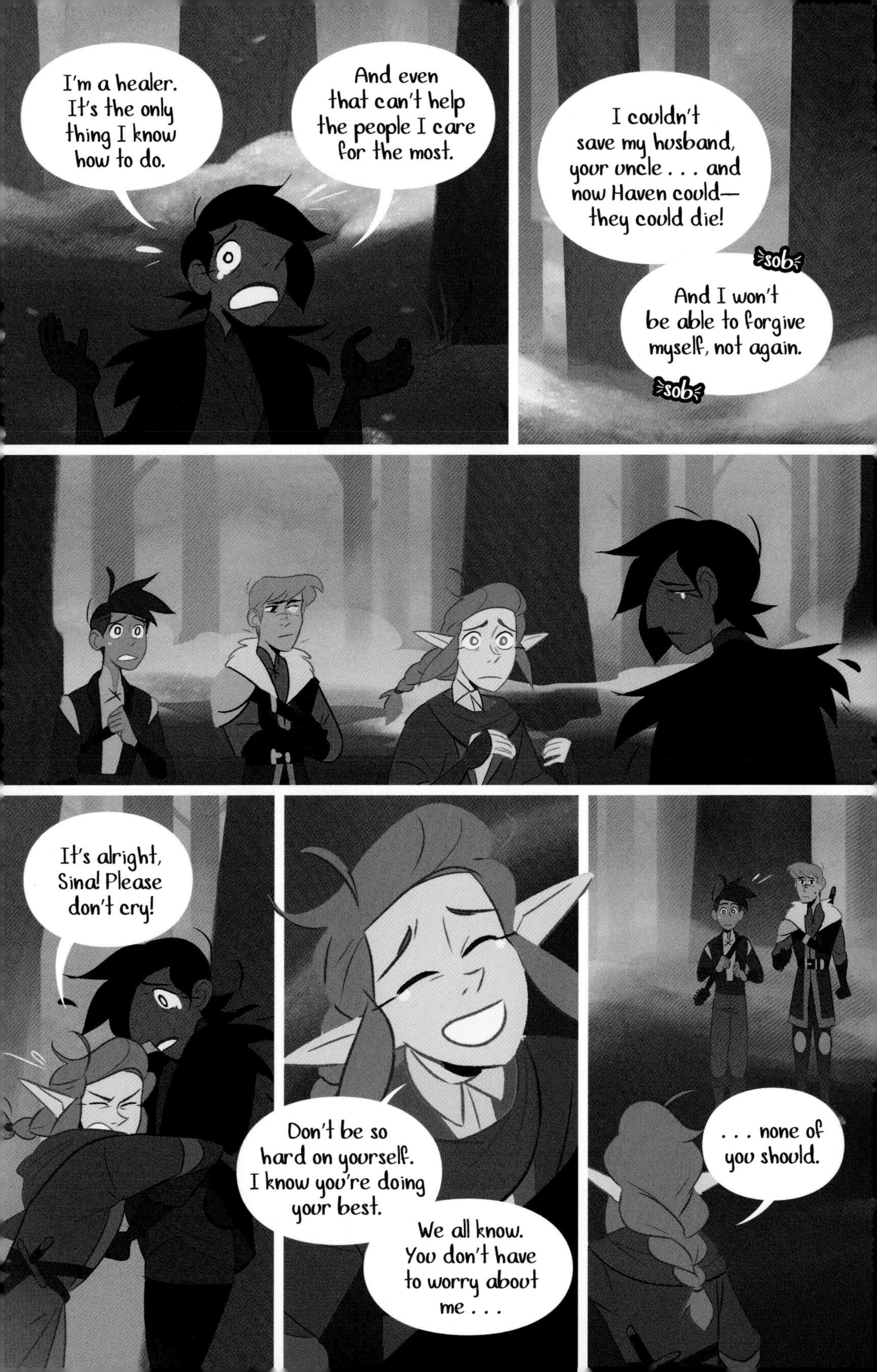

I'm a healer. It's the only thing I know how to do.
And even that can't help the people I care for the most.
I couldn't save my husband, your uncle . . . and now Haven could— they could die!
sob
And I won't be able to forgive myself, not again.
sob
It's alright, Sina! Please don't cry!
Don't be so hard on yourself. I know you're doing your best.
We all know. You don't have to worry about me . . .
. . . none of you should.

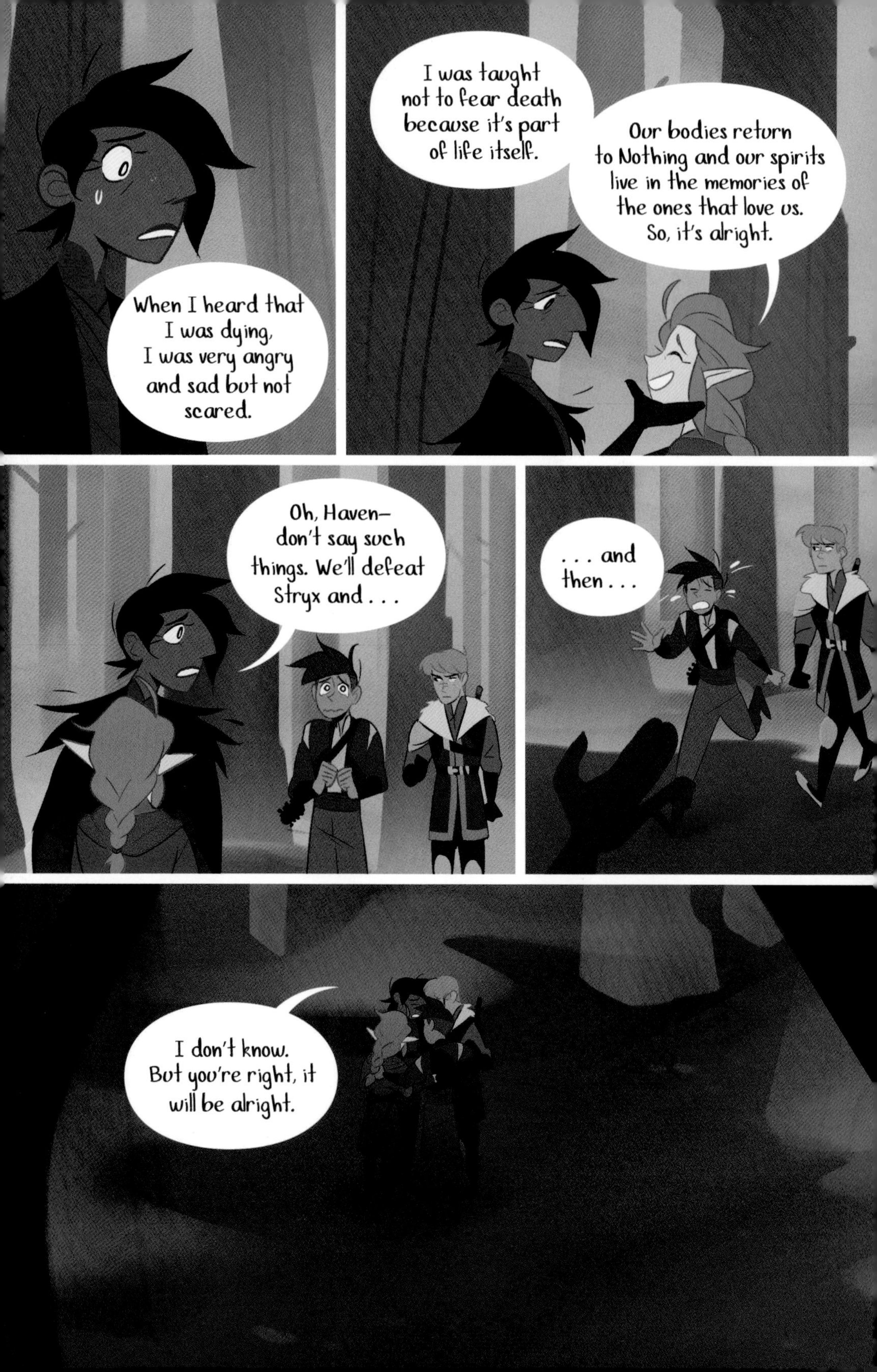
When I heard that I was dying, I was very angry and sad but not scared.
I was taught not to fear death because it's part of life itself.
Our bodies return to Nothing and our spirits live in the memories of the ones that love us. So, it's alright.
Oh, Haven— don't say such things. We'll defeat Stryx and . . .
. . . and then . . .
I don't know. But you're right, it will be alright.

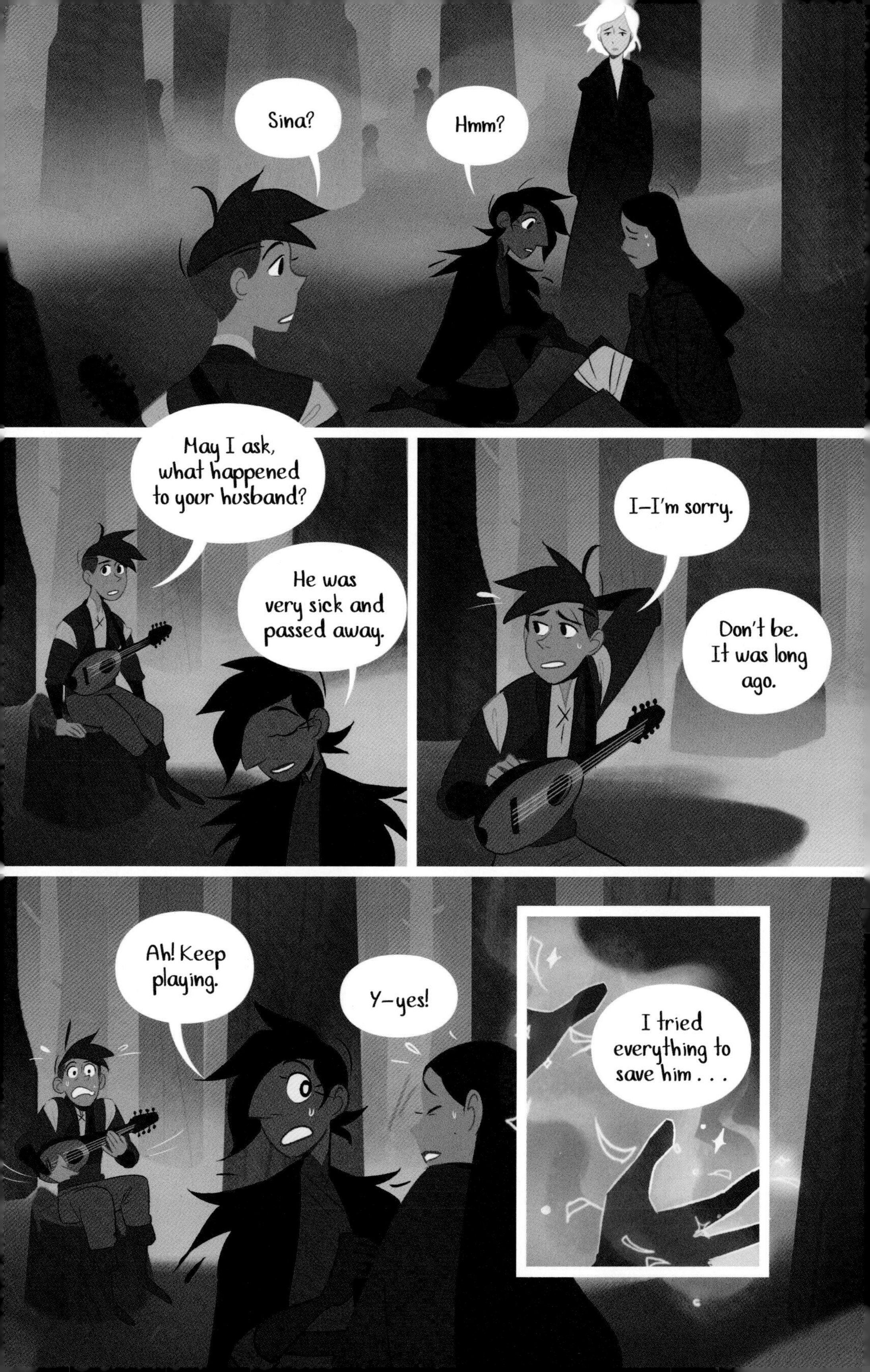
Sina?
Hmm?
May I ask, what happened to your husband?
He was very sick and passed away.
I—I'm sorry.
Don't be. It was long ago.
Ah! Keep playing.
Y—yes!
I tried everything to save him . . .

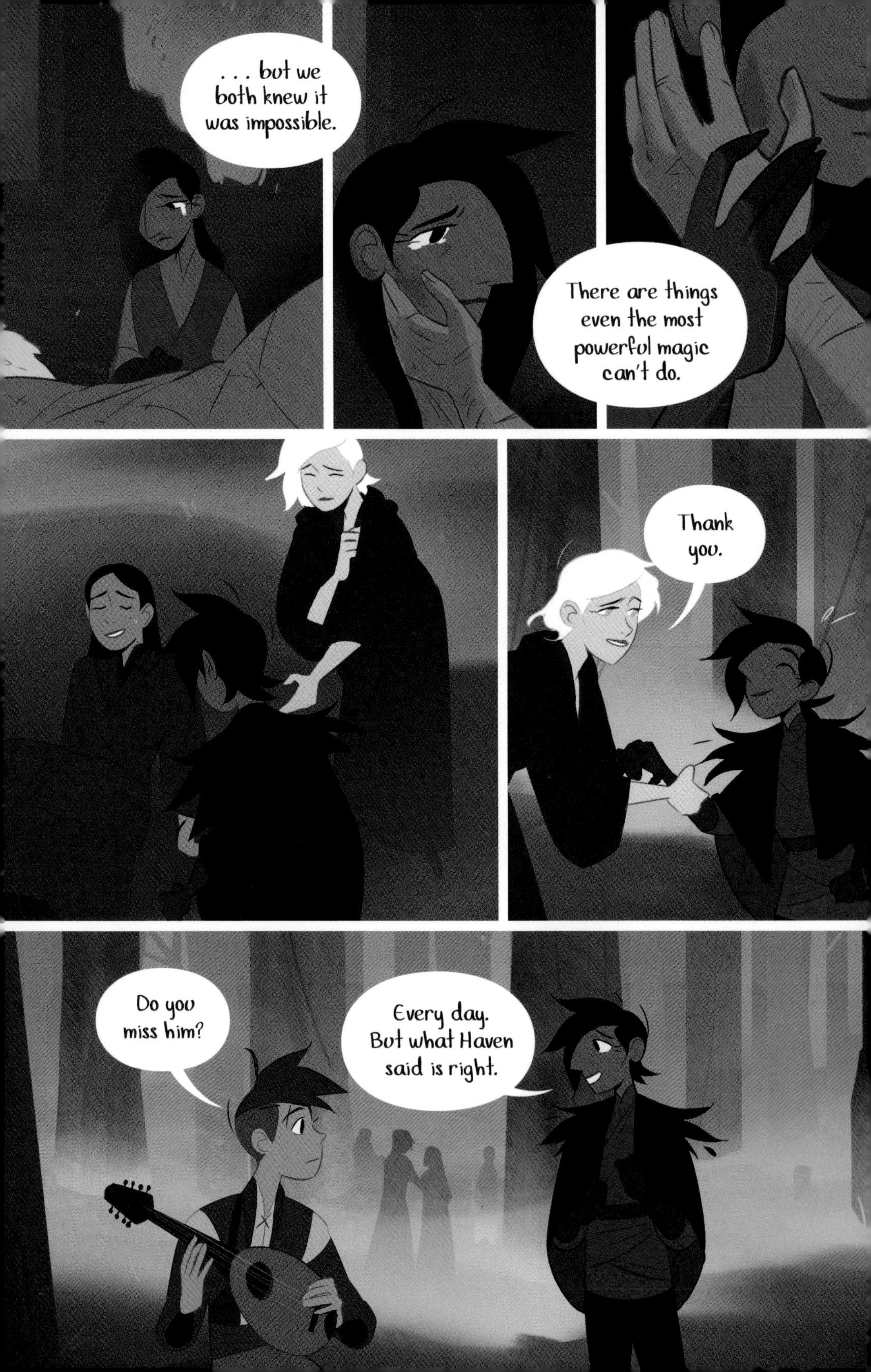
. . . but we both knew it was impossible.
There are things even the most powerful magic can't do.
Thank you.
Do you miss him?
Every day. But what Haven said is right.

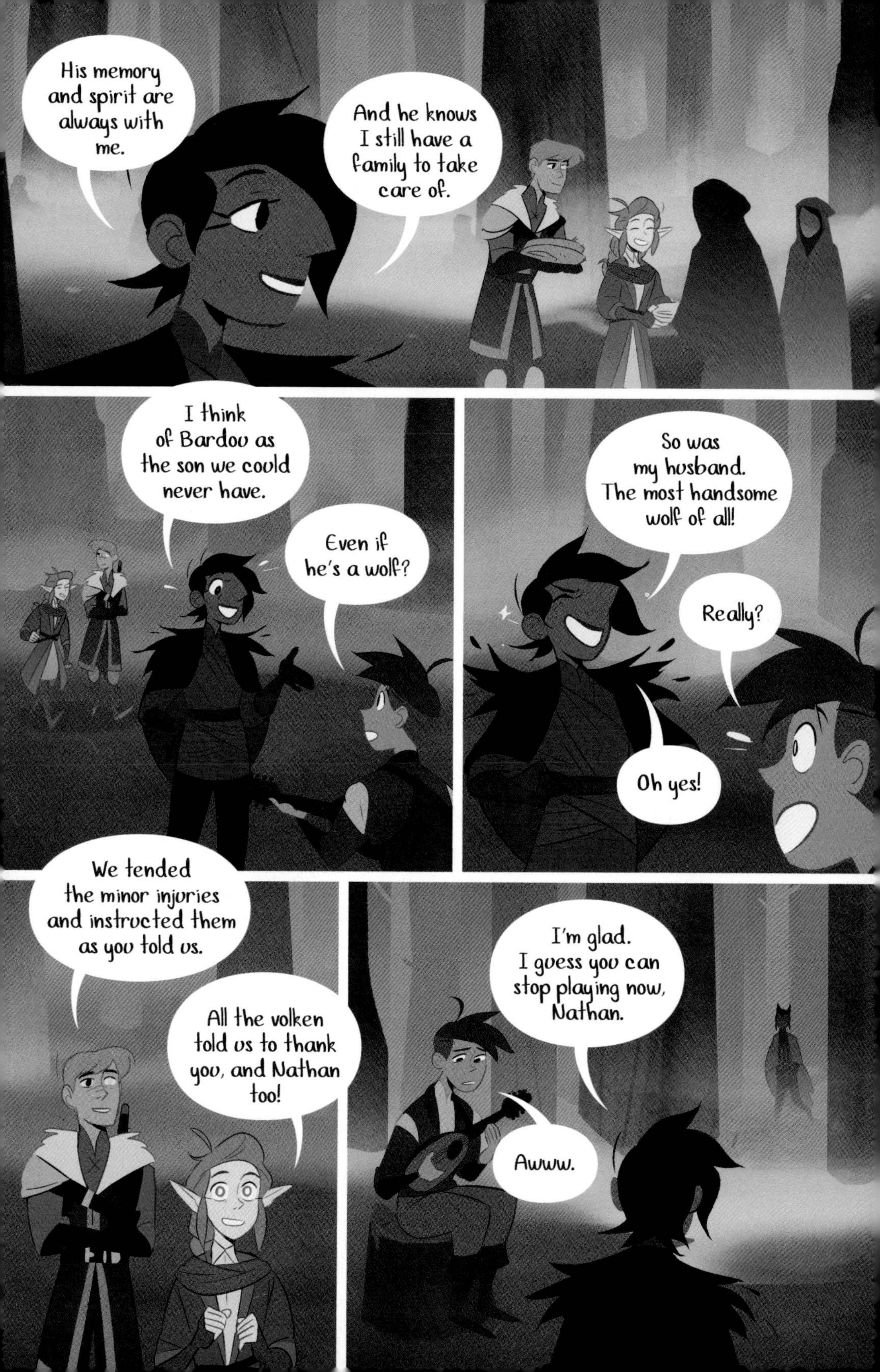
His memory and spirit are always with me.
And he knows I still have a family to take care of.
I think of Bardou as the son we could never have.
Even if he's a wolf?
So was my husband. The most handsome wolf of all!
Really?
Oh yes!
We tended the minor injuries and instructed them as you told us.
All the volken told us to thank you, and Nathan too!
I'm glad. I guess you can stop playing now, Nathan.
Awww.

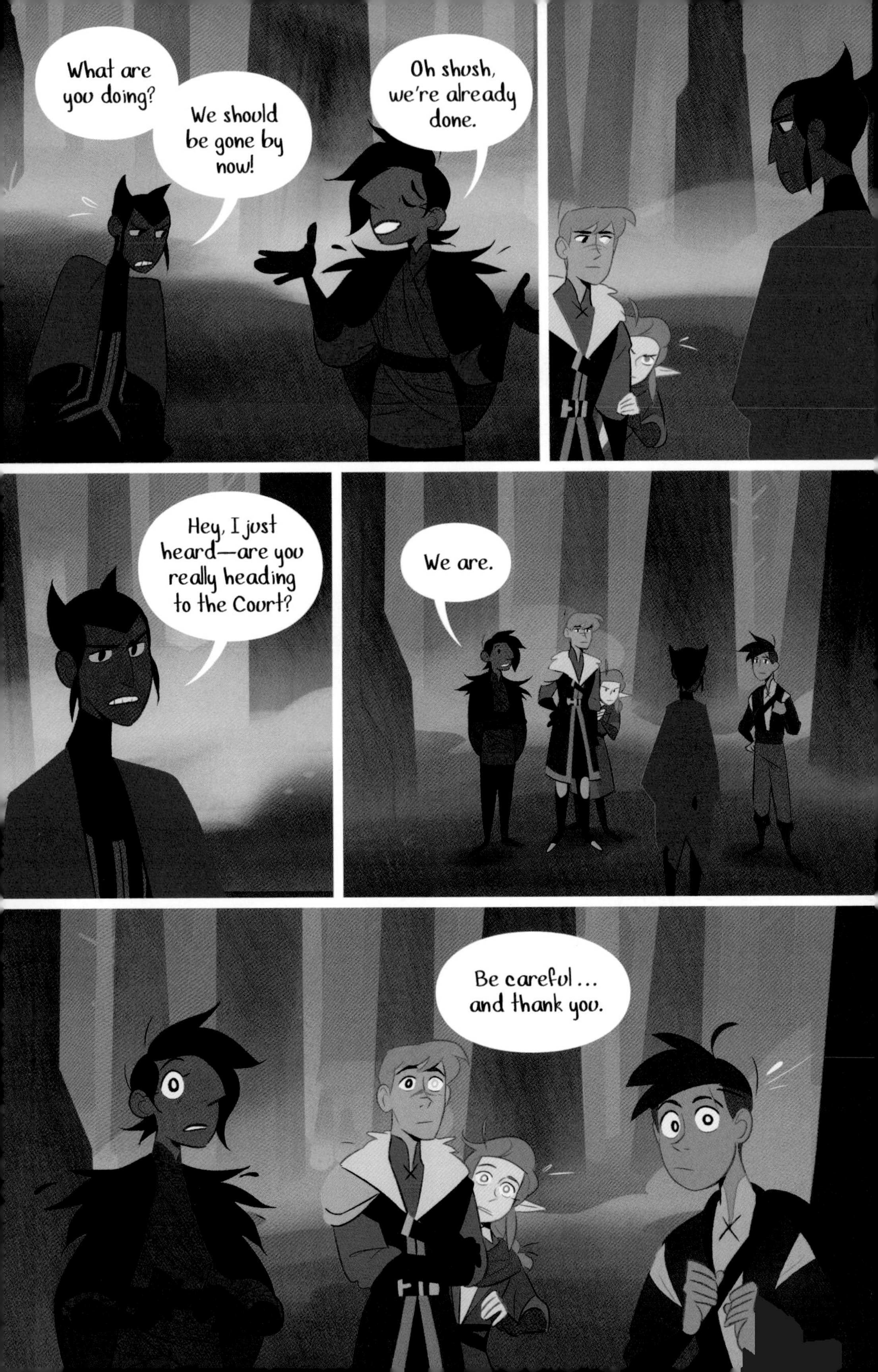
What are you doing?
We should be gone by now!
Oh shush, we're already done.
Hey, I just heard—are you really heading to the Court?
We are.
Be careful... and thank you.

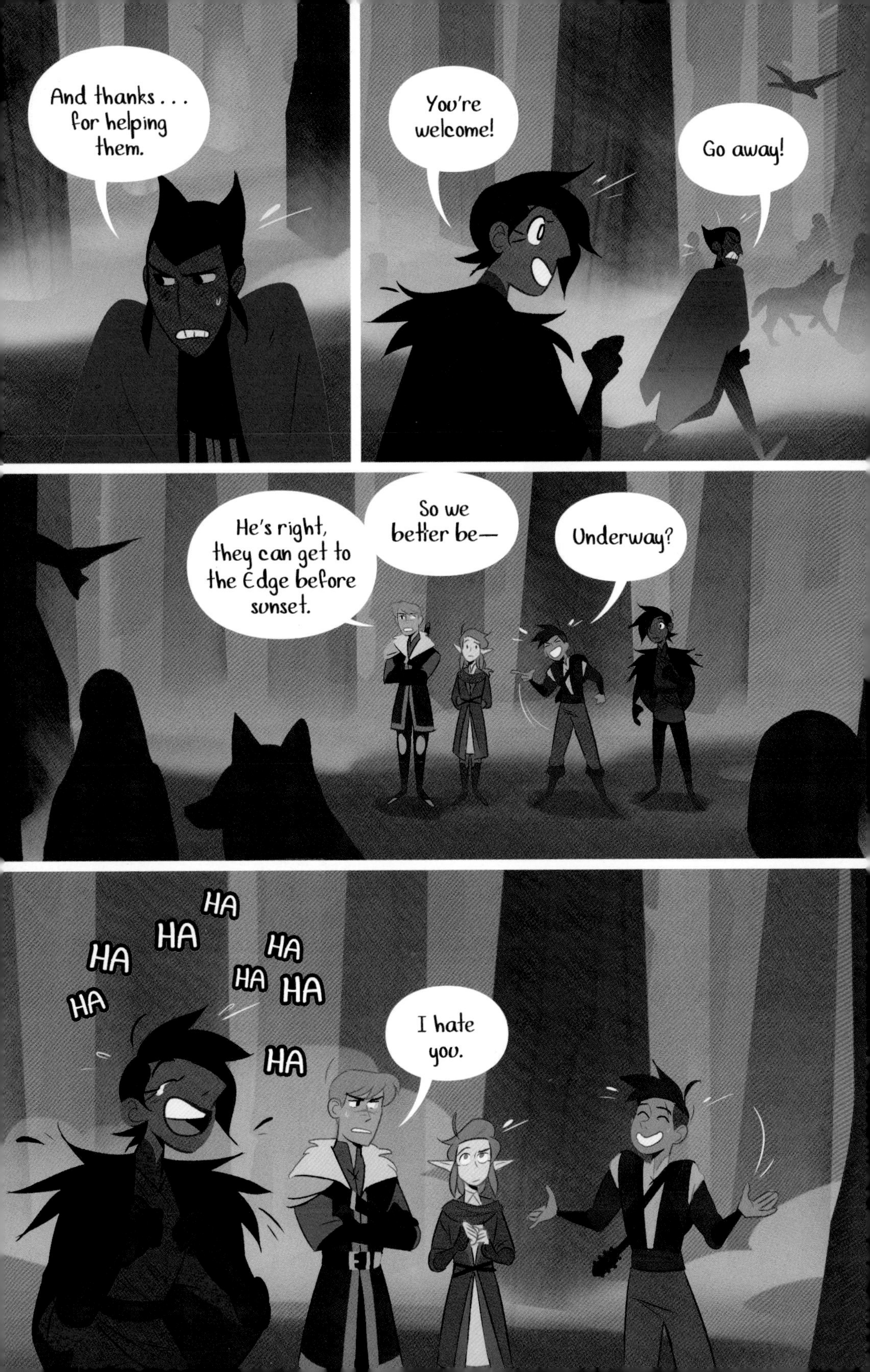
And thanks . . . for helping them.
You're welcome!
Go away!
He's right, they can get to the Edge before sunset.
So we better be—
Underway?
HA
HA
HA
HA
HA
HA HA
HA
I hate you.

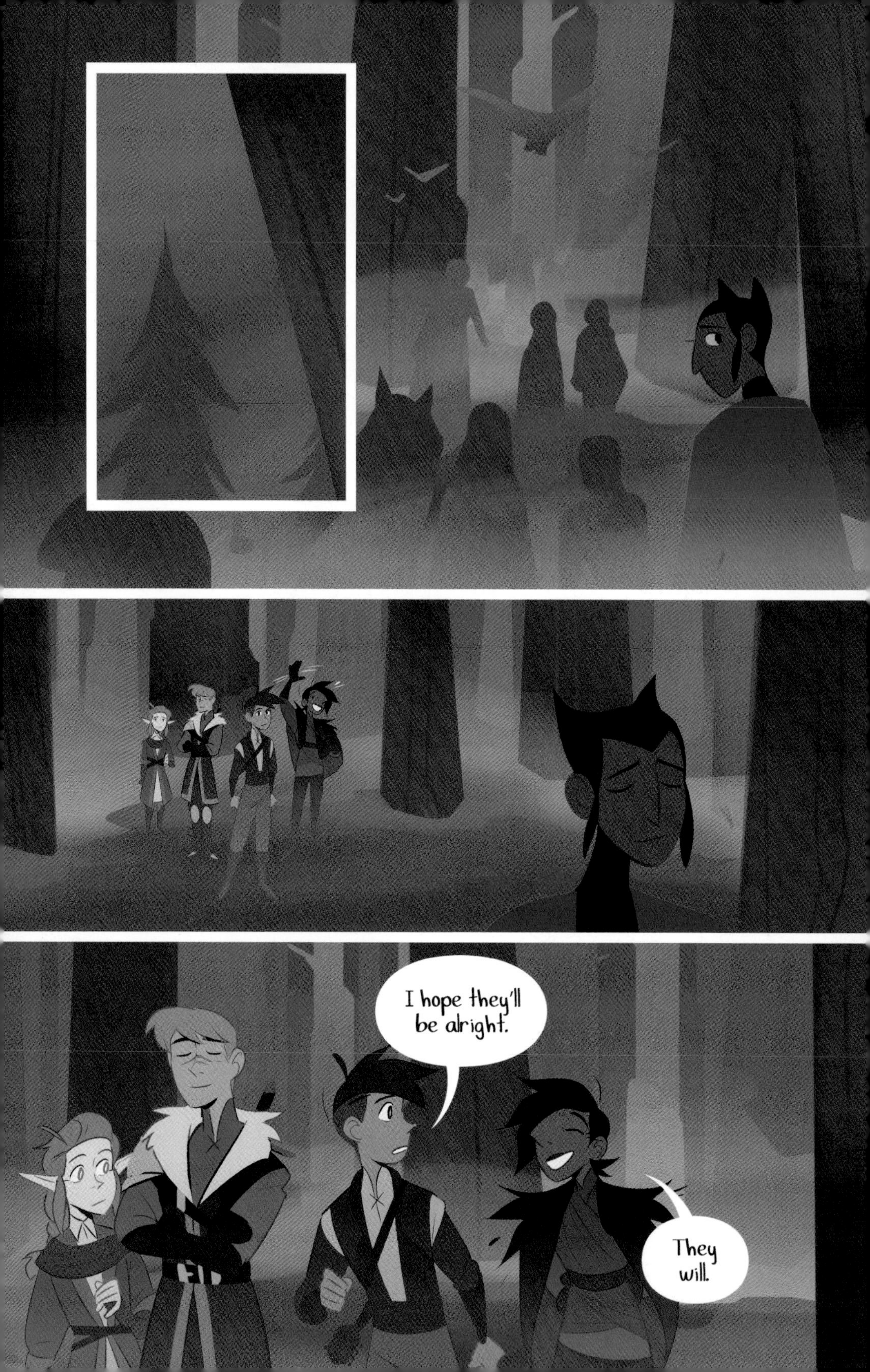
I hope they'll be alright.
They will.

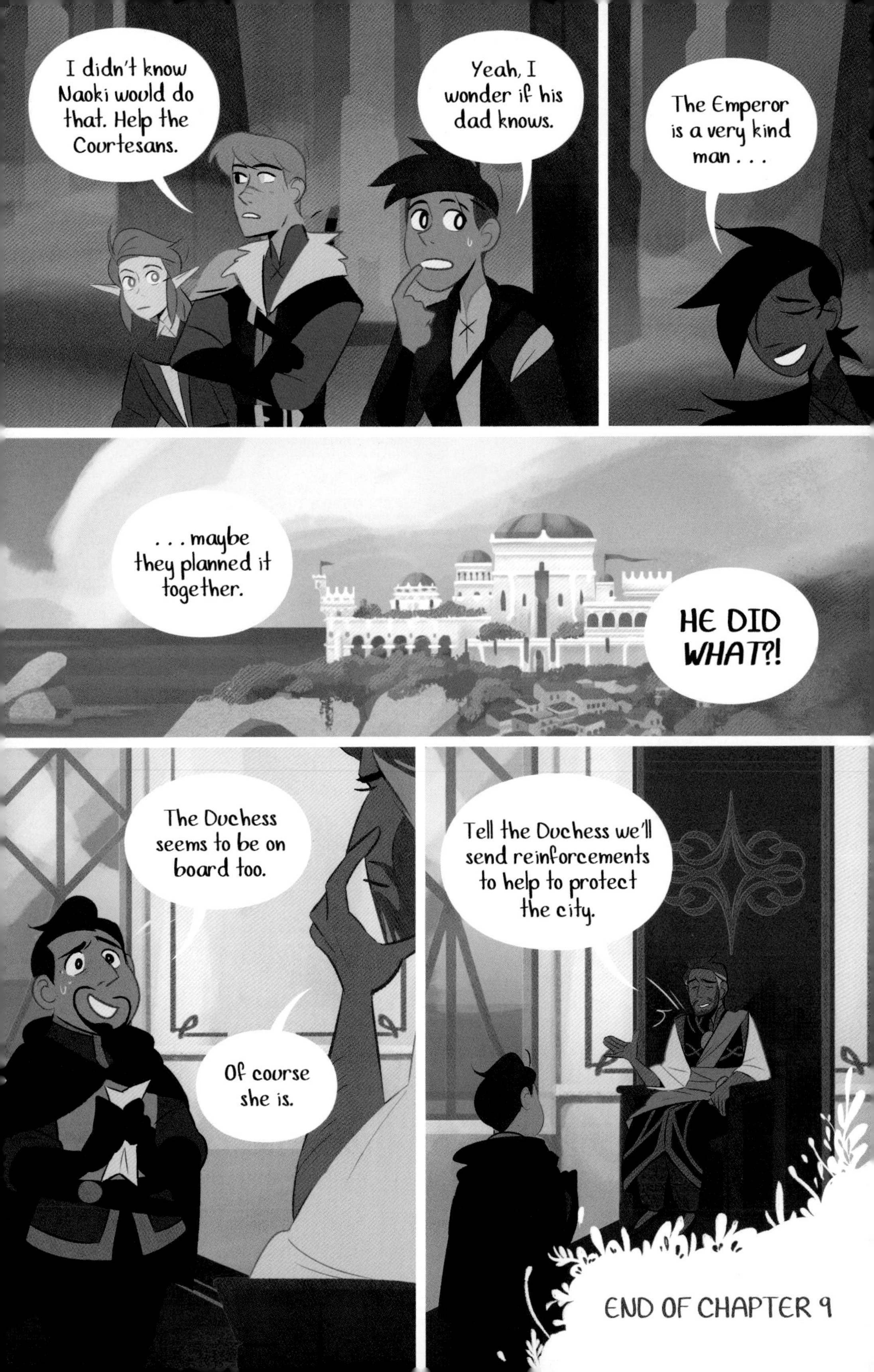
I didn't know Naoki would do that. Help the Courtesans.
Yeah, I wonder if his dad knows.
The Emperor is a very kind man . . .
. . . maybe they planned it together.
HE DID WHAT?!
The Duchess seems to be on board too.
Of course she is.
Tell the Duchess we'll send reinforcements to help to protect the city.
END OF CHAPTER 9

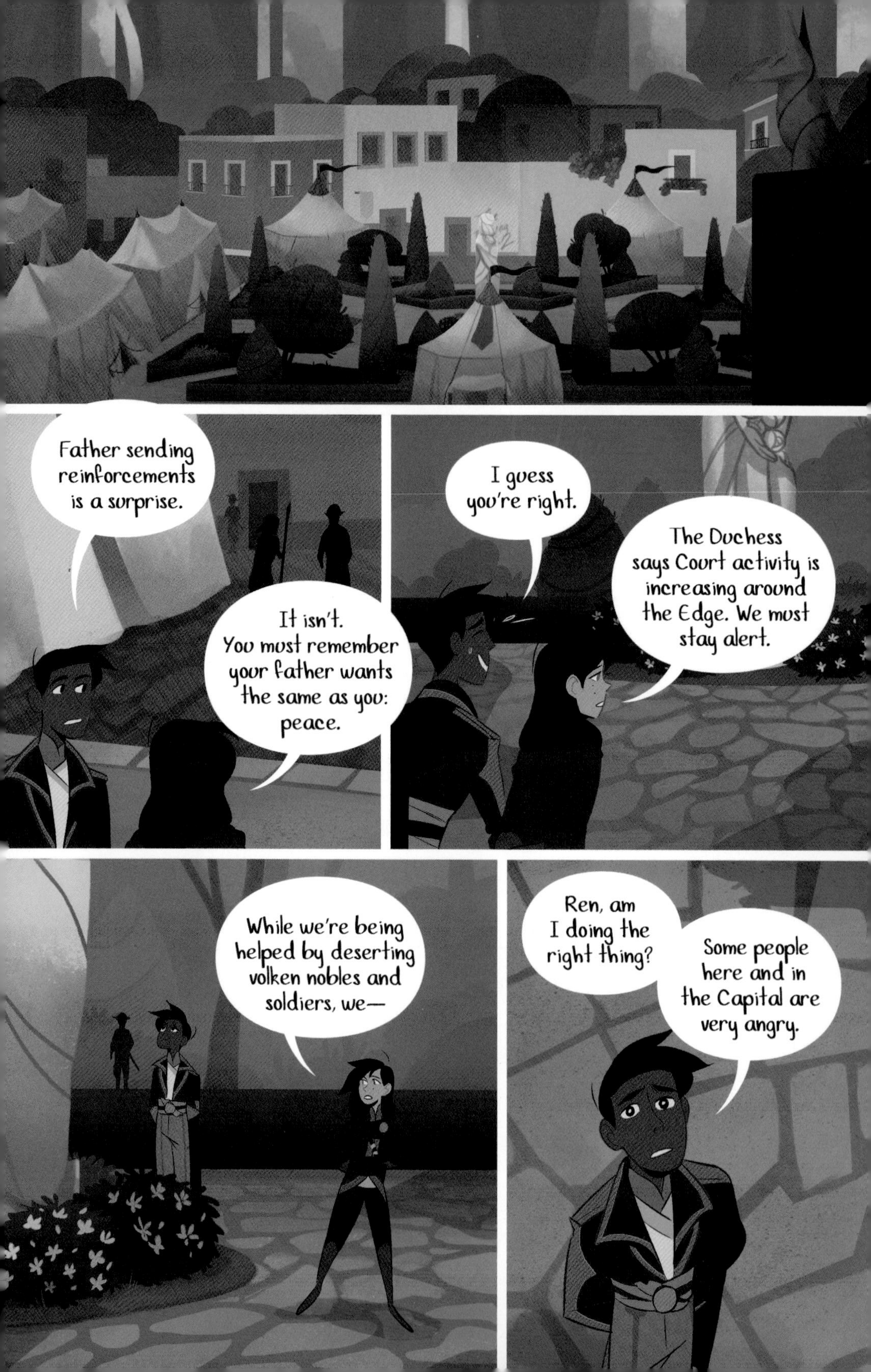
Father sending reinforcements is a surprise.
It isn't. You must remember your father wants the same as you: peace.
I guess you're right.
The Duchess says Court activity is increasing around the Edge. We must stay alert.
While we're being helped by deserting volken nobles and soldiers, we—
Ren, am I doing the right thing?
Some people here and in the Capital are very angry.

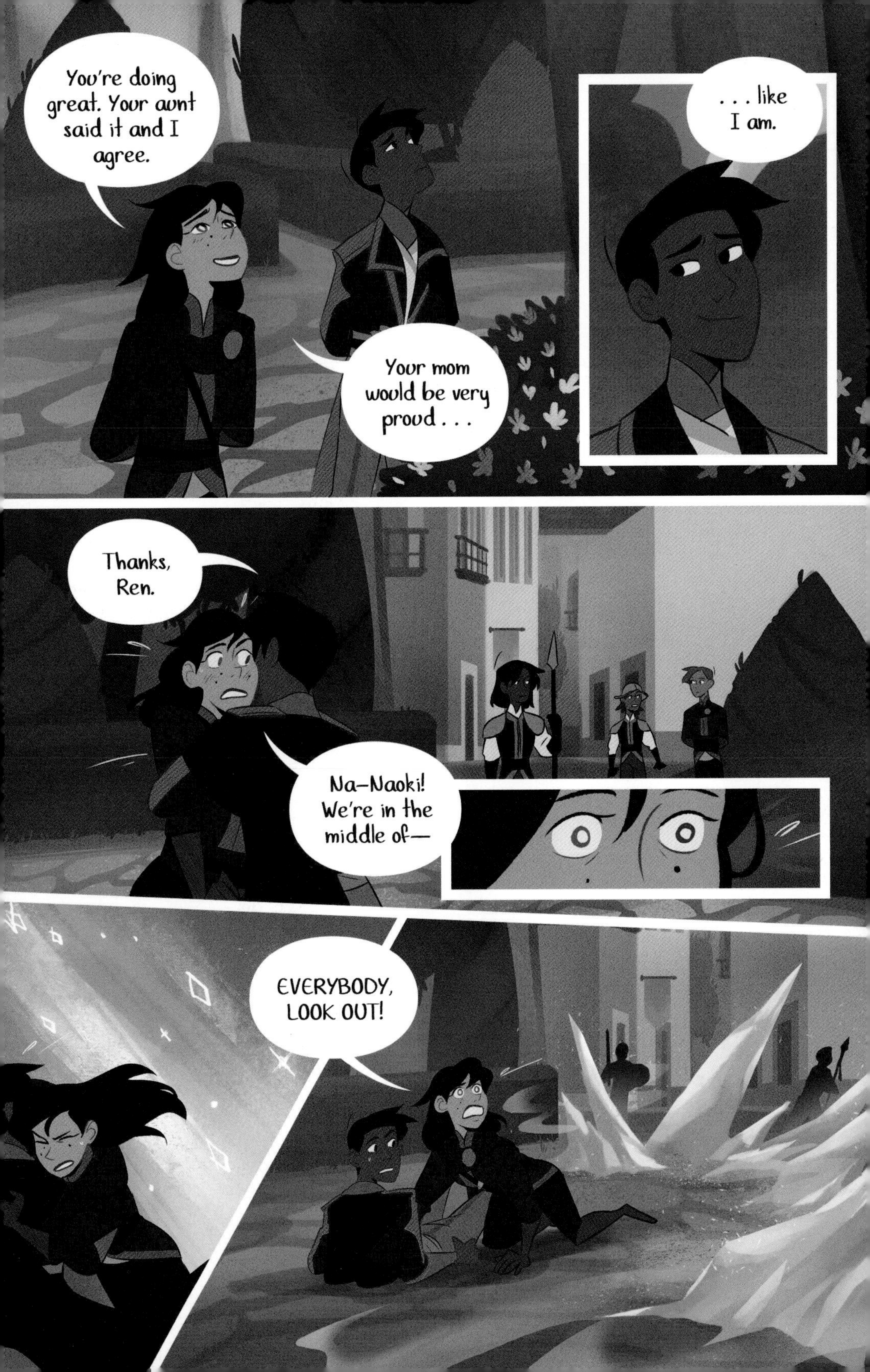
You're doing great. Your aunt said it and I agree.
Your mom would be very proud . . .
. . . like I am.
Thanks, Ren.
Na-Naoki! We're in the middle of—
EVERYBODY, LOOK OUT!

Chapter 10
Prepare for Trouble
Aww, aren't you adorable? The weirdo and his pet.
I should've known you'd come back . . .

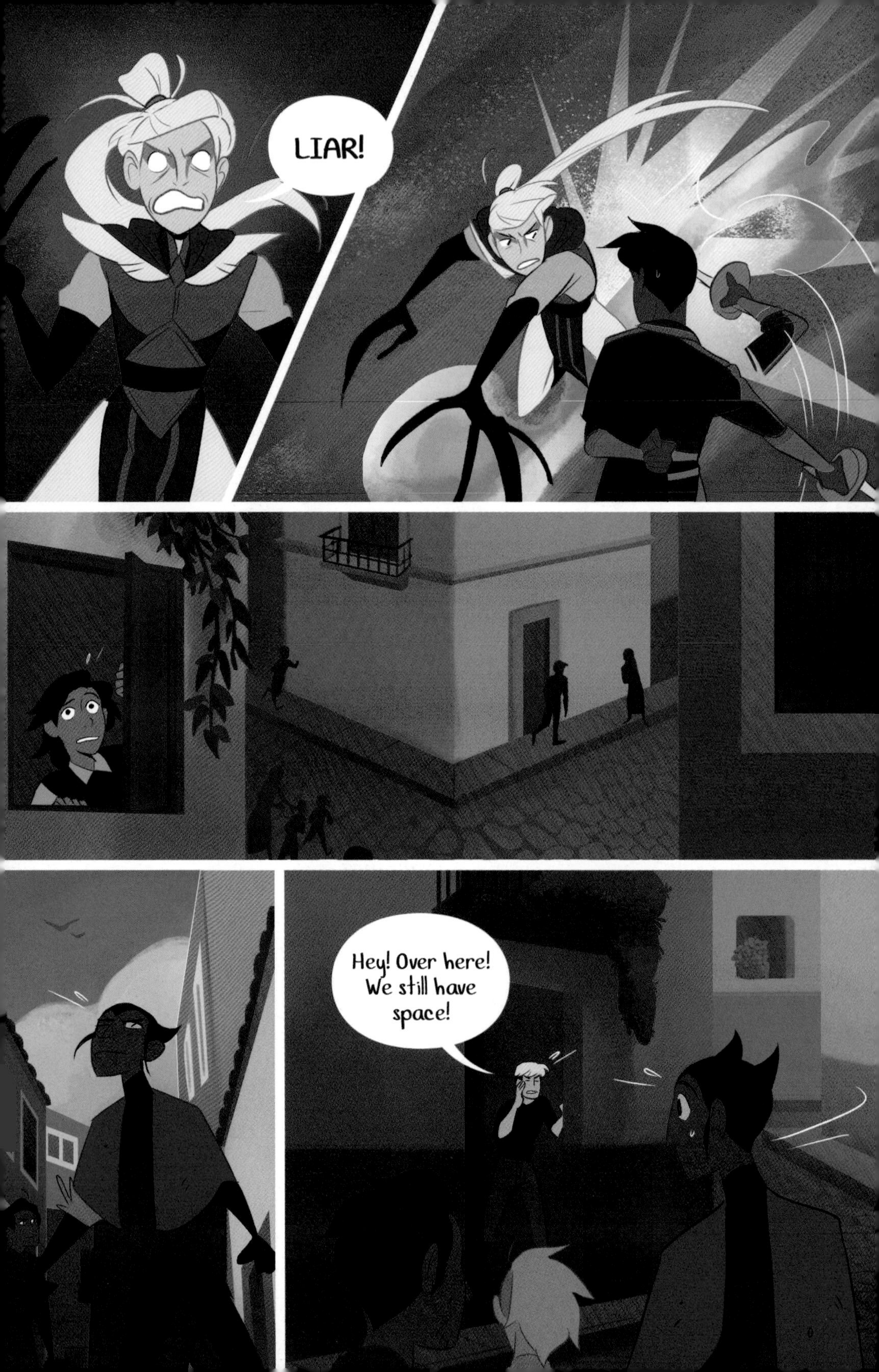
LIAR!
Hey! Over here! We still have space!

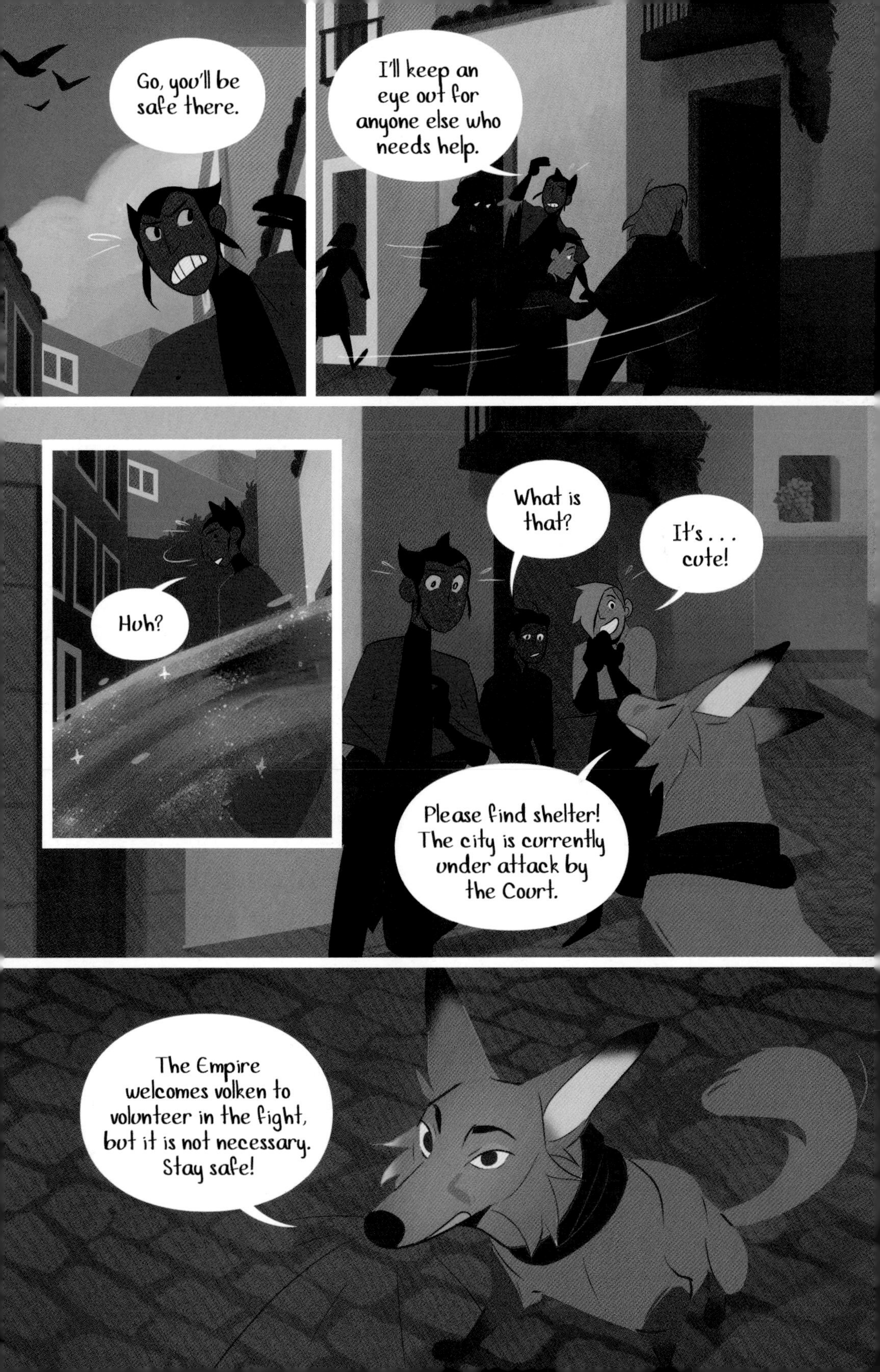
Go, you'll be safe there.
I'll keep an eye out for anyone else who needs help.
Huh?
What is that?
It's . . . cute!
Please find shelter! The city is currently under attack by the Court.
The Empire welcomes volken to volunteer in the fight, but it is not necessary. Stay safe!

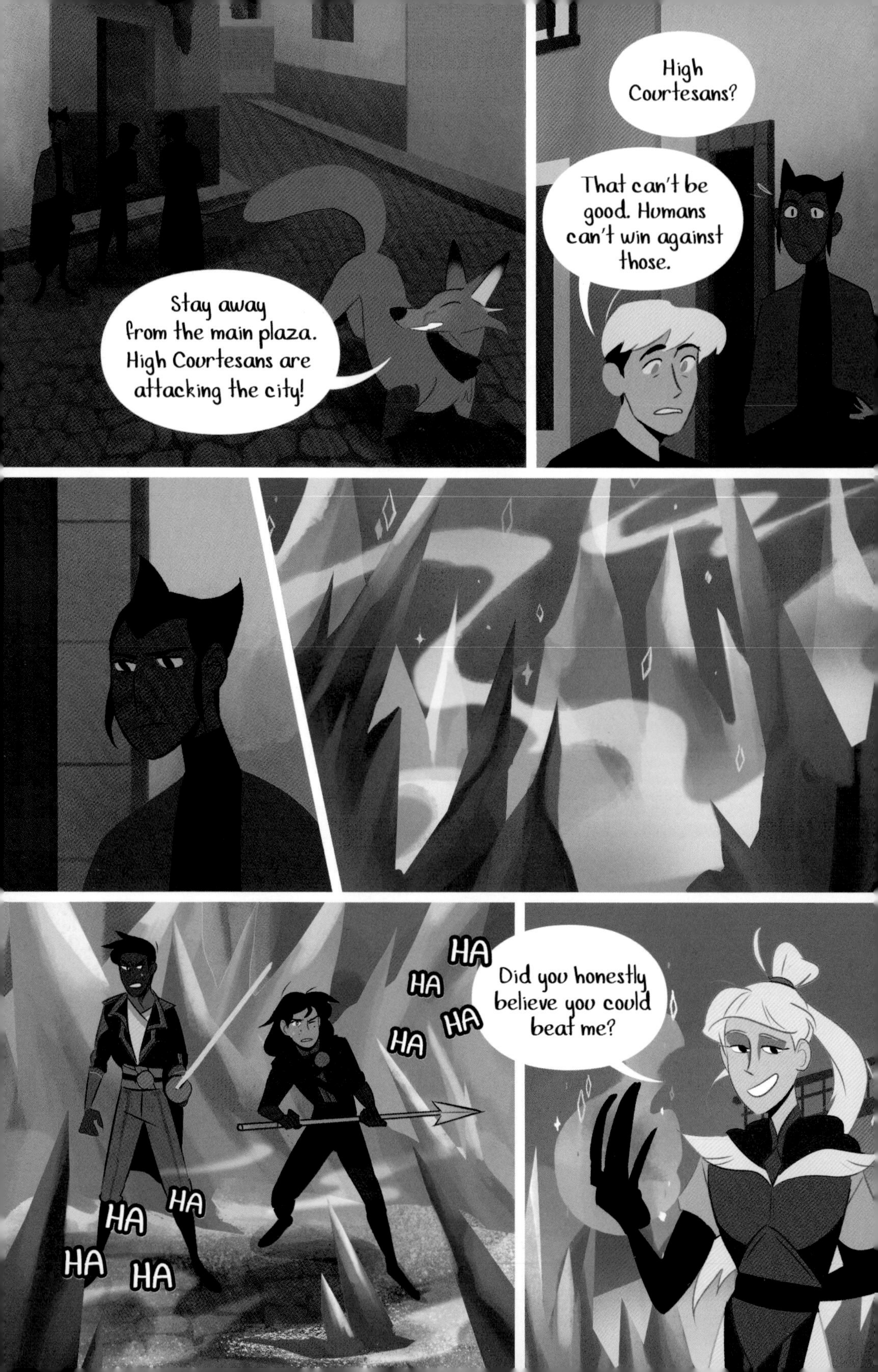
Stay away from the main plaza. High Courtesans are attacking the city!
High Courtesans?
That can't be good. Humans can't win against those.
HA
HA
HA
HA
HA
HA
HA
HA
Did you honestly believe you could beat me?

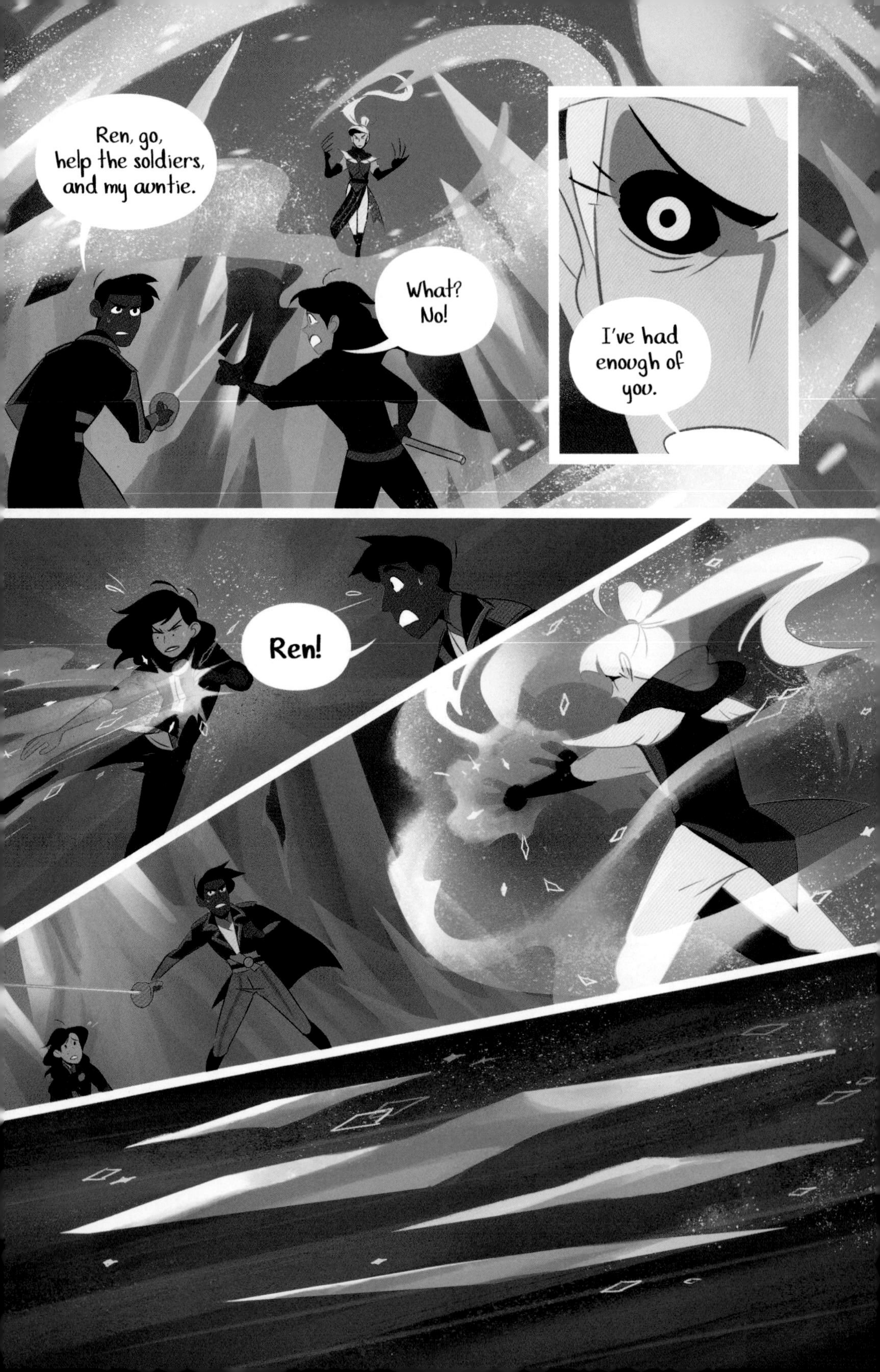
Ren, go, help the soldiers, and my auntie.
What? No!
I've had enough of you.
Ren!

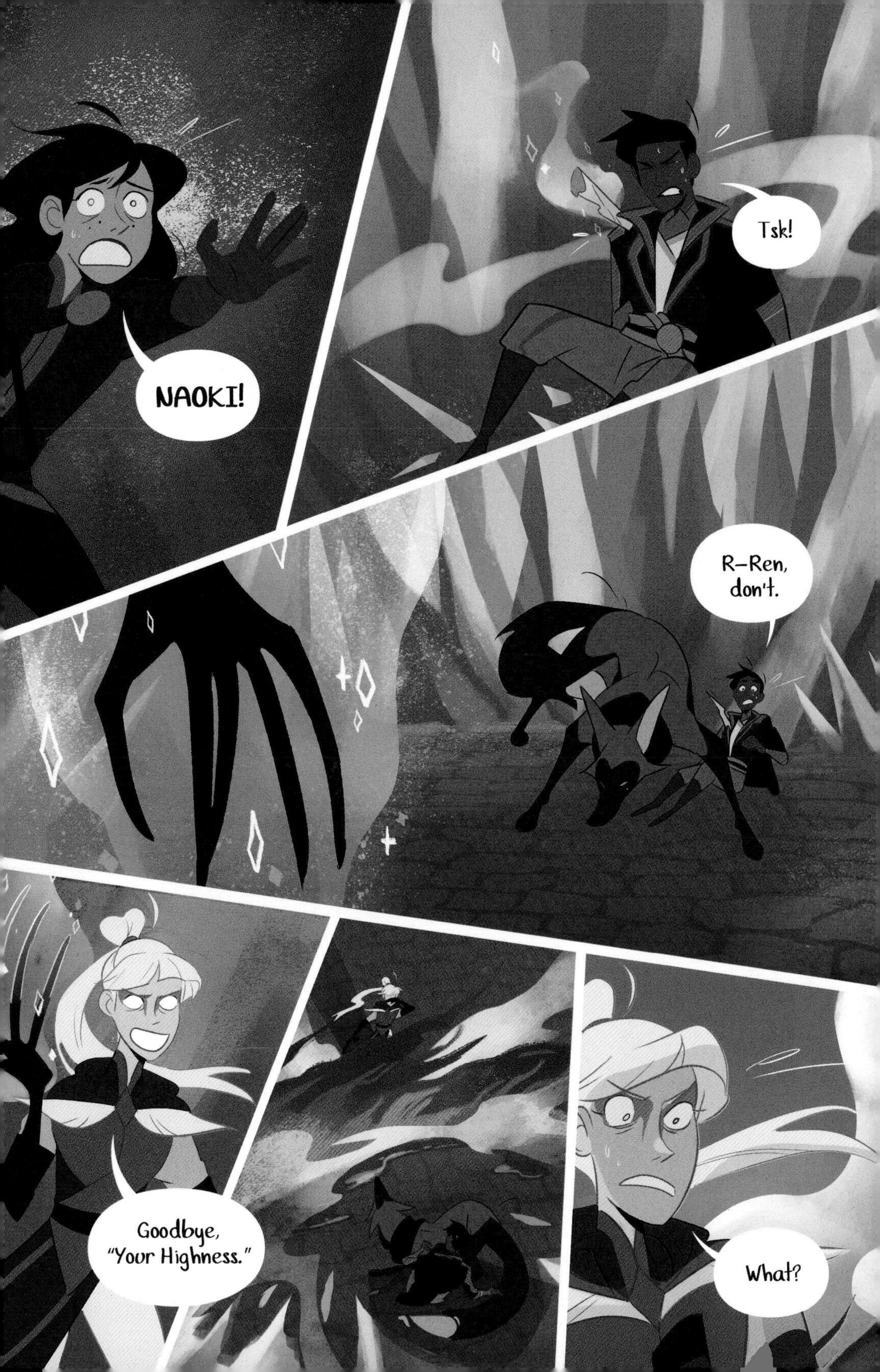
NAOKI!
Tsk!
R-Ren, don't.
Goodbye, "Your Highness."
What?

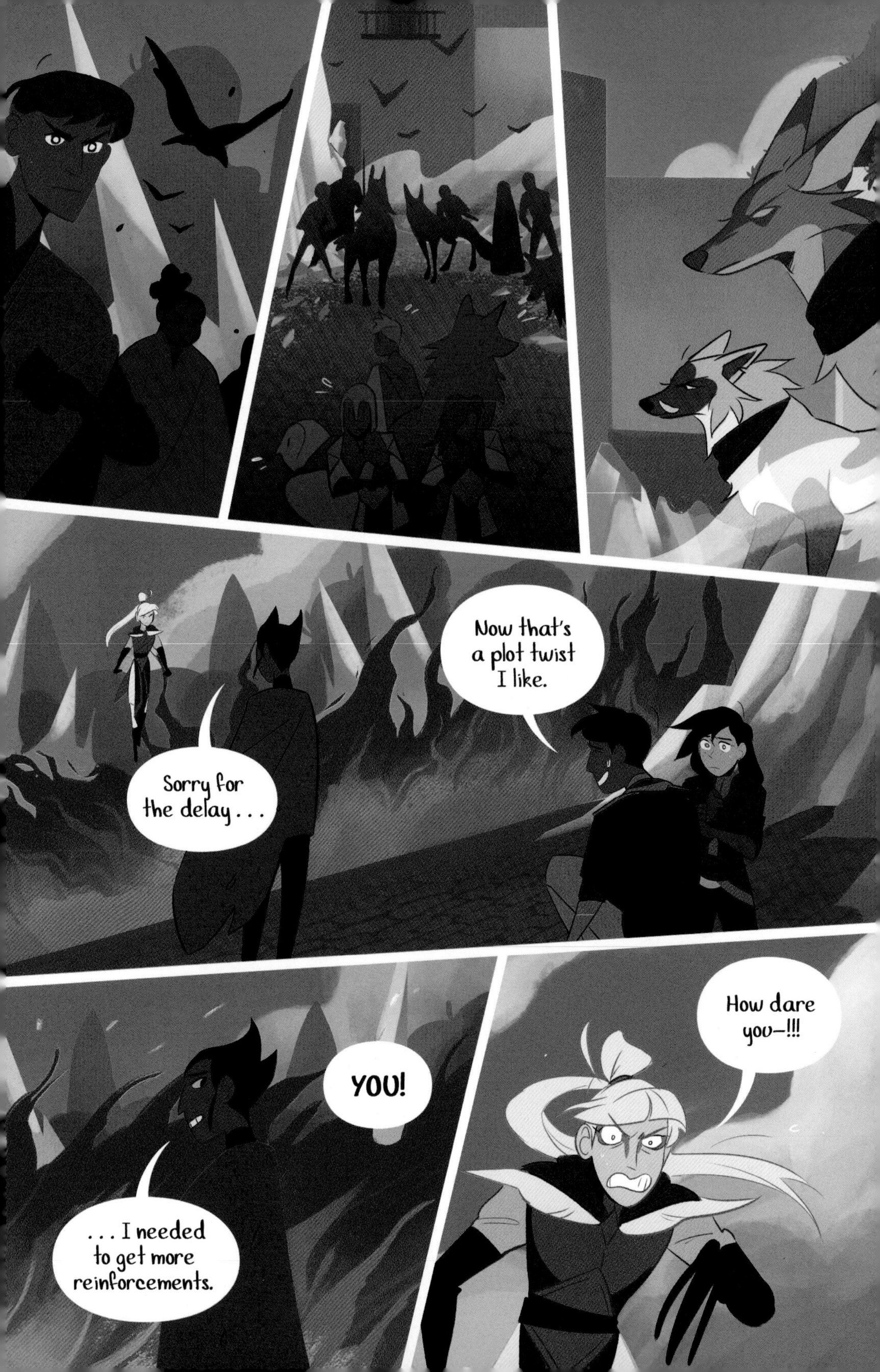
Now that's a plot twist I like.
Sorry for the delay . . .
. . . I needed to get more reinforcements.
YOU!
How dare you–!!!

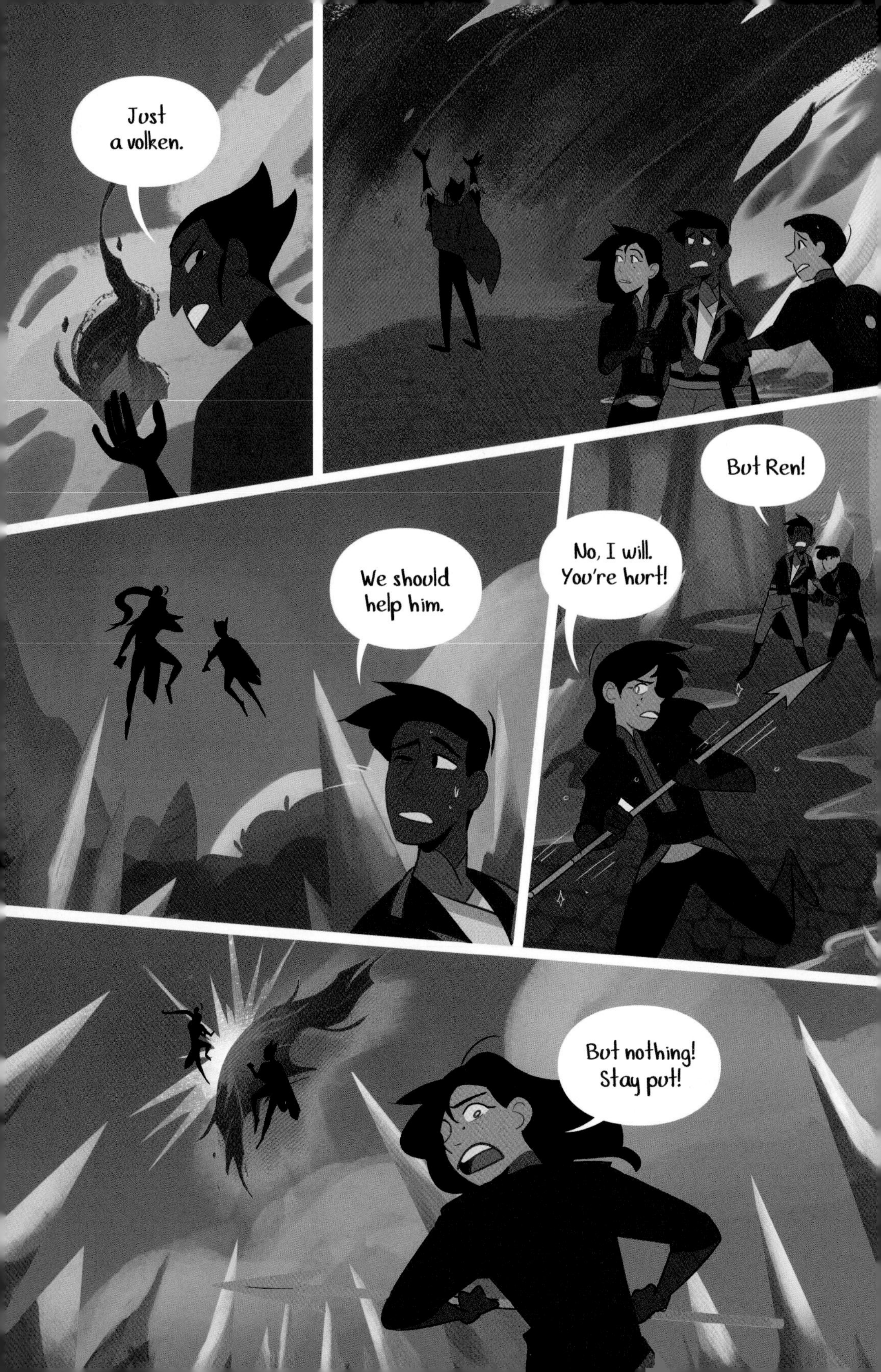
Just a volken.
But Ren!
We should help him.
No, I will. You're hurt!
But nothing! Stay put!

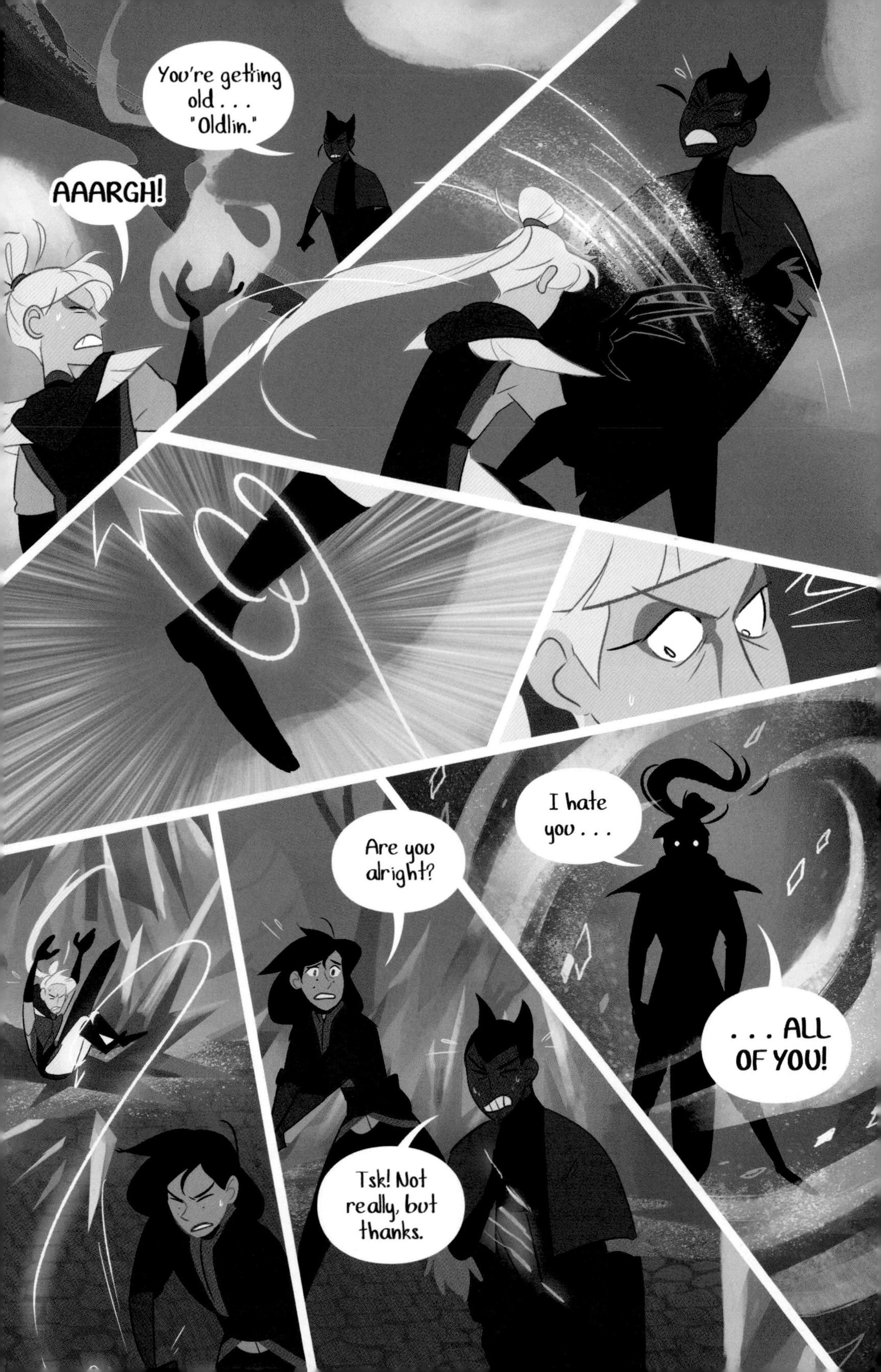
You're getting old . . . "Oldlin."
AAARGH!
I hate you . . .
Are you alright?
. . . ALL OF YOU!
Tsk! Not really, but thanks.

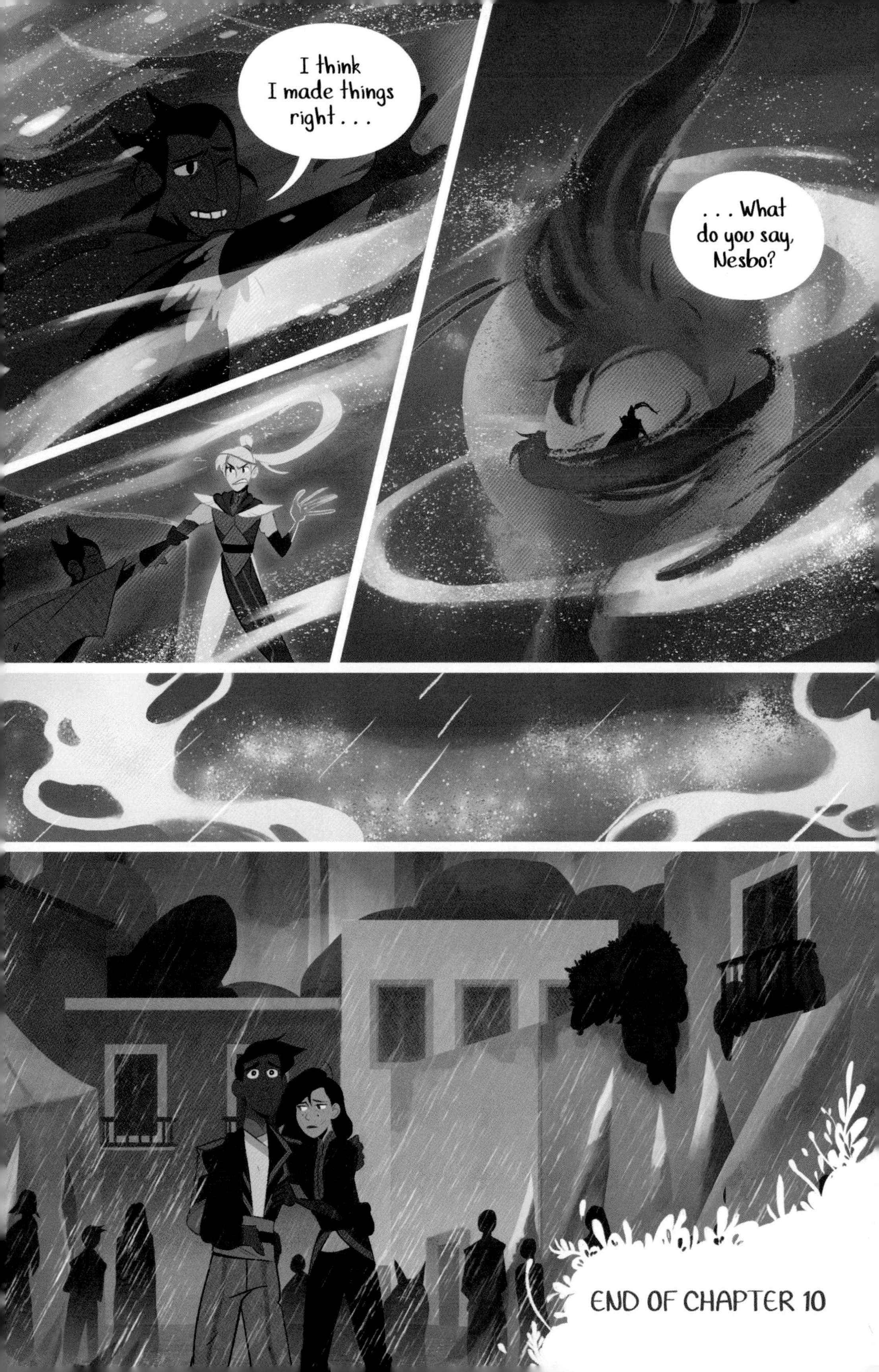
I think I made things right . . .
. . . What do you say, Nesbo?
END OF CHAPTER 10

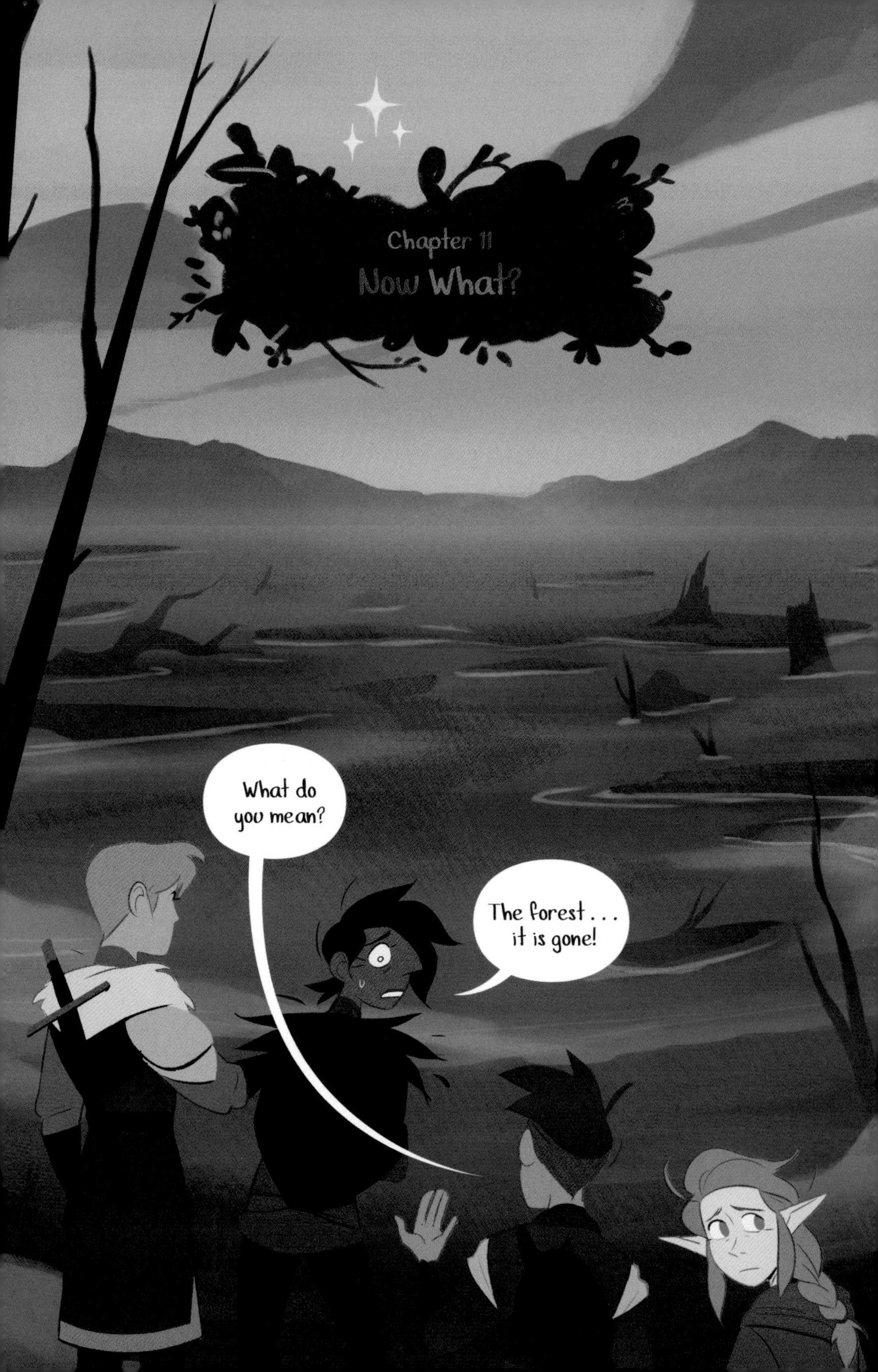
Chapter 11
Now What?
What do you mean?
The forest . . . it is gone!

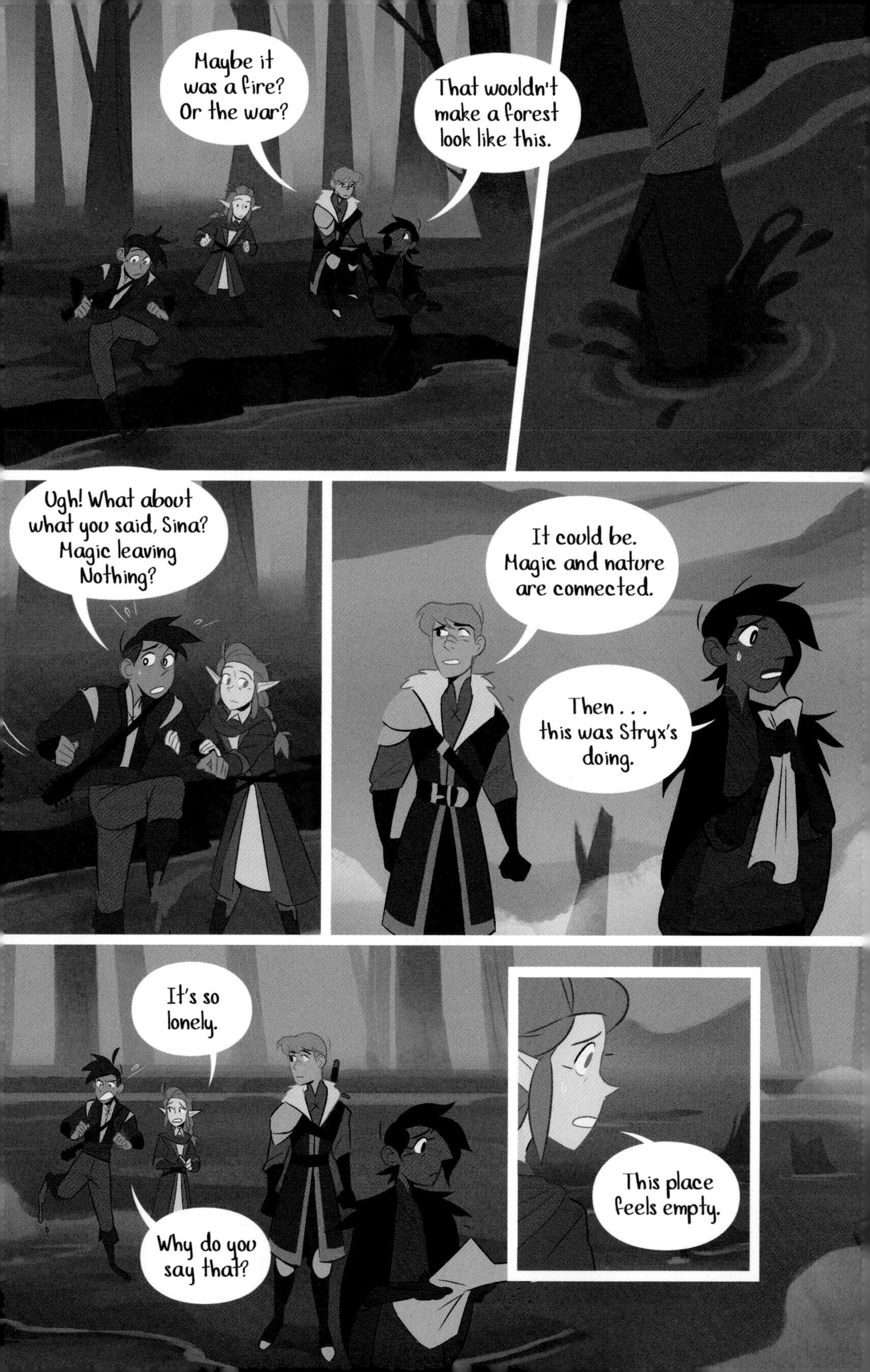
Maybe it was a fire? Or the war?
That wouldn't make a forest look like this.
Ugh! What about what you said, Sina? Magic leaving Nothing?
It could be. Magic and nature are connected.
Then . . . this was Stryx's doing.
It's so lonely.
Why do you say that?
This place feels empty.

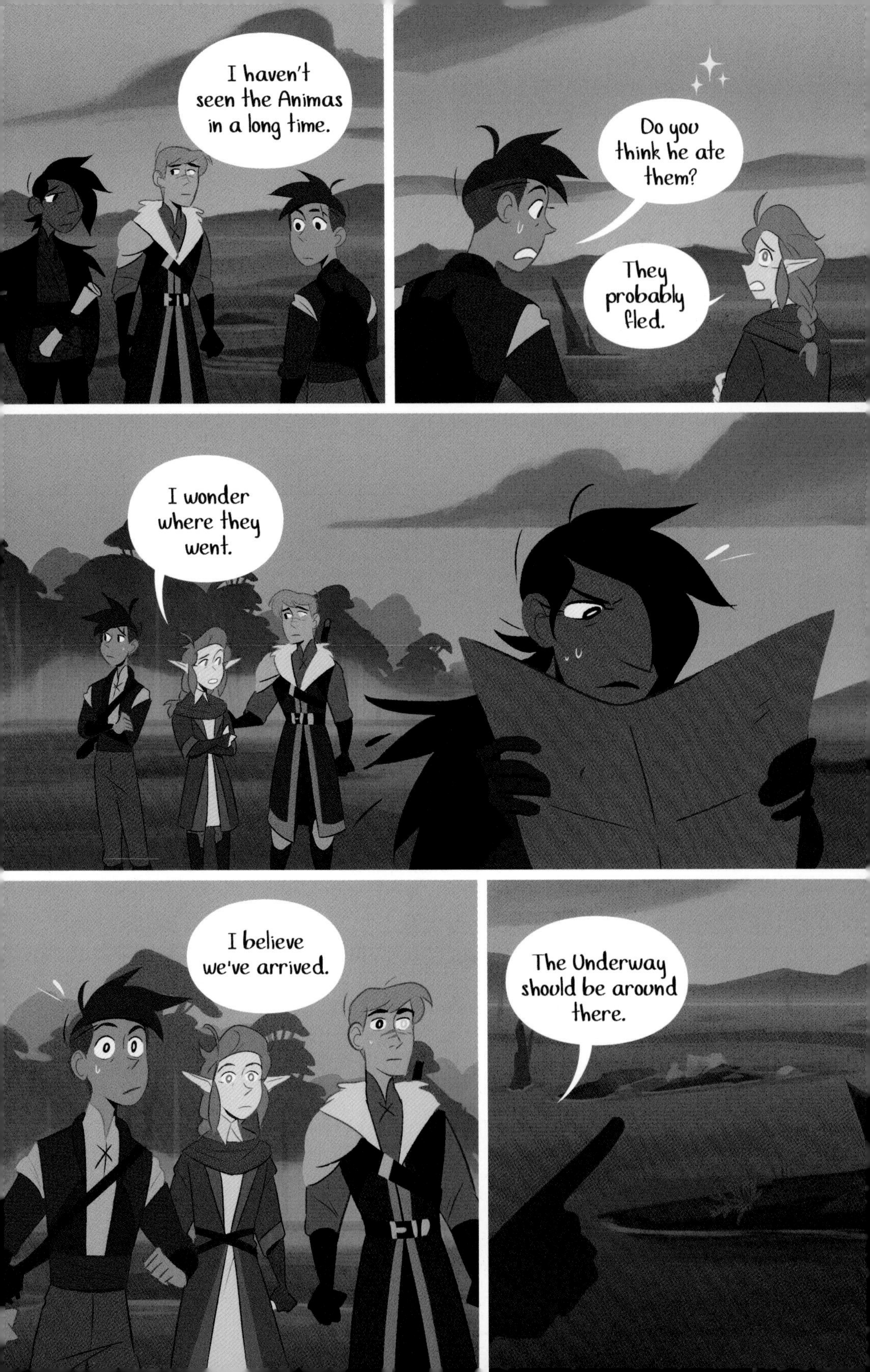

I haven't seen the Animas in a long time.
Do you think he ate them?
They probably fled.
I wonder where they went.
I believe we've arrived.
The Underway should be around there.

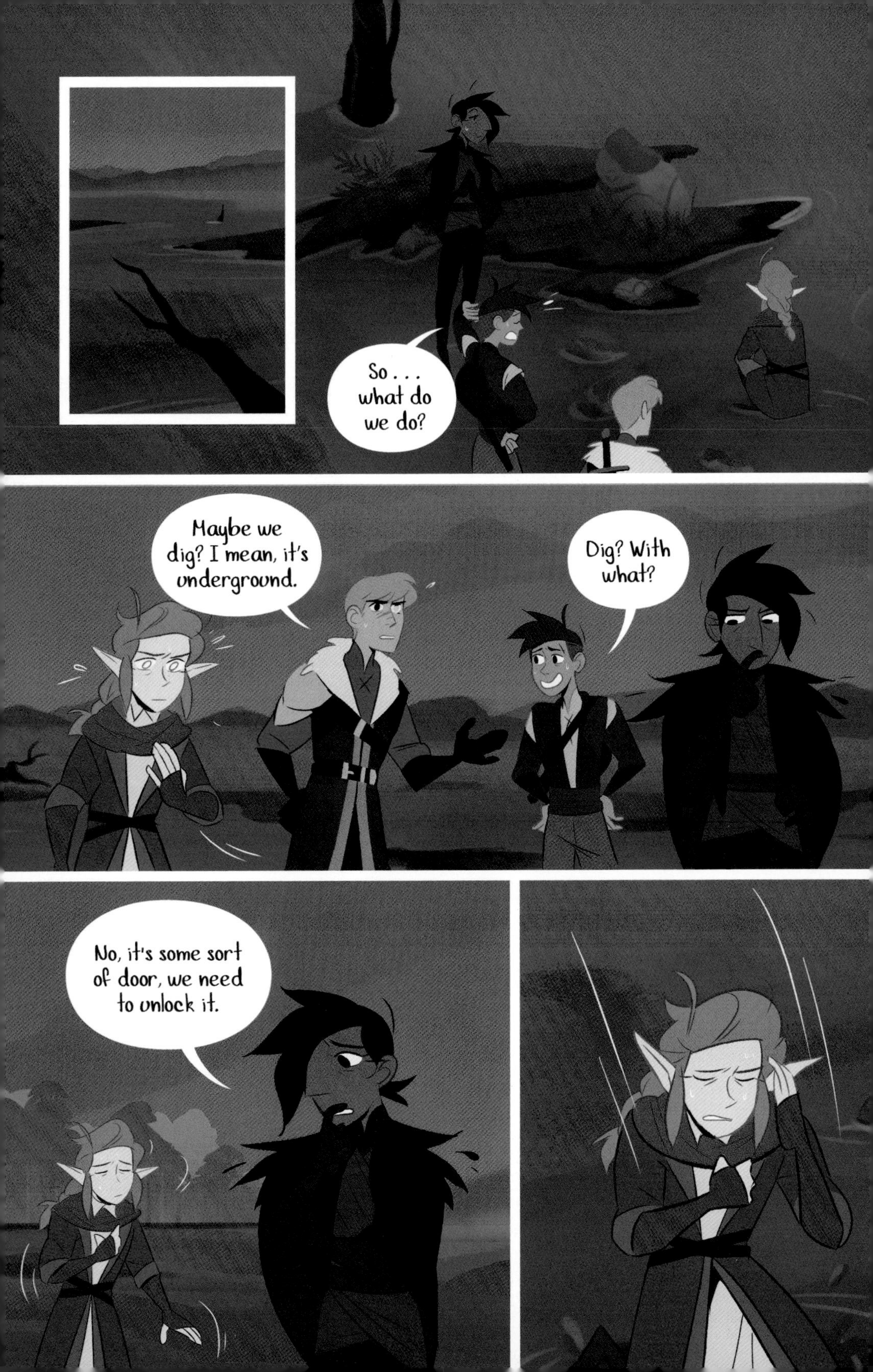
So . . . what do we do?
Maybe we dig? I mean, it's underground.
Dig? With what?
No, it's some sort of door, we need to unlock it.

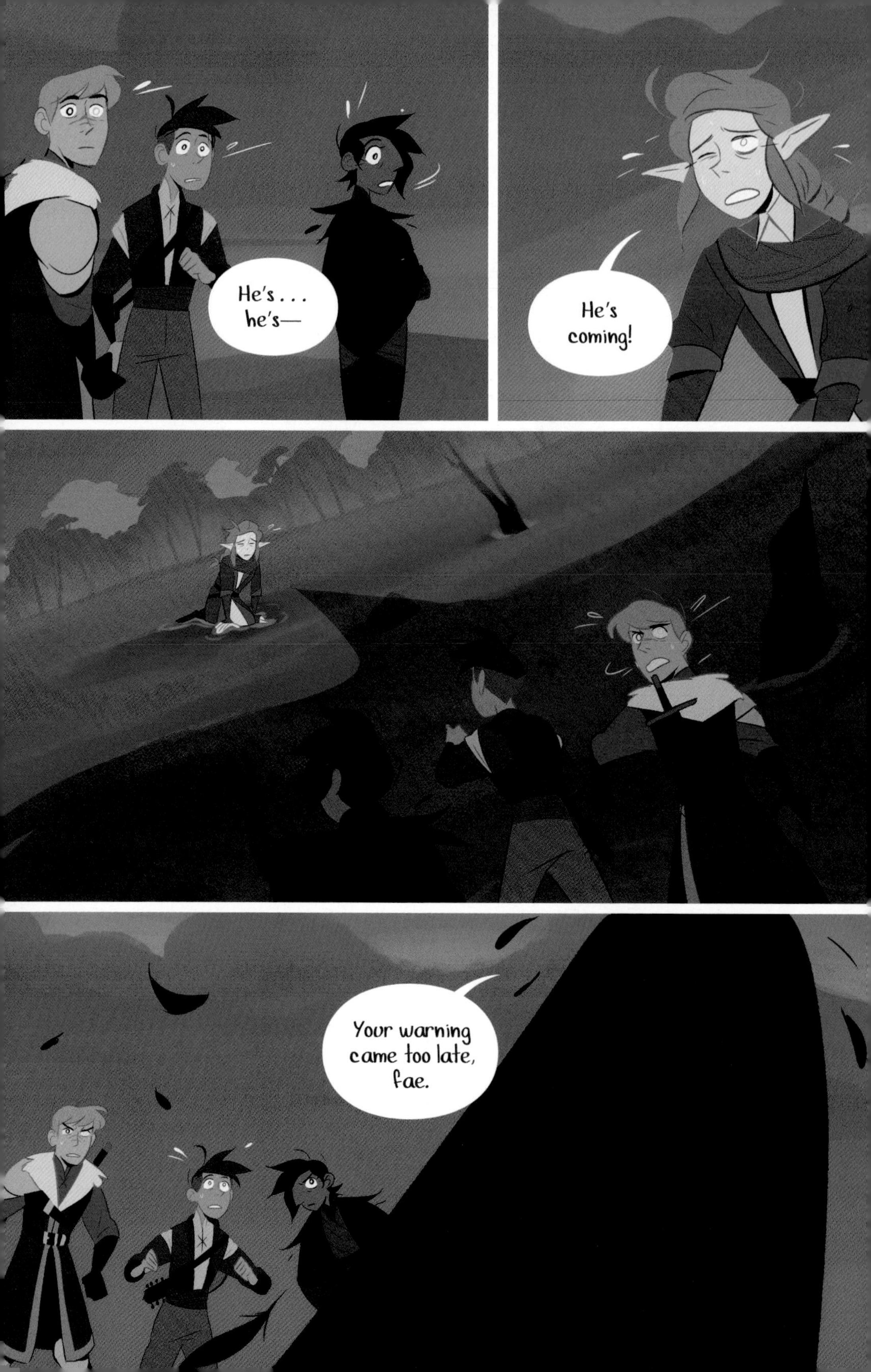
He's . . .
he's—
He's coming!
Your warning came too late, fae.

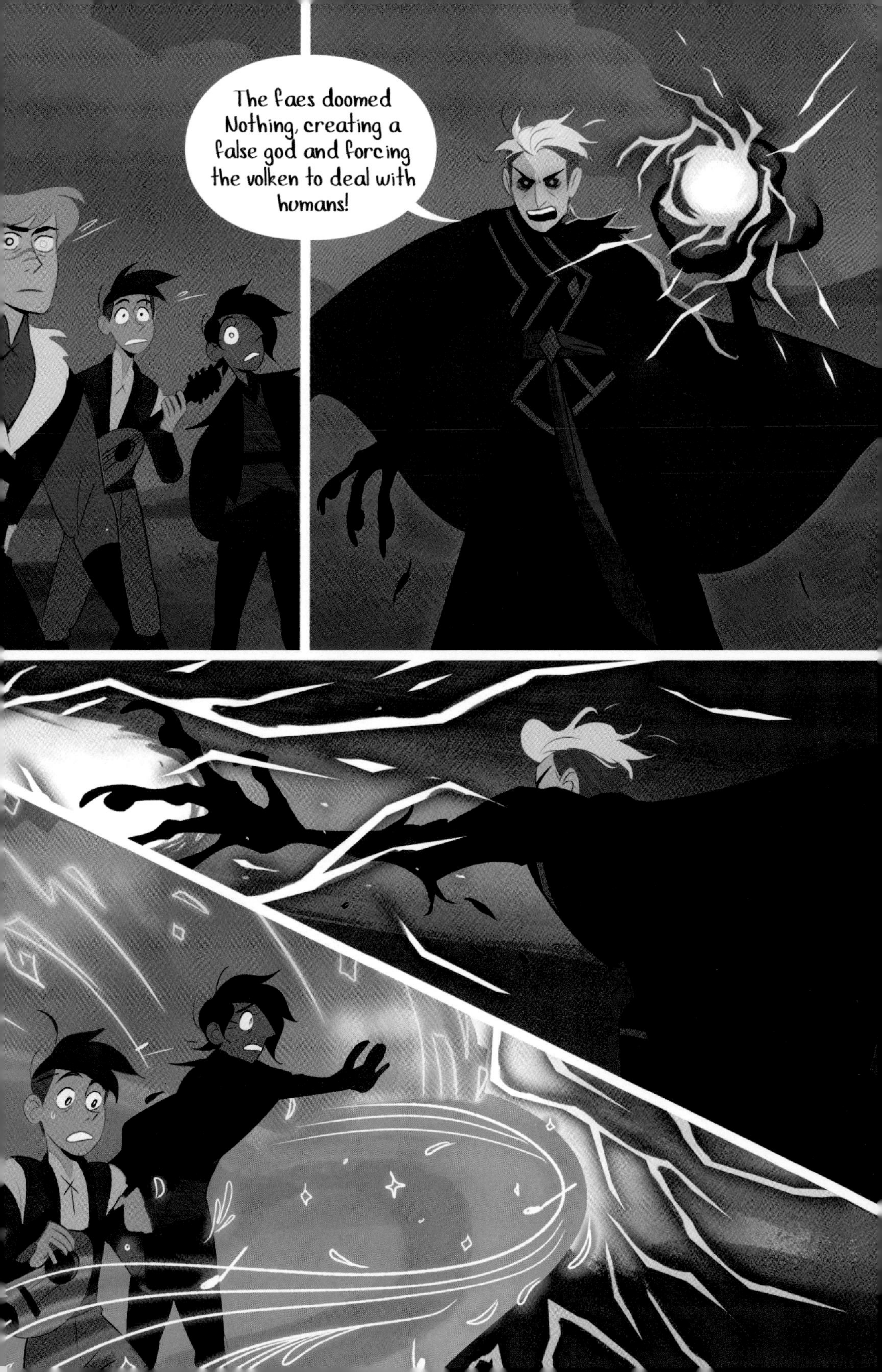
The faes doomed Nothing, creating a false god and forcing the volken to deal with humans!

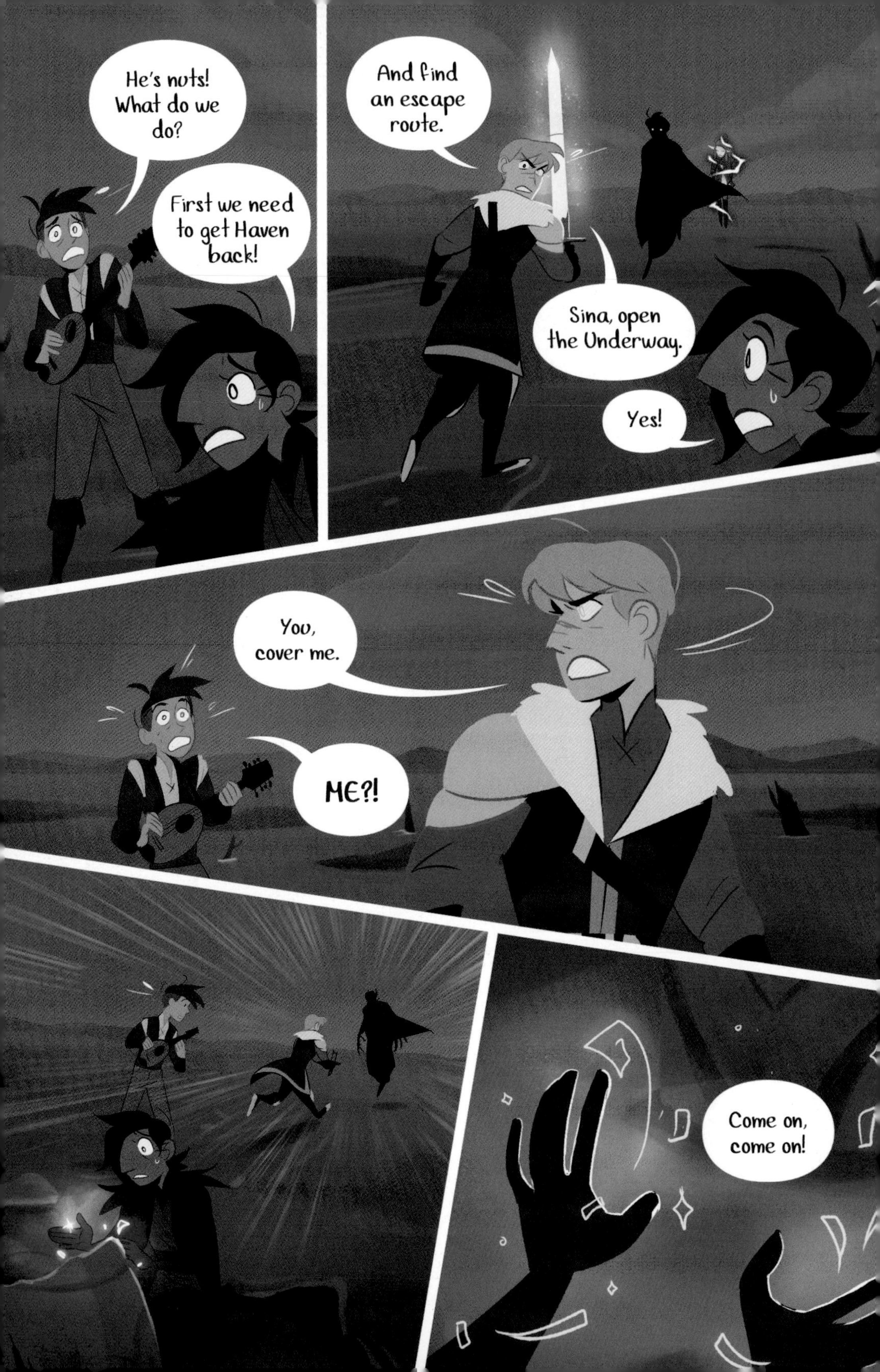
He's nuts! What do we do?
First we need to get Haven back!
And find an escape route.
Sina, open the Underway.
Yes!
You, cover me.
ME?!
Come on, come on!

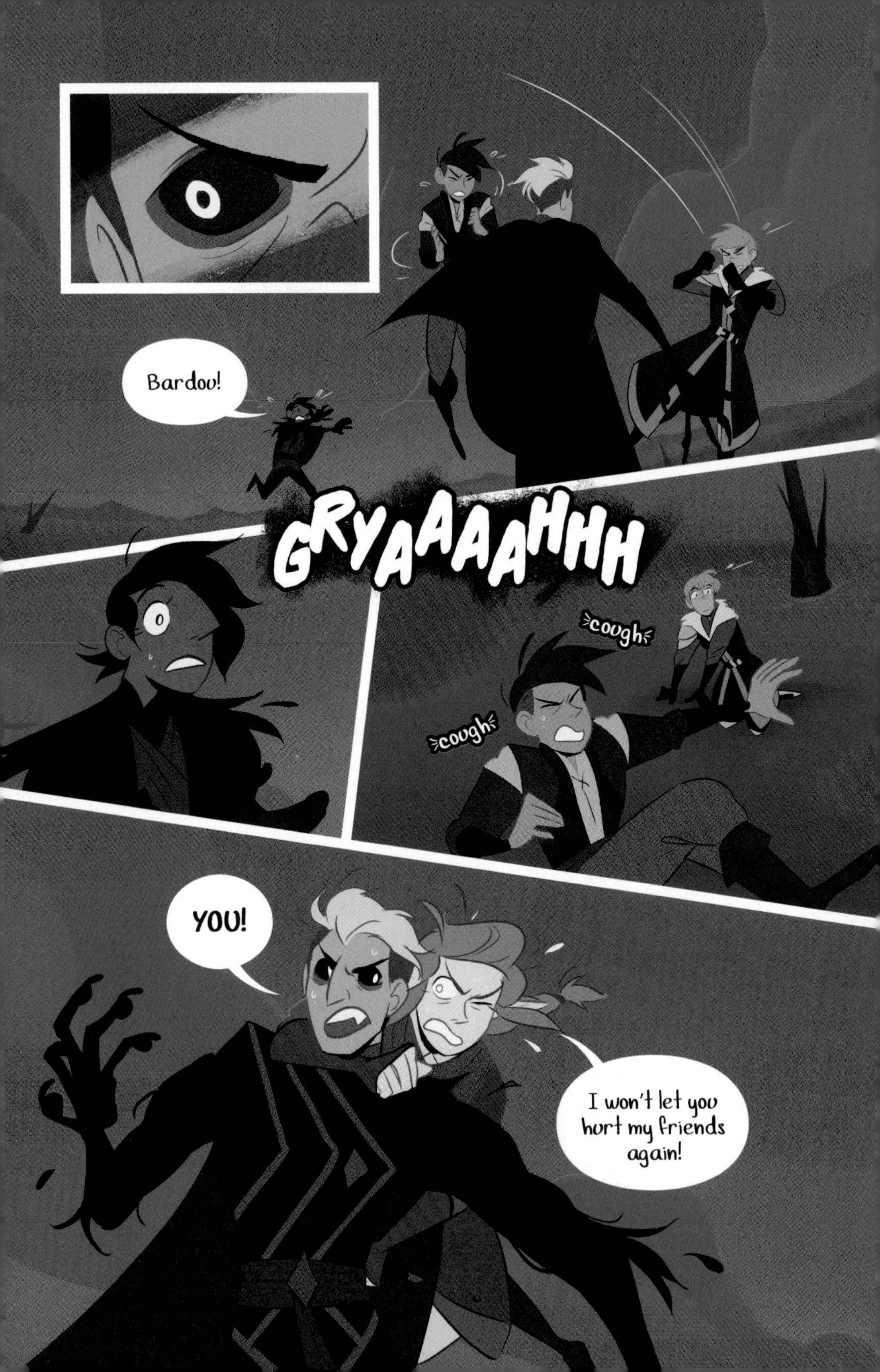
Bardou!
GRYAAAAHHH
cough
cough
YOU!
I won't let you hurt my friends again!

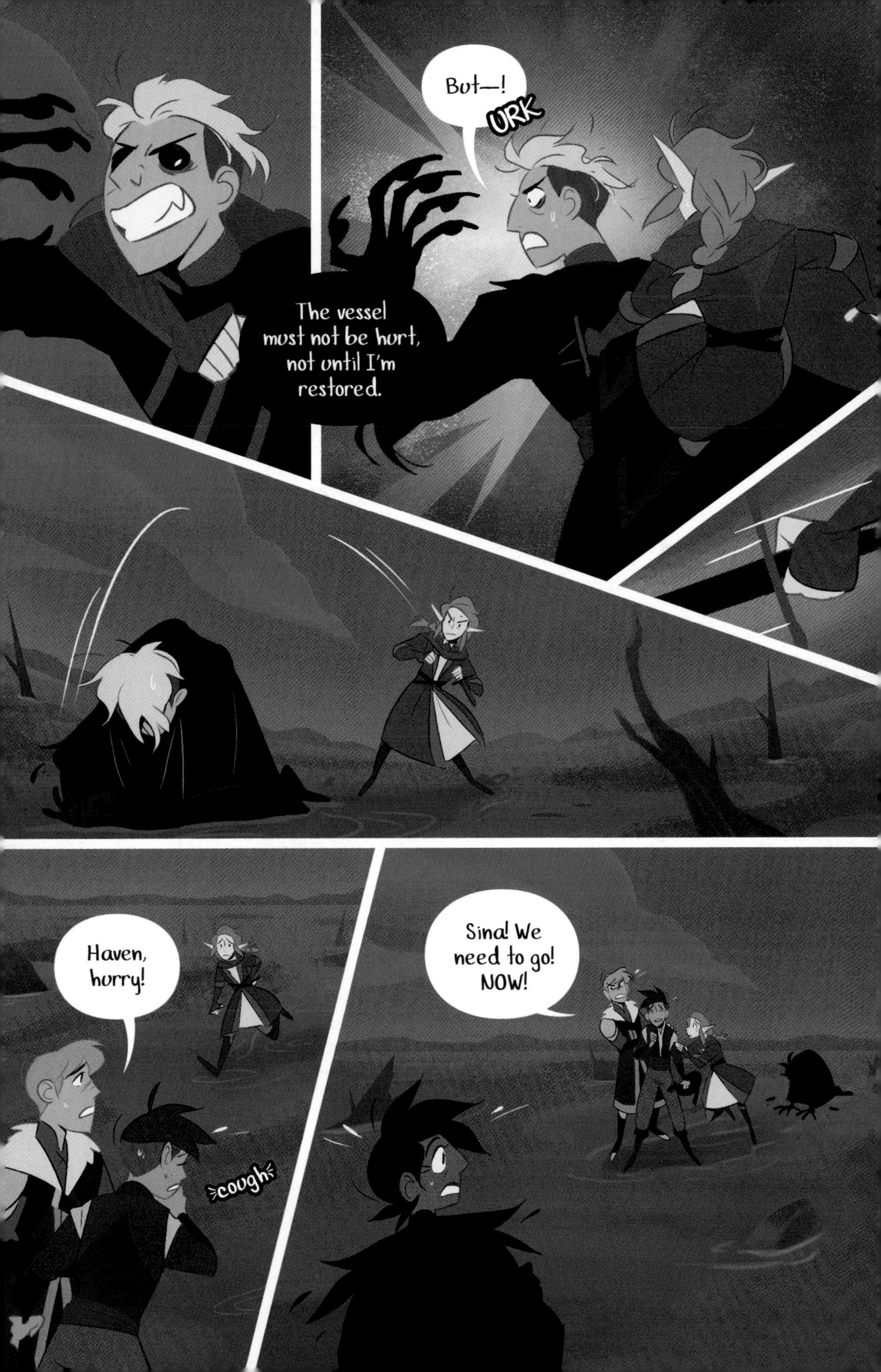
But—!
URK
The vessel must not be hurt, not until I'm restored.
Haven, hurry!
cough
Sina! We need to go! NOW!

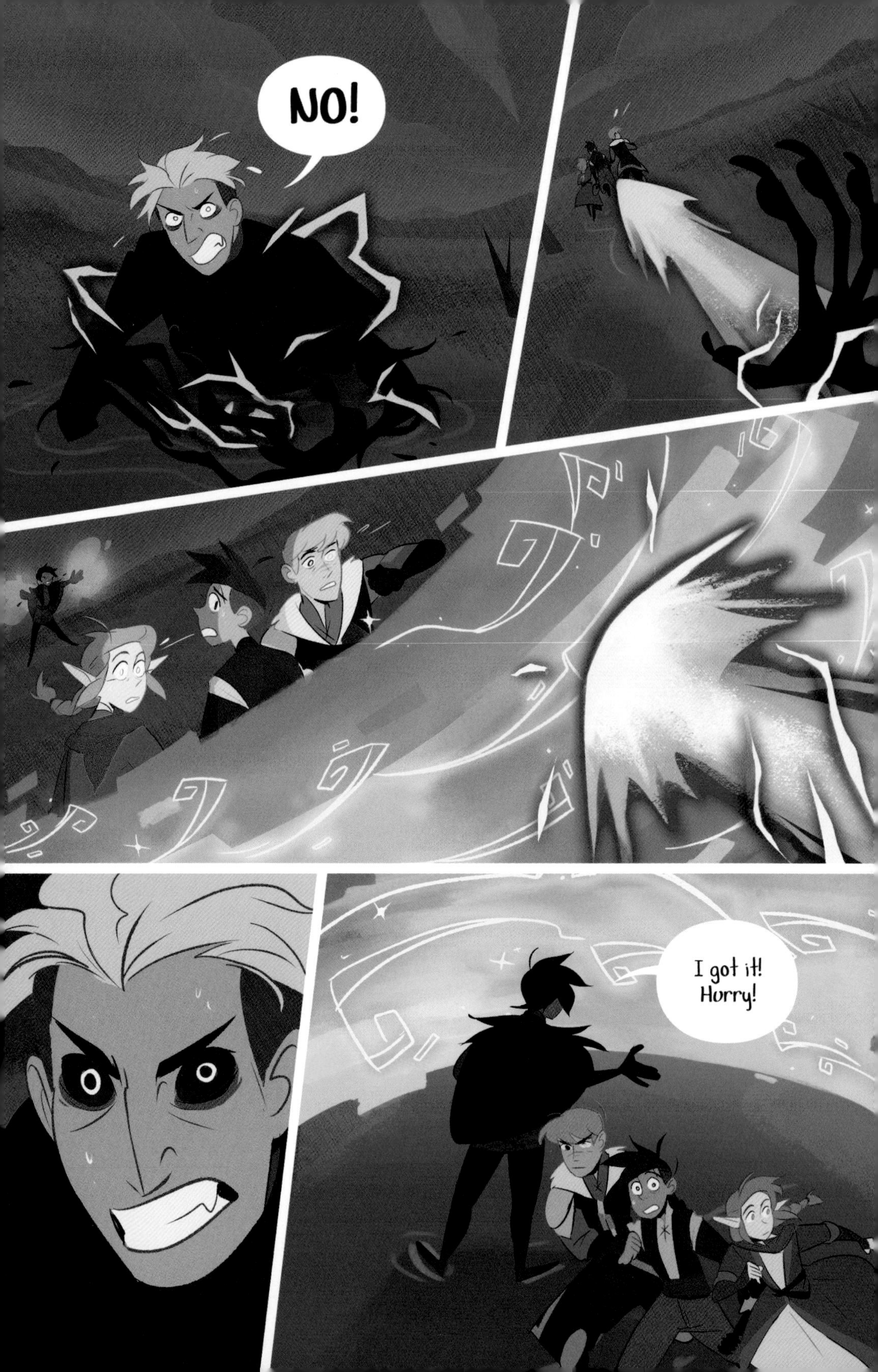
NO!
I got it! Horry!

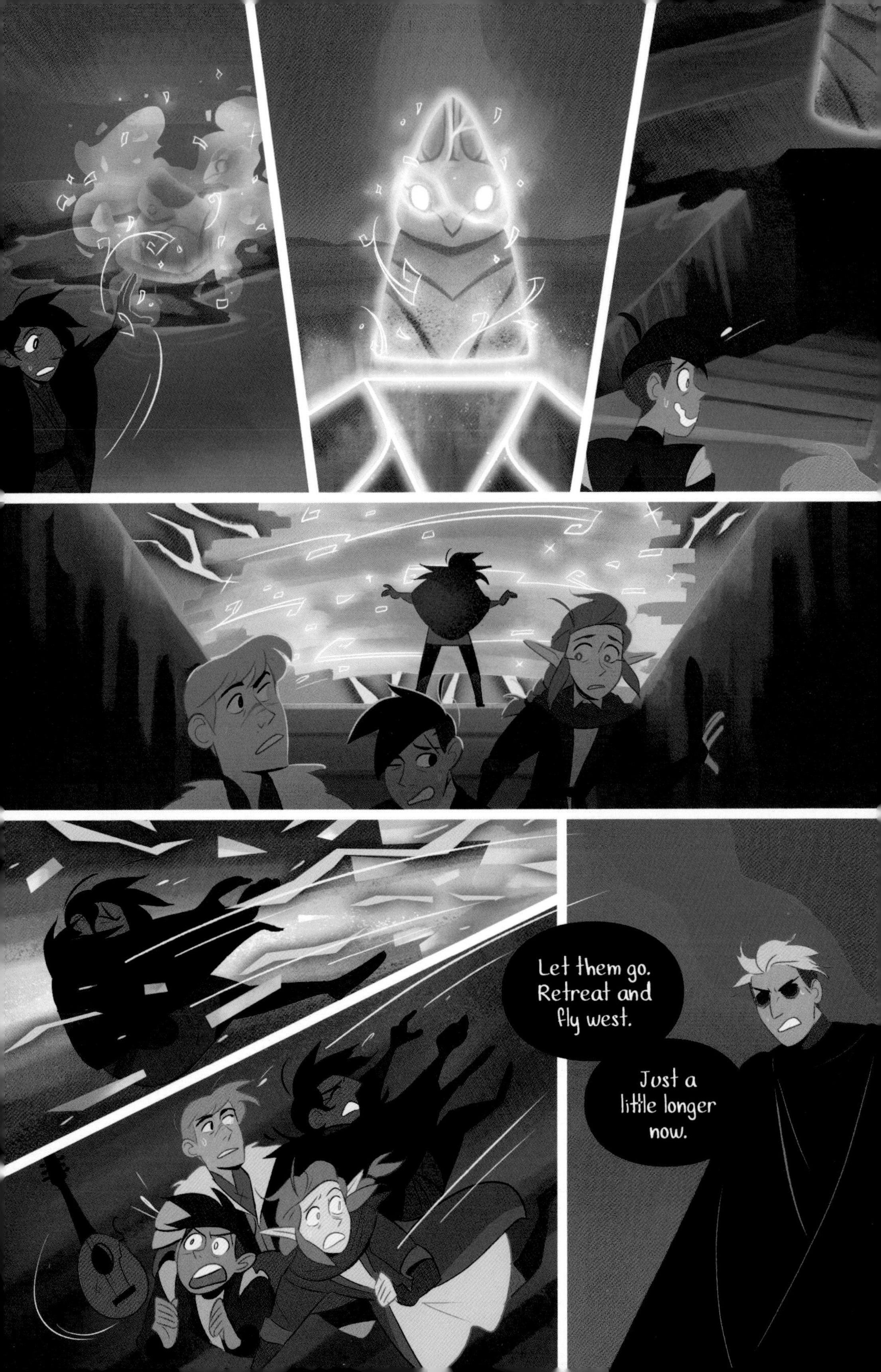
Let them go. Retreat and fly west.
Just a little longer now.

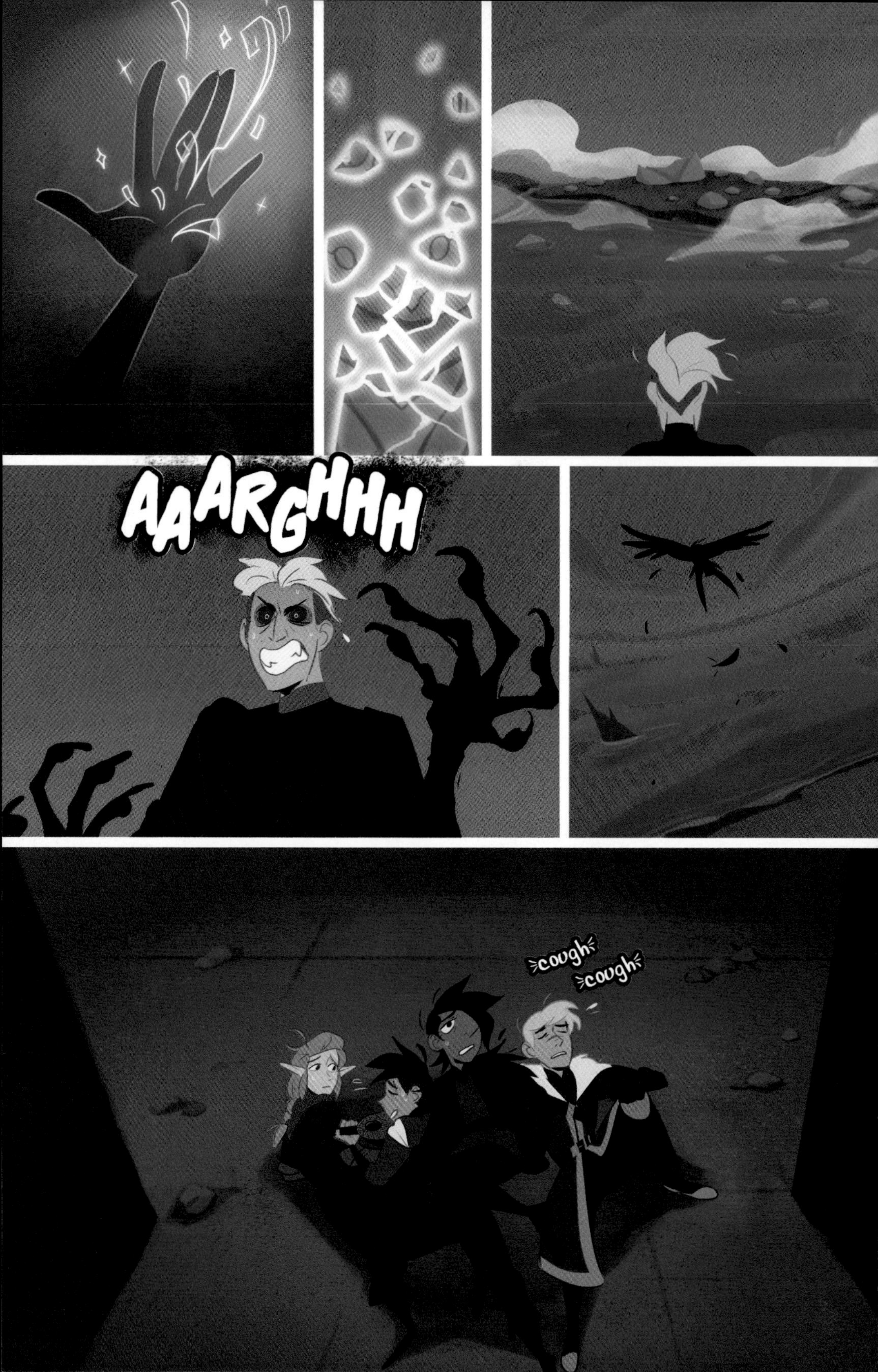
AAARGHHH
cough
cough

END OF CHAPTER 11

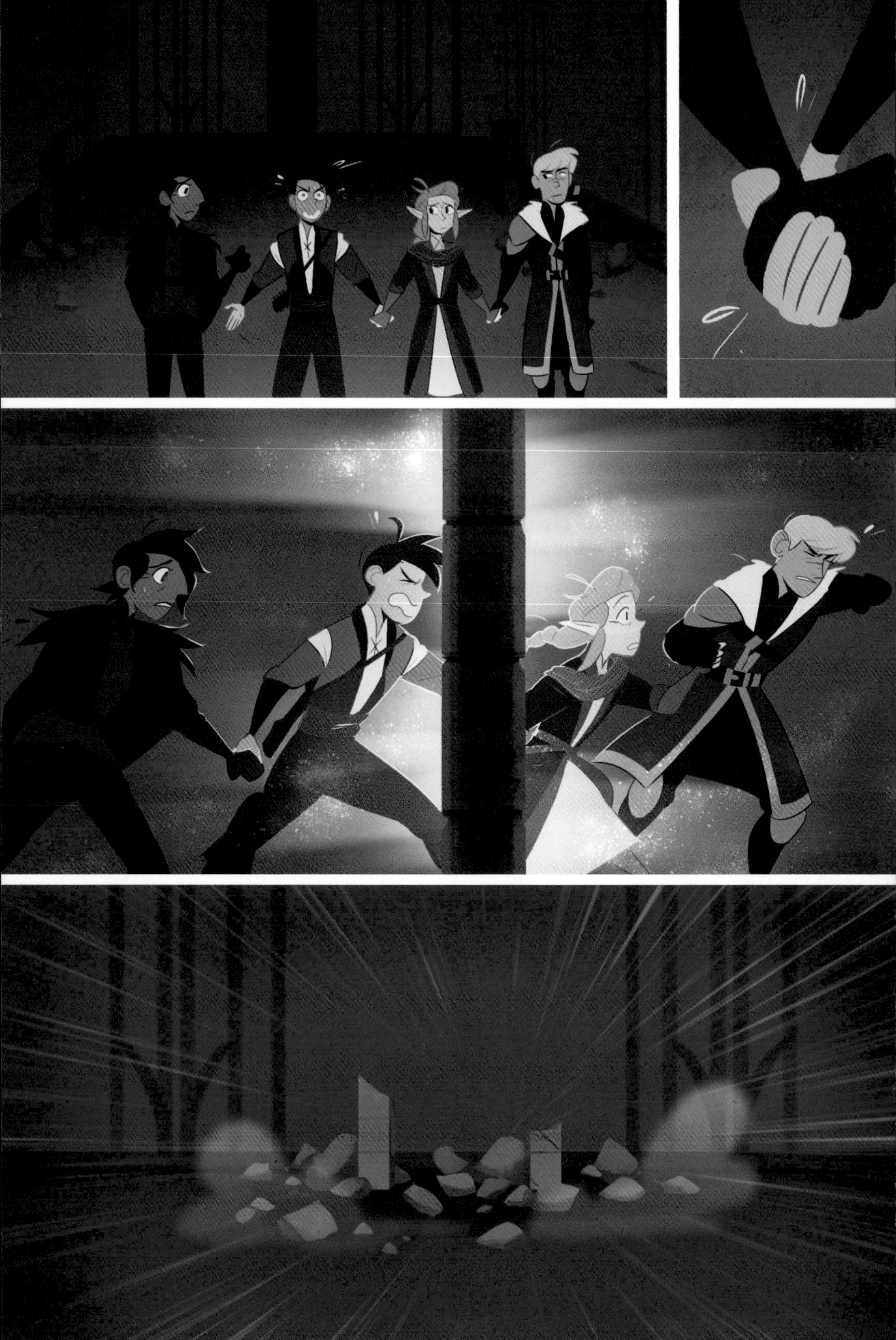

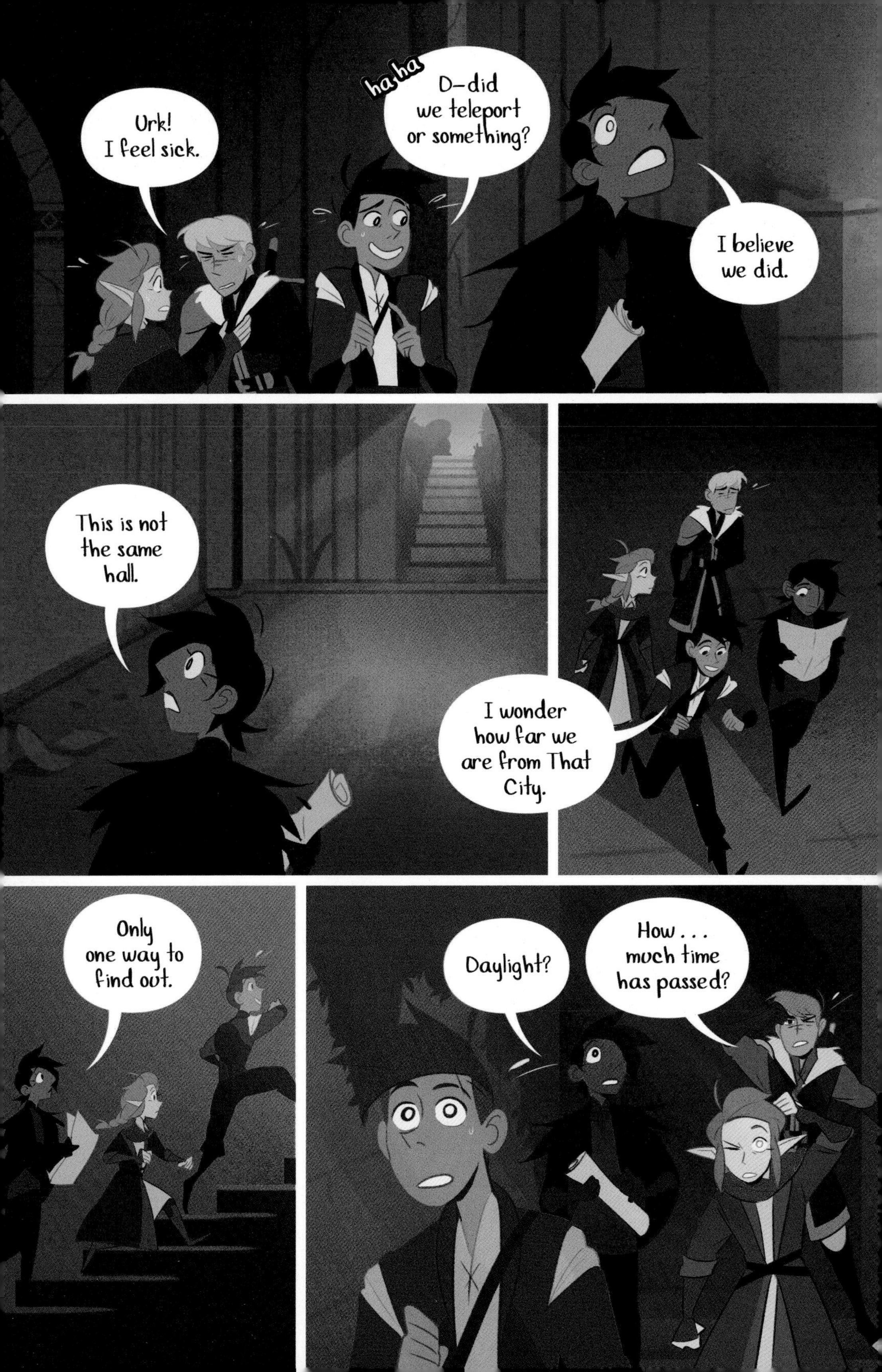
Urk!
I feel sick.
ha ha
D-did
we teleport
or something?
I believe
we did.
This is not
the same
hall.
I wonder
how far we
are from That
City.
Only
one way to
find out.
Daylight?
How . . .
much time
has passed?

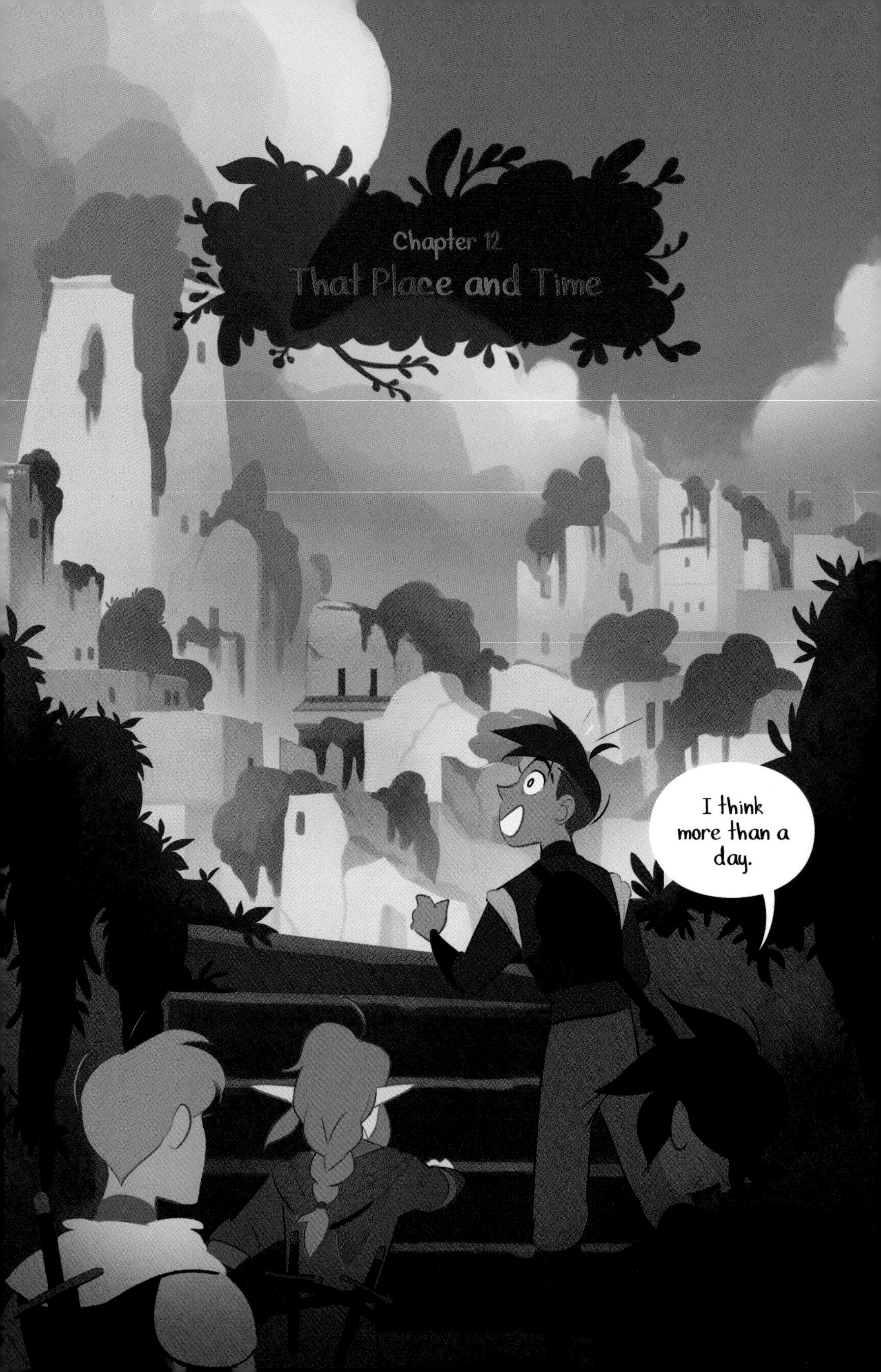
Chapter 12
That Place and Time
I think more than a day.

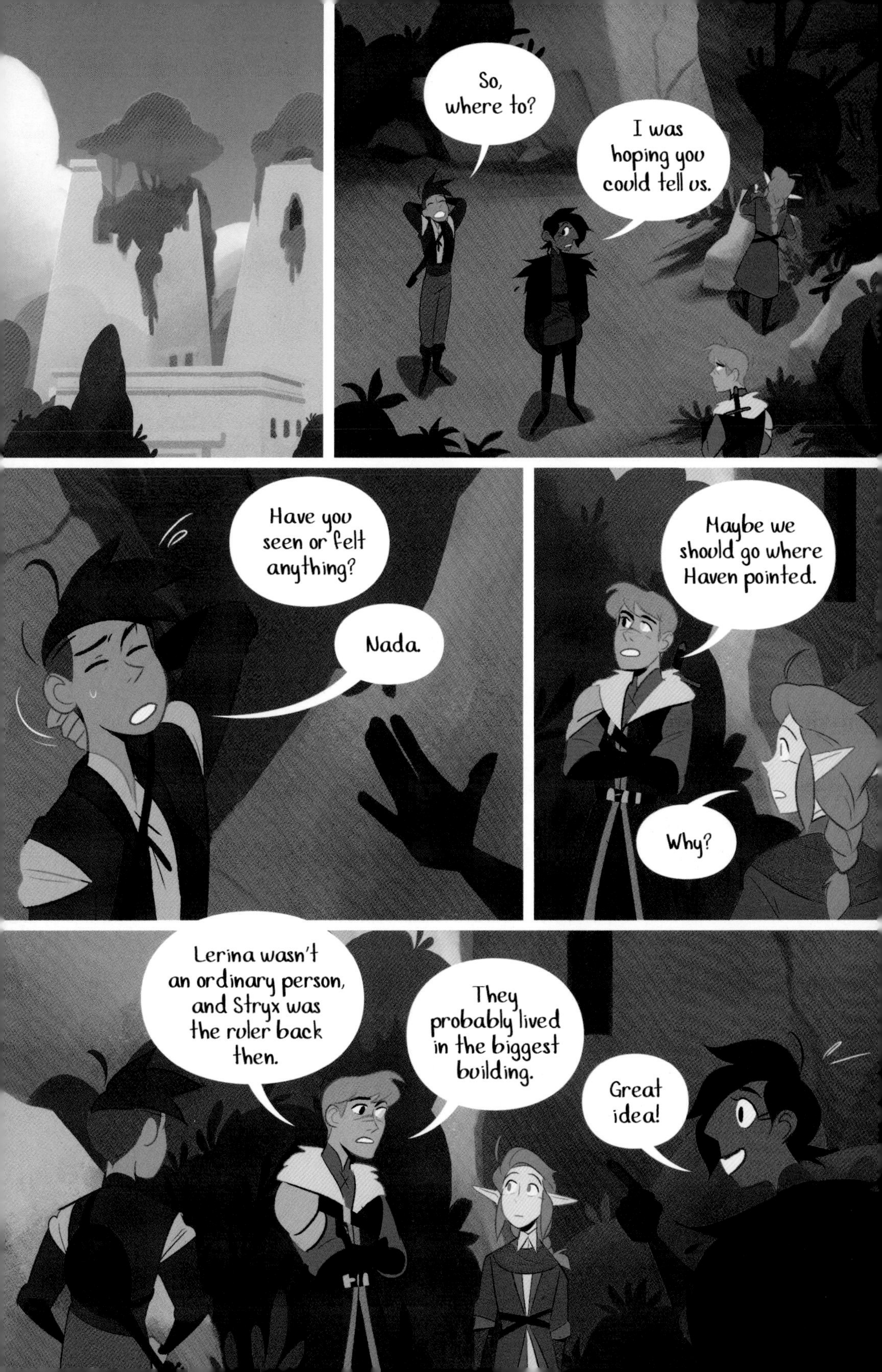
So, where to?
I was hoping you could tell us.
Have you seen or felt anything?
Nada.
Maybe we should go where Haven pointed.
Why?
Lerina wasn't an ordinary person, and Stryx was the ruler back then.
They probably lived in the biggest building.
Great idea!

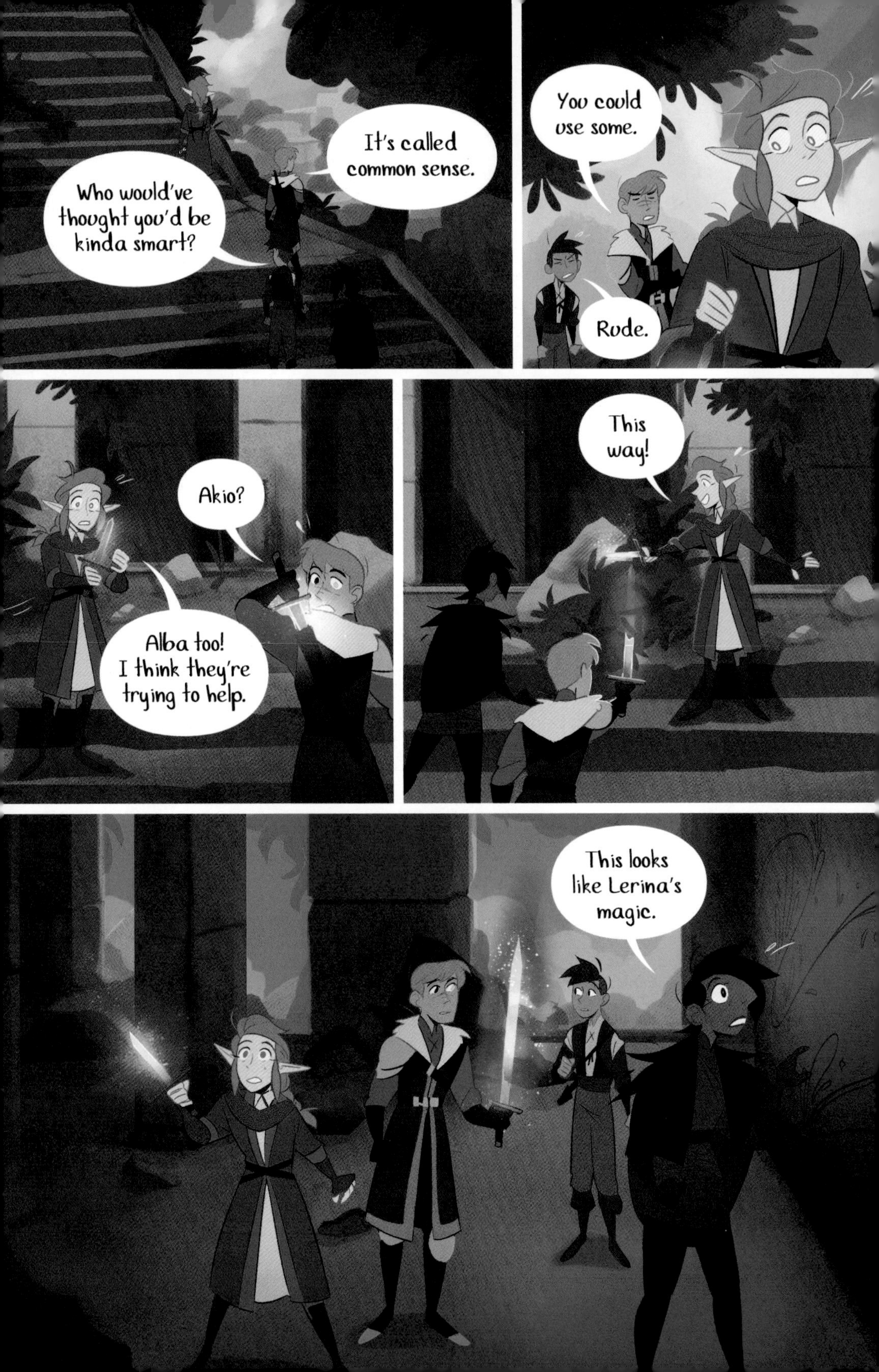
It's called common sense.
Who would've thought you'd be kinda smart?
You could use some.
Rude.
Akio?
Alba too! I think they're trying to help.
This way!
This looks like Lerina's magic.

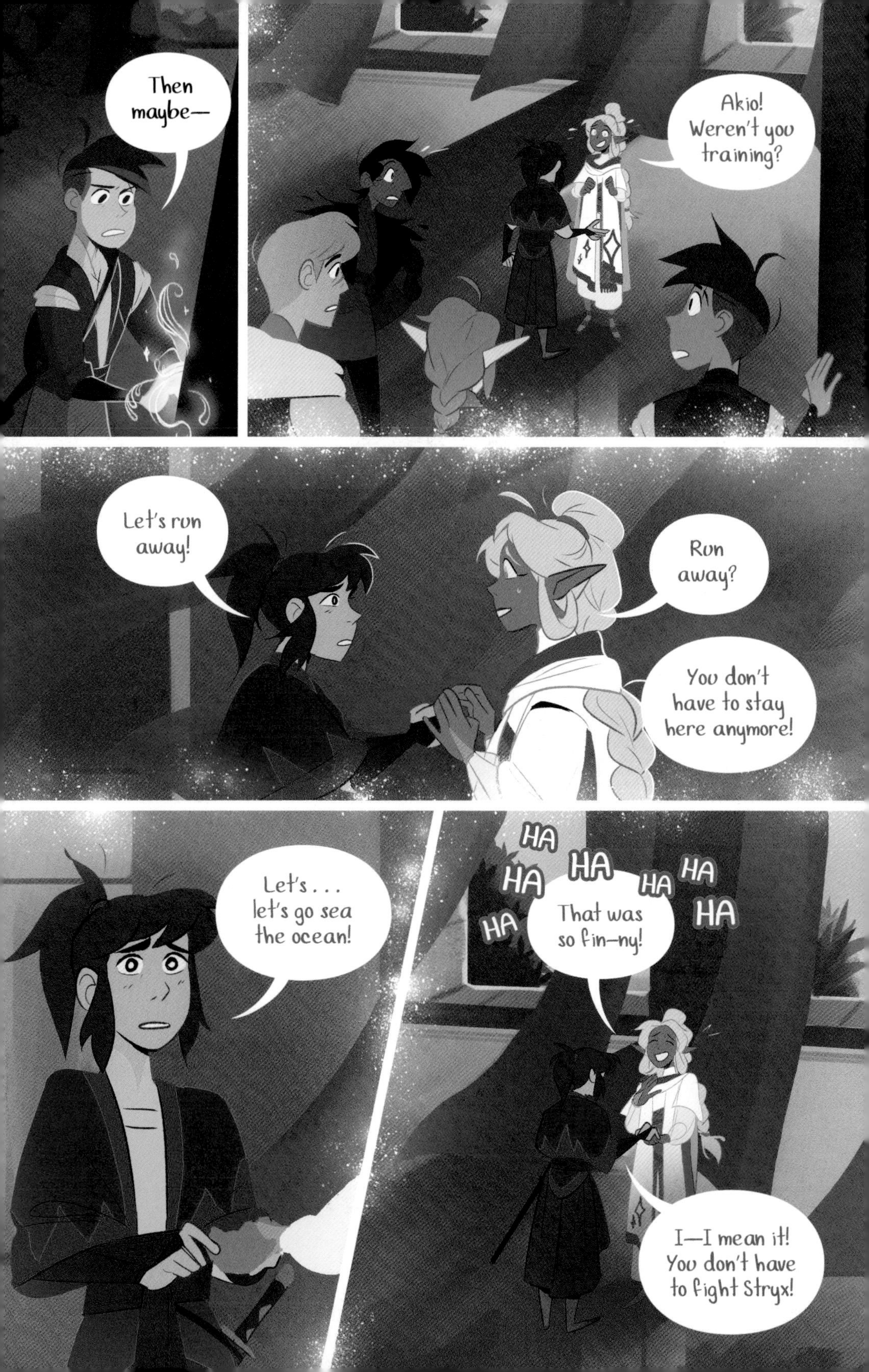

Then maybe—
Akio! Weren't you training?
Let's run away!
Run away?
You don't have to stay here anymore!
Let's . . . let's go sea the ocean!
HA HA HA HA HA HA HA
That was so fin—ny!
I—I mean it! You don't have to fight Stryx!

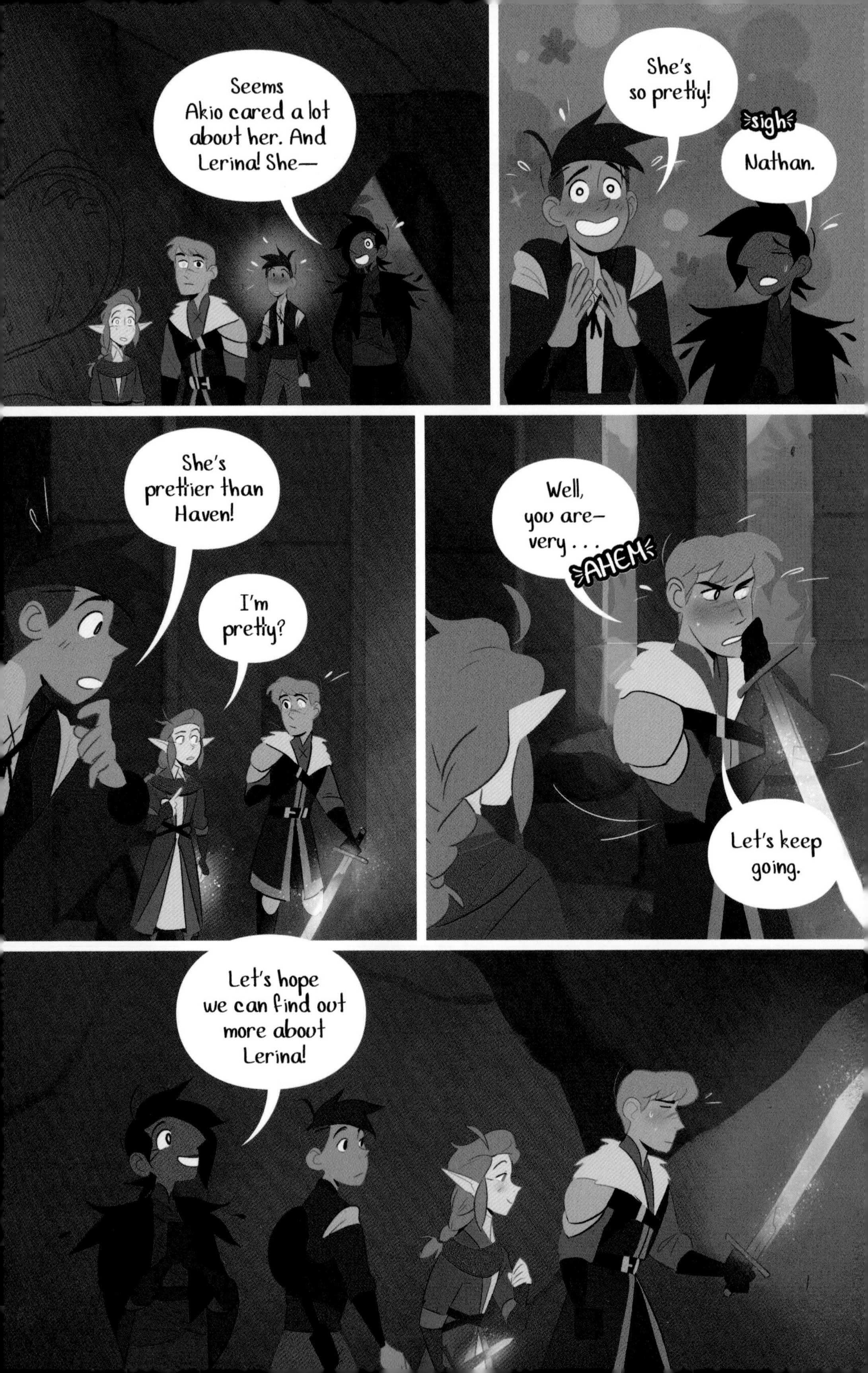
Seems Akio cared a lot about her. And Lerina! She—
She's so pretty!
sigh
Nathan.
She's prettier than Haven!
I'm pretty?
Well, you are— very . . .
AHEM
Let's keep going.
Let's hope we can find out more about Lerina!

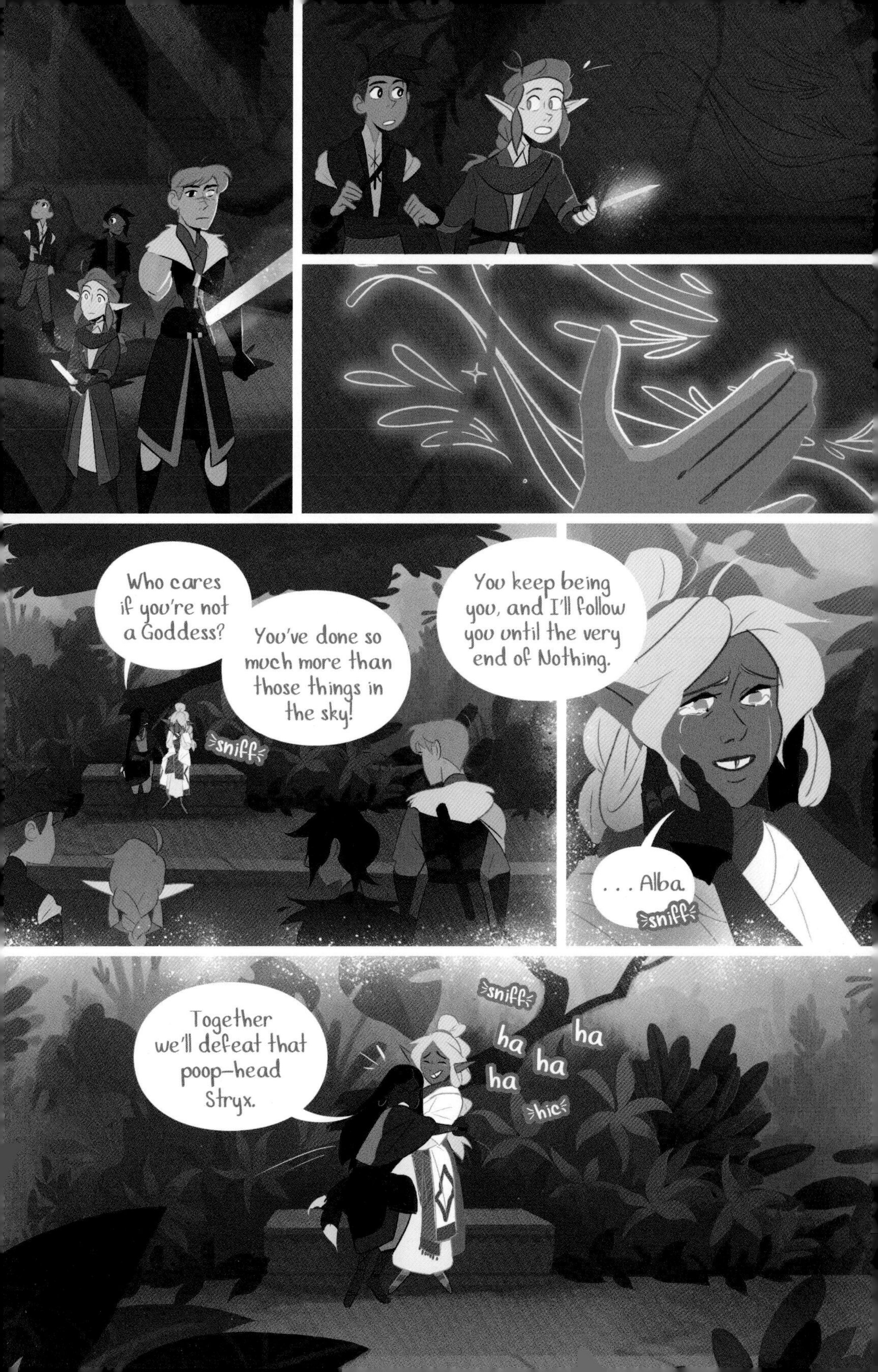
Who cares if you're not a Goddess?
You've done so much more than those things in the sky!
sniff
You keep being you, and I'll follow you until the very end of Nothing.
. . . Alba.
sniff
Together we'll defeat that poop-head Stryx.
sniff
ha
ha
ha
ha
hic

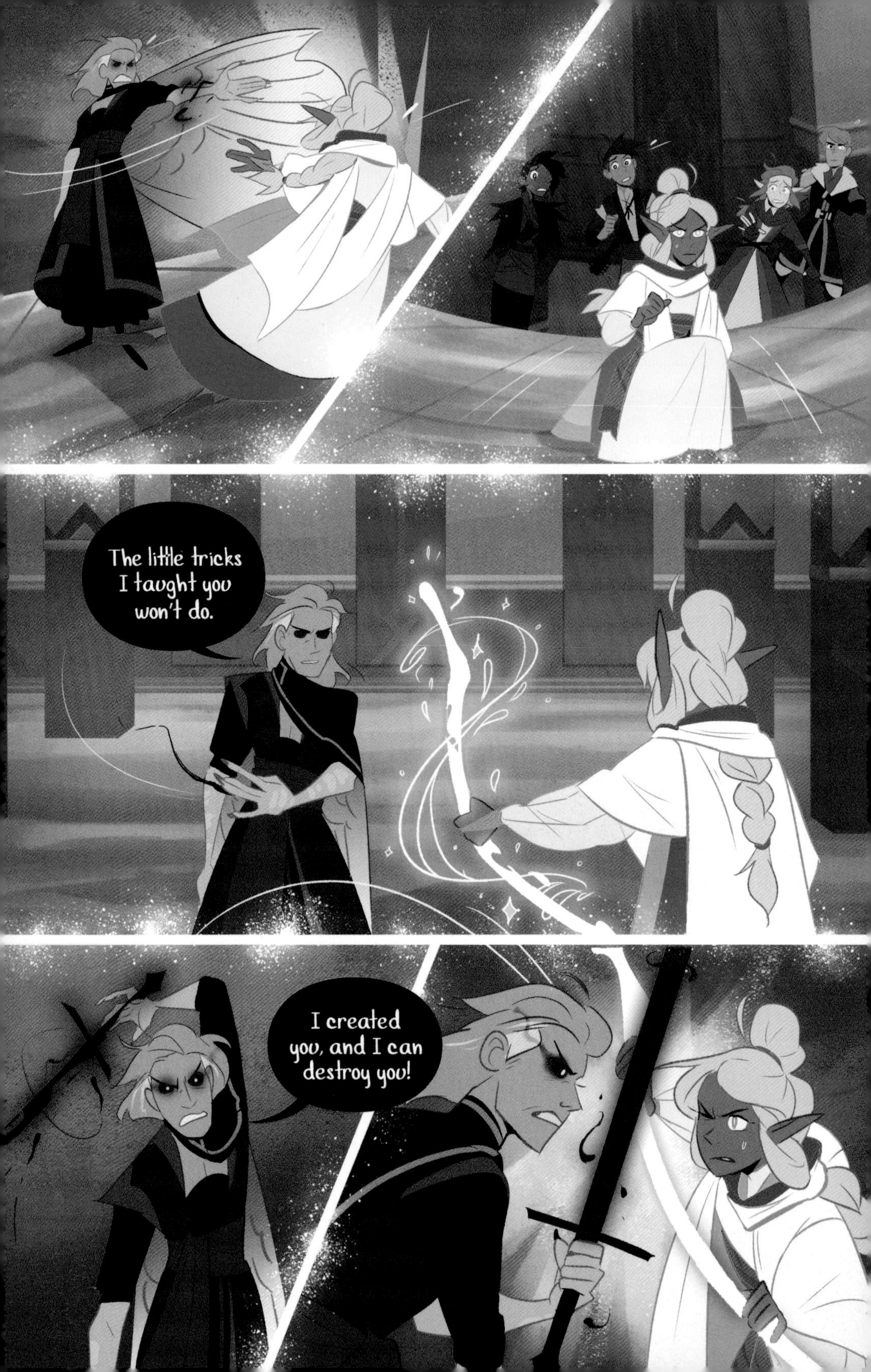
The little tricks I taught you won't do.
I created you, and I can destroy you!

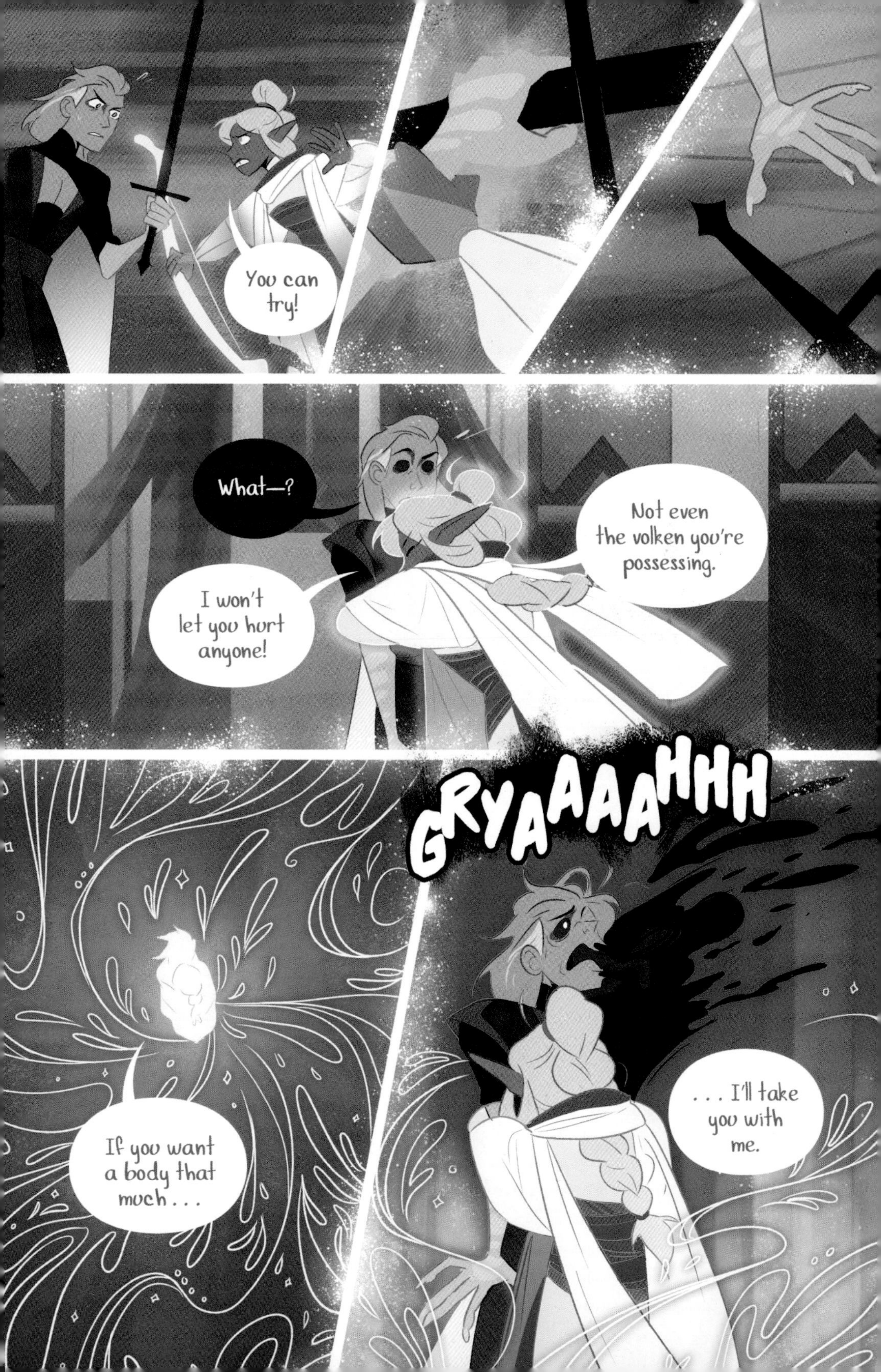
You can try!
What—?
Not even the volken you're possessing.
I won't let you hurt anyone!
GRYAAAAAHHH
If you want a body that much . . .
. . . I'll take you with me.

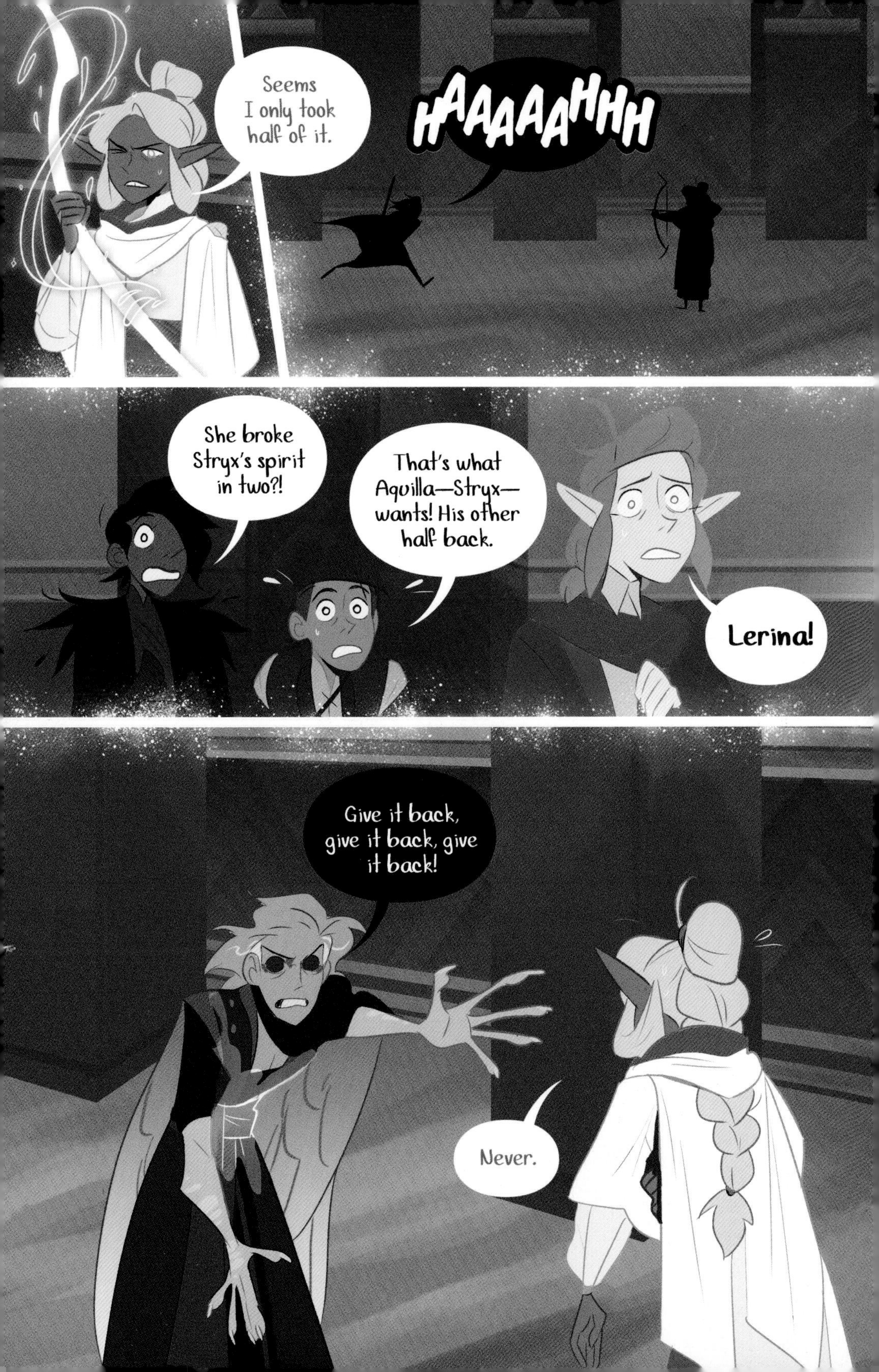
Seems I only took half of it.
HAAAAAHHH
She broke Stryx's spirit in two?!
That's what Aquilla—Stryx—wants! His other half back.
Lerina!
Give it back, give it back, give it back!
Never.

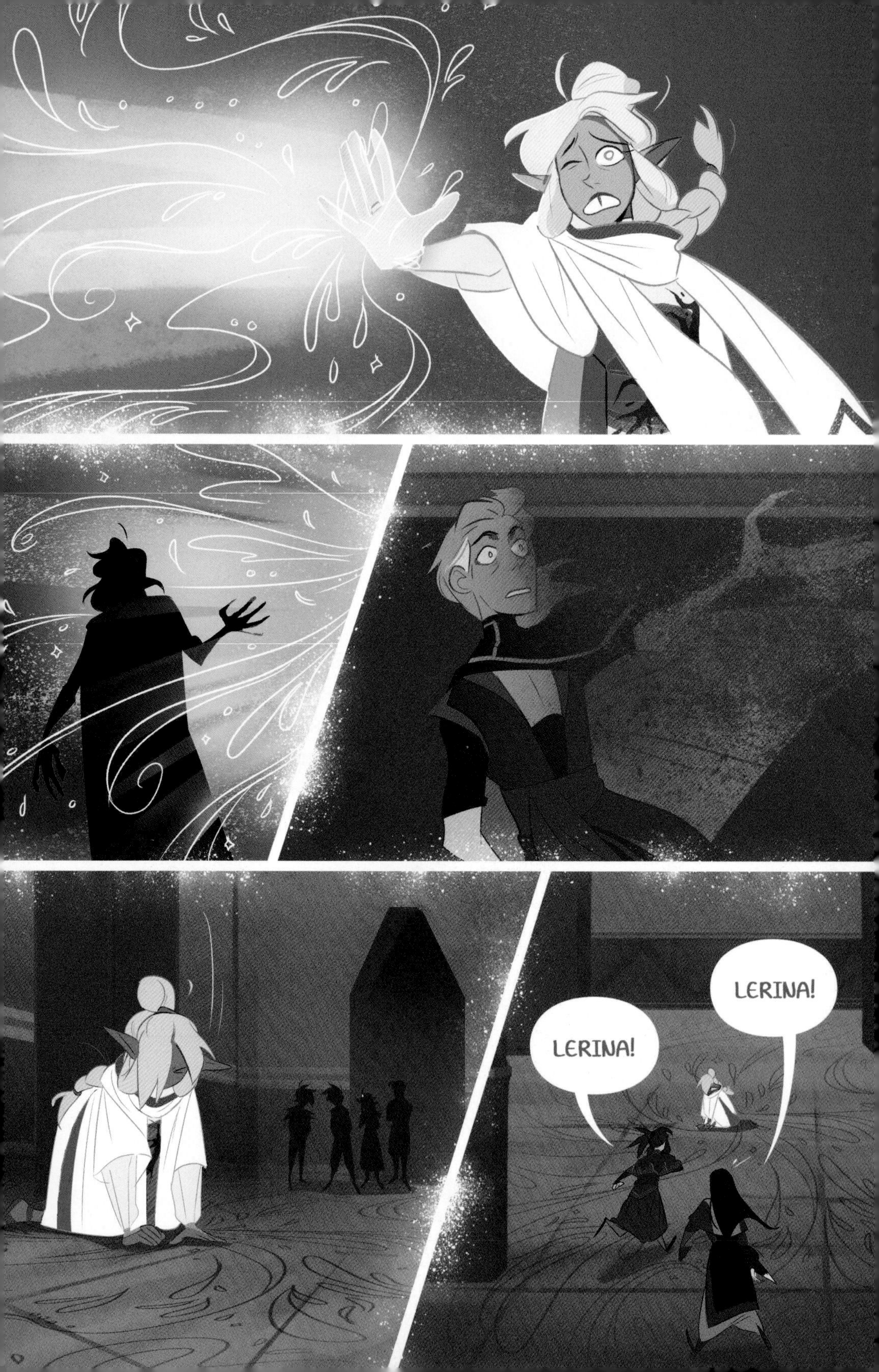
LERINA!
LERINA!

END OF CHAPTER 12

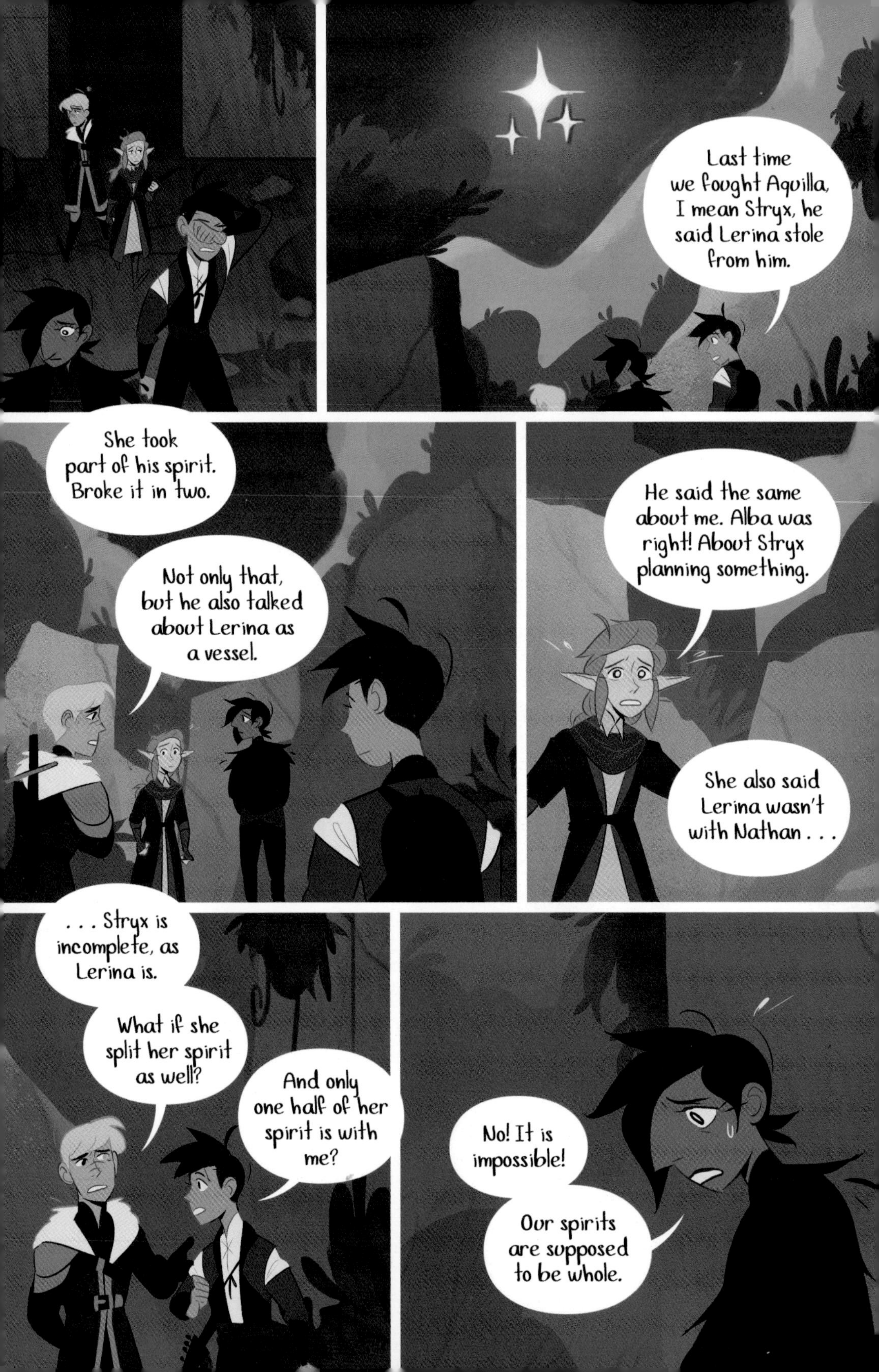
Last time we fought Aquilla, I mean Stryx, he said Lerina stole from him.
She took part of his spirit. Broke it in two.
Not only that, but he also talked about Lerina as a vessel.
He said the same about me. Alba was right! About Stryx planning something.
She also said Lerina wasn't with Nathan . . .
. . . Stryx is incomplete, as Lerina is.
What if she split her spirit as well?
And only one half of her spirit is with me?
No! It is impossible!
Our spirits are supposed to be whole.

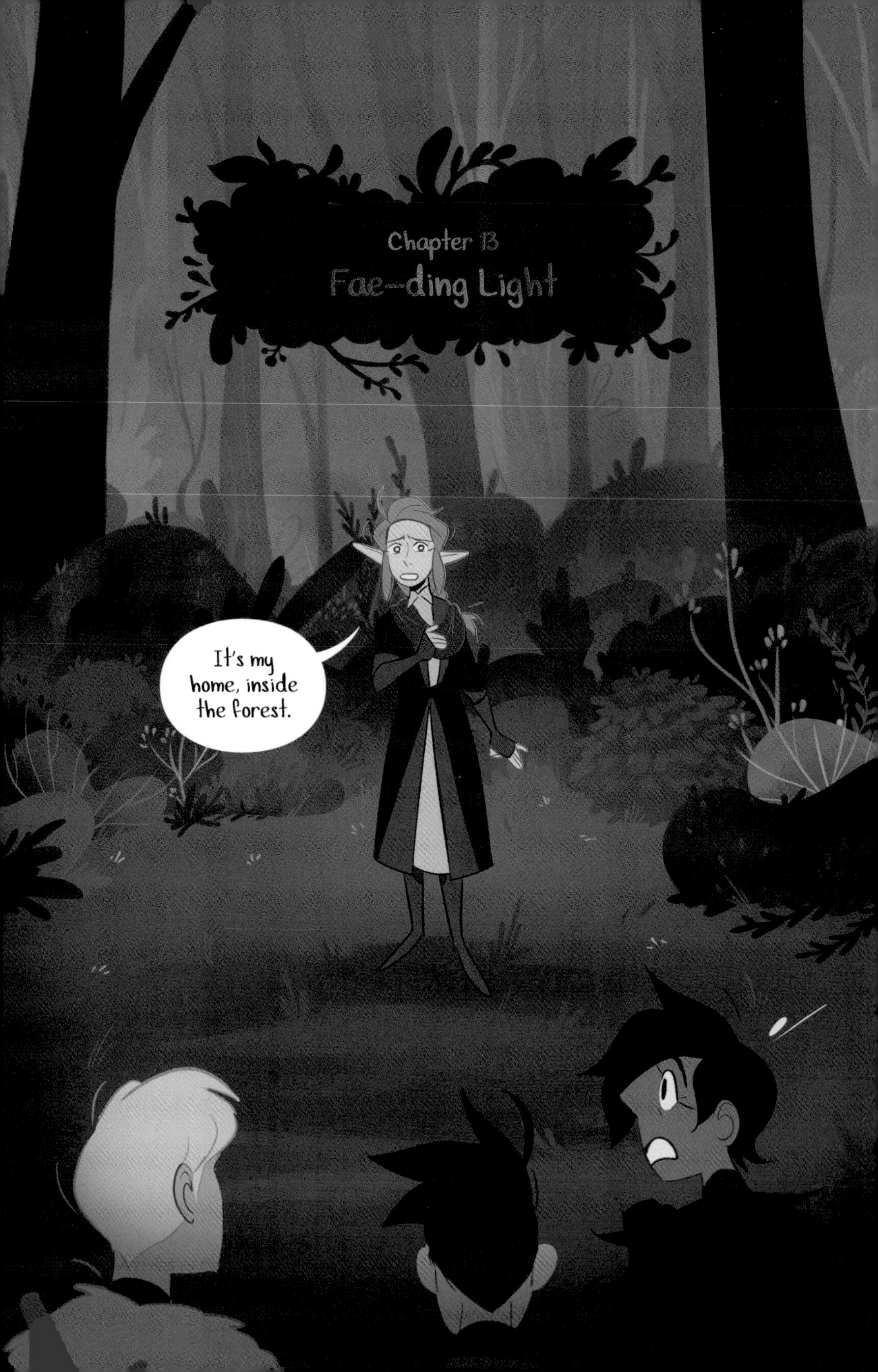
Chapter 13
Fae-ding Light
It's my home, inside the forest.

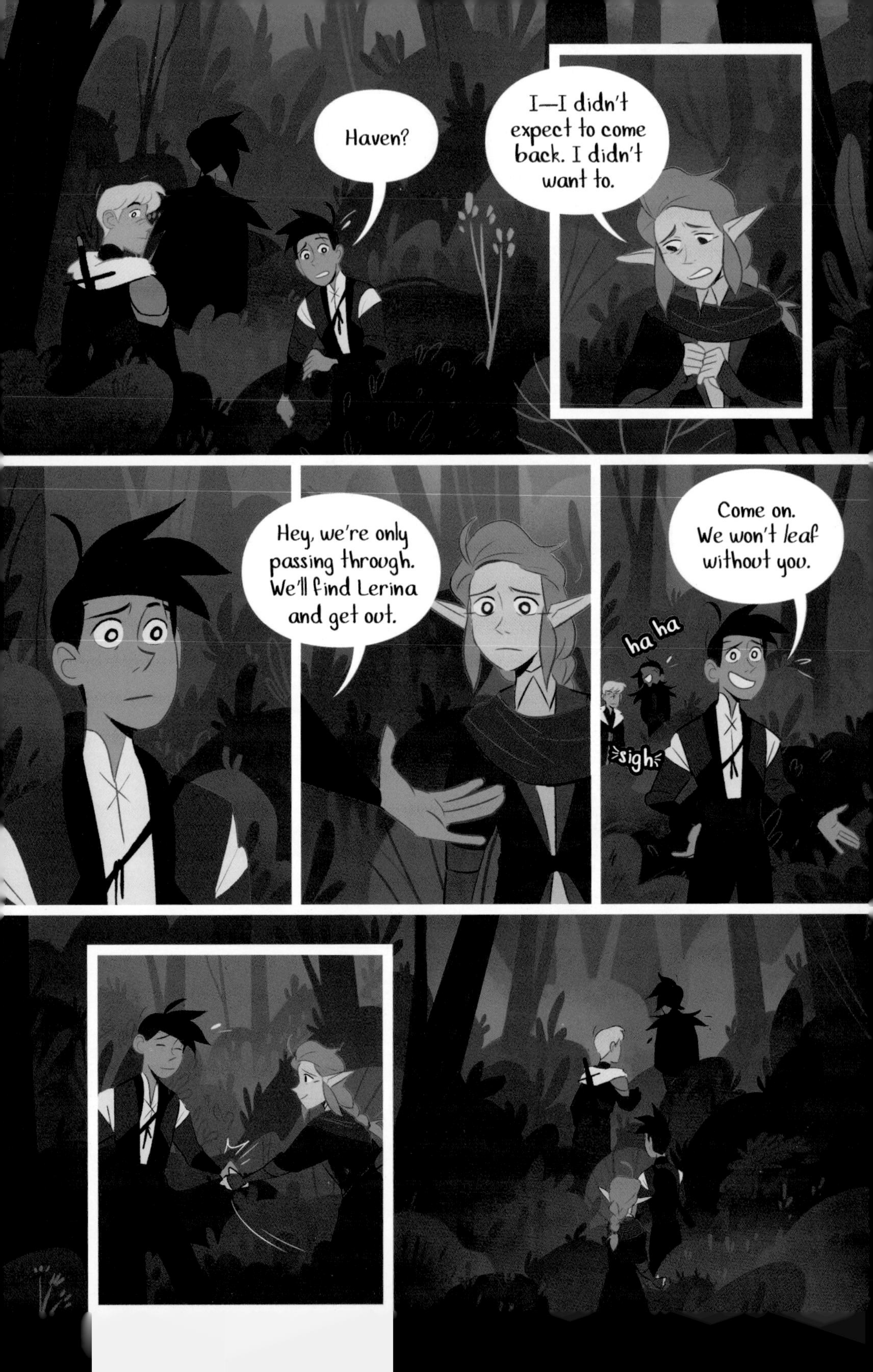
Haven?
I—I didn't expect to come back. I didn't want to.
Hey, we're only passing through. We'll find Lerina and get out.
Come on. We won't *leaf* without you.
ha ha
sigh

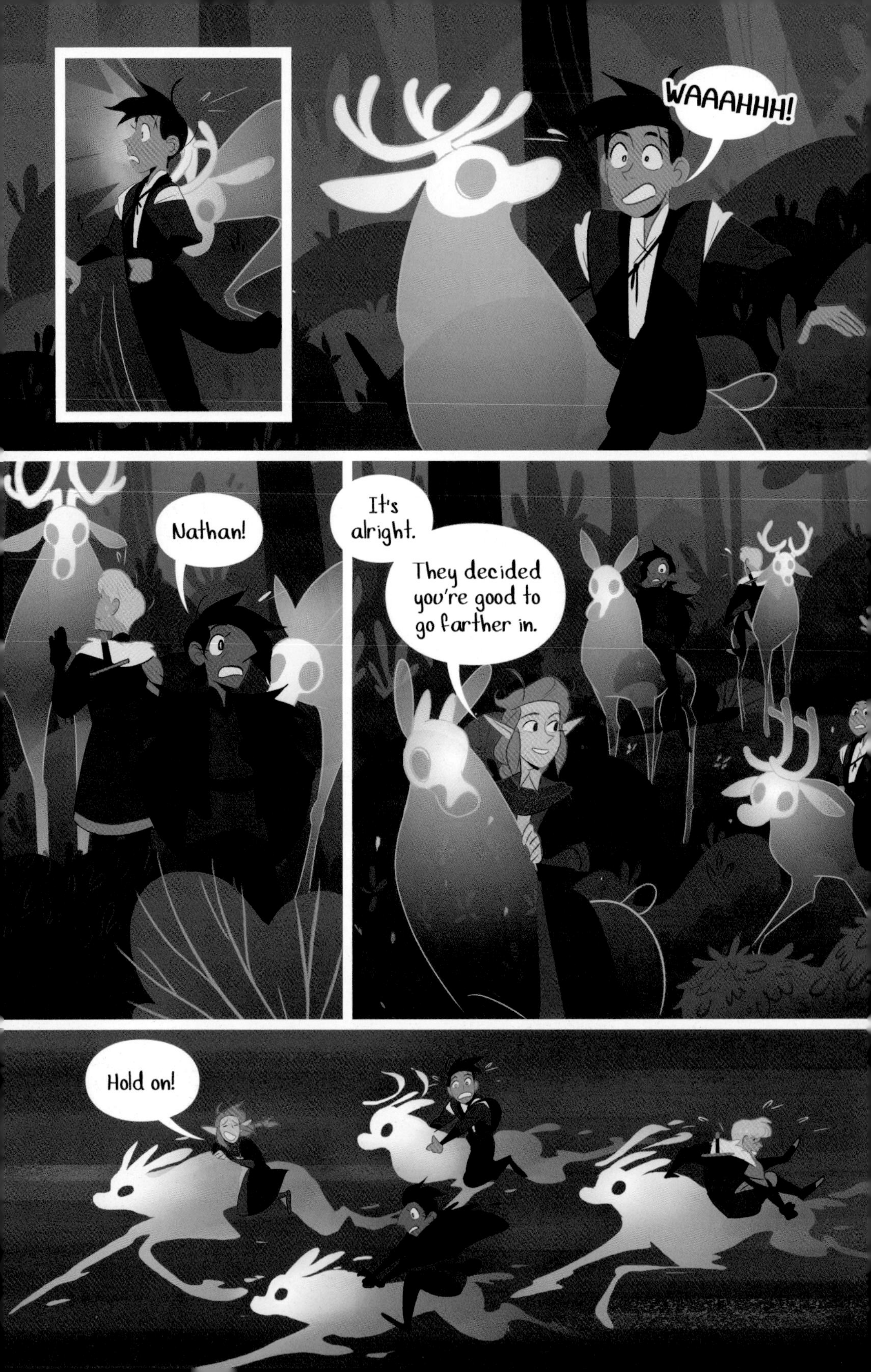
WAAAHHH!
Nathan!
It's alright.
They decided you're good to go farther in.
Hold on!

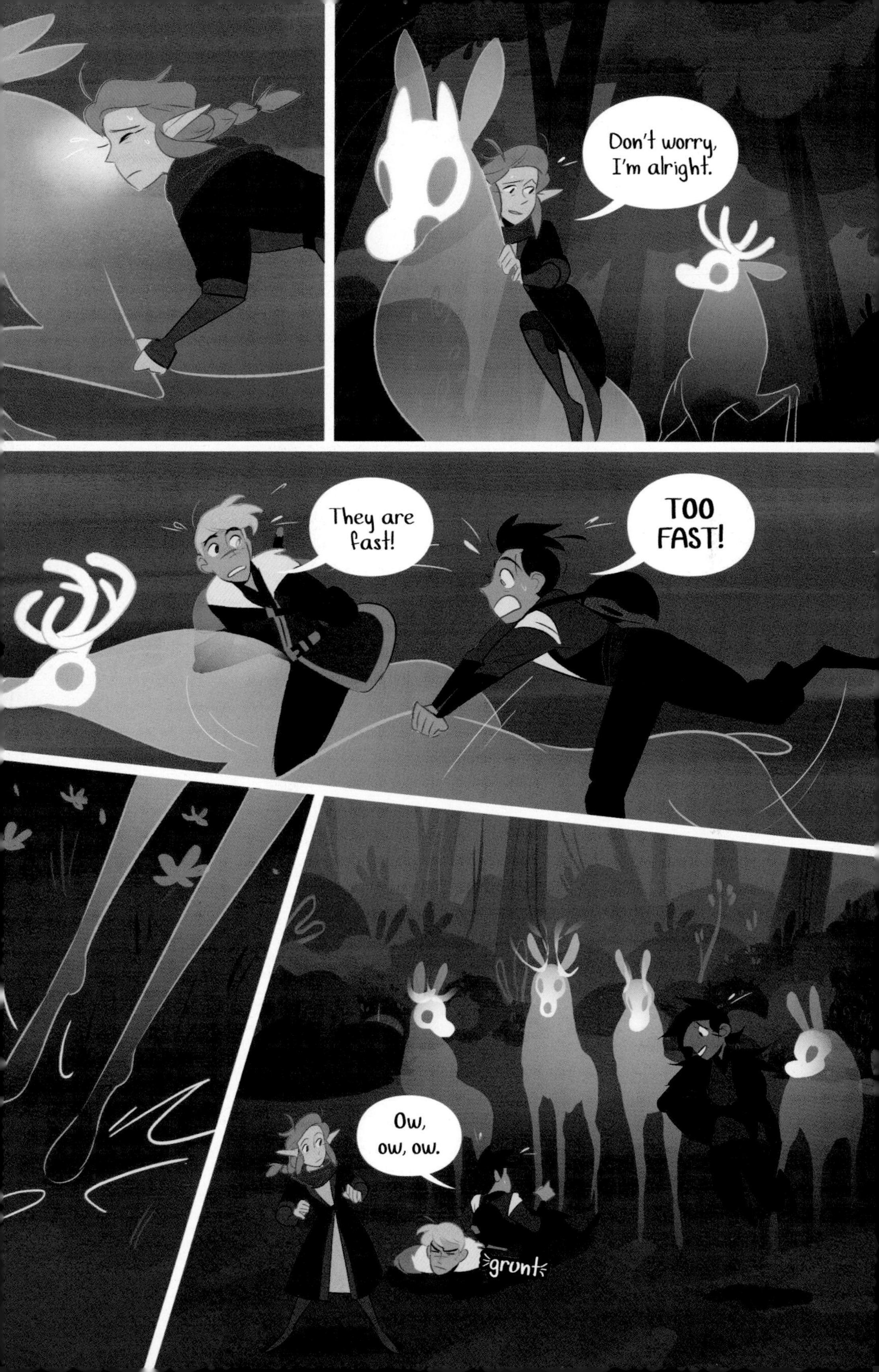
Don't worry,
I'm alright.
They are
fast!
TOO
FAST!
Ow,
ow, ow.
grunt

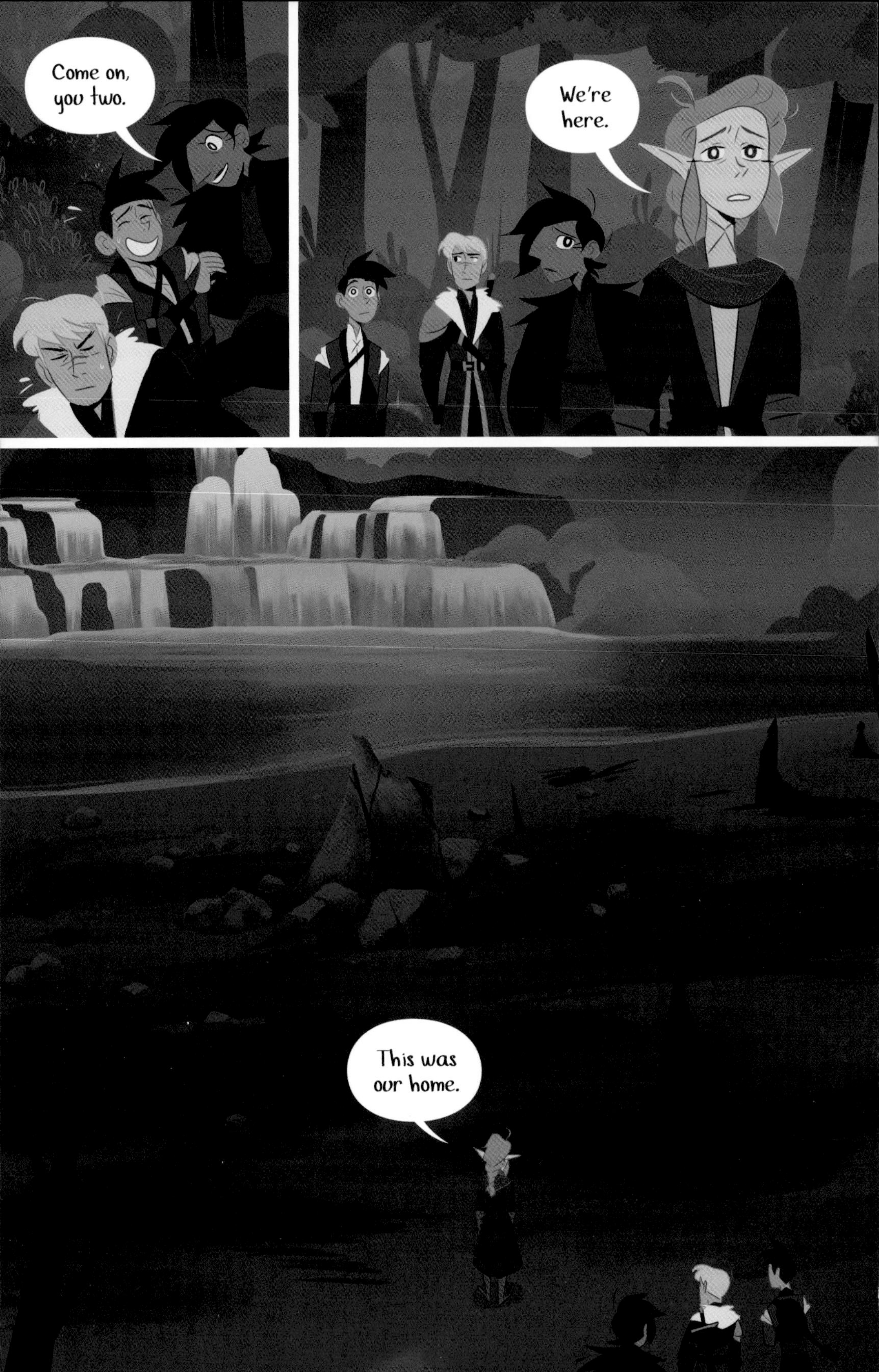
Come on, you two.
We're here.
This was our home.

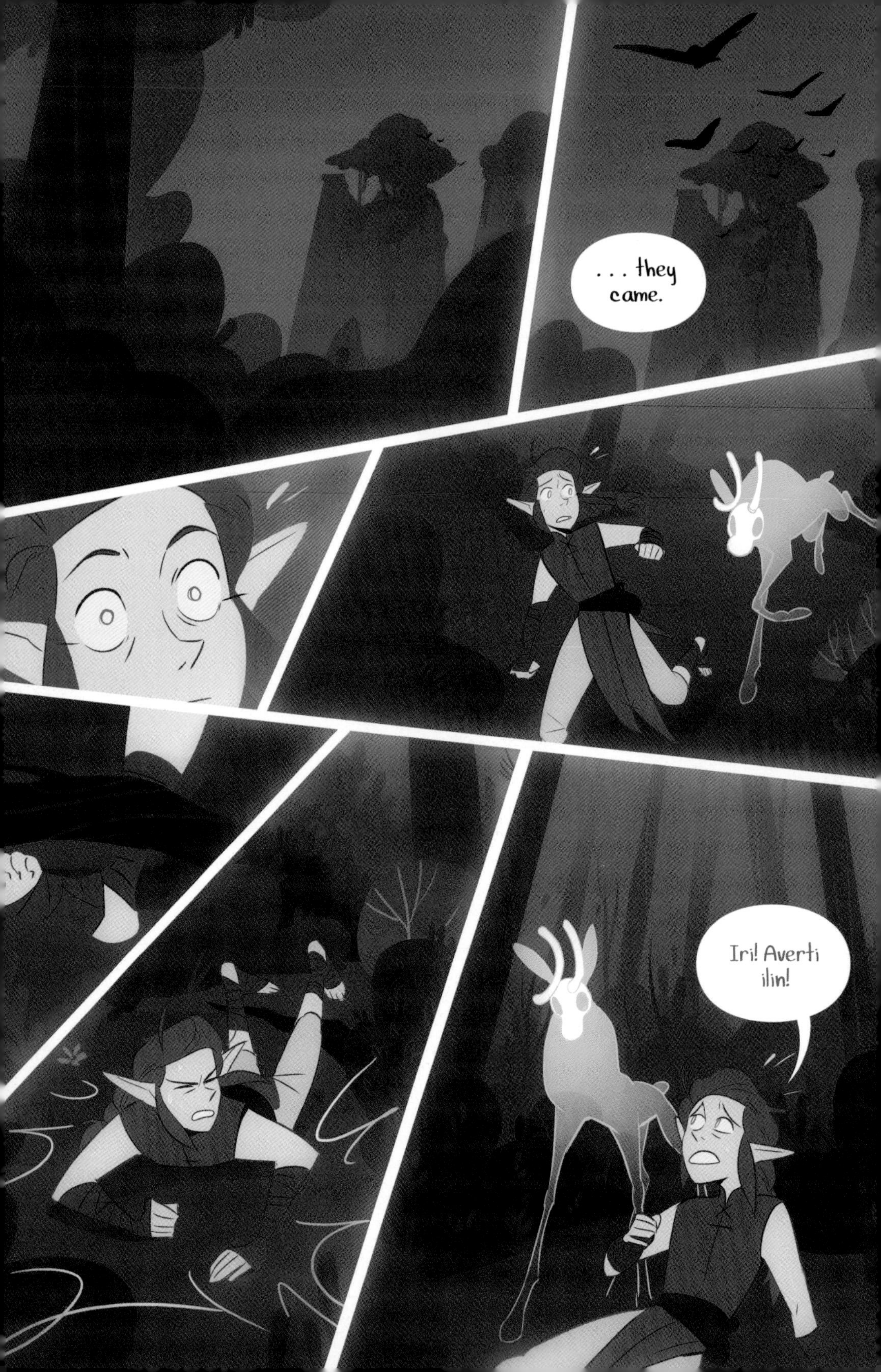
. . . they came.
Iri! Averti ilin!

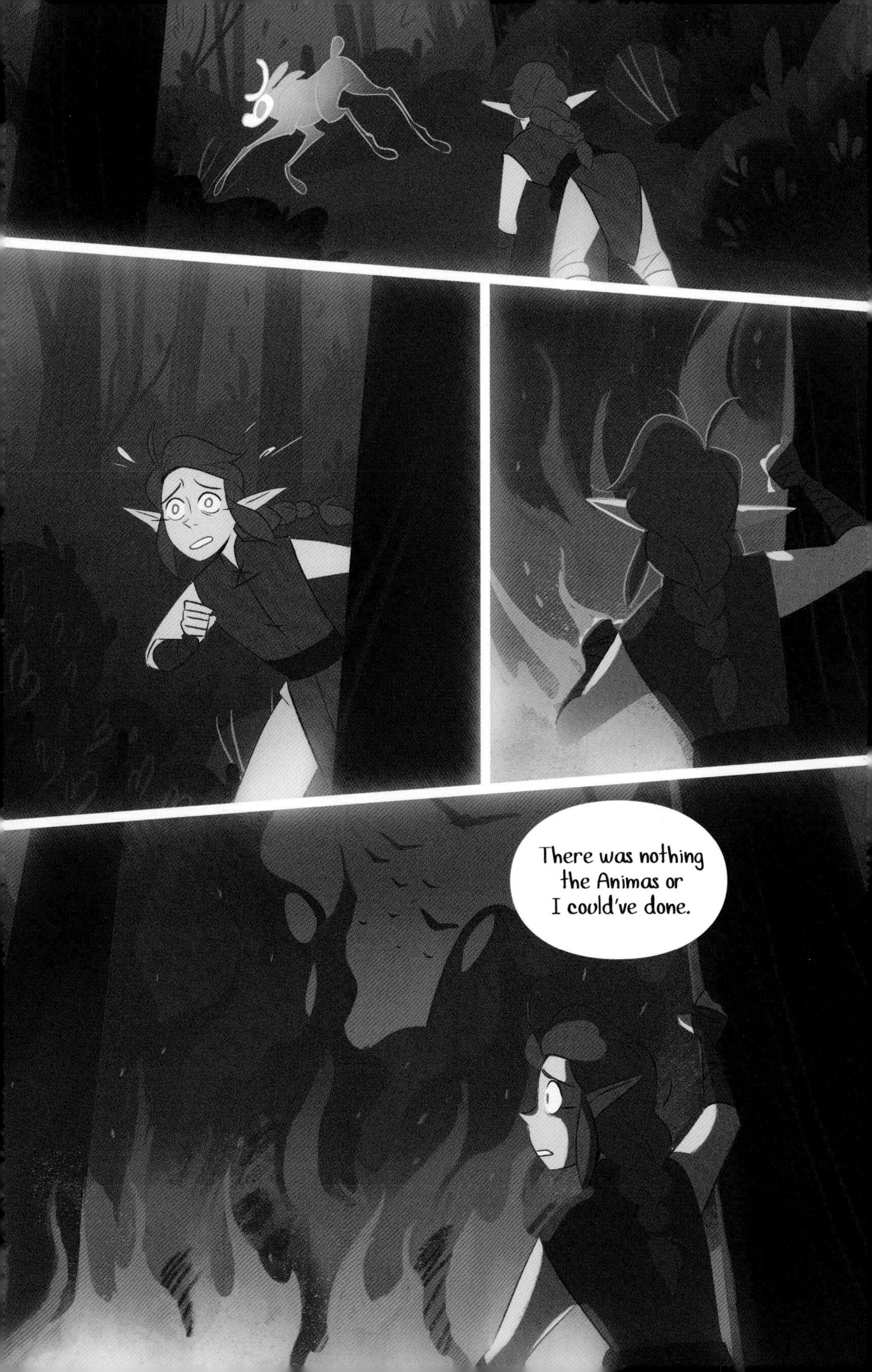
There was nothing
the Animas or
I could've done.

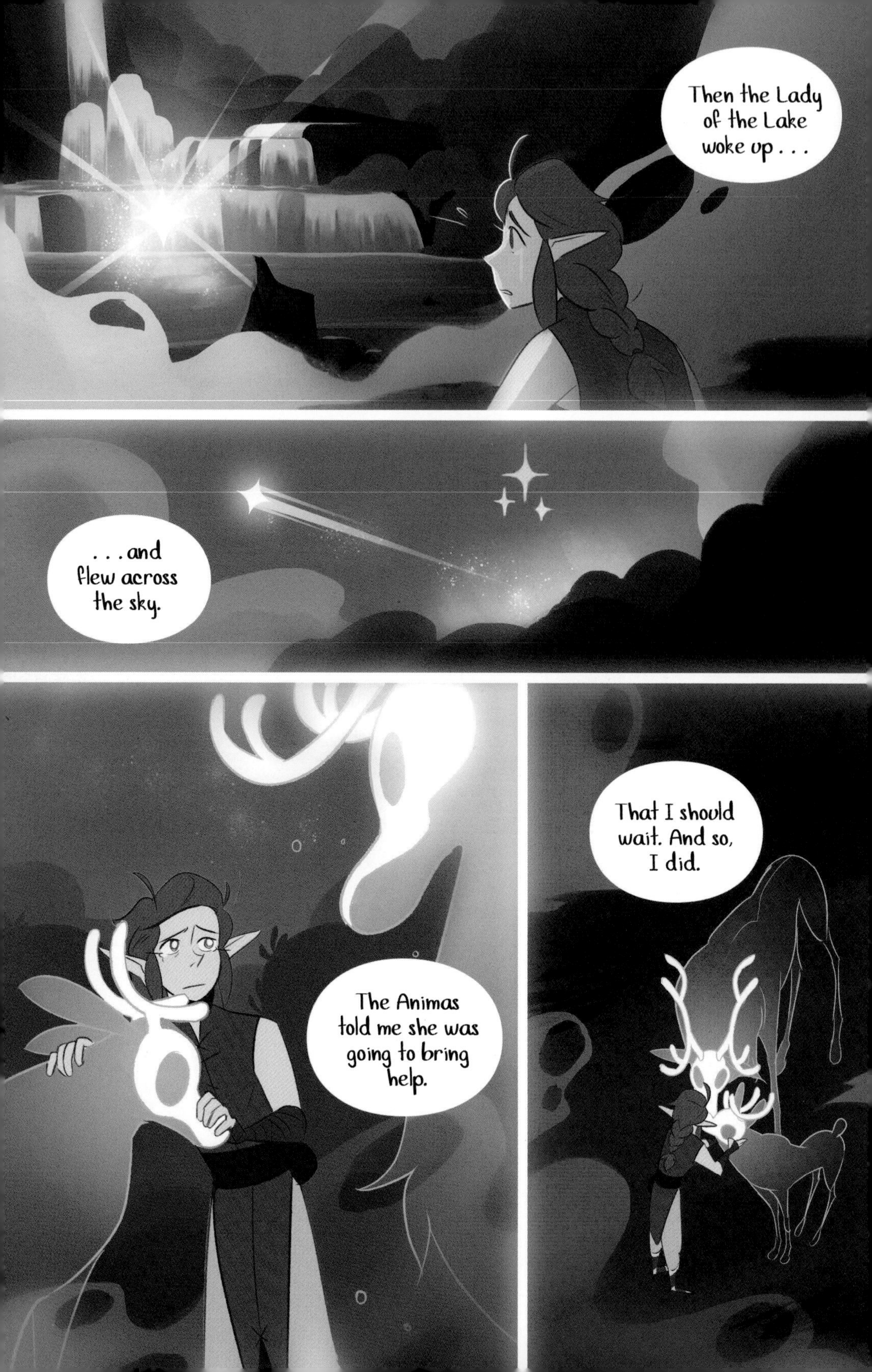
Then the Lady of the Lake woke up . . .
. . . and flew across the sky.
The Animas told me she was going to bring help.
That I should wait. And so, I did.

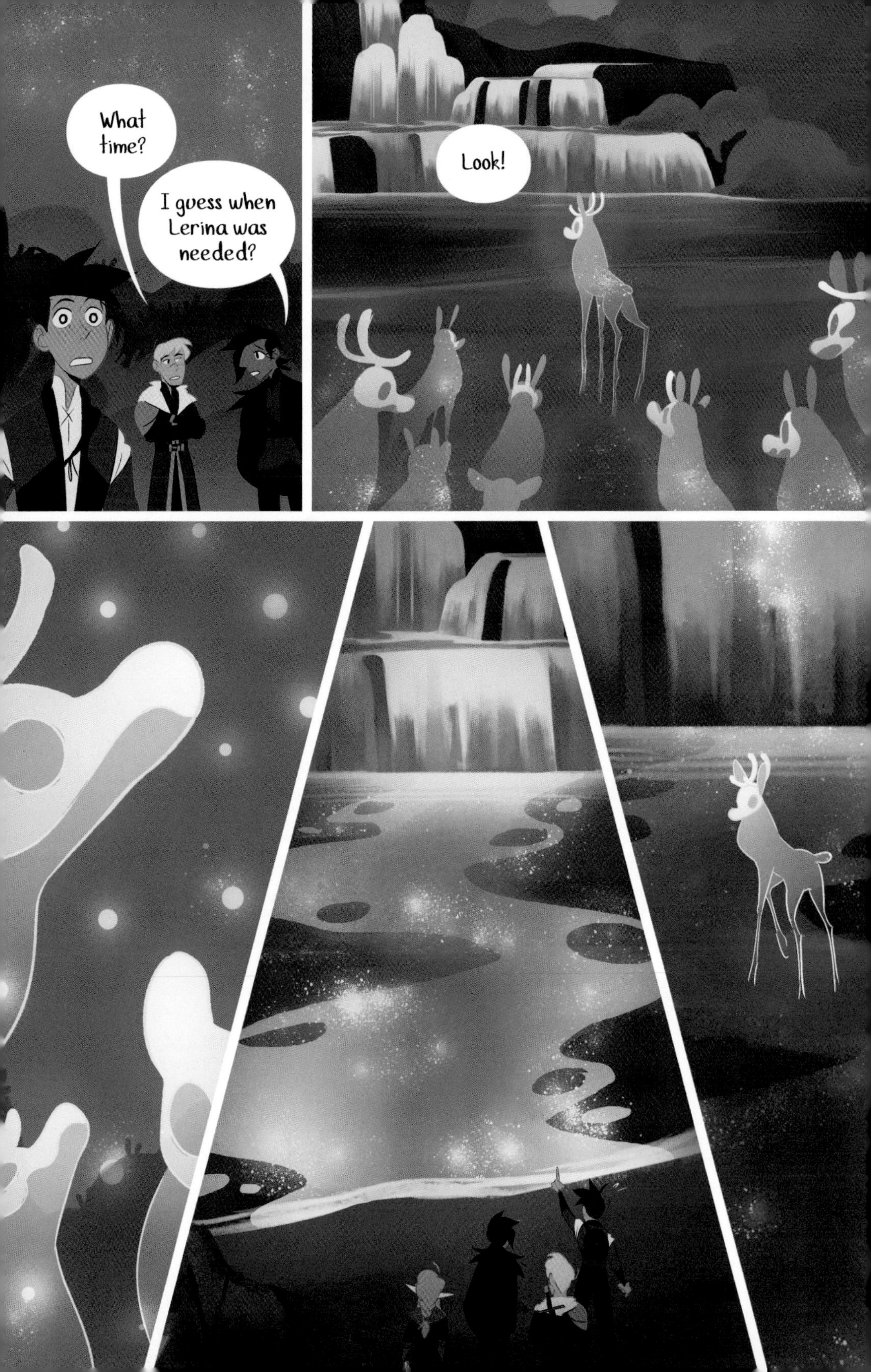

What time?
I guess when Lerina was needed?
Look!

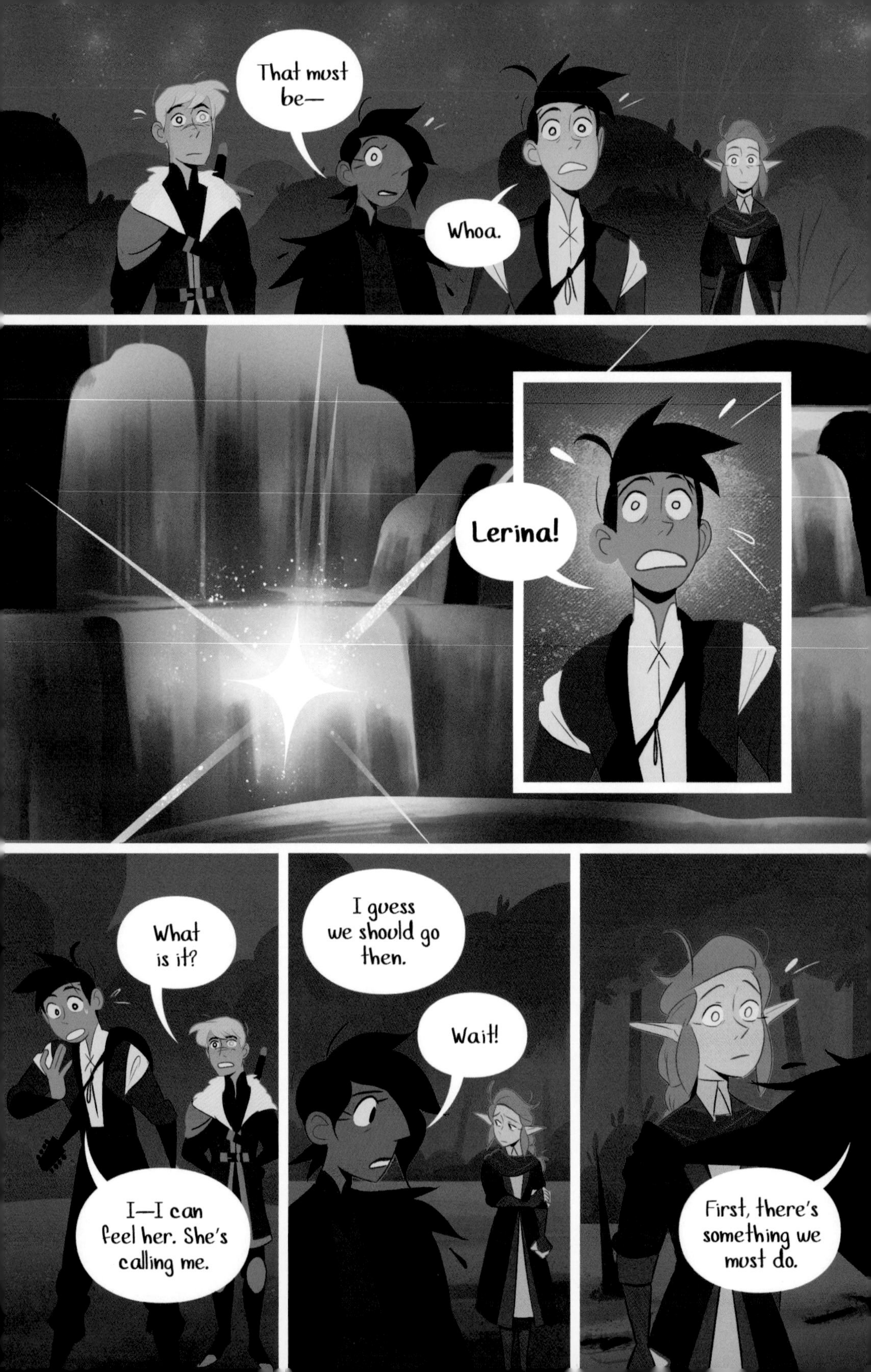
That must be—
Whoa.
Lerina!
What is it?
I—I can feel her. She's calling me.
I guess we should go then.
Wait!
First, there's something we must do.

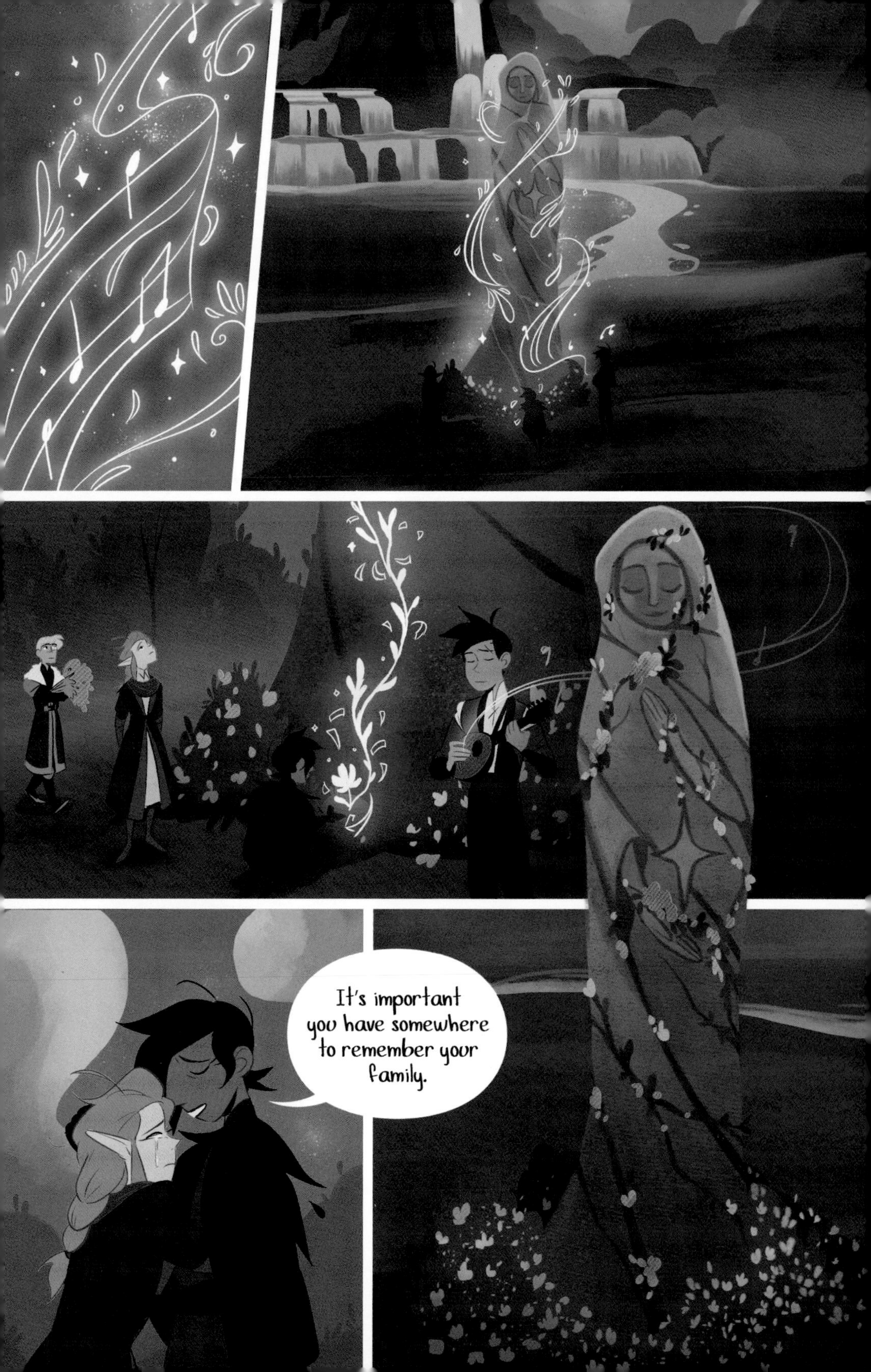
It's important you have somewhere to remember your family.

END OF CHAPTER 13

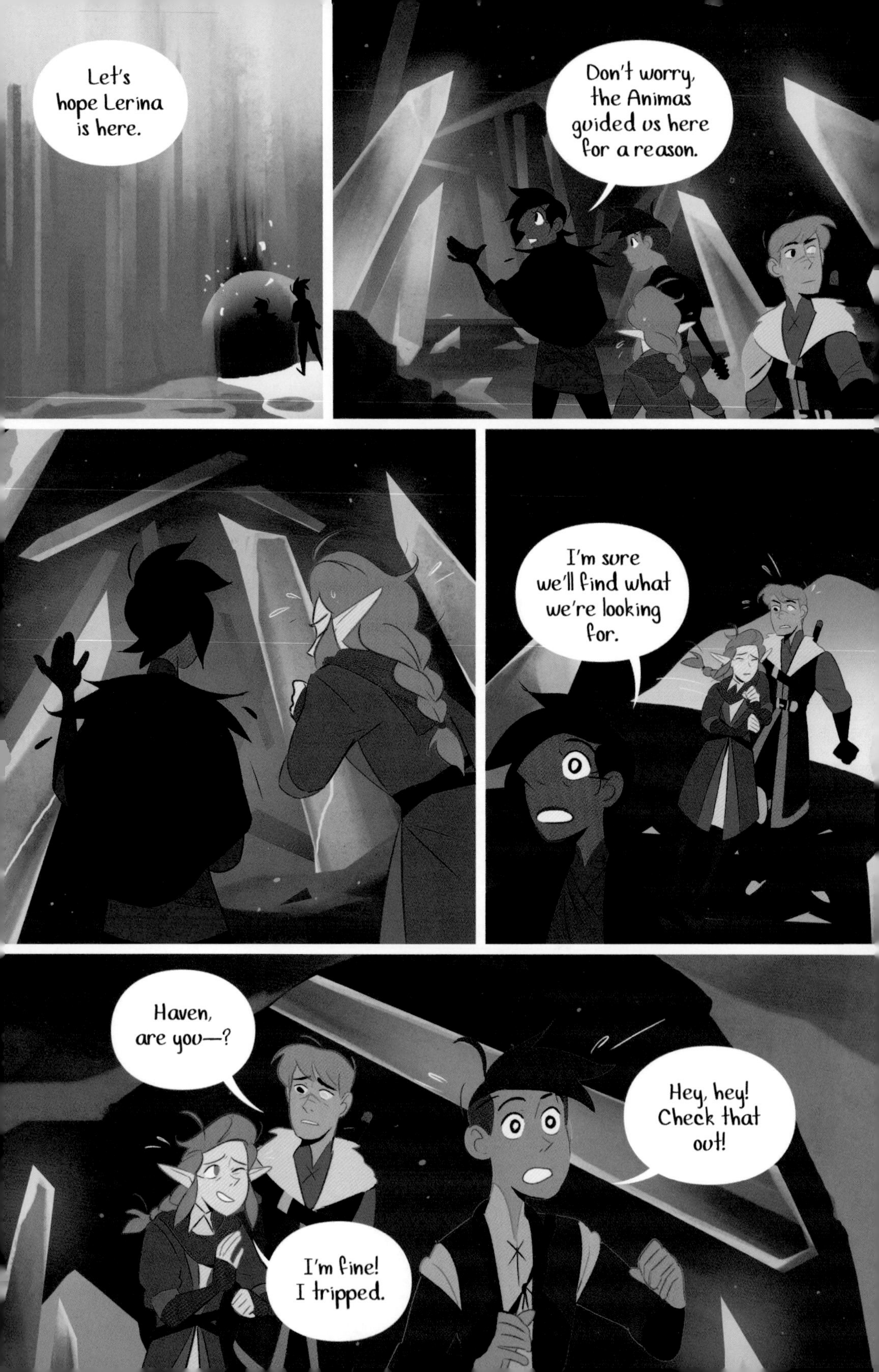
Let's hope Lerina is here.
Don't worry, the Animas guided us here for a reason.
I'm sure we'll find what we're looking for.
Haven, are you—?
I'm fine! I tripped.
Hey, hey! Check that out!

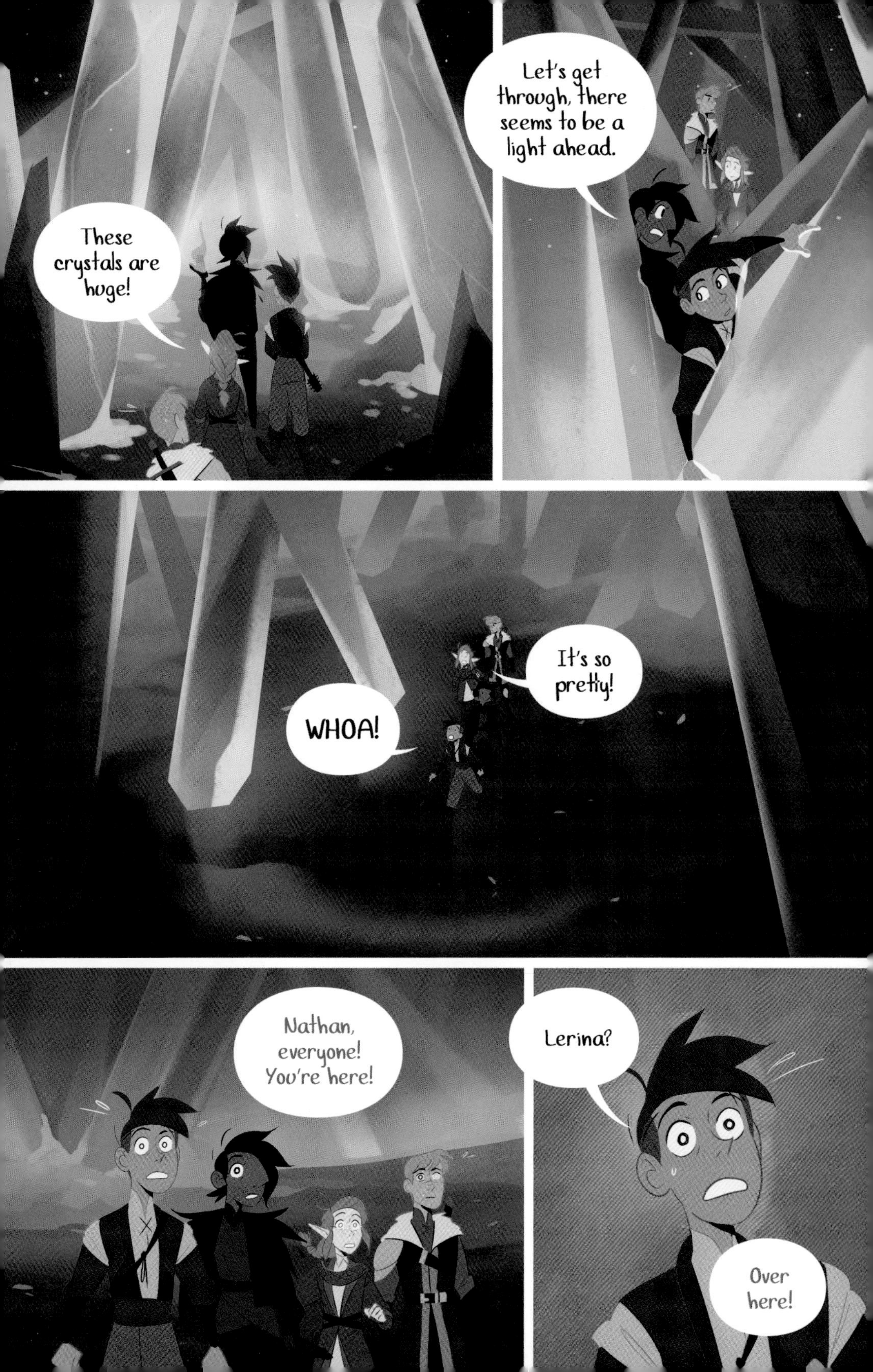
These crystals are huge!
Let's get through, there seems to be a light ahead.
WHOA!
It's so pretty!
Nathan, everyone! You're here!
Lerina?
Over here!

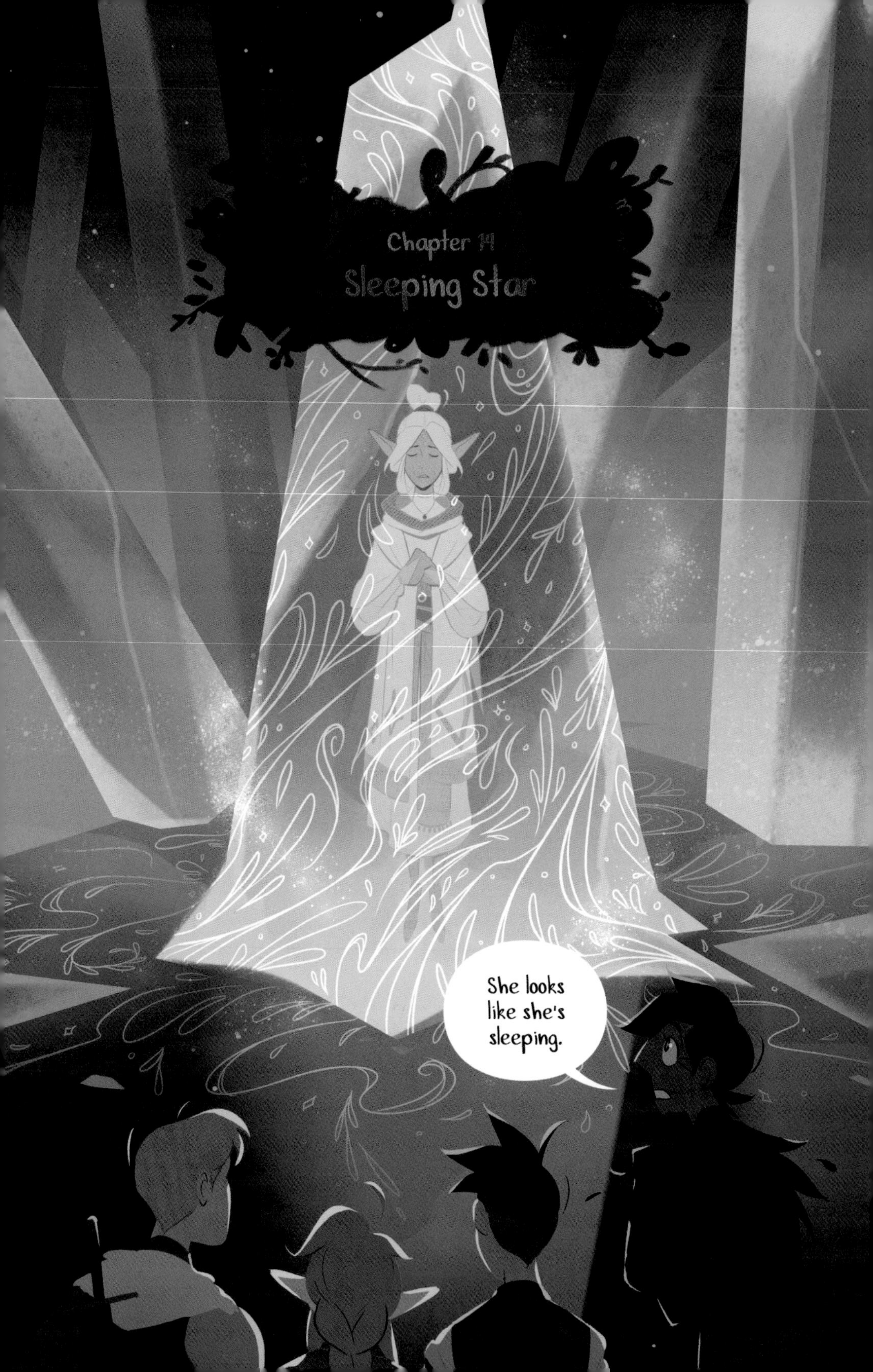
Chapter 14
Sleeping Star
She looks like she's sleeping.

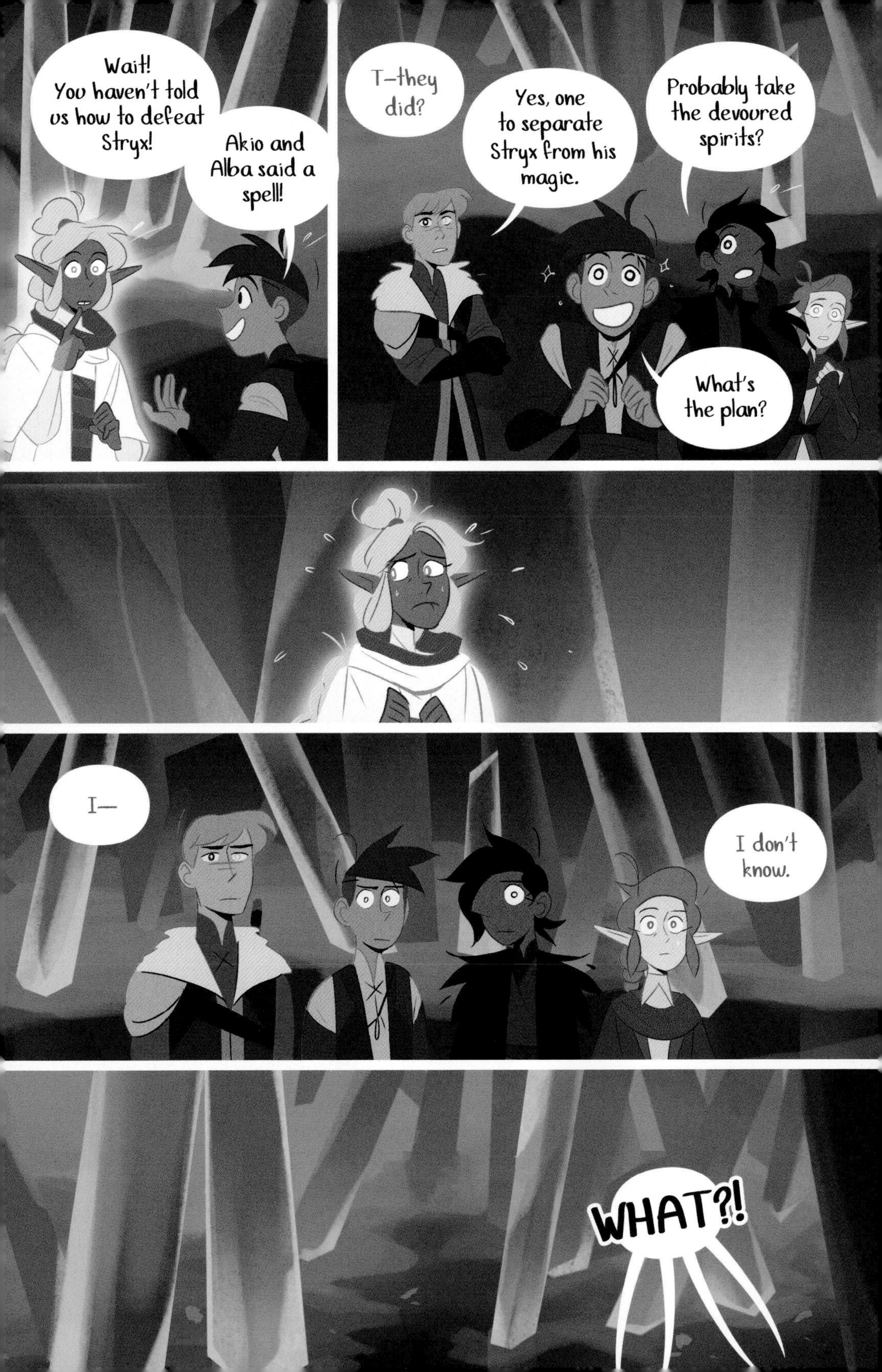
Wait!
You haven't told us how to defeat Stryx!
Akio and Alba said a spell!
T—they did?
Yes, one to separate Stryx from his magic.
Probably take the devoured spirits?
What's the plan?
I—
I don't know.
WHAT?!

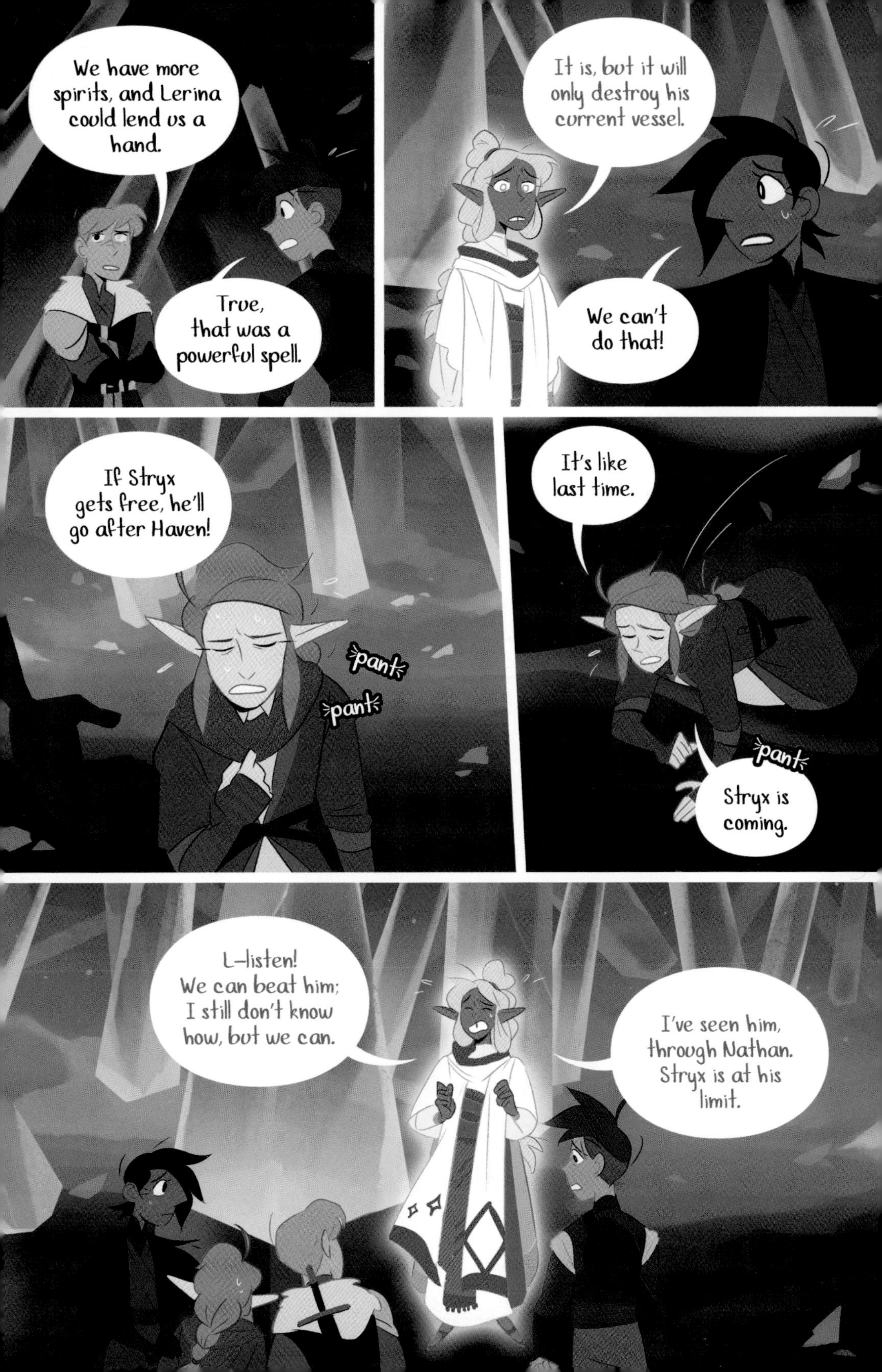
We have more spirits, and Lerina could lend us a hand.
True, that was a powerful spell.
It is, but it will only destroy his current vessel.
We can't do that!
If Stryx gets free, he'll go after Haven!
pant
pant
It's like last time.
pant
Stryx is coming.
L-listen! We can beat him; I still don't know how, but we can.
I've seen him, through Nathan. Stryx is at his limit.

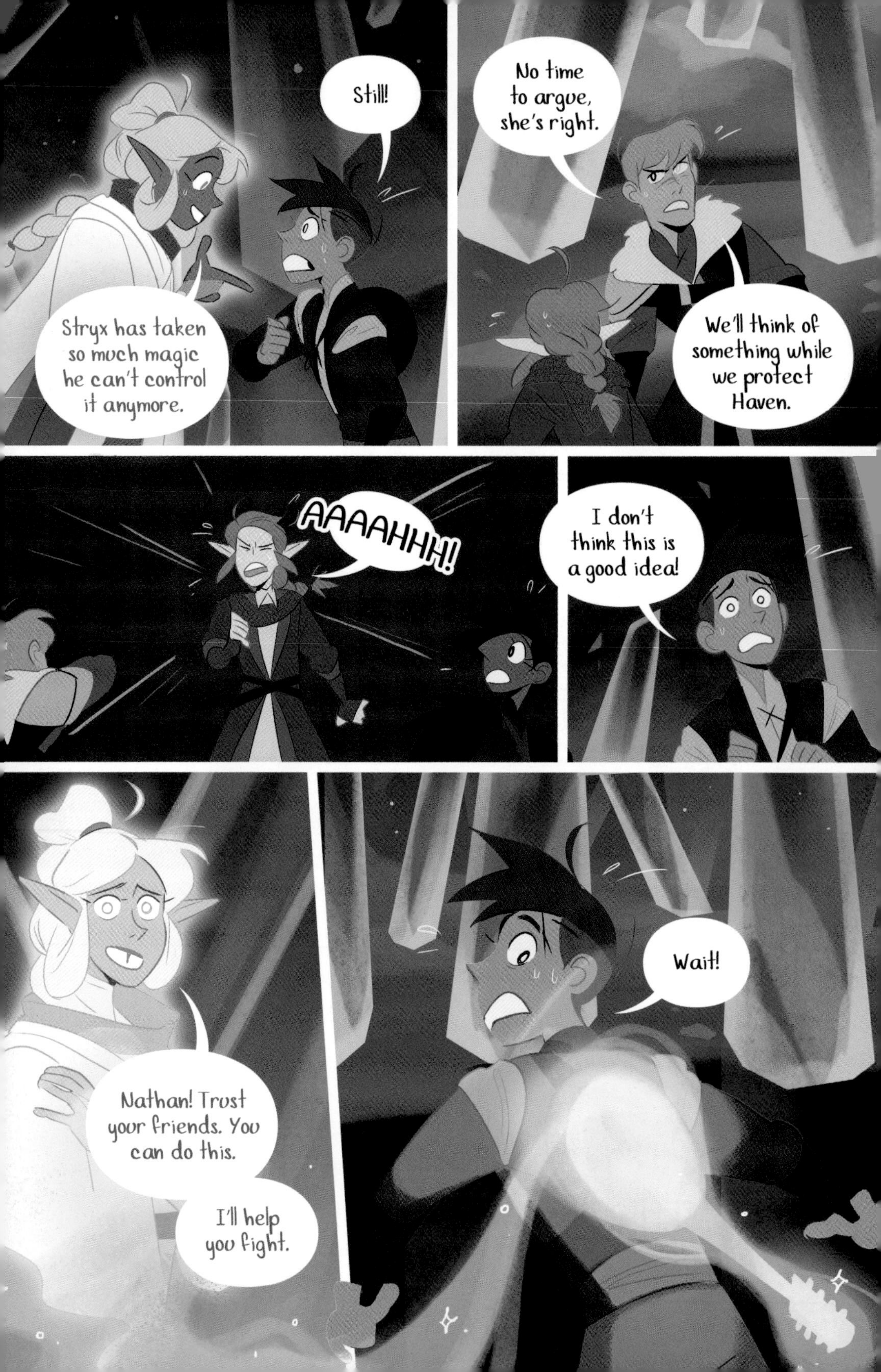
Still!
Stryx has taken so much magic he can't control it anymore.
No time to argue, she's right.
We'll think of something while we protect Haven.
AAAAHHH!
I don't think this is a good idea!
Nathan! Trust your friends. You can do this.
I'll help you fight.
Wait!

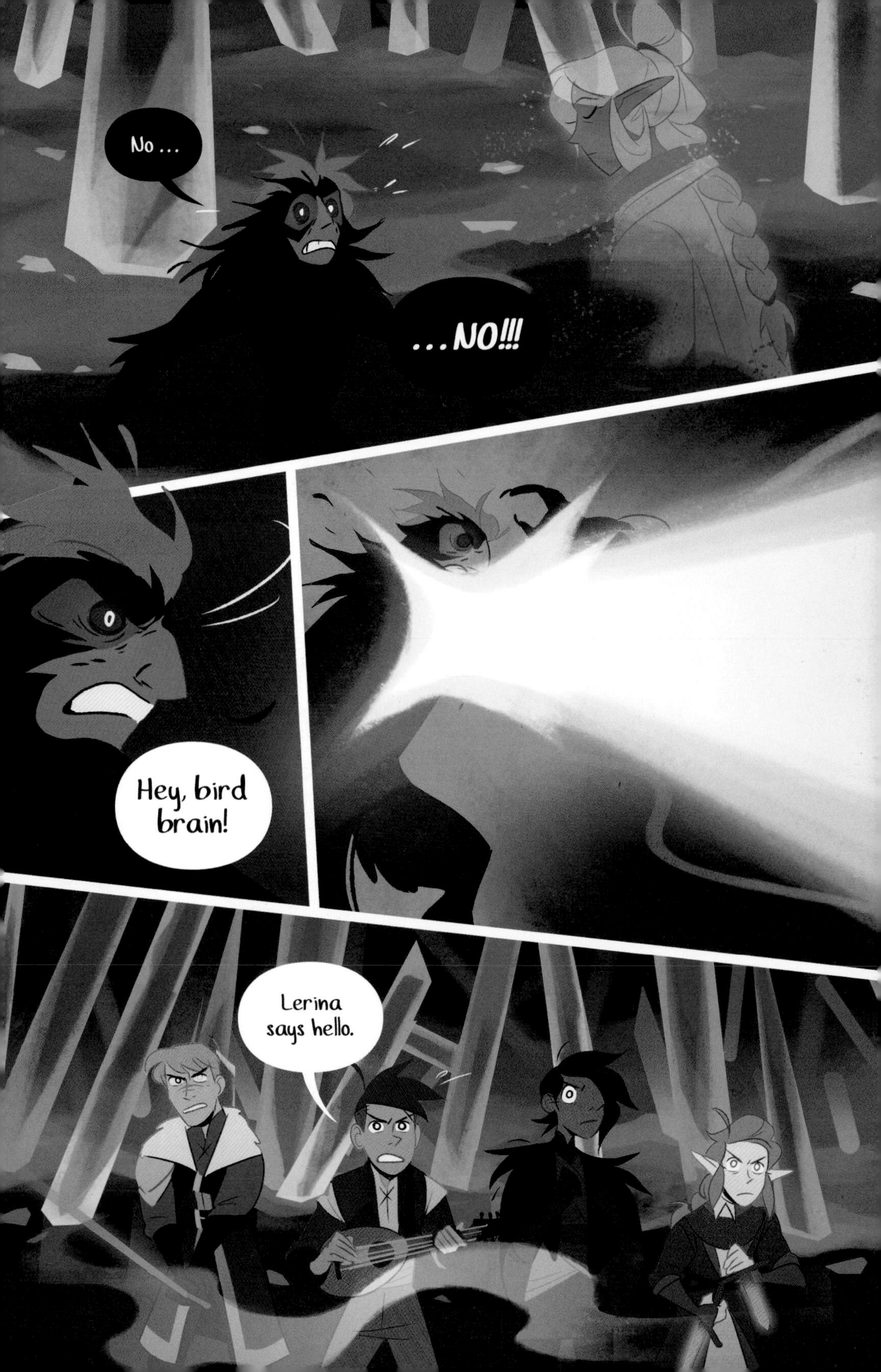
No . . .
. . . NO!!!
Hey, bird brain!
Lerina says hello.

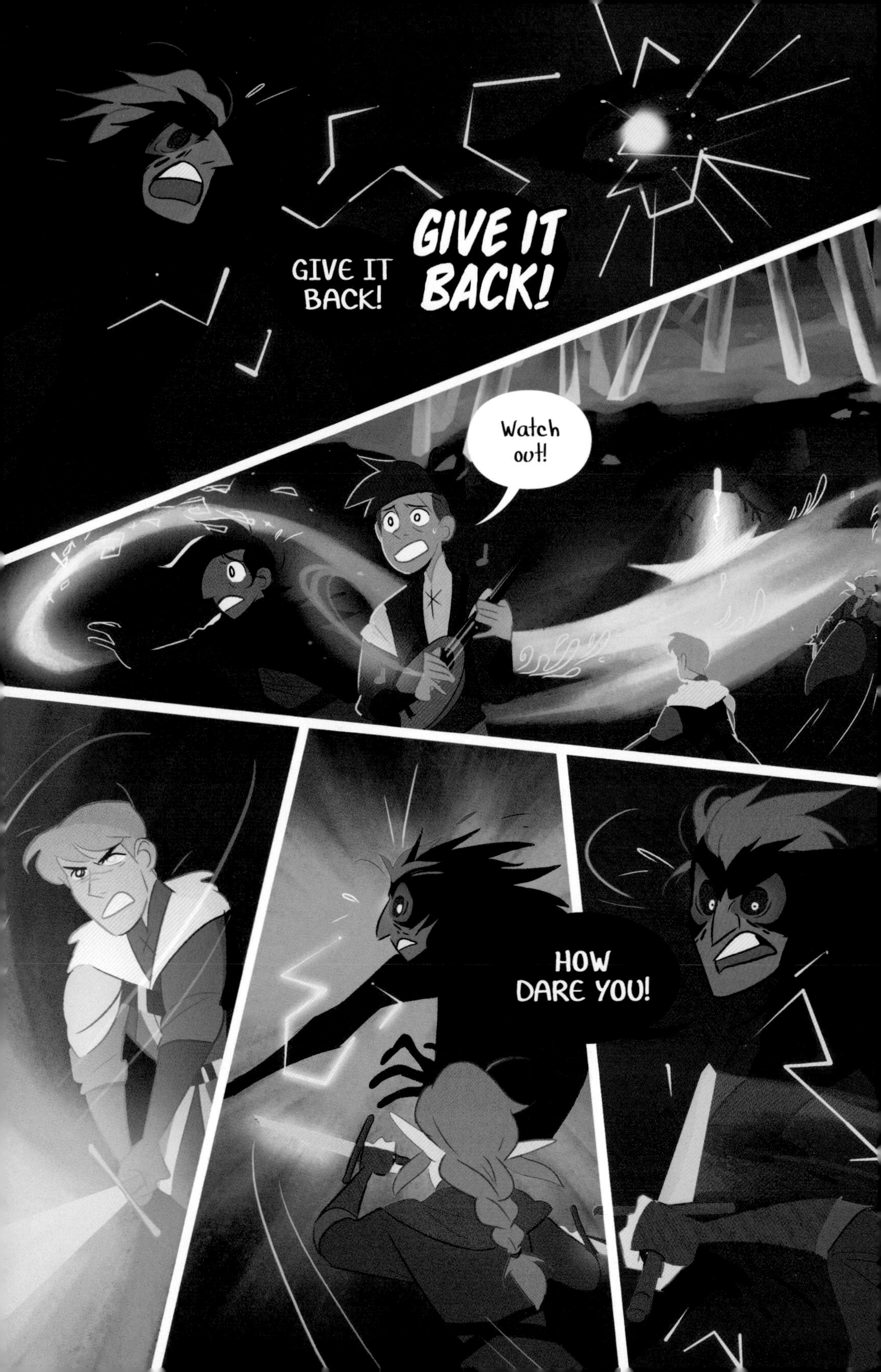
GIVE IT BACK!
GIVE IT BACK!
Watch out!
HOW DARE YOU!

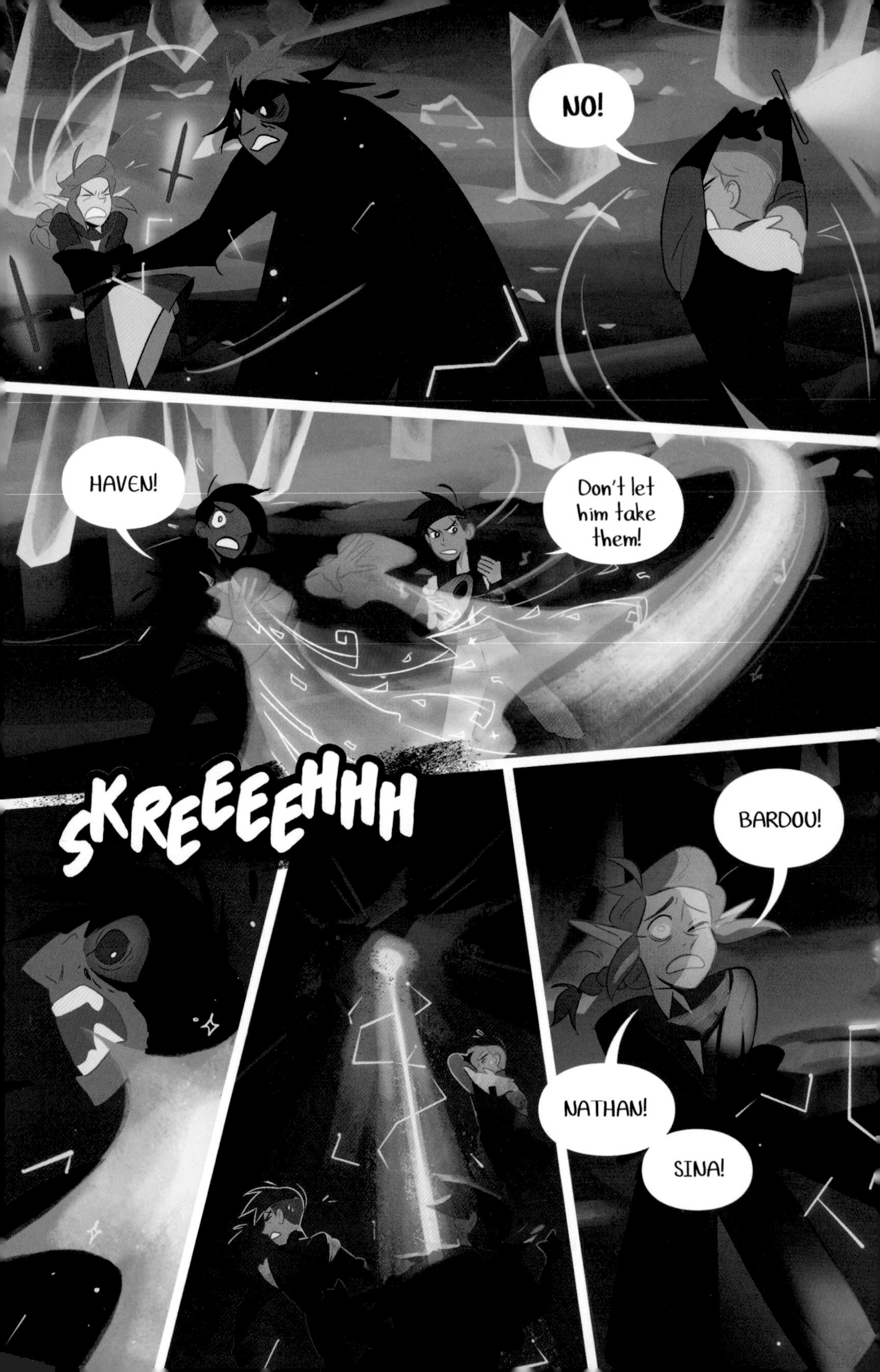
NO!
HAVEN!
Don't let him take them!
SKREEEEHHH
BARDOU!
NATHAN!
SINA!

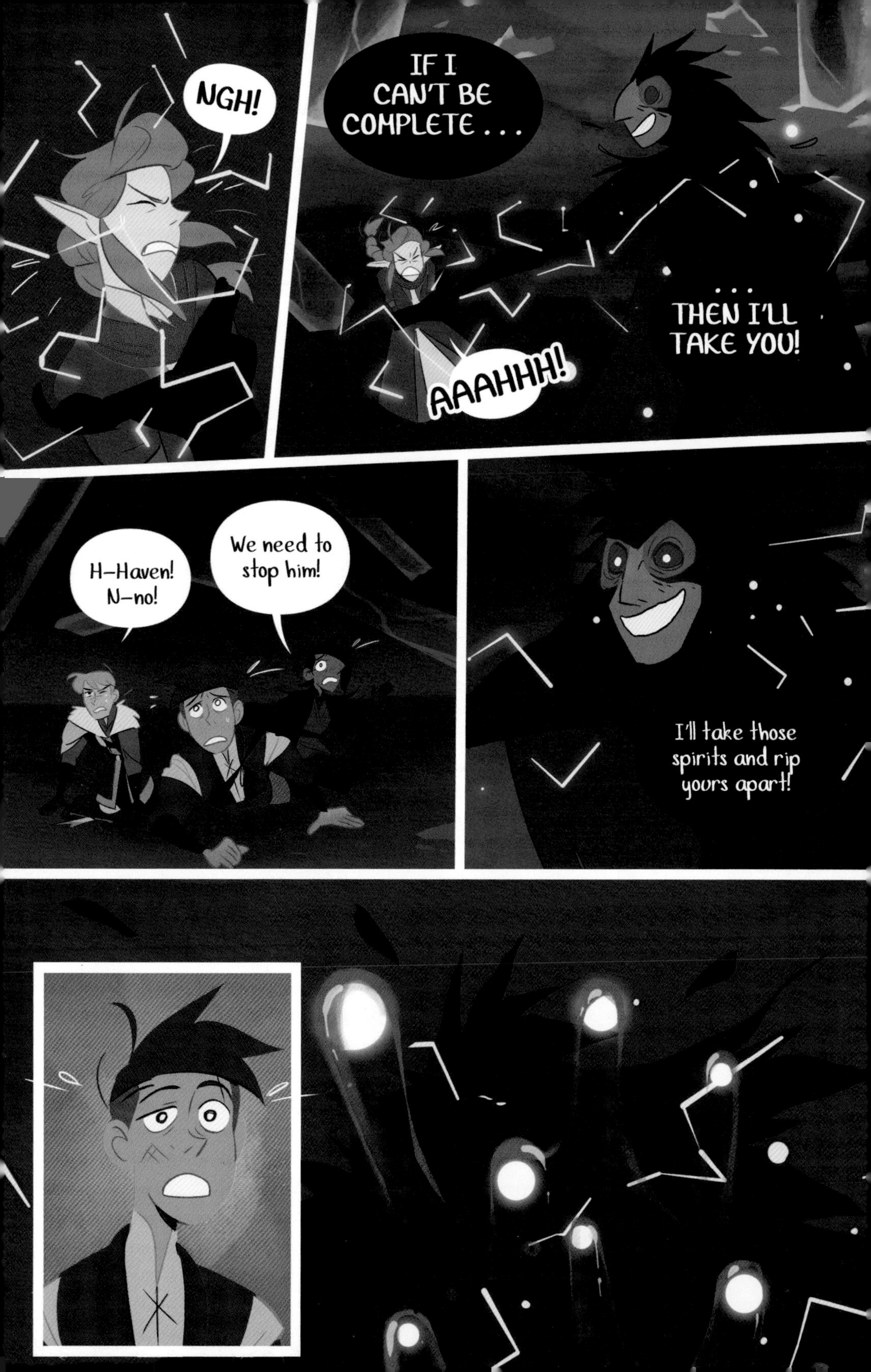
NGH!
IF I CAN'T BE COMPLETE . . .
AAAHHH!
. . . THEN I'LL TAKE YOU!
H–Haven! N–no!
We need to stop him!
I'll take those spirits and rip yours apart!

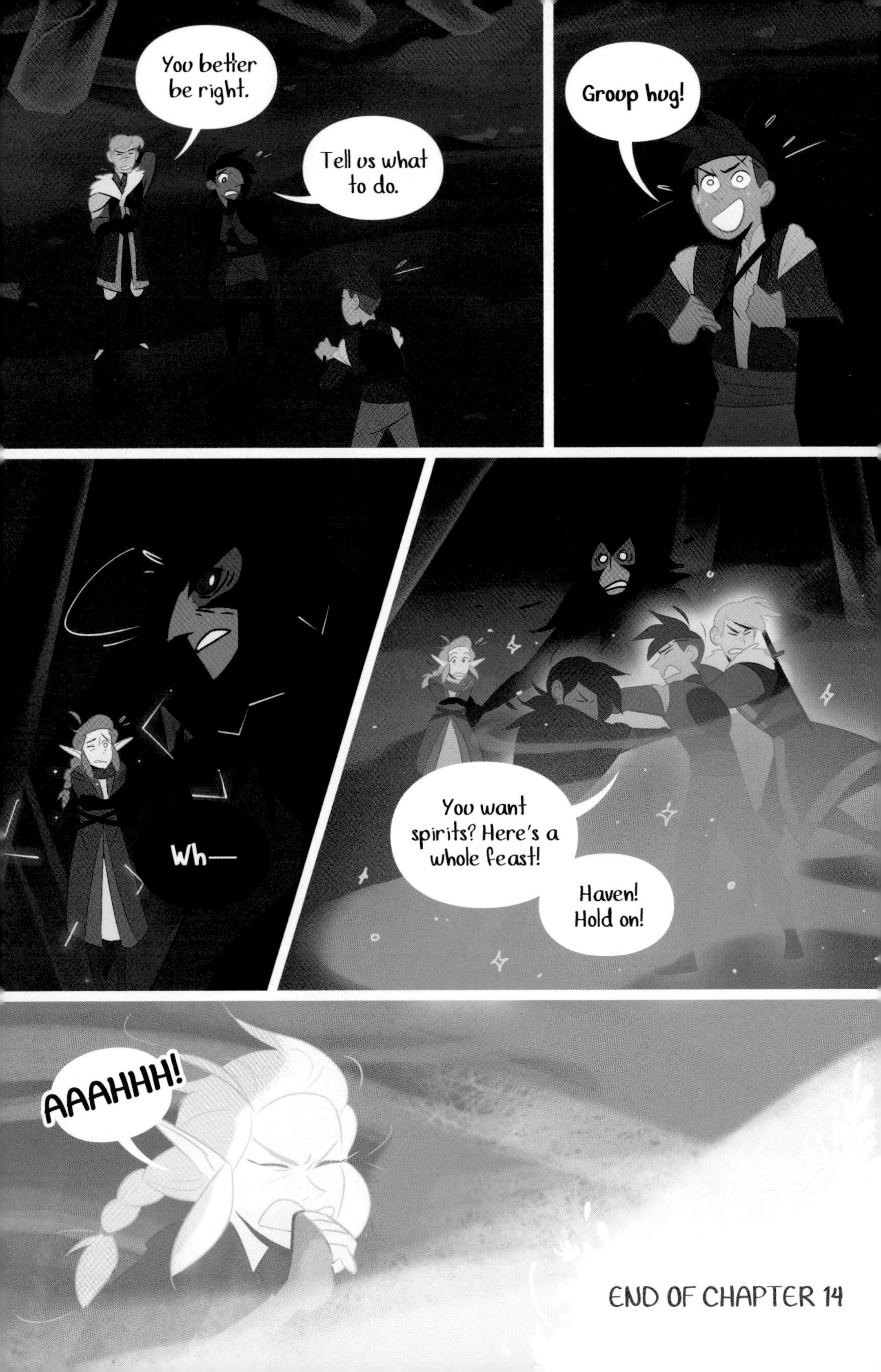
You better be right.
Tell us what to do.
Group hug!
Wh—
You want spirits? Here's a whole feast!
Haven! Hold on!
AAAHHH!
END OF CHAPTER 14

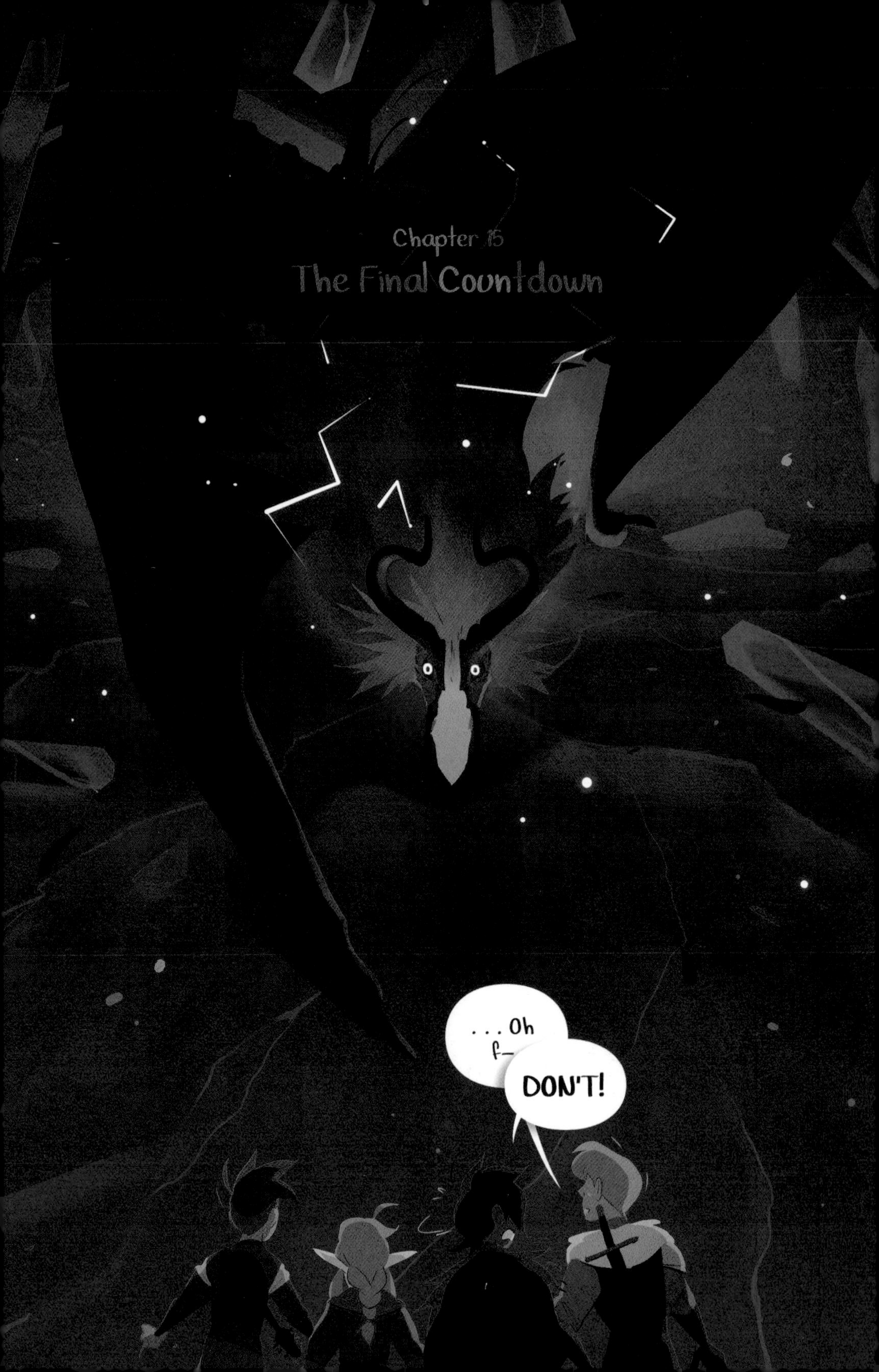
Chapter 15
The Final Countdown
. . . Oh
f—
DON'T!

SKREEEEHHH
He's gone. I—
I can't feel Stryx anymore!
It worked! He's trapped!
EEEEEE
SKREEEE
Look out!

We don't know what that thing will do!
We have to stop it.
Everyone!
SKREEEEEEE
Haven, are you okay to fight?
I am, more than ever.
We have to get him down, Sina, cover us.
On it!
Right! Nathan?

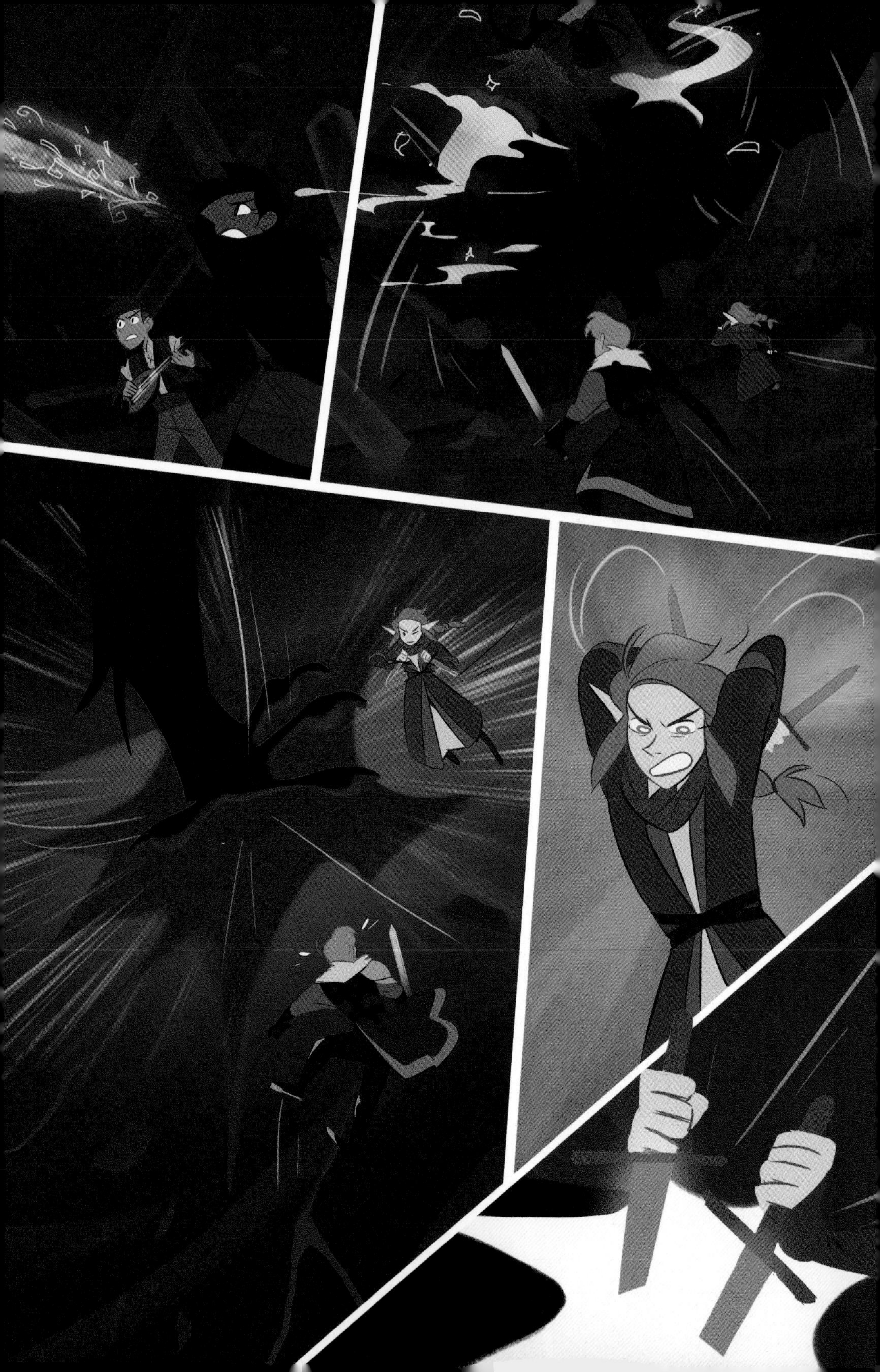

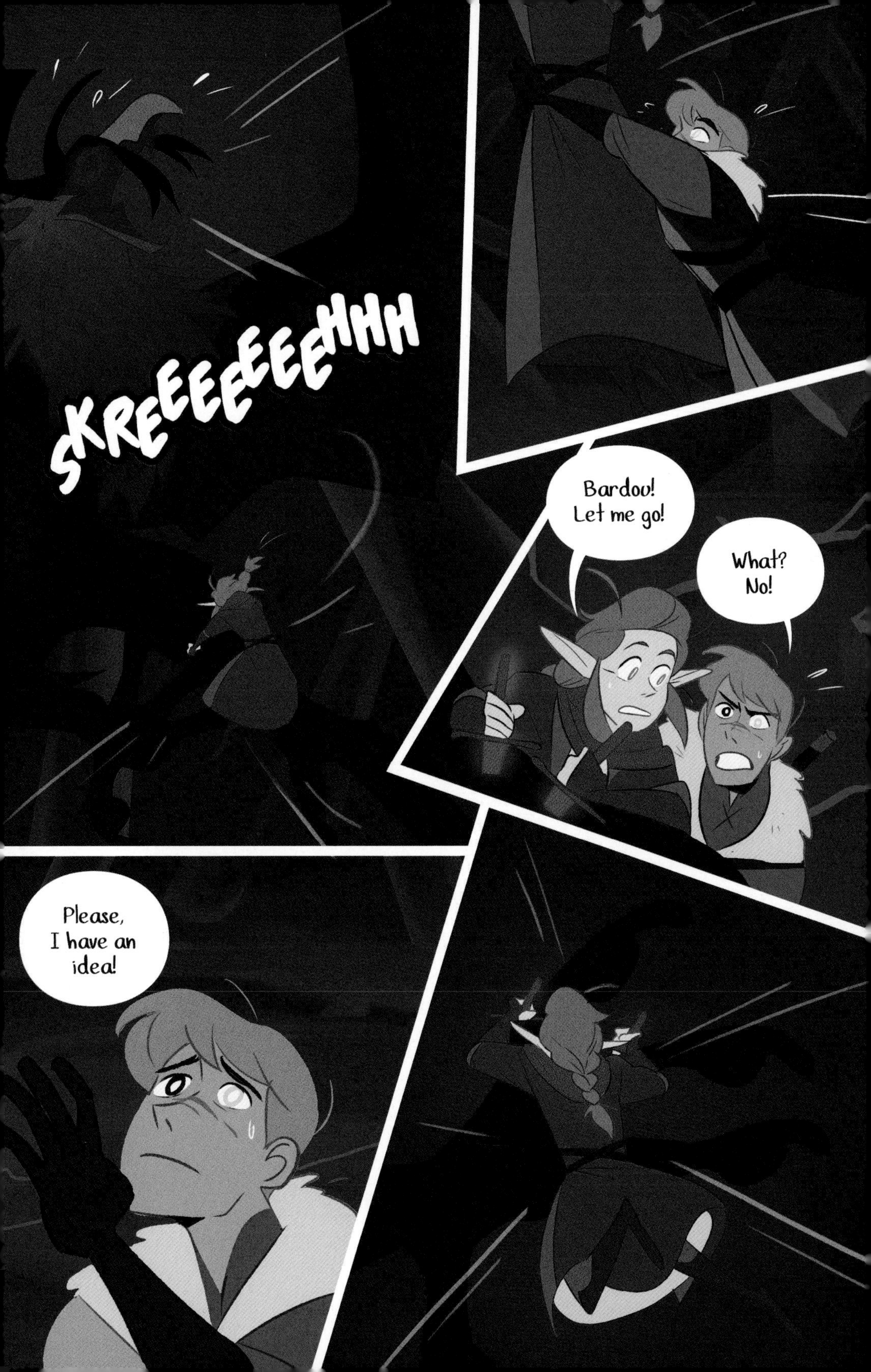
SKREEEEEEEHHH
Bardou! Let me go!
What? No!
Please, I have an idea!

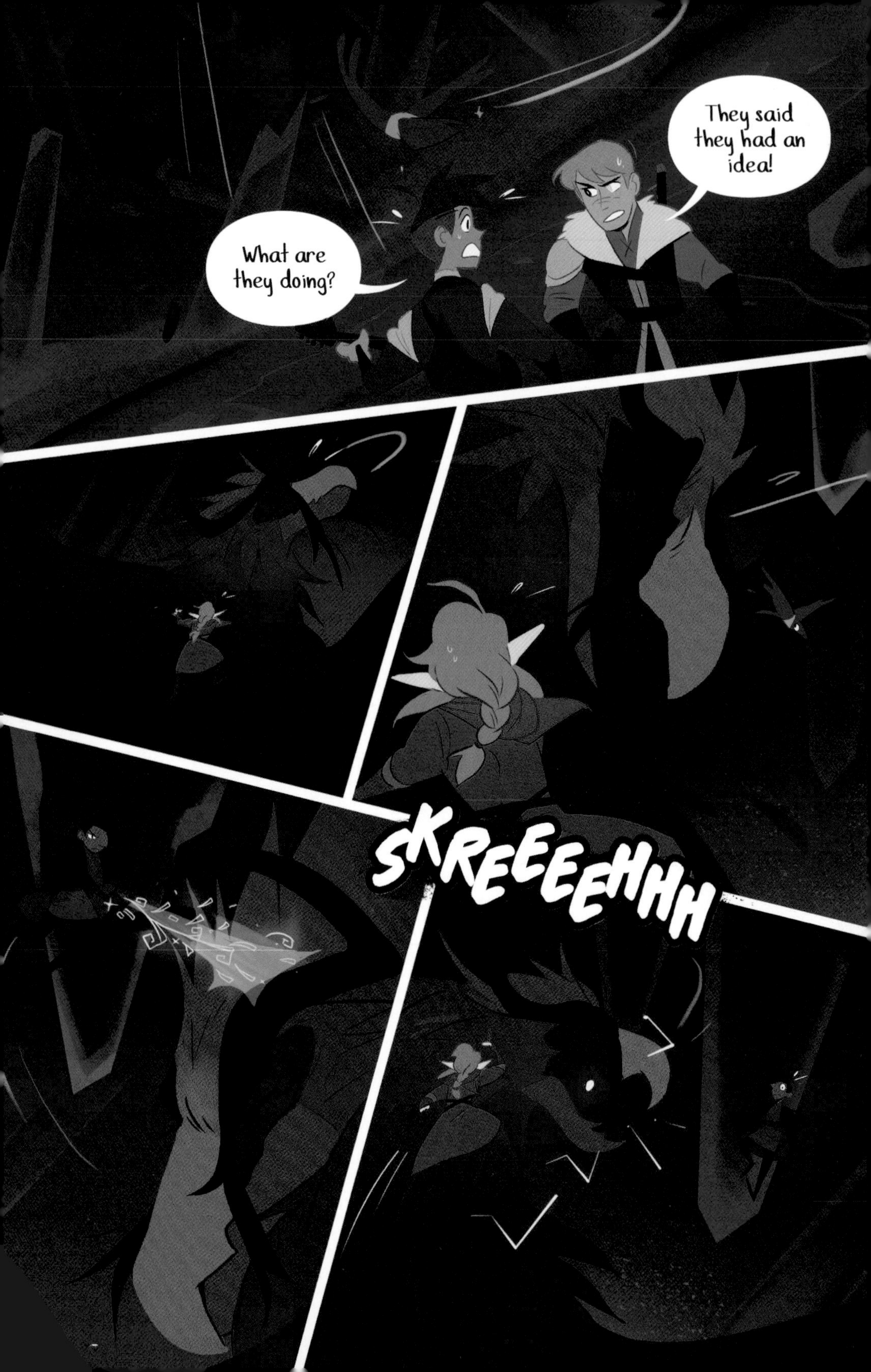
They said they had an idea!
What are they doing?
SKREEEEHHH

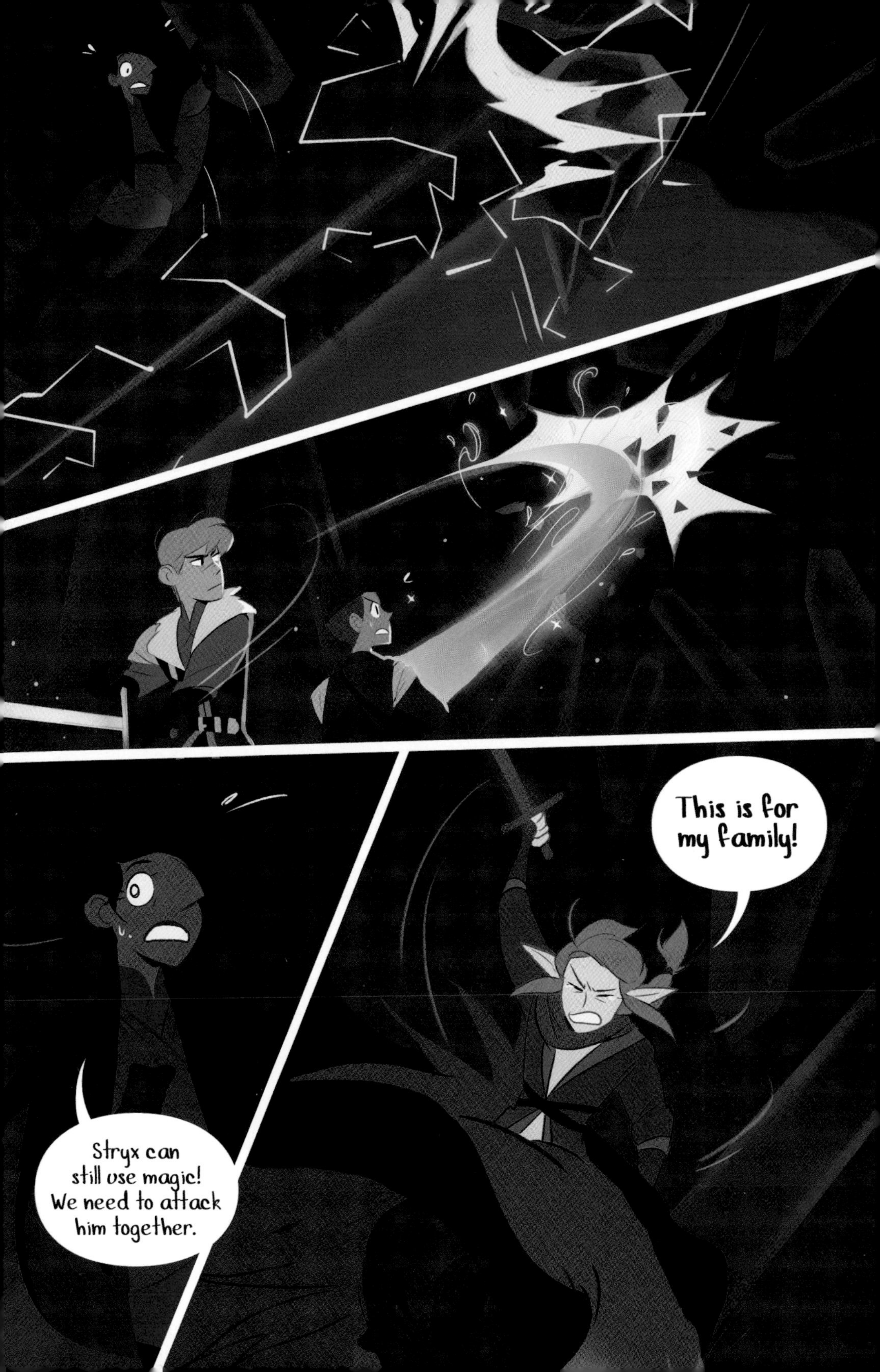
This is for my family!
Stryx can still use magic! We need to attack him together.

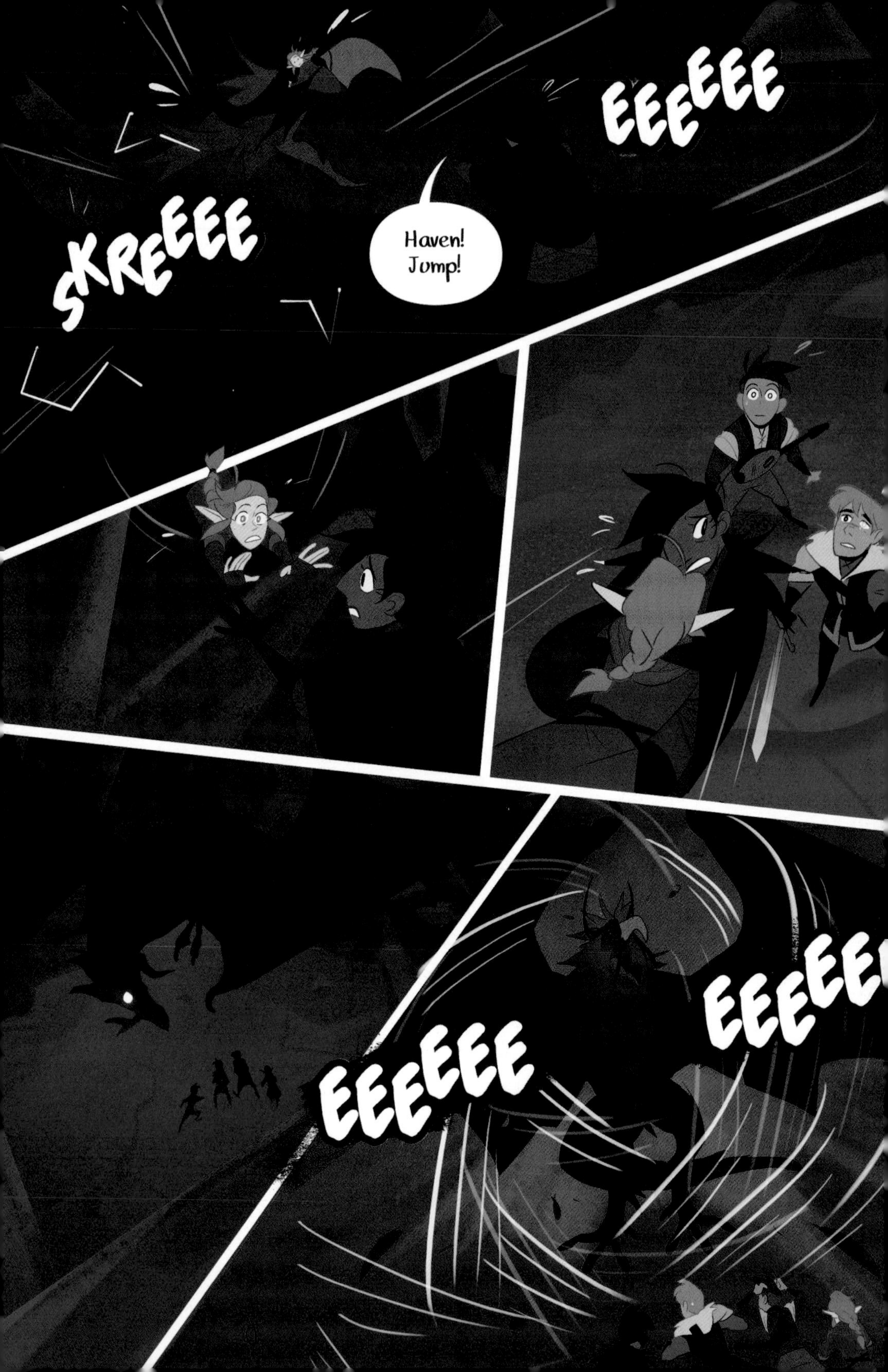
EEEEEE
SKREEEE
Haven! Jump!
EEEEEE
EEEEEE

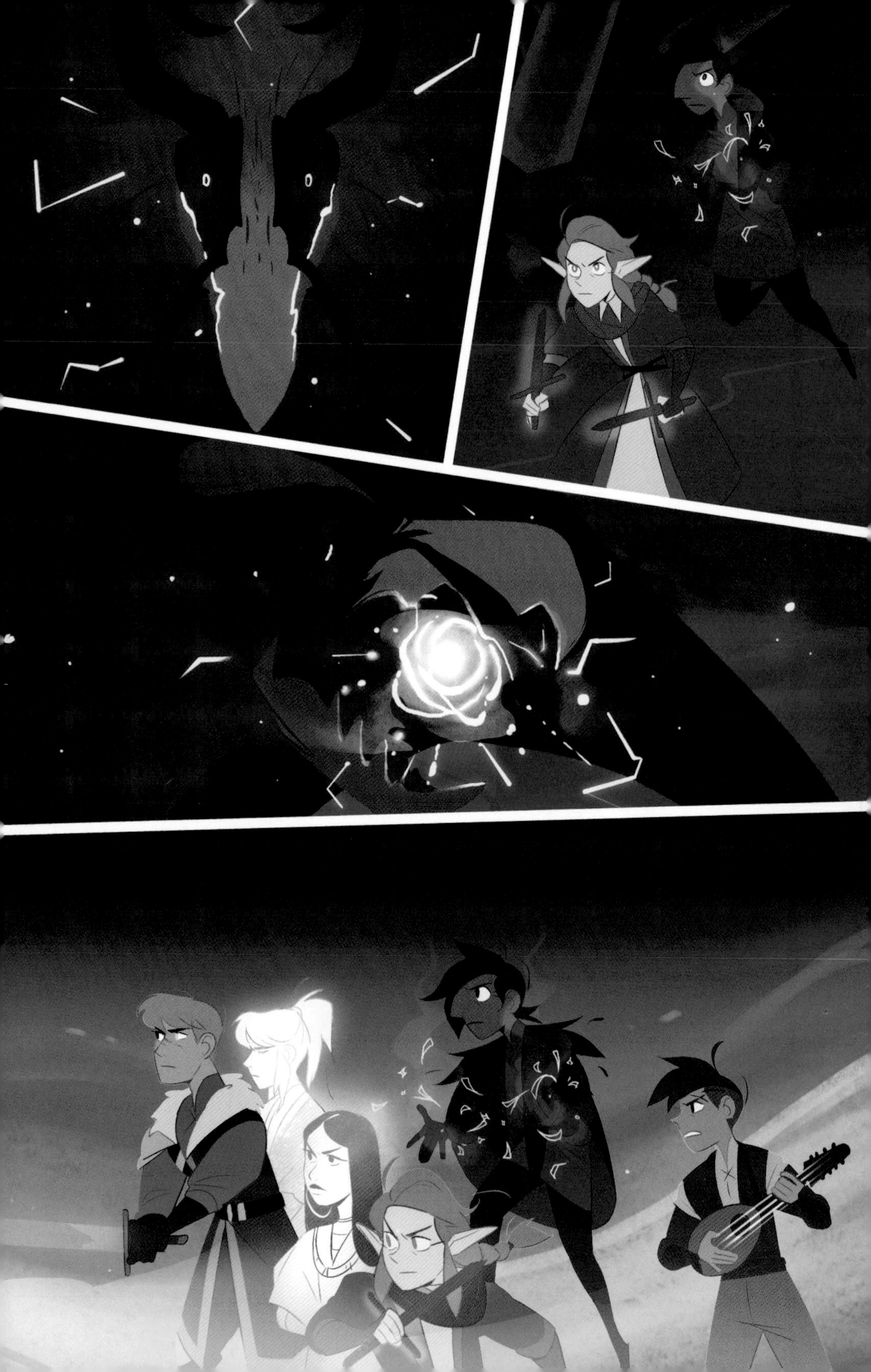

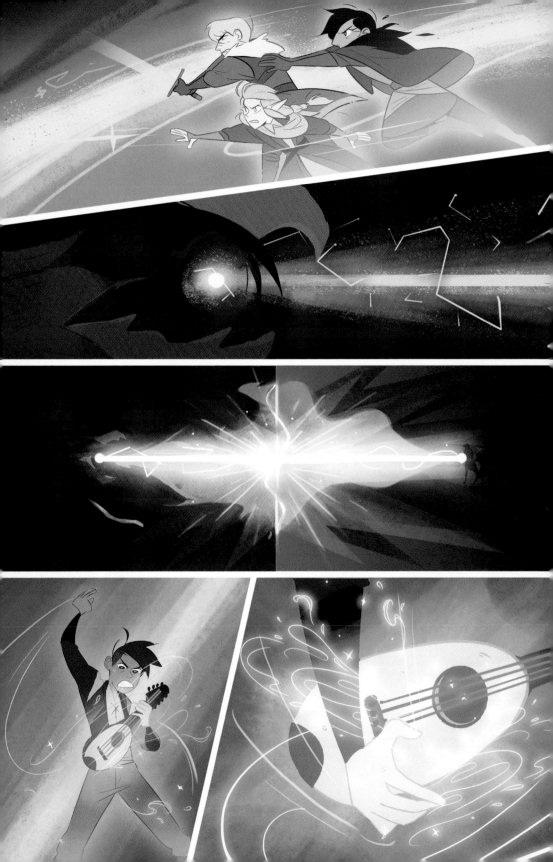

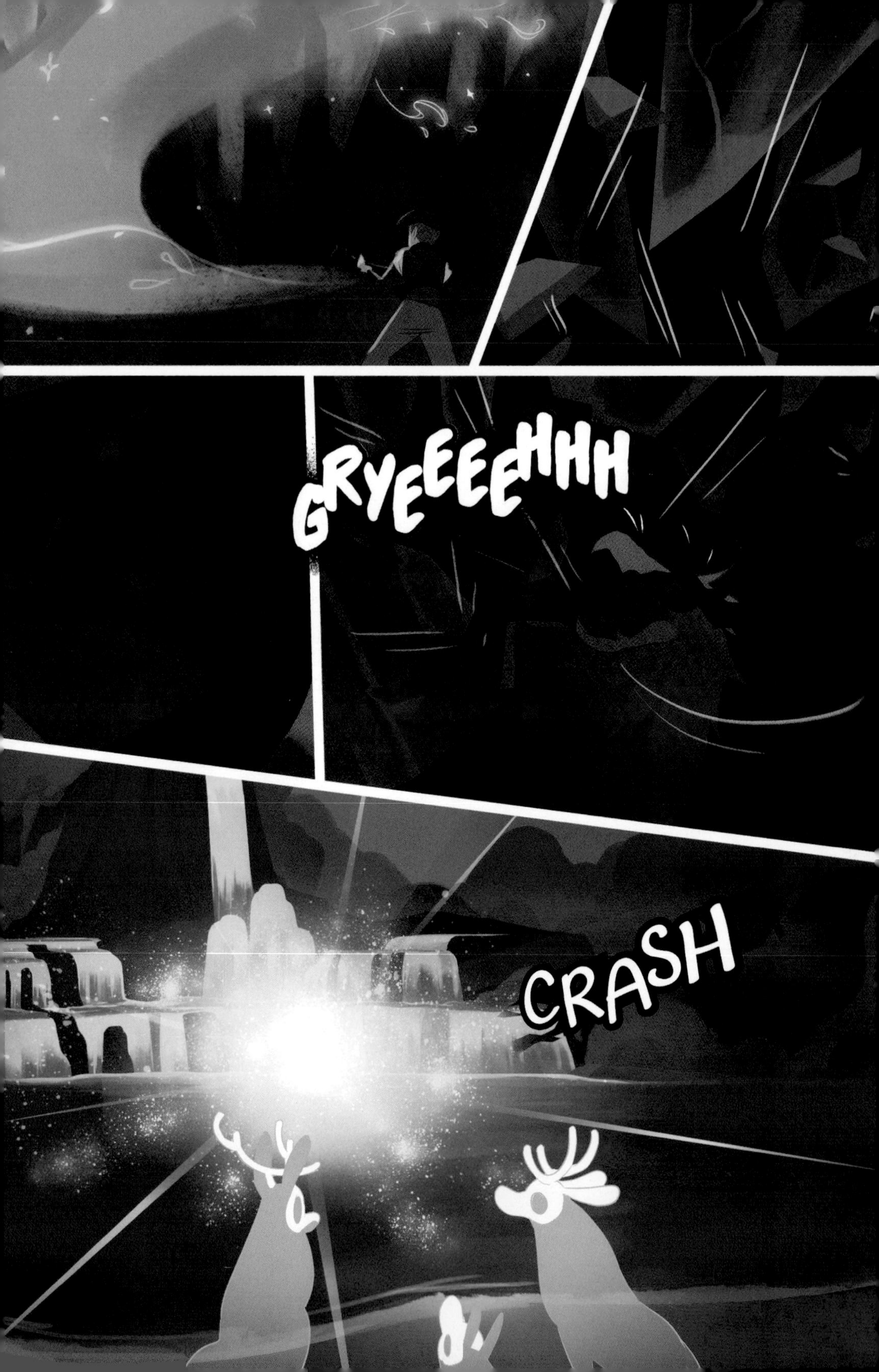
GRYEEEEHHH
CRASH

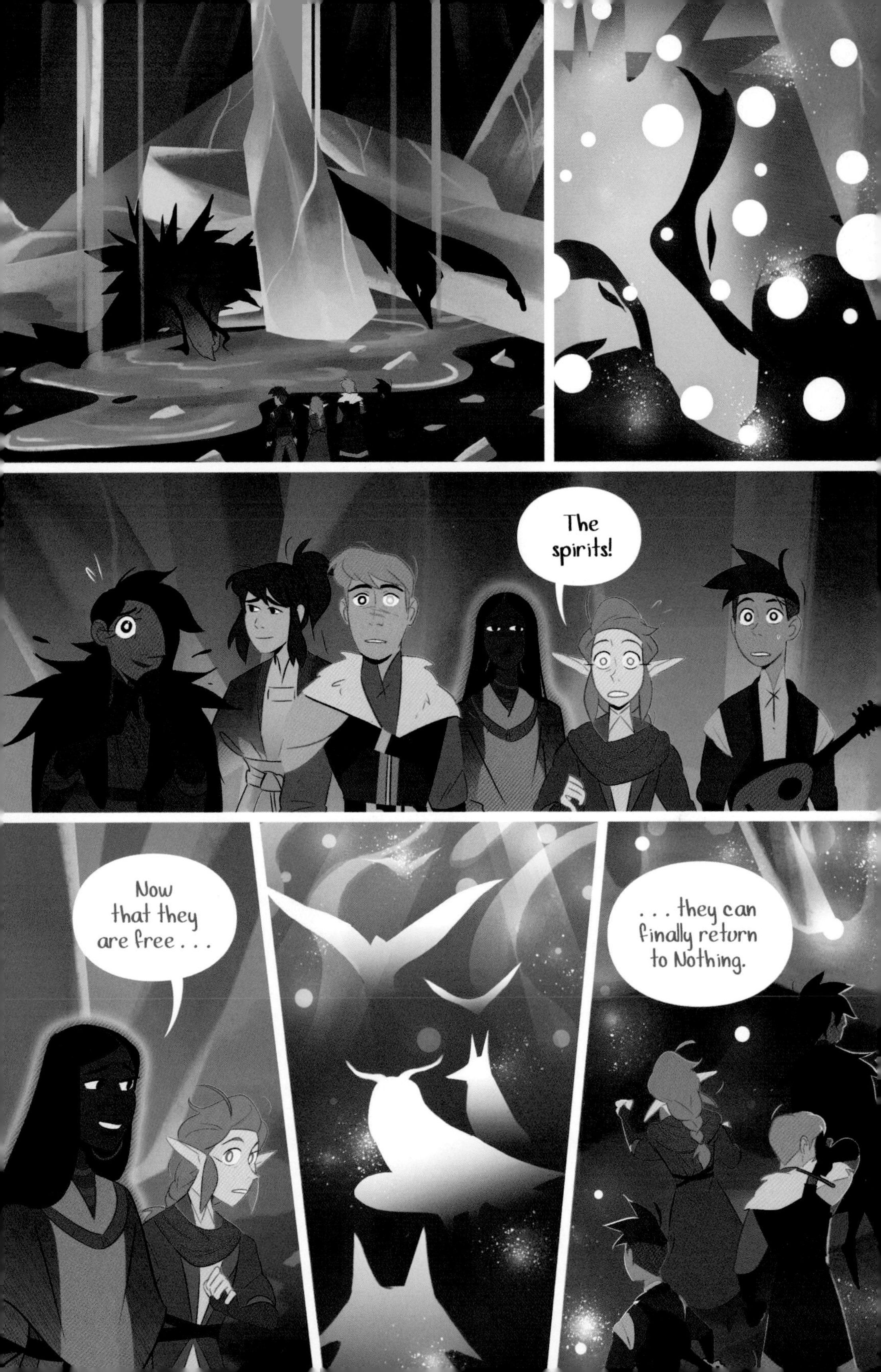
The spirits!
Now that they are free . . .
. . . they can finally return to Nothing.

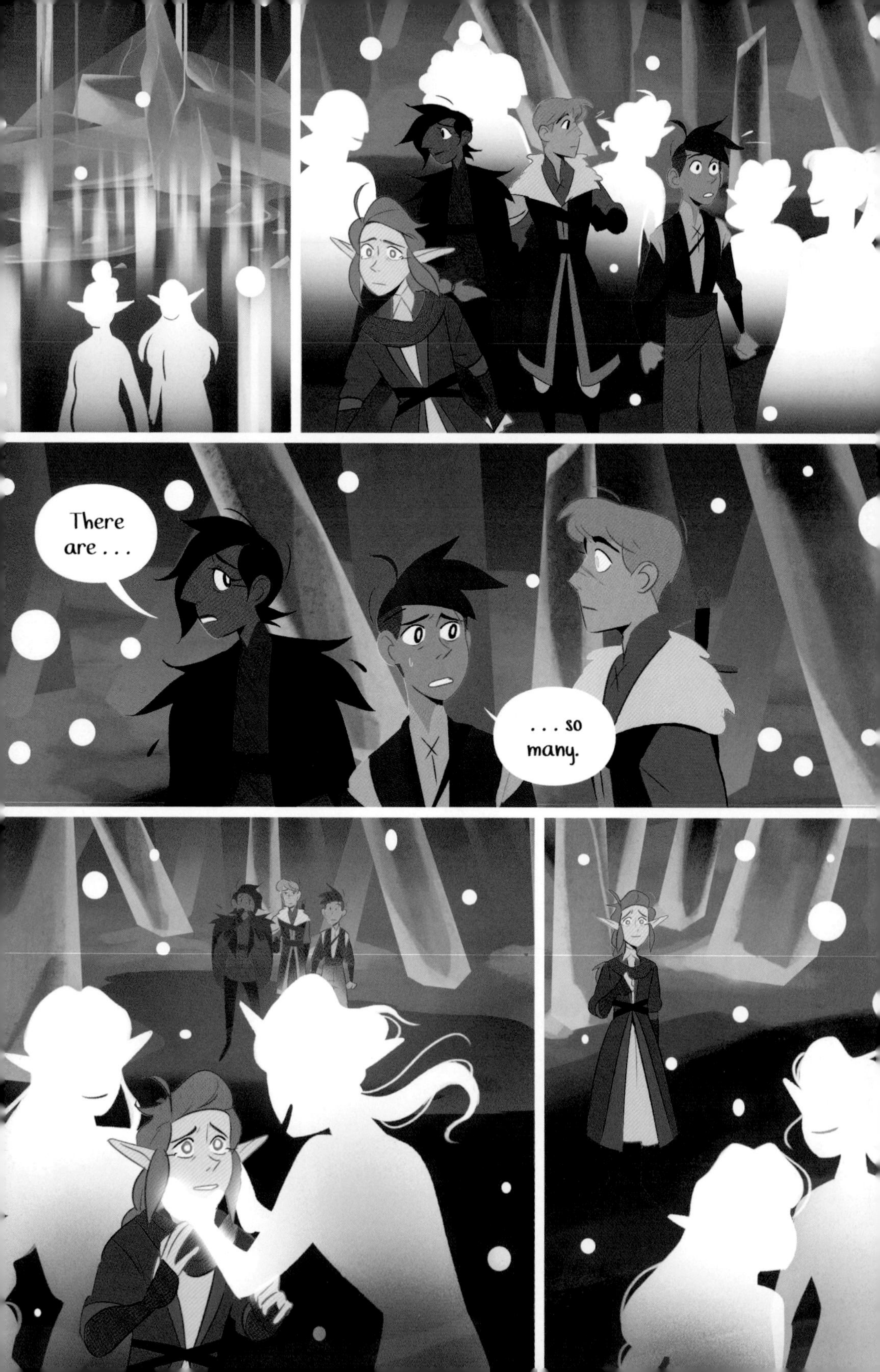
There are . . .
. . . so many.

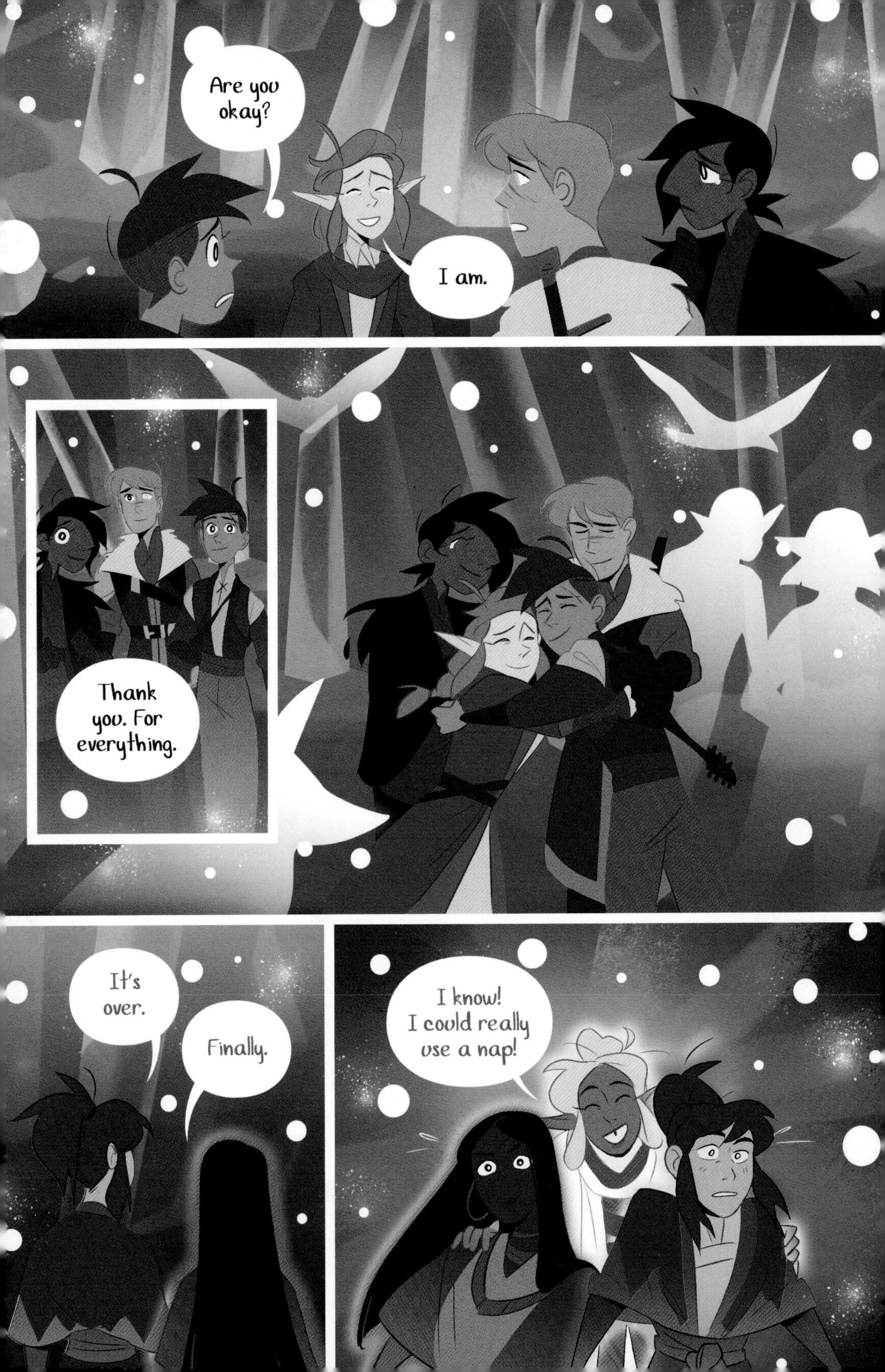
Are you okay?
I am.
Thank you. For everything.
It's over.
Finally.
I know! I could really use a nap!

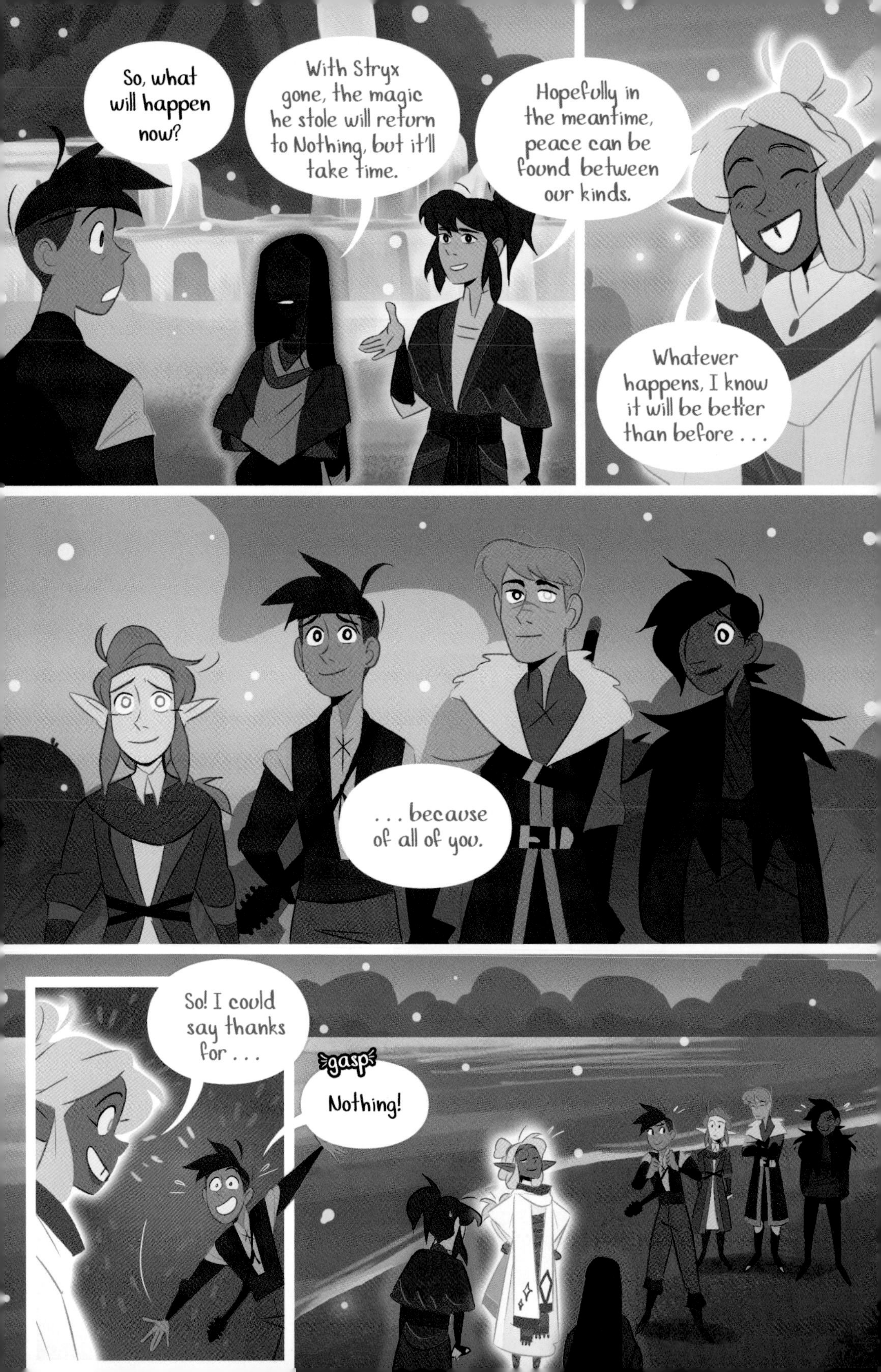

So, what will happen now?
With Stryx gone, the magic he stole will return to Nothing, but it'll take time.
Hopefully in the meantime, peace can be found between our kinds.
Whatever happens, I know it will be better than before . . .
. . . because of all of you.
So! I could say thanks for . . .
gasp
Nothing!

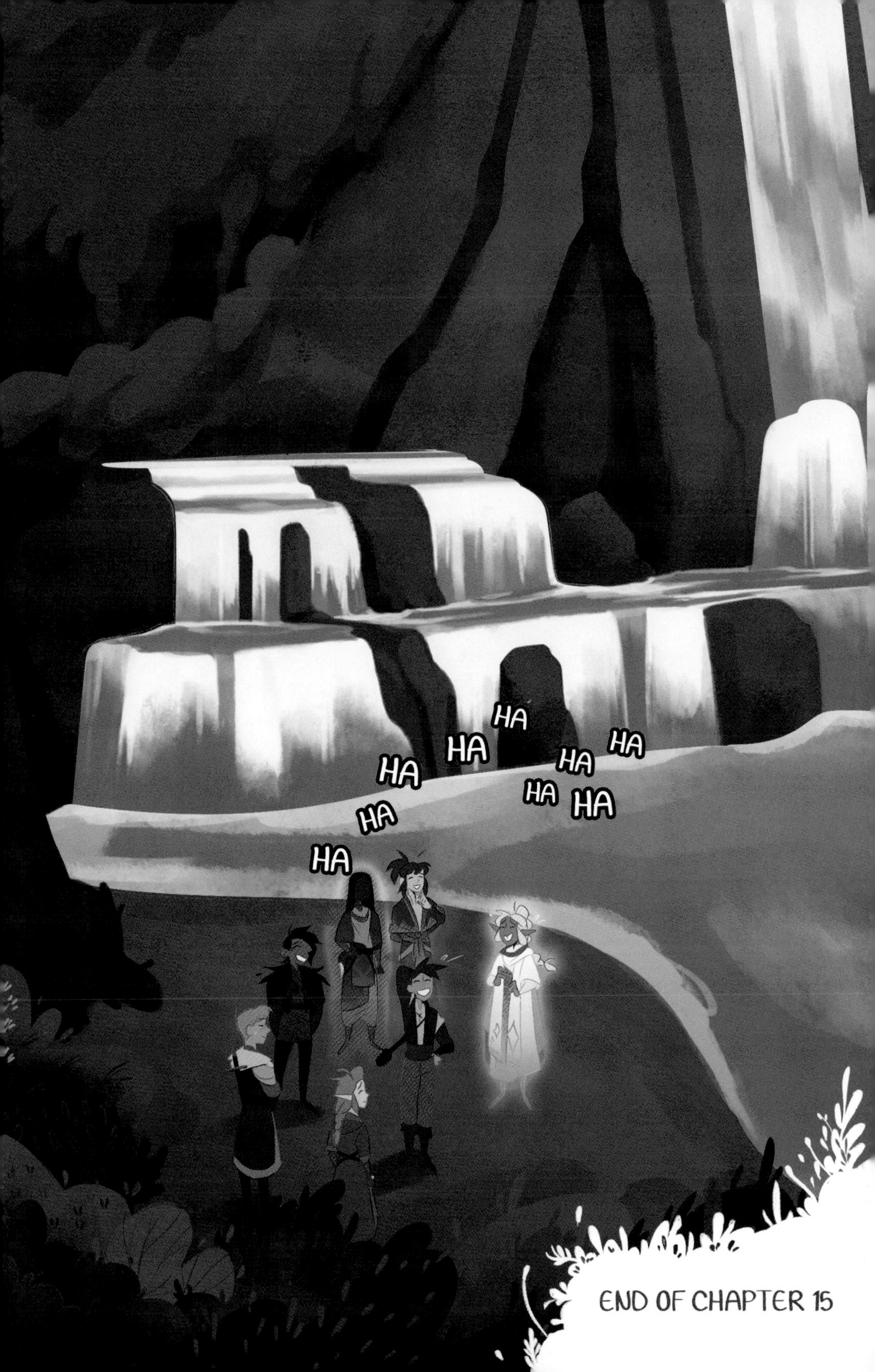
HA
HA
HA
HA
HA
HA
HA
HA
HA
END OF CHAPTER 15

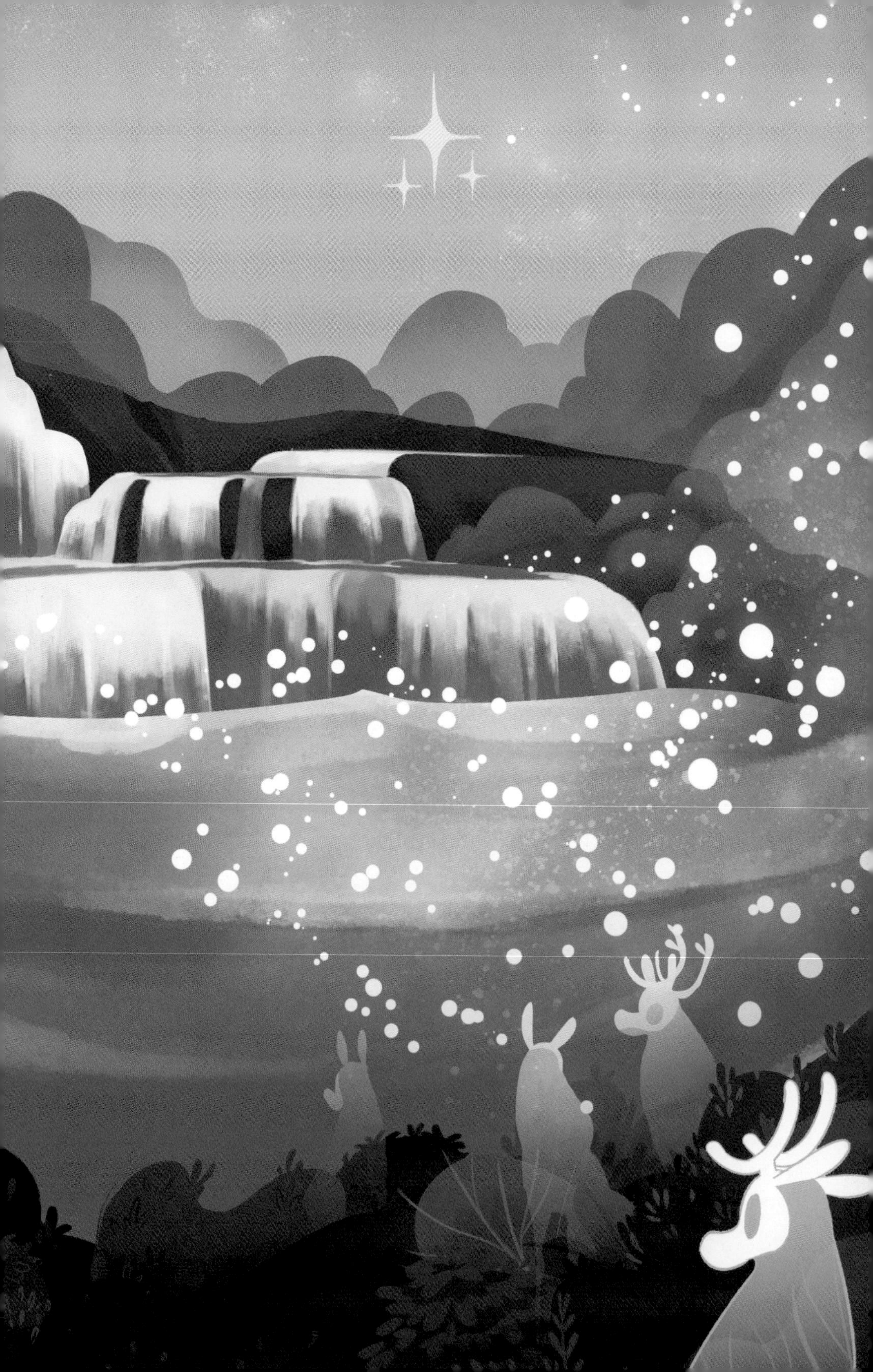

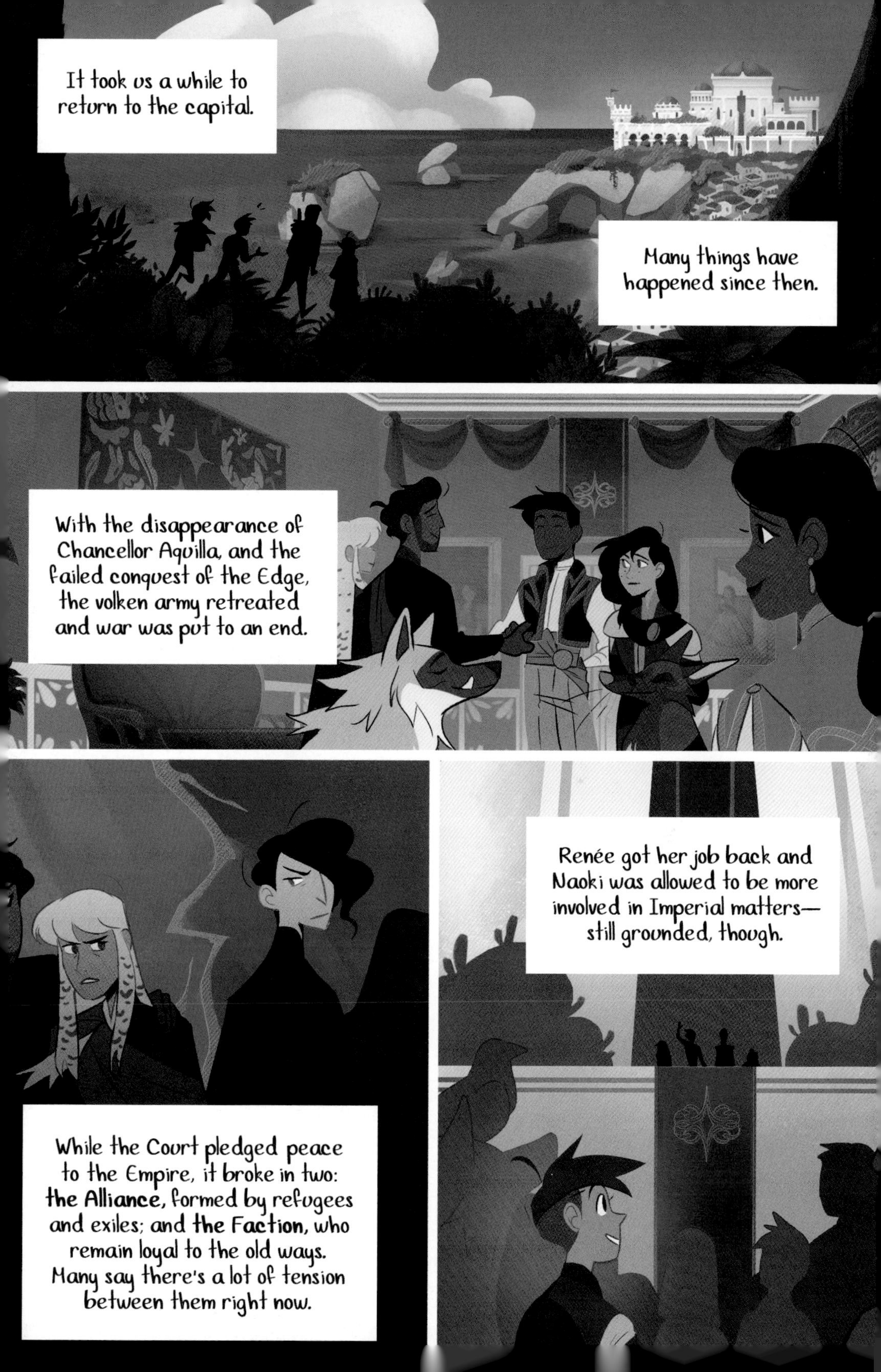
It took us a while to return to the capital.
Many things have happened since then.
With the disappearance of Chancellor Aquilla, and the failed conquest of the Edge, the volken army retreated and war was put to an end.
While the Court pledged peace to the Empire, it broke in two: **the Alliance**, formed by refugees and exiles; and **the Faction**, who remain loyal to the old ways. Many say there's a lot of tension between them right now.
Renée got her job back and Naoki was allowed to be more involved in Imperial matters—still grounded, though.

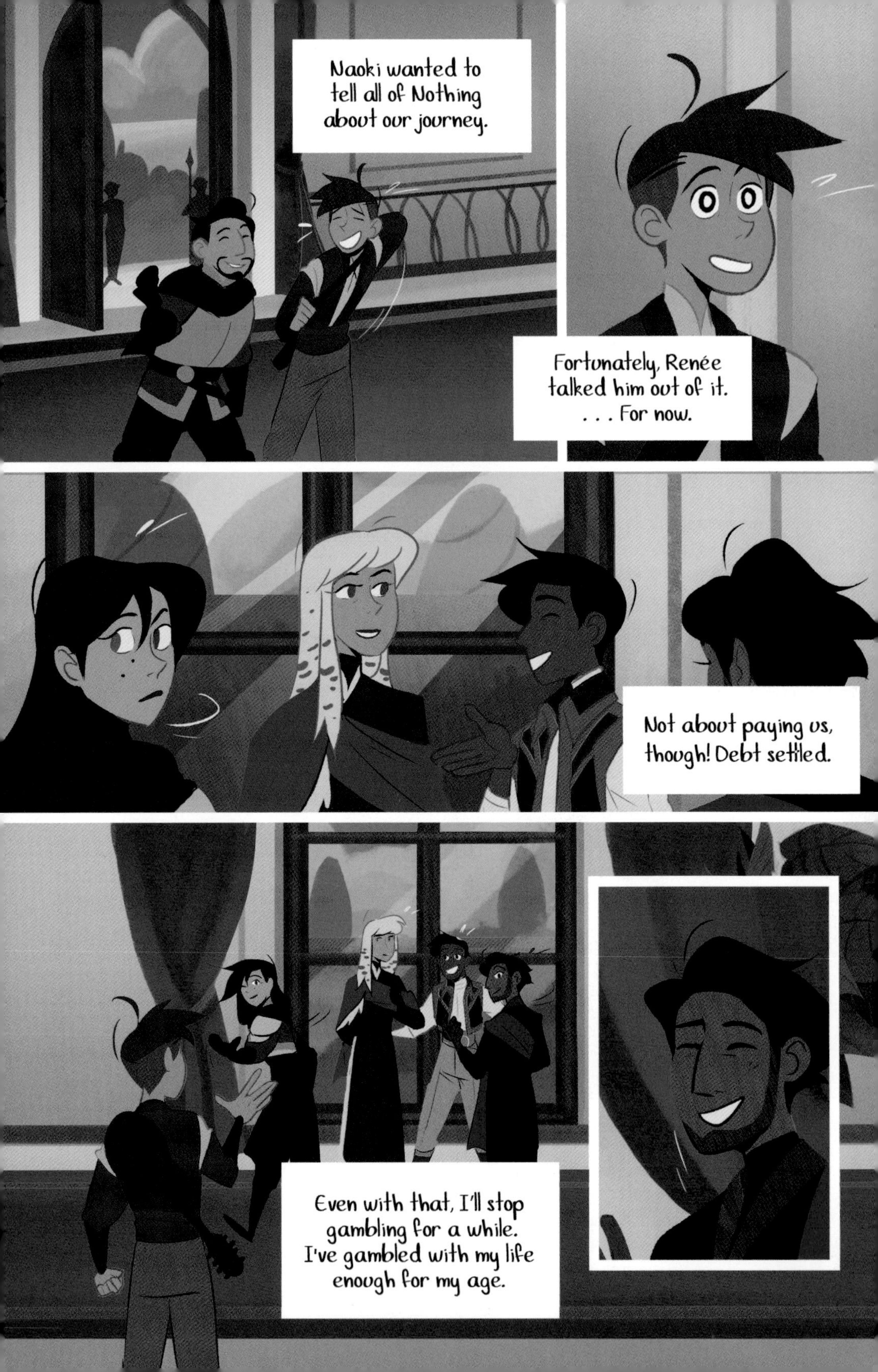
Naoki wanted to tell all of Nothing about our journey.
Fortunately, Renée talked him out of it. . . . For now.
Not about paying us, though! Debt settled.
Even with that, I'll stop gambling for a while. I've gambled with my life enough for my age.

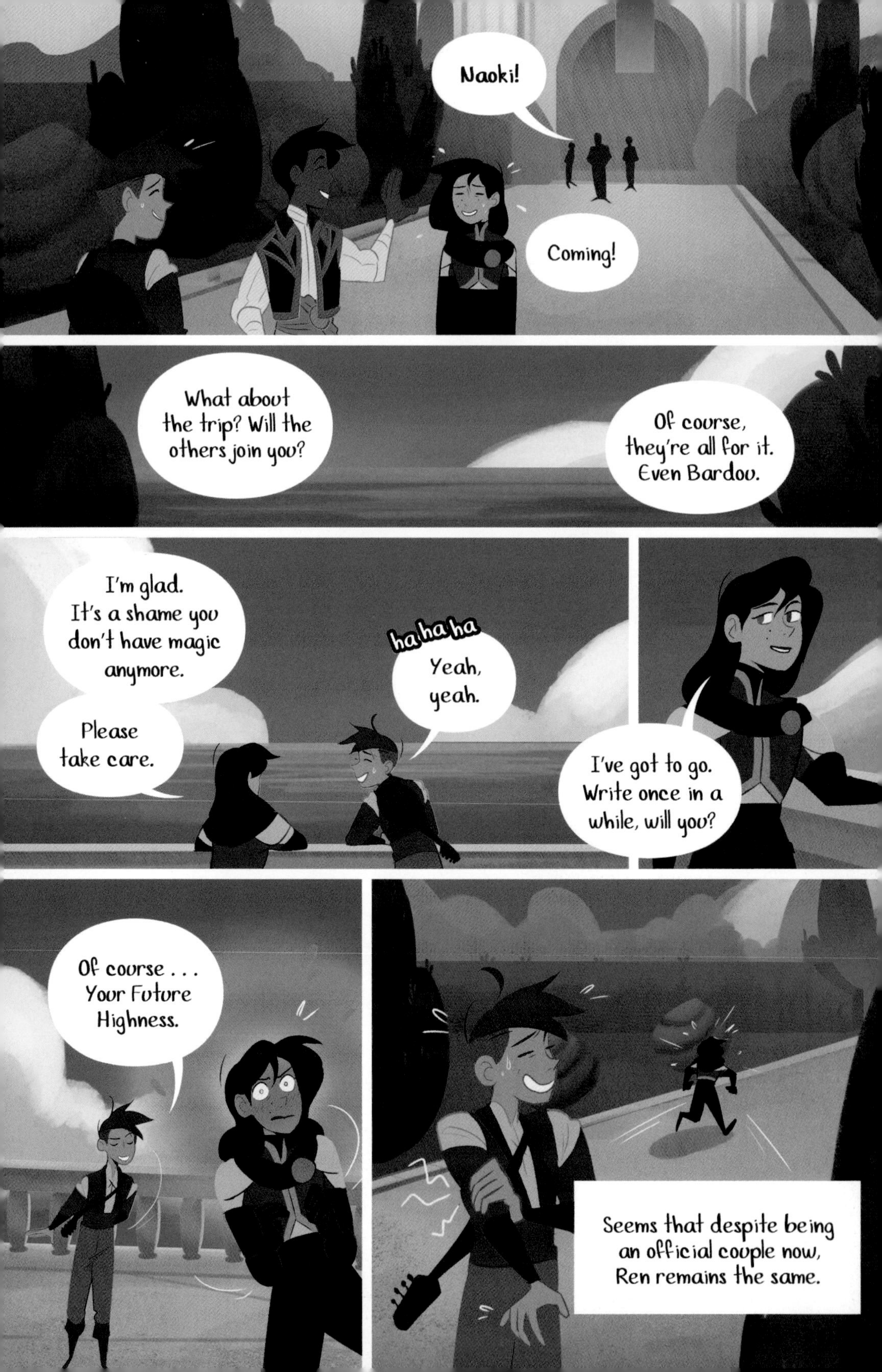
Naoki!
Coming!
What about the trip? Will the others join you?
Of course, they're all for it. Even Bardou.
I'm glad. It's a shame you don't have magic anymore.
Please take care.
ha ha ha
Yeah, yeah.
I've got to go. Write once in a while, will you?
Of course . . . Your Future Highness.
Seems that despite being an official couple now, Ren remains the same.

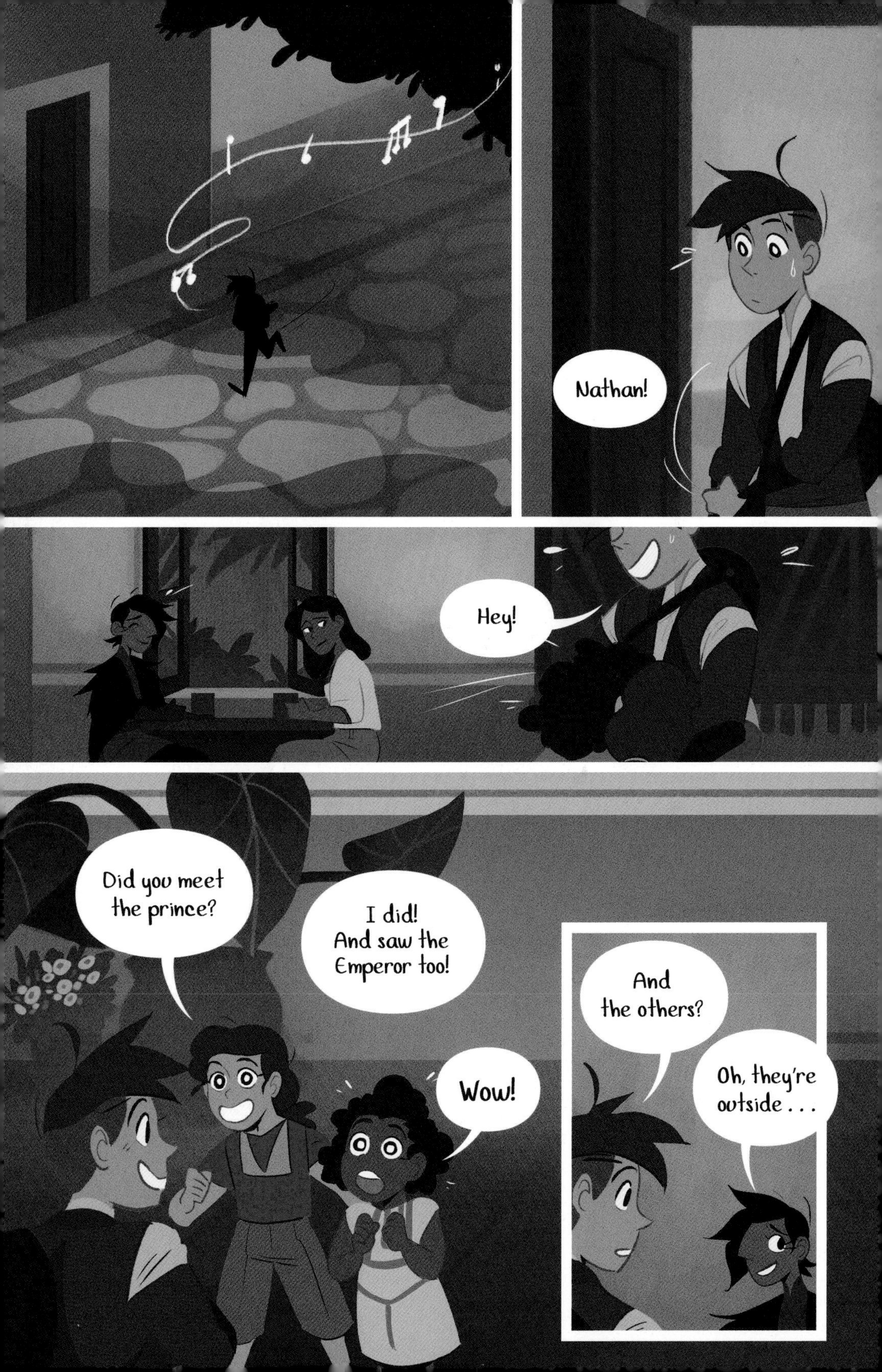
Nathan!
Hey!
Did you meet the prince?
I did! And saw the Emperor too!
Wow!
And the others?
Oh, they're outside . . .

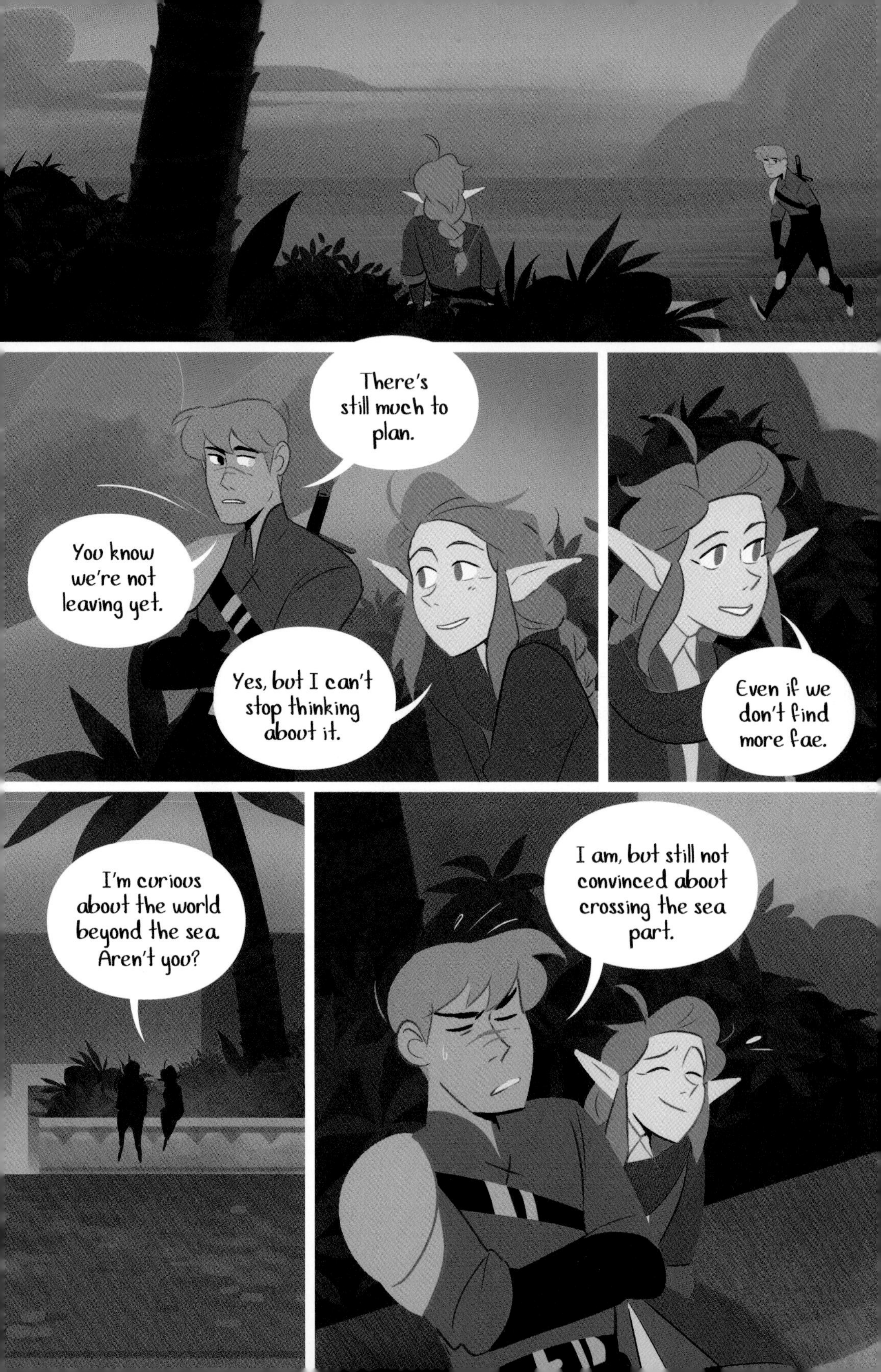
There's still much to plan.
You know we're not leaving yet.
Yes, but I can't stop thinking about it.
Even if we don't find more fae.
I'm curious about the world beyond the sea Aren't you?
I am, but still not convinced about crossing the sea part.

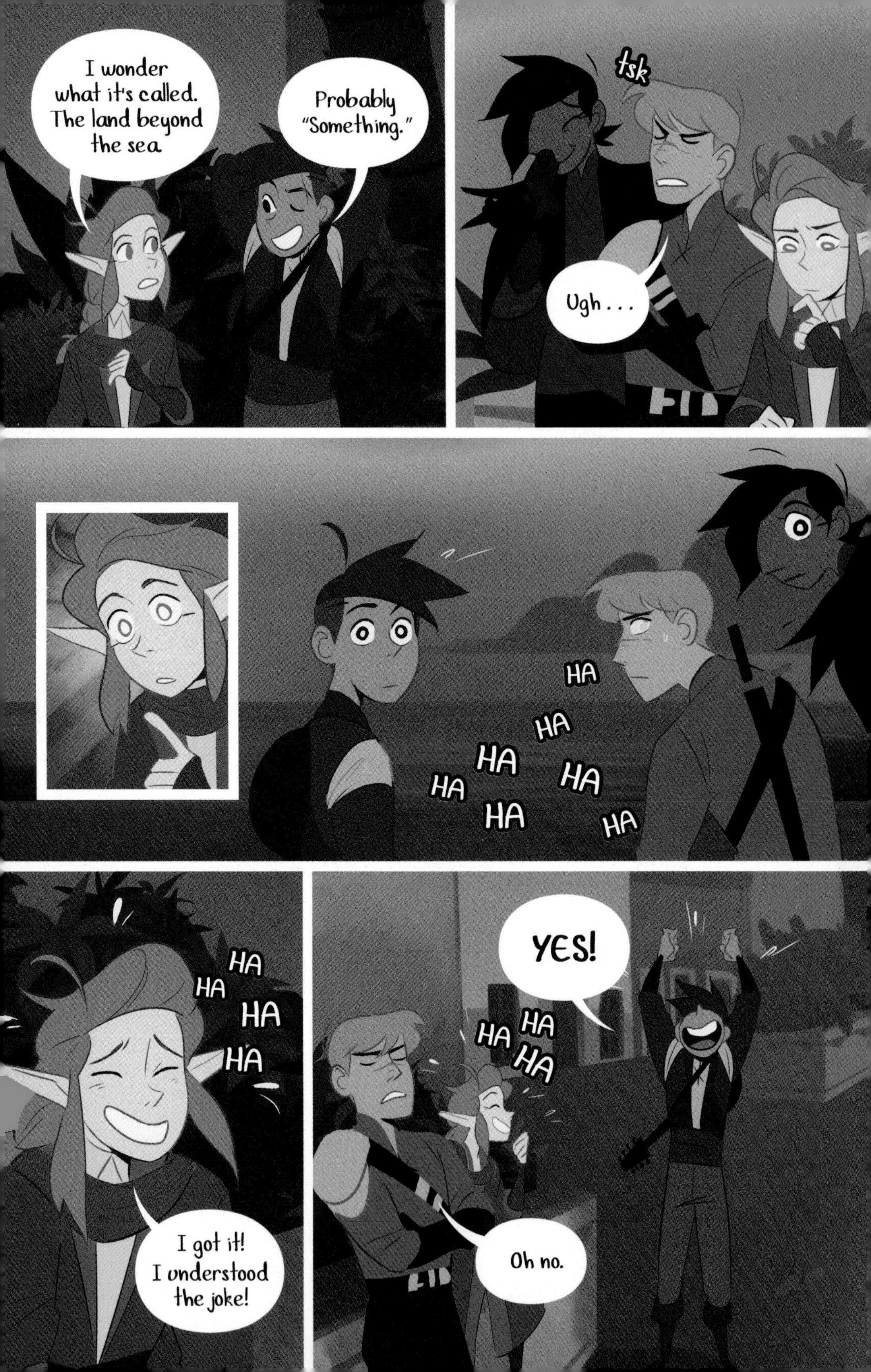
I wonder what it's called. The land beyond the sea
Probably "Something."
tsk
Ugh . . .
HA
HA
HA
HA
HA
HA
HA
HA
HA
HA
HA
I got it! I understood the joke!
YES!
HA
HA
HA
Oh no.

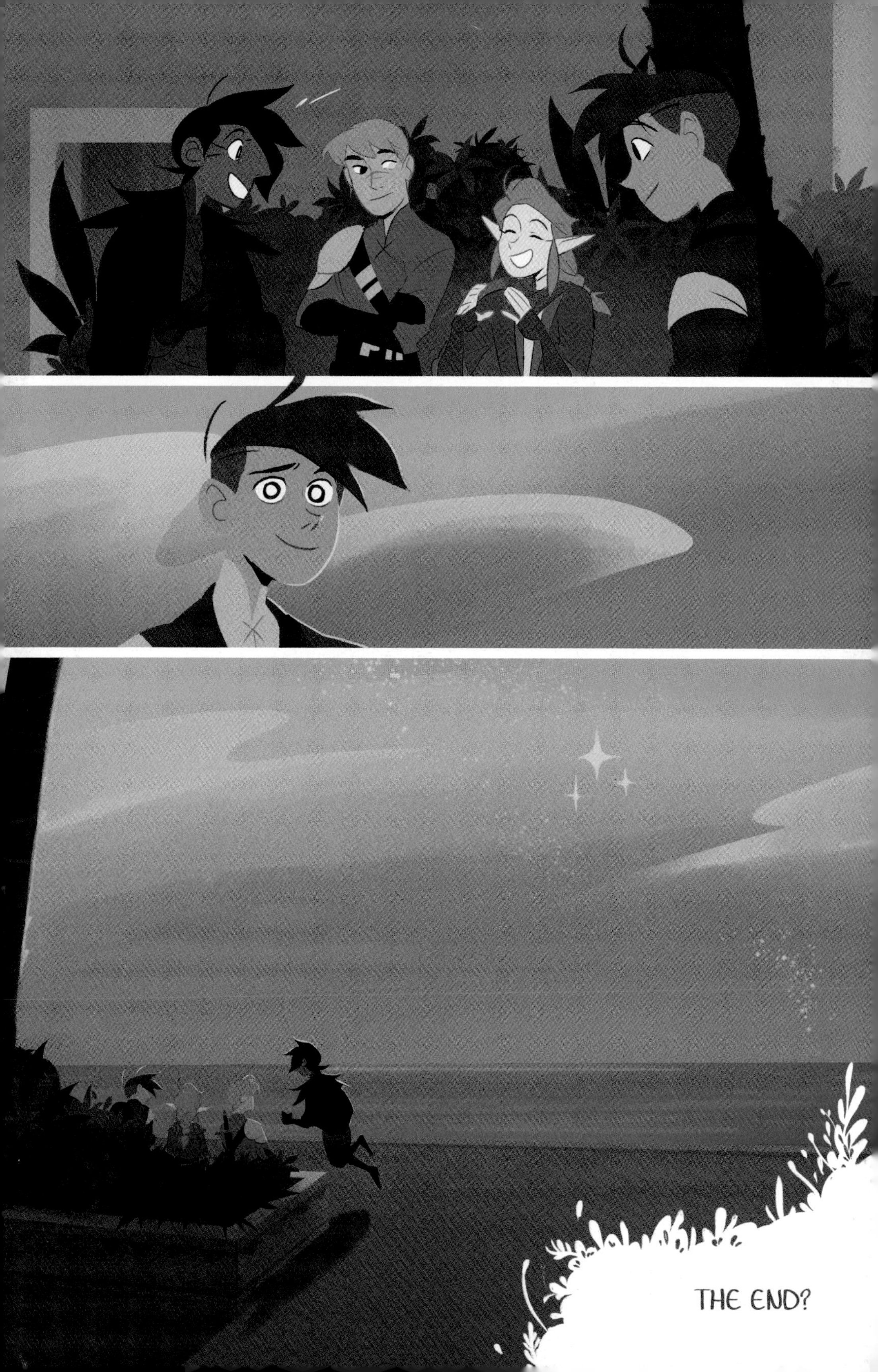
THE END?

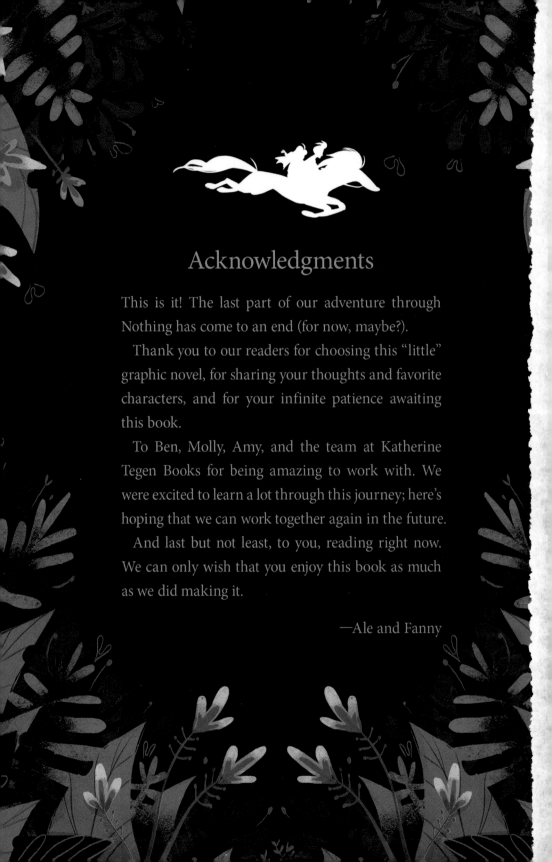

Acknowledgments

This is it! The last part of our adventure through Nothing has come to an end (for now, maybe?).

Thank you to our readers for choosing this "little" graphic novel, for sharing your thoughts and favorite characters, and for your infinite patience awaiting this book.

To Ben, Molly, Amy, and the team at Katherine Tegen Books for being amazing to work with. We were excited to learn a lot through this journey; here's hoping that we can work together again in the future.

And last but not least, to you, reading right now. We can only wish that you enjoy this book as much as we did making it.

—Ale and Fanny